Philip James Bailey

Festus

A Poem

Philip James Bailey

Festus
A Poem

ISBN/EAN: 9783744770057

Printed in Europe, USA, Canada, Australia, Japan

Cover: Foto ©Andreas Hilbeck / pixelio.de

More available books at **www.hansebooks.com**

FESTUS:

A POEM

BY

PHILIP JAMES BAILEY,

BARRISTER AT LAW.

EIGHTEENTH AMERICAN EDITION.

NEW YORK:

S. A. ROLLO,

169 & 170 FULTON-STREET,

OPPOSITE ST. PAUL'S CHURCH.

1860.

PREFACE

TO THE AMERICAN EDITION.

WE here present to the American public a book which has produced no little sensation in England, and which has been, for some time, known to many in this country. But although the first edition was issued six years since, it has had but a limited circulation among us; and it is believed that in republishing "FESTUS," we not only perform a work which its merits demand, but open, for the first time, to many who will appreciate it, a great and original poem. The peculiar value of the second English edition, from which this is printed, consists in the "Proem," which was not attached to the first. Having placed at the end of the volume some of the highest literary opinions in England, we will not intrude any analysis of our own. But a word upon one point. With many minds, it will be difficult to acquit the author from the charge of irreverence. For this purpose, we refer to his vindication in the Proem and in the body of the work ; by which the reader will perceive that he is free from irreverence in spirit, whatever question there may be as to the propriety of certain forms of expression. As to the extravagances, which all will discover, they are the extravagances of deep and eloquent passion — the luxuriant overgrowth of a profoundly rich soil. With all its faults, "Festus" is a great poem — a mine of thought and imagery. It is perfectly safe to pronounce it one of the most powerful and splendid productions of the age.

DEDICATION.

***

My FATHER! unto thee to whom I owe
  All that I am, all that I have and can;
Who madest me in thyself the sum of man
  In all his generous aims and powers to know,
  These first-fruits bring I; nor do thou forego
Marking when I the boyish feat began,
Which numbers now near three years from its plan,
  Not twenty summers had imbrowned my brow.
Life is at blood-heat every page doth prove.
  Bear with it. Nature means Necessity.
If here be aught which thou canst love, it springs
  Out of the hope that I may earn that love
More unto me than immortality;
  Or to have strang my harp with golden strings.

1838.

PROEM.

Without all fear, without presumption, he
Who wrote this work would speak respecting it
A few brief words, and face his friend the world;
Revising, not reversing, what hath been.
   Poetry is itself a thing of God;
He made His prophets poets; and the more
We feel of poesie do we become
Like God in love and power, — under-makers.
All great lays, equals to the minds of men,
Deal more or less with the Divine, and have
For end some good of mind or soul of man.
The mind is this world's, but the soul is God's;
The wise man joins them here all in his power.
The high and holy works, amid lesser lays,
Stand up like churches among village cots;
And it is joy to think that in every age,
However much the world was wrong therein,
The greatest works of mind or hand have been
Done unto God.   So may they ever be!
It shows the strength of wish we have to be great,
And the sublime humility of might.
   True fiction hath in it a higher end
Than fact; it is the possible compared
With what is merely positive, and gives
To the conceptive soul an inner world,
A higher, ampler, Heaven than that wherein
The nations sun themselves.   In that bright state

Are met the mental creatures of the men
Whose names are writ highest on the rounded crown
Of Fame's triumphal arch; the shining shapes
Which star the skies of that invisible land,
Which, whosoe'er would enter, let him learn; —
'T is not enough to draw forms fair and lively,
Their conduct likewise must be beautiful;
A hearty holiness must crown the work,
As a gold cross the minster-dome, and show,
Like that instonement of divinity,
That the whole building doth belong to God.
And for the book before us, though it were,
What it is not, supremely little, like
The needled angle of a high church spire,
Its sole end points to God the Father's glory,
From all eternity seen; making clear
His might and love in saving sinful man.
One bard shows God as he deals with states and kings;
Another, as He dealt with the first man;
Another, as with Heaven and earth and hell;
Ours, as He loves to order a chance soul
Chosen out of the world, from first to last.
And all along it is the heart of man
Emblemed, created and creative mind.
It is a statued mind and naked heart
Which is struck out.   Other bards draw men dressed
In manners, customs, forms, appearances,
Laws, places, times, and countless accidents
Of peace or polity: to him these are not;
He makes no mention, takes no compt of them: —
But shows, however great his doubts, sins, trials,
Whatever earthborn pleasures soil man's soul,
What power soever he may gain of evil,
That still, till death, time is; that God's great Heaven
Stands open day and night to man and spirit;
For all are of the race of God, and have
In themselves good.   The life-writ of a heart,

Whose firmest prop and highest meaning was
The hope of serving God as poet-priest,
And the belief that He would not put back
Love-offerings, though brought to Him by hands
Unclean and earthy, e'en as fallen man's
Must be; and most of all, the thankful show
Of His high power and goodness in redeeming
And blessing souls that love Him, spite of sin
And their old earthy strain, — these are the aims,
The doctrines, truths, and staple of the story.
What theme sublimer than soul being saved?
'T is the bard's aim to show the mind-made world
Without, within; how the soul stands with God,
And the unseen realities about us.
It is a view of life spiritual
And earthly.   Let all look upon it, then,
In the same light it was drawn and colored in;
In faith, in that the writer too hath faith,
Albeit an effect, and not a cause.
Faith is a higher faculty than reason,
Though of the brightest power of revelation,
As the snow-headed mountain rises o'er
The lightning, and applies itself to Heaven.
We know in day-time there are stars about us,
Just as at night, and name them what and where
By sight of science; so by faith we know,
Although we may not see them till our night,
That spirits are about us, and believe,
That, to a spirit's eye, all Heaven may be
As full of angels as a beam of light
Of motes.   As spiritual, it shows all
Classes of life, perhaps, above our kind,
Known to tradition, reason, or God's word,
Whose bright foundations are the heights of Heaven.
As earthly, it embodies most the life
Of youth, its powers, its aims, its deeds, its failings;
And, as a sketch of world-life, it begins

And ends, and rightly, in Heaven and with God;
While Heaven is also in the midst thereof.
    God, or all good, the evil of the world,
And man, wherein are both, are each displayed.
The mortal is the model of all men.
The foibles, follies, trials, sufferings —
And manifest and manifold are they —
Of a young, hot, unworld-schooled heart that has
Had its own way in life, and wherein all
May see some likeness of their own, — 't is these
Attract, unite, and, sunlike, concentrate
The ever-moving system of our feelings.
The hero is the world-man, in whose heart
One passion stands for all, the most indulged.
The scenes wherein he plays his part are life,
A sphere whose centre is co-heavenly
With its divine original and end.
Like life, too, as a whole, the story hath
A moral, and each scene one, as in life, —
One universal and peculiar truth —
Shining upon it like the quiet moon,
Illustrating the obscure unequal earth; —
And though these scenes may seem to careless eyes
Irregular and rough and unconnected,
Like to the stones at Stonehenge, — though convolved,
And in primeval mystery, — still an use,
A meaning, and a purpose may be marked
Among them of a temple reared to God: —
The meaning alway dwelling in the word,
In secret sanctity, like a golden toy
Mid Beauty's orbed bosom.   Scenes of earth
And Heaven are mixed, as flesh and soul in man.
    Now, the religion of the book is this,
Followed out from the book God writ of old.
All creatures being faulty by their nature,
And by God made all liable to sin,
God only could atone — and unto none

Except himself — for universal sin.
It is thus that God did sacrifice to God,
Himself unto Himself, in the great way
Of Triune mystery. His death, as man,
Was real as our own; and as, except
In the destruction of all life, there could
Be no atonement for its sin, while life
Doth necessarily result from God,
As thought and outward action from ourselves,
So the atonement must be to and by Him;
Which makes it justice equally with love;
For all His powers and attributes are equal,
And must make one in any act of His;
And every act of God is infinite.
He acts through all in all: the truth we know,
He doth Himself inbreathe; the ill we do,
He hath atoned for; and the Scriptures show
That God doth suffer for the sins of those
Whom He hath made, that are liable to sin.
In all of us He hath His agony;
We are the cross, and death of God, and grave.
Him love then all the more, and worship Him
Who lived and died, and rose from death for us,
And is and reigns forever God in all.
Let each man think himself an act of God,
His mind a thought, his life a breath of God;
And let each try, by great thoughts and good deeds,
To show the most of Heaven he hath in him.
  Many who read the word of life, much doubt
Whether salvation be of grace or faith,
Election, or repentance, or good works,
Or God's high will: reconcile all of them.
Each of the persons of the Triune God
Hath had His dispensation, hath it now;
The Father by His prophets, and the Son
In His own days, by His own deeds; and now
The Spirit, by the ministry of Christ;

And thus, by law, by gospel, and by grace,
The scheme of God's salvation is complete.
Salvation, then, is God-like, threefold; or
That under one or other, all may come;
By will of God alone, by faith in Christ,
And by repentance, and good works, and grace.
So there is one salvation of the Father,
One of the Son, another of the Spirit;
Each, the salvation of the Three in One.
The mortal in this lay is saved of will,
In manner as this hymn unfolds, which hath
Just warranty for every word from God's.

O God! Thou wondrous One in Three,
    As mortals must Thee deem;
Thou only canst be said to be,
    We but at best to seem.
For Thou dost save, and Thou may'st slay,
    Canst make a mortal soul
In Thee eternal; in a day
    Wilt bring to nought the whole.

Thou hardenest, and Thou openest hearts,
    As in Thy Word is shown;
Thou savest and destroyest parts,
    By Thy right will alone.
Let down Thy grace, then, Lord! on all
    Whom Thou wilt save to live;
Oh! if they stumble, stop their fall!
    Oh! if they fall, forgive!

They are forgiven from the first,
    They are predestined Thine;
And though in sin they were the worst,
    In Thee they are divine.

They are, and were, and will be, Lord!
  In one, in Heaven, in Thee,
Yea with the Spirit, and the Word,
  One God in Trinity.

These principles and doctrines pending not
Upon the action of the poem here,
But over and above it, influencing
Nevertheless the story, as the course
Of stars enwoven with our system, earth,
Vary the view of this life's hemisphere,
And mingle it more palpably with Heaven,
And with its changeless, ceaseless, boundless God.
It is thus that by creating to and from
Eternity, and multiplying ever
His own one Being through the universe,
He doth eternize happiness, and make
Good infinite by making all in Him.
There is but one great right and good; and ill
And wrong are shades thereof, not substances.
Nothing can be antagonist to God.
  Necessity, like electricity,
Is in ourselves and all things, and no more
Without us than within us, and we live,
We of this mortal mixture, in the same law
As the pure colorless intelligence
Which dwells in Heaven, and the dead Hadëan shades,
We will and act and talk of liberty;
And all our wills and all our doings both
Are limited within this little life.
Free-will is but necessity in play,—
The clattering of the golden reins which guide
The thunder-footed coursers of the sun.
The ship which goes to sea informed with fire, —
Obeying only its own iron force,
Reckless of adverse tide, breeze dead, or weak

As infant's parting breath, too faint to stir
The feather held before it, — is as much
The appointed thrall of all the elements,
As the white-bosomed bark which wooes the wind,
And when it **dies** desists.   And thus with man;
However contrary he set his heart
To God, he is but working out His will;
And, at an infinite angle, more or less
Obeying his own soul's necessity.
He only hath freewill whose will is fate.
   Evil and good are God's right hand and left.
By ministry of evil good is clear,
And by temptation virtue; as of yore
Out of the grave rose God.   Let this be deemed
Enough to justify the portion weighed
To the great spirit Evil, named herein.
If evil seem the most, yet good most is:
As water may be deep and pure below
Although the face be filmy for a time.
And if the spirit of evil seem more in
The work than God, it **is but to** work His will,
Who therefore **is all that** the other seems.
And evil is in almost every scene
Of life more or less forward.   Above all
The mystery of the Trinity is held,
Whose mystery is its reasonableness.
All that is said of Deity is said
In love and reverence.   Be it so conceived
What comes before and after the great world, —
Deep in the secretest abyss of Light,
And Being's most reserved immensity —
God alone knows eternally, who rends
The mantling Heavens with his hands; but with
The present is communion creatural:
He liveth in the sacrament of life.
And for the soul of man delineate here —
The outline half invisible — is shown

The self-sought grace, the self-aspiring truth
And natural religion of the heart
Contrasting Godhood with humanity
Ever; whereas the Spirit aye **unites.**
Temptation, and its workings in the heart
Whose faint and false resistance but assists, —
Ambition, thirst of secret lore, joy, love —
Riverlike, doubling sometimes on itself—
Adventure, pleasure, travel heavenly
And earthly, friendship, **passion,** poesie,
Viewed ever in their spiritual end —
And power, celestial happiness and **earth's**
Millennial foretaste, ill annihilate,
The restoration of the angels lost,
And one salvation universal given
To all create, — all **these, related, form,**
With **much beside, the body of the work:—**
The islands, seas, and mainland of its orb.
　Thus much then for this book. It aims to mark
The various beliefs as well as doubts
Which hold or search by turns the mind of youth
Unresting anywhere. Its heresies,
If such they be, are charitable ones; —
For they who read not in the **blest belief**
That all souls may be saved, read to no end.
We were made to be saved. **We are of God.**
Nor bates the book one tittle of the truth,
To smoothe its way to favor **with the fearful.**
　All rests with **those who read. A work or thought**
Is what each makes it to himself, **and may**　　·
Be full of great dark meanings, like the sea,
With shoals of life rushing; **or** like the air,
Benighted with the wing of the wild dove,
Sweeping miles broad o'er the far western **woods,**
With mighty glimpses of the central light —
Or may be nothing — bodiless, spiritless.

Now therefore to his work and to the world
The writer bids, God speed!   It matters not
If they agree or differ.   Each perchance
May bear true witness to another end.
Let then what hath been, be.   It boots not here
To palliate misdoings.   'T were less toil
To build Colossus than to hew a hill
Into a statue.   Hail and farewell, all!

FESTUS.

Scene — *Heaven.*

God.

Eternity hath snowed its years upon them;
And the white winter of their age is come,
The World and all its worlds; and all shall end.
Seraphim.   God! God! God!
    As flames in skies
    We burn and rise
    And lose ourselves in Thee!
    Years on years!
    And nought appears
    Save God to be.
    God! God! God!
    To us no thought
    Hath Being brought
    Toward Thee that doth not move!
    Years on years!
    And what appears
    Save God to love?
    God! God! God!
    All Thou dost make
    Lies like a lake
    Below Thine infinite eye:
    Years on years!
    And all appears
    Save God to die.
Cherubim.   As sun and star,

How high or far,
Show but a boundless sky;
So creature mind
Is all confined
To show Thee, God, most High.
The sun still burns,
The sun still turns
Round, round himself and round;
So creature mind
To self's confined,
But Thou God hast no bound!
Systems arise,
Or a world dies,
Each constant hour in air;
But creature mind,
In Heaven confined,
Lives on like Thee, God! there.

SERAPHIM AND CHERUBIM. God! God! God!
Thou fill'st our eyes
As were the skies
One burning, boundless sun!
While creature mind,
In path confined,
Passeth a spot thereon.
God! God! God!

LUCIFER. Ye thrones of Heaven, how bright,
how pure ye are:
How have ye brightened since I saw ye first!
How have I darkened since ye saw me last!
What is the dark abyss of fire, and what
The ravenous heights of air, o'er which I reign,
In agony of glory, to these seats?
The loathsome cavern of the oracle,
O'er which ye rise in templed majesty,
Filled with the incense of all worshippers,
And echoing with the eloquence of God,
Which rolls in sunny clouds around the heavens.
Yet must I work through world and life my fate;
And winding through the wards of human hearts,

Steal their incarnate strength. Death does his work
In secret and in joy intense, untold,
As though an earthquake smacked its mumbling lips
O'er some thick peopled city. But for me,
Exists nor peace nor pleasure, **even** here,
Where all beside, the very faintest thought,
Is **rapture.** I will speak to God as erst.
Father **of** spirit, as the sun of air!
Beginning of all ends, and **end of** all
Beginnings, throughout whole Eternity;
From whom Eternity and **every** power
Perfect, and pure cause, **is and** emanates!
Originator without origin!
End without end! Creator **of all ages,**
And sabbath of all Being; **who hast** made
All numbers sacred, **who art all and** one!
At whose right hand **the wisdom of** all worlds
Combined, is **only fearful foolishness**
Or inarticulate **madness,—and Thou,** Lord!
Maker and Perfecter of all, the one!
Being above all Being, **God the** Life!
Who **art** the way whereon **the** world proceeds
From God, all-making, and whereby returns
The ever generated universe!—
Who rulest all worlds in the law of light,
Thy nature and their own; who art before
All ages, angels, blessed, times and worlds!
Word that in every world art safe to save
All souls, impregned with spirit, God-begot!
And Thou eternal spirit-Deity!
The sanctifier of **the** universe!
Being, **and** Life, and spirit, who dost **make,**
Destroyest, recreatest, makest God!
God one **and** Trine! Thou seest me here again;
Still, sunlike, though eclipsed, of blinding power
And fiery cause, and everness of ill;
Behold I bow before Thee; hear Thou me!
GOD.
What wouldst thou, Lucifer?

LUCIFER.   There is a youth
Among the sons of men I fain would have
Given up wholly to me.
                          GOD.
                              He is thine,
To tempt.
      LUCIFER.   I thank Thee, Lord!
                          GOD.
                                    Upon his soul
Thou hast no power.   All souls are mine for aye.
And I do give thee leave to this that he
May know my love is more than all his sin,
And prove unto himself that nought but God
Can satisfy the soul He maketh great.
      LUCIFER.   Thou God art all in one! Thy infinite
Bounds Being.   Thou hast said the world shall end
The world is perfect, as concerns itself,
And all its parts and ends; not as towards Thee.
So man is likest and unlikest God,
Of all existence; therefore doth as much
Resemble Thee as any act a mind.
In him of whom I ask, I seek once more
To tempt the living world, and then depart.
      THE HOLY GHOST.   And I will hallow him to
          the ends of Heaven,
That though he plunge his soul in sin like a sword
In water, it shall nowise cling to him.
He is of Heaven.   All things are known in Heaven,
Ere aimed at upon earth.   The child is chosen.
      SAINTS.   Another soul
                  The Holy one
              Hath chosen out of earth;
                  And there is none
                Throughout the whole
              Like worthy of his birth.
      GUARDIAN ANGEL.   Oh! who hath joy like
          mine? was I not here
When from Thy boundless bosom, as a star
Out of the air, that soul was kindled, Lord!

And given to me to guard and guide — while both,
Mid starry strains out of the depths of Heaven,
Fell at Thy feet in worship ? — joy of joys !
To you, ye saints and angels, let me speak ;
For ye I see rejoice with me.   Ye know
What 't is to triumph o'er temptation, what
To fall before it ; how the young spirit faints —
The virgin tremor, the heart's ebb and flow,
When first some vast temptation calmly comes
And states itself before it, like the sun
Low looming in the west, above the wave
Of wimpling streamlet, ere its waters grow.
To size aortal.   Than the Fiend himself
There is no greater evil.   Less the shame
Of yielding, more the glory of conquering,
In him, to whom he goes, this soul elect.
From infancy through childhood, up to youth,
Have I this soul attended ; marked him blest
With all the sweet and sacred ties of life ; —
The prayerful love of parents, pride of friends,
Prosperity, and health and ease, the aids
Of learning, social converse with the good
And gifted, and his heart all-lit with love,
Like to the rolling sea with living light ; —
Hopeful and generous and earnest ; rich
In commune with high spirits, loving truth
And wisdom for their own divinest selves :
Tracking the deeds of the world's glory, or
Conning the words of wisdom, Heaven-inspired,
As on the soul, in pure effectual ray,
The bright, transparent atoms, thought by thought,
Fall fixed for evermore.   And thus his days,
Through sunny noon, or mooned eve, or night
Star-armied, shining through the deathless air,
All radiantly elapsed, in good or joy.
All this, for long, I marked.   There grew at length,
A change within his spirit ; and I feared
A fatal and a final fall from good.
God's love seemed lost upon him.   He became

Heart-deadened.   Watching, warning, vain, I fled
Hither to intercede with God our Lord,
To bless him with salvation.   We may plead
Alway for those we love, by leave divine.
Nor knew I till this moment, with all Heaven,
That, in the righteous providence of God,
That soul was saved.   Thou knowest, Lord! the
        mould
Of mortals, and the **infinite end whereto**
The souls Thou savest are predestinate;
Oh! be Thy mercy mighty to this soul,
Fiend-threatened; nor permit him who presides
O'er Hell's eternal holocaust, too far
To **tempt or** tamper with the heart of man! —
                    GOD.
My mercy doth outstretch the **universe;**
Shall it not **be** sufficient for one soul?
    LUCIFER.   I **am the** wrath of God unto myself,
And made by Him **to do** my part.   Do thou
Thine! they are far enough apart I ween.
    GUARDIAN ANGEL.   The heaven-strung chords
        of man's immortal **soul**
Are not for thee to wither at thy will.
Bear witness, all ye blessed, to the word; —
Angels, intelligences, sons of God!
Ye who know nought but truth, feel nought but
        love,
Will nought but bliss, do nought but righteousness
Whose life was ere the Heavens were conceived,
The stars begotten, or the ages born;
Ye many ordered hierarchies, which are
The love, truth, justice, majesty, and might,
Dominion, glory, wisdom, bliss of God;
Ye through whose ministry of mercy — His
Immediate, ever instant, active, all
Spirits and worlds are governed — age by **age**
Gazing and gaining glory; ye who stand,
Stirless, before the throne, entranced in joy;
Or ye, whose life is to present all souls

Reborn to their Creator; or to search
The golden globed skies for deeds of grace;
And ye who move all Heavens, in whose names
The name of God is, as in angels' all;
The crown, the wisdom, the intelligence,
Kindness, and strength and beauty, splendor, worth,
Original and rule; and ye who move
Restless around the throne, the burning seven,
The virtue, power, salvation, fire, and rest,
Blessing and praise of God; and ye who rule
Regions or kingdoms, states, tribes, families,
Ages and times, and seasons, and events;
Systems and elements, material powers,
Mental and spiritual; or ye who bear
Souls from the heaven to earth, from earth to heaven,
Ye tenants of the archetypal worlds
And spiritual spheres; and you, ye saints!
Freed once on earth into the liberty
Of the necessity which is of God;
Yours are the many multitudes of stars,
And bliss and power for ever, ye are gods!
And live an endless life, bespoken here;
Bear witness, all, that happiness succeeds
To godliness; and that, despite of sin,
The world may recognize in all time's scenes,
Though belts of clouds bar half its burning disk,
The overruling, overthrowing power,
Which by our creature purposes works out
Its deeds, and by our deeds its purposes.

    LUCIFER. God! for thy glory only can I act,
And for thy creatures' good. When creatures stray
Farthest from Thee, then warmest towards them burns
Thy love, even as yon sun beams hotliest on
The earth when distant most.

GOD.

                                   The earth whereon
He dwells, this grain selected from the sands
Of life, dies with him.

LUCIFER.   God! I go to do
Thy will.

GOD.

    Thou, too, who watchest o'er the world
Whose end I fix, prepare to have it judged.
  ANGEL OF EARTH. Let me not then have
    watched o'er it in vain.
From age to age, from hour to hour I still
Have hoped it would grow better — hope so now:
'T is better than it once was, and hath more
Of mind and freedom than it ever had.
I love it more than ever. Thou didst give
It to me as a child. To me earth is
Even as the boundless universe to Thee;
Nay, more! for Thou couldst make another. It is
My world. Take it not from me, Lord! Thou,
    Christ,
Mad'st it the altar where thou offeredst up
Thyself for the creation. Let it be
Immortal as Thy love. And altars are
Holy; and sister angels, sister orbs
Hail it afar as such. Oh! I have heard
World question world and answer; seen them weep
Each other if eclipsed for one red hour,
And of all worlds most generous was mine,
The tenderest and the fairest.
  LUCIFER.   Knowest thou not
God's son to be the brother and the friend
Of spirit everywhere? Or hath thy soul
Been bound for ever to thy foolish world?
  ANGEL. Star unto star speaks light, and world
    to world
Repeats the password of the universe
To God; the name of Christ — the one great word
Well worth all languages in earth or Heaven.
  SON OF GOD. Think not I lived and died for
    thine alone,
And that no other sphere hath hailed me Christ.
My life is ever suffering for love.

In judging and redeeming worlds is spent
Mine everlasting being.
    LUCIFER.   Earth he next
Will judge; for so saith God.
    ANGEL OF EARTH.   Be it not, Lord!
Thou art a God of goodness and of love;
He is the evil of the universe,
And loveth not the earth, Thy Son, nor Thee.
Thou knowest best.
    LUCIFER.   Behold now all yon worlds!
The space each fills shall be its successor.
Accept the consolation!
    ANGEL OF EARTH.   Earth! oh, Earth
    LUCIFER. 'T is earth shall lead destruction; she
        shall end.
The stars shall wonder why she comes no more
On her accustomed orbit, and the sun
Miss one of his eleven of light; the moon,
An orphan orb, shall seek for earth for aye,
Through time's untrodden depths and find her not;
No more shall morn, out of the holy east,
Stream o'er the amber air her level light;
Nor evening, with the spectral fingers, draw
Her star-sprent curtain round the head of earth;
Her footsteps never thence again shall grace
The blue sublime of heaven.   Her grave is dug.
I see the stars, night-clad, all gathering
In long and dark procession.   Death's at work.
And, one by one, shall all yon wandering worlds,
Whether in orbed path they roll, or trail,
In an inestimable length of light,
Their golden train of tresses after them,
Cease; and the sun, centre and sire of light,
The keystone of the world-built arch of heaven,
Be left in burning solitude.   The stars,
Which stand as thick as dewdrops on the fields
Of heaven, and all they comprehend, shall pass.
The spirits of all worlds shall all depart
To their great destinies; and thou and I,

Greater in grief than worlds, shall live as now.
In hell's dark annals there is something writ,
Which shall amaze man yet.   There! to thy earth!
   ANGEL OF EARTH. There is a blind world, yet
      unlit by God,
Rolling around the extremest edge of light;
Where all things are disaster and decay,
The outcast of all being; no one thing
Fitting another: that is fit for thee.
Be that thy world! but not the living earth.
Stretch forth Thy shining shield, oh God! the
    heavens,
Over the prostrate earth, an armed friend,
And save her from the swift and violent hell
Her beauty hath enchanted! from the wrath
Of love like his, oh save her, though by death!
            GOD.
Destruction and salvation are the hands
Upon the face of time.   When both unite,
The day of death dawns.   Every orb exists
Unto its preappointed end: and earth,
My creature, the elect of worlds, ere all
Is saved.   The world shall perish as a worm
Upon destruction's path; the universe
Evanish like a ghost before the sun,
Yea like a doubt before the truth of God,
Yet nothing more than death shall perish.   Then,
Rejoice ye souls of God, regenerate,
Ye indwellers divine of Deity;
In Him ye are immortal as Himself!
   SON OF GOD.   O'er all things are eternity and
      change,
And special predilection of our God.
Thou who createst souls, as the sun clouds,
Out of the sea of spirit, sire of both
The first and second natures of Thy Son,
In whom the maker and the made make one,
Deific spirit! who in every world
Payeth creation's penalties; in all,

Is heir of God and nature, and in Thee,
And in self-worship, Deifies himself!
And you blest spirits for whom I died, for **whom,**
Forefated, fore-atoned for from the first,
All heaven reserves the fulness of its bliss;
Creator and created! witness, both,
How I have loved ye, as God-natured life
Alone can love and suffer!   Let the earth
And every orb, the offspring of all air,
Perish; but all I die for, live for **me.**

GOD.

The earth shall not **be** when her **sabbath ends,**
In the high close of order.
    LUCIFER.   Heaven, farewell!
Hell is more bearable than nothingness.
    THRONES.   Thou, God, **art Lord of mercy! and**
        Thy thoughts
Are high above the star-dust of the world!
    DOMINATIONS. **Yet** o'er   the   meanest   atom
        reignest Thou
Omnipotent as o'er the universe!
    POWERS.   Thy might is self-creative, **and Thy**
        works,
Immortal, temporal, destructible,
Are ever in Thy sight and blessed there!
The heavens are Thy bosom, and Thine **eye**
Is high **o'er** all existence; yea the worlds
Are but **Thy** shining foot-prints upon space!
    PRINCEDOMS.   Eternal Lord! Thy strength com-
        pels the worlds,
And bows the heads of ages; **at Thy voice**
Their unsubstantial essence **wears away.**
    VIRTUES.   All-favoring **God! we glory** but in
        Thee.
Ye **Heavens exalt,** expand yourselves! they come,
The infinite generations, all Divine,
Of Deity, our brethren and our friends!
    ARCHANGELS.   Thou who hast thousand names,
        as night hath stars,

Which light Thee up to eye create, yet not
One thousandth part illumine Thy boundlessness,
Nor that abyss of Being 'midst of which
Thy countless wonders constellate themselves;
Thy light, the light we dwell in shall at last
Fulfil the universe, and all be bliss;
The consummation of all ages come.
We praise Thee for Thy mercies, and for this,
The first, and last, and greatest of all boons.
   ANGELS.   Thee God! we praise
     Through our ne'er sunsetting days,
     And Thy just ways,
     Divine:
     In Thy hand is every spirit,
     And the meed the same may merit;
     All which all the worlds inherit
     Are Thine!
     It is not unto creatures given
     To scale the purposes of Heaven,
     Alway just and kind;
     But before Thy mighty breath,
     Life and spirit, dust and death,
     The boundless All is driven,
     Like clouds by wind.
  ANGEL OF EARTH. Woe! woe at last in Heaven!
     Earth to death is given;
     The ends of things hang still
     Over them as a sky;
     Do what we will,
     All's for eternity!

SCENE — *Wood and Water — Sunset.*

FESTUS *alone.*

FESTUS.   This is to be a mortal and immortal!
To live within a circle, — and to be
That dark point where the shades of all things around

Meet, mix, **and deepen.   All** things unto me
Show their **dark sides**! somewhere there must **be**
Oh! I feel like **a seed in the cold earth;**   [light.
Quickening at heart, and pining **for the air**!
Passion **is** destiny.   The heart is **its own**
Fate.   It is well youth's gold **rubs off so soon.**
The heart gets dizzy with its **drunken dance,**
And the voluptuous vanities **of life**
Enchain, enchant, and cheat my **soul no more.**
My spirit is on **edge.**   I can enjoy
Nought which has not the honied **sting of sin ;**
That **soothing** fret which makes the **young untried,**
Longing to **be** beforehand with their **nature,**
In dreams and **loneness** cry, they die **to live ;**
That wanton whetting of the soul, **which while**
It gives a finer, **keener edge for** pleasure,
Wastes more and dulls the sooner. Rouse **thee,**
      heart;
Bow of my life thou yet art full of spring!
My quiver still hath many purposes.
Yet what is worth a thought of all things here?
How mean, how miserable every care!
How doubtful, **too, the system** of the mind!
And then the **ceaseless, changeless, hopeless round**
Of weariness and **heartlessness and woe**
And vice and vanity!   Yet these make life;
The life at **least** I witness if **not feel.**
No matter! we are immortal.   **How I wish**
I could **love men! for amid all life's quests**
There seems but worthy one — to do men good.
It matters not how long we live but how.
For as the parts **of one manhood while here**
We live in every **age : we think and feel**
And feed upon the coming **and the gone**
As **much as on the now** time.   **Man is one :**
And **he hath one** great heart.   **It is thus we feel,**
With **a** gigantic throb athwart the sea,
Each others' rights and wrongs; thus **are we men.**
Let us think less of men and **more of God!**

Sometimes the thought comes swiftening over us,
Like a small bird winging the still blue air;
And then again, at other times, it rises
Slow, like a cloud which scales the skies all breath-
　　　less,
And just over head lets itself down on us.
Sometimes we feel the wish across the mind
Rush, like a rocket tearing up the sky,
That we should join with God and give the world
The slip: but while we wish, the world turns round,
And peeps us in the face — the wanton world;
We feel it gently pressing down our arm —
The arm we had raised to do for truth such wonders;
We feel it softly bearing on our side —
We feel it touch and thrill us through the body —
And we are fools and there's an end of us.
'Tis a fine thought that sometime end we must.
There sets the sun of suns! dies in all fire,
Like Asher's death-great monarch.　God of might!
We love and live on power.　It is spirit's end.
Mind must subdue.　To conquer is its life.
Why mad'st Thou not one spirit, like the sun,
To king the world?　And oh! might I have been
That sun-mind, how I would have warmed the
　　　world
To love and worship and bright life!
　　　Lucifer, *suddenly appearing.*　　　Not thou!
Hadst thou more power the more wouldst thou mis-
　　　use.
　　Festus.　Who art thou, pray?　I saw thee not
　　　before.
It seems as thou hadst grown out of the air.
　　Lucifer.　Thou knowest me well.　Though
　　　stranger to thine eye,
I am not to thy heart.
　　Festus.　　　　　　　I know thee not.
　　Lucifer.　Come nearer! Look on me! I am
　　　above thee;
Beneath thee, and around thee, and before thee.

Festus.   Why, **art** thou **all things, or dost go**
          through all ?
A spirit, or embodied blast of **air**?
I feel thou art **a spirit.**
    Lucifer.   Yea I am.
    Festus.   I knew it ! I am glad, yet tremble **so.**
What hours upon hours have I longed for this,
And hoped that thought or prayer might produce !
I have besought the stars, with tears, to send
A power unto me ; and have set the clouds
Until I thought I saw one coming : **but**
The shadowy giant alway thinned away,
And I was fated unimmortalized.
What shall I do ?   Oh ! let **me** kneel to **thee !**
    Lucifer.   Nay, rise ! and **I**'ll not **say, for thine**
          own sake,
That thou **dost pray in private to the Devil.**
    Festus.   **Father of** lies thou liest !
    Lucifer.   I am he !
It is enough **to** make the Devil merry,
To think that men call on me momently,
Deeming me ever dungeoned fast in Hell ;
Swearers and swaggerers jeer at my name ;
And oft indeed it is a special jest
With witling gallants.   Let me once appear !
Woe 's me ! they faint and shudder — pale and **pray ;**
The burning oath which quivered **on the lip,**
Starts back and sears and blisters up the **tongue ;**
Confusion ransacks the abandoned heart,
Quells the bold blood, and o'er the vaulted brow
Slips **the** white woman-hand.   To judgment, ho !
The very pivot of the **earth seems** snapped ;
And down they drop like ruins to repent.
Such be the bravery of mighty man !
    Festus.   **I must** be mad ; **or** mine eye cheats **my**
          brain ;
And this strange phantom comes from overthought,
Like the white lightning from a day too hot.
It must be so.   But I will pass it.

LUCIFER.   Stay!
FESTUS. Oh save me God! He is reality!
LUCIFER.   And now thou kneel'st to Heaven.
      Fye, graceless boy!
Mocking thy Maker with a cast-off prayer;
For had not I the first fruits of thy faith?
   FESTUS. Tempter, away! From all the crowds
      of life
Why single me? Why score the young green bole
For fellage? Go! Am I the youngest, worst?
No! Light the fires of hell with other souls;
Mine shall not burn with thee.
   LUCIFER.   Thou judgest harshly.
Can I not touch thee without slaying thee?
   FESTUS. Why art thou here? What wouldst
      thou have with me?
   LUCIFER. 'Fore all I would have gentle words
      and looks.
   FESTUS. I pray thee, go!
   LUCIFER. I cannot quit thee yet.
But why so sad? Wilt kneel to me again?   ·
This leafy closet is most apt for prayer.
   FESTUS. Yes; I will pray for thee and for myself.
   LUCIFER. Waste not thy prayers! I scatter them:
      they reach
No further than thy breath — a yard or so.
And as for me, I heed them, need them not.
My nature God knows and hath fixed; and He
Recks little of the manners of the world;
Wicked He holdeth it and unrepentant.
   FESTUS. Therefore the more some ought to pray.
   LUCIFER.   To blow
A kiss, a bubble and a prayer hath like
Effect and satisfaction.
   FESTUS.   Let me hence!
Go tell thy blasphemics and lies elsewhere.
Thou scatter prayer! Make me Thy minister
One moment God! that I may rid the world
For ever of its evil. Oh! Thine arm!

LUCIFER. **Canst rid** thyself?

FESTUS.   Alas, **no.**   Get thee gone !
Can nought insult thee nor provoke thy flight ?

LUCIFER. I laugh alike at ruin and redemption.
I am the one which knows nor hope nor fear ;
Which ne'er knew good nor e'er can know the **worst.**
What thinkest thou can anger me, or harm ? ·

FESTUS. · Wherefore didst thou quit Hell ? **To**
    drag me there ?

LUCIFER. Thou **wilt not guess mine** errand.
    Deem'st thou aught   ·
Which God had made all evil ? **Me He made.**
Oft I do good ; and thee **to serve** I come.

FESTUS. Did I not hear thee boast with **thy last**
    breath
Not to have known what good was ?

LUCIFER.   From myself
I know it not ; yet God's will I must **work.**
I come I say to scrve thee.

FESTUS.   Well ! I would
Thou never hadst : but speak thy purpose straight.

LUCIFER. **I heard** thy prayer **at** sunset. I **was**
    here.
I saw thy secret longings, unsaid thoughts,
Which prey upon the breast like night-fires on
A heath.   I know thy heart by heart.   I **read**
The tongue when still as well as when it moves.
And thou didst pray to God.   Did He attend ?
Or turn His eye from the great glass of **things,**
Wherein he worshippeth eternally
Himself, to thee one moment ?   He **did not.**
I tell thee nought **He cares for men.**   I came
And come to proffer thee the earth ; to set
Thee on a throne — the **throne of will** unbound —
To crown thy **life with** liberty and joy,
And make thee free and mighty even as I am !

FESTUS. I would not be as thou **art** for Hell's
    throne ;
Add Earth's — add Heaven's !

LUCIFER.   I knew thy proud high heart.
To test its worth and mark I held it brave,
In shape and being thus myself I came ;
Not in disguise of opportunity —
Not as some silly toy which serves for most —
Not in the mask of lucre, lust nor power —
Not in a goblin size nor cherub form —
But as the soul of Hell and evil came I
With leave to give the kingdom of the world —
The freedom of thyself.
   FESTUS.   Good ; prove thy powers.
   LUCIFER. Do I not prove them ? Who but I,
     that have
Immortal might o'er mine own mind, and o'er
All hearts and spirits of the living world,
Would share it with another, or forego,
One hour, the great enjoyment of the whole ?
And who but I give men what each loves best ?
   FESTUS. Open the Heavens and let me look on
     God !
Open my heart and let me see myself!
Then I 'll believe thee.
   LUCIFER.   ., Thou shalt not believe
For that I give thee, but for that I am.
Believe me first ; then I will prove myself.
Though sick I know thee of the joys of sense,
Yet those thou lovest most I will make pure,
And render worthy of thy love ; unfilm them,
That so thou mayst not dally with the blind.
Thou shalt possess them to their very souls.
Pleasure and love and unimagined beauty ;
All, all that be delicious, brilliant, great,
Of worldly things are mine, and mine to give.
   FESTUS. What can be counted pleasure after
     love ?
Like the young lion which hath once lapped blood,
The heart can ne'er be coaxed back to aught else.
   LUCIFER. I will sublime it for thee all to bliss :
As yet it hath but made thee wretched.

FESTUS. Spirit,
It is not bliss I seek ; I care not for it.
I am above the low delights of life.
The life I live is in a dark cold cavern,
Where I wander up and down feeling for something
Which is to be — and must be — what, I know not ;
But the incarnation of my destiny
Is nigh.
    LUCIFER. It is thy fate which weighs upon thee.
Necessity sits on humanity,
Like to the world on Atlas' neck. 'T is this,
And the sultry sense of overdrawn life.
    FESTUS. True ;
The worm of the world hath eaten out my heart.
    LUCIFER. I will renew it in thee. It shall be
The bosom favorite of every beauty,
Even like a rosebud. Thou shalt render happy,
By naming who may love thee. Come with me.
    FESTUS. I have a love on earth, and one in
        Heaven.
    LUCIFER. Thou shalt love ten as others love
        but one!
    FESTUS. Oh! I was glad when something in me
        said
Come, let us worship beauty! and I bowed ;
And went about to find a shrine ; but found
None that my soul, when seeing, said enough, to.
Many I met with where I put up prayers,
And had them more than answered ; and at such
I worshipped, partly because others did ;
Partly because I could not help myself.
But none of these were for me ; and away
I went champing and choking in proud pain ;
In a burning wrath that not a sea could slake.
So I betook me to the sounding sea ;
And overheard its slumberous mutterings
Of a revenge on man ; whereat almost
I gladdened, for I felt savage as the sea.
I had only one thing to behold, the sea ;

I had only one thing to believe, I loved;
Until that lonesome sameness grew sublime
And darkly beautiful as death, when some
Bright soul regains its star-home, or as Heaven
Just when the stars falter forth, one by one,
Like the first words of love from a maiden's lips.
There are points from which we can command our
          life;
When the soul sweeps the future like a glass;
And coming things, full freighted with our fate,
Jut out, dark, on the offering of the mind.
Let them come! Many will go down in sight;
In the billow's joyous dash of death go down.
At last came love; not whence I sought nor thought
          it;
As on a ruined and bewildered wight
Rises the roof he meant to have lost for ever.
On came the living vessel of all love;
Terrible in its beauty as a serpent,
Rode down upon me like a ship full sail
And bearing me before it, kept me up
Spite of the drowning speed at which we drave
On, on, until we sank both.   Was not this love?
    LUCIFER.   Why, how can I tell?   I am not in
          love;
But I have oft times heard mine angels call
Most piteously on their lost loves in Heaven;
And, as I suffer, I have seen them come;
Seen starlike faces peep between the clouds,
And Hell become a tolerable torment.
Some souls lose all things but the love of beauty;
And by that love they are redeemable;
For in love and beauty they acknowledge good;
And good is God — the great Necessity.
I have not told thee half I will do for thee.
All secrets thou shalt ken — all mysteries construe.
At nothing marvel.   All the veins which stretch,
Unsearchable by human eyes, of lore
Most precious, most profound, to thine shall bare

And vulgar **lie** like dust. The world within,
The world above thee, and the dark domain,
Mine own thou shalt o'er rule; and he alone
Who rightly can esteem such high delights,
He only merits—he alone shall have.
    FESTUS.   And if I have shall I be happier?
What is pleasure?   What, happiness?
    LUCIFER.   **It is that**
I vouchsafe to thee.
    FESTUS.   **Am I** tempted thus
Unto my fall?
    LUCIFER.   God wills or **lets it be.**
How thinkest thou?
    FESTUS.   **That I** will go with thee.
    LUCIFER.   From God I come.
    FESTUS.   I do believe thee, spirit,
He will not let thee harm me.   Him I love,
And thee I fear not.   I obey Him.
    LUCIFER.   Good.
Both time and case are urgent.   Come away!
    FESTUS.   Give **me a** breathing-time to fortify,
Within myself, the promise I have made.
    LUCIFER.   Expect **me,** then, at midnight, here.
       Remember,
That thou canst any time repent.
    FESTUS.   Ay, true.   [*Goes.*
    LUCIFER.   Repentance never yet did **aught on**
       earth;
It undoes many good things.   **Of all men,**
Heaven shield me from the wretch **who can repent**

SCENE — *Water* **and** **Wood** — *Midnight.*

FESTUS, *alone.*

All things are calm, **and** fair, and passive.   Earth
Looks as if lulled upon an angel's lap
Into a breathless dewy sleep: so still,

That we can only say of things, they **be**!
The lakelet now, no longer vexed with gusts,
Replaces on her breast the pictured moon   [time
Pearled round with **stars**. Sweet imaged scene of
To come, perchance, when this vain life o'erspent,
Earth may some purer beings' presence bear;
Mayhap even God may walk among his saints,
In eminence and brightness like **yon moon**,
Mildly outbeaming all **the beads of light**
Strung o'er night's proud **dark brow**. How
          strangely fair
Yon round still star, which looks half suffering from,
And half rejoicing in **its own** strong fire;
Making itself a lonelihood of light,
Like Deity, where'er in Heaven it dwells.
How can the beauty of material things
So win **the** heart and work upon the mind,
Unless like-natured with them ? Are great things
And thoughts of the same blood ? They have like
          effect.   -
    LUCIFER.   **Why** doubt on mind ? What matter
          how we call   -
That which all feel to be their noblest part ?
Even spirits have a better and a worse :
For every thing created **must have form.**
Passions they have, somewhat **like thine;** but less
Of grossness and that downwardness of **soul**
Which **men have.** It is true they have **no earth;**
For what they live **on is** above themselves.
    FESTUS.   There seems a sameness among things;
          for mind
And matter speak, in causes, **of one God.**
The inward and the outward worlds are like;
The pure and gross but differ in degree.
Tears, feeling's bright embodied form, **are** not
More pure than dewdrops, Nature's tears, which **she**
Sheds in her own breast for the fair which die.
The sun insists on gladness; but **at** night,
When he is gone, poor Nature loves **to** weep.

LUCIFER. **There is less** real difference among
things
Than men imagine.   They overlook the mass,
But fasten each on some particular crumb,
Because they feel that they can equal **that,**
Of doctrine, or belief, or party cause.
  FESTUS. That is the madness of the **world — and**
that
Would I **remove.**
  LUCIFER.   It is imbecility,
Not madness.
  FESTUS.   Oh! the brave and good who **swerve**
A worthy cause can only one way fail;
By perishing therein.   Is it to fail?
No; every great or good man's death is a step
Firm set towards their end — the **end** of being;
Which is the good **of all and love of God.**
The world **must have great minds, even** as great
spheres
Or **suns,** to govern **lesser** restless minds,
While they stand still and burn with life; to keep
Them in their places, and to light and heat them.
If I desire immortal life for aught,
It is to learn the mystery of mind
And somewhat more of God.   Let others rule
Systems or succor saints, if such things please;
To live like light or die in light like dew,
Either! I should be blest.
  LUCIFER.   **It may not be.**
For as we do no **see the sun himself,**
It is but the light about him, like a **ring**
Of glory round the forehead of **a saint, so**
God thou wilt never see.   His **unveiled love**
Were terrible, too much for man to meet.
  FESTUS. Men have a **claim on** God; and none
who hath
A heart of kindness, reverence and love,
But dare look God in the face and ask His smile.
He dwells in no fierce light — no cloud of flame;

And if it were, Faith's eye can look through **Hell,**
And through the solid world.   We must all **think**
On **God.**   Yon water must reflect the sky.
Midnight!   Day hath too much light for us,
To see things spiritually.   Mind and Night
Will meet, though in silence, like forbidden **lovers,**
With whom to see each other's sacred form
Must satisfy.   The stillness of deep bliss,
Sound as the **silence** of the **high** hill-top
Where **thunder finds no echo** — like God's voice
Upon the worldling's proud, **cold, rocky heart** —
Fills full the sky ; and the eye shares with **Heaven**
That look, **so like to** feeling, which the **bright**
And glorious things of Nature **ever wear.**
There is **much to** think **and** feel of things beyond
This earth ; **which** lie, **as we** deem, upwards — far
From the day's glare and riot — they are Night's!
Oh ! **could we** lift the future's sable shroud !
    LUCIFER.   Behind a shroud **what** should thou
        see but death ?
    FESTUS.   Spirit is like the thread whereon are
        strung
The beads **or worlds of** life.   It may **be here,**
It may be there that I shall **live** again ;
In yon strange world whose long nights know no star,
But seven fair maidlike moons attending **him**
Perfect his sky — perchance in one of those —
But live again I shall wherever it be.
We long to learn the future — love to guess.
    LUCIFER.   The science of the future is to **man,**
But **what** the shadow of the wind might be.
Such thoughts are vain and **useless.**
    FESTUS.   Forced on us.
    LUCIFER.   All things are of necessity.
    FESTUS.   Then best.
But the **good are** never fatalists.   The bad
Alone act by necessity, they say.
    LUCIFER.   It matters not what men assume to be ;
Or good, **or** bad, they are **but what they are.**

FESTUS. What is necessity ? Are we, and thou,
And all the **worlds,** and the whole infinite
We cannot **see,** but working out God's thoughts ?
And have we no self-action ? Are all God ?
LUCIFER. Then hath He sin and all absurdity.
FESTUS. Yet, if created Being have free-will,
Is it not wrong to judge it may traverse
God's own high will, and yet impossible
To think on 't otherwise ?
LUCIFER.   It may **be so.**
All creature wills, and all their ends and powers
Must come within the **boundless scope** of God's.
FESTUS. And all our powers are **but weaknesses**
To what we shall have, **and to that God hath.**
Doth not the wish, **too, point the likelihood**
Of life to **come ?**
LUCIFER.   **Boys wish** that they were kings.
And so with thee. A deathless spirit's state,
Freed from gross form and bodily weightiness,
Seems kingly by the side of souls like thine.
And boys and men will likely both be balked.
What if it be, that spirit, **after** death,
Is loosed like flesh into its elements ?
The worlds which man hath constellated, hold
No fellowship in nature ; **nor** perchance
As he hath systematized life, mind, **and soul.**
But sooth to say, I know **not aught of** this.
I have no kind. No nature **like to me**
Exists. And human **spirits must at least**
Sleep till the day of doom, **if it ever be.**
FESTUS. Hast **never known one free from**
       body?
LUCIFER.   None.
FESTUS. Why **seek then to** destroy them ?
LUCIFER.   It is my part.
Let ruin bury ruin. Let it be
Woe here, woe there, woe, woe, be everywhere !
It is not for me to know, nor thee, the end
Of evil. I inflict and thou must **bear.**

The arrow knoweth not its end and aim.
And I keep rushing, ruining along
Like a great river rich with dead men's souls.
For if I knew, I might rejoice ; and that
To me by Nature is forbidden. I know
Nor joy nor sorrow ; but a changeless tone
Of sadness like the nightwind's is the strain
Of what I have of feeling. I am not
As other spirits, — but a solitude
Even to myself ; I the sole spirit sole.
    FESTUS. Can none of thine immortals answer
      me ?
    LUCIFER. None, mortal !
    FESTUS. Where then is thy vaunted power ?
    LUCIFER. It is better seen as thus I stand apart
From all. Mortality is mine — the green
Unripened universe. But as the fruit
Matures, and world by world drops mellowed off
The wrinkling stalk of Time, as thine own race
Hath seen of stars now vanished — all is hid
From me. My part is done. What after comes
I know not more than thou.
    FESTUS.   Raise me a spirit !
Awake ye dead ! out with the secret, death !
The grave hath no pride nor the rise-again.
Let each one bring the bane whereof he died.
Bring the man his, the maiden hers ! Oh ! half
Mankind are murderers of themselves or souls.
Yea, what is life but lingering suicide ?
Wake, dead ! Ye know the truth ; yet there ye lie
All mingling, mouldering, perishing together
Like run sand in the hour-glass of old Time.
Death is the mad world's asylum. There is peace ;
Destruction's quiet and equality.
Night brings out stars as sorrow shows us truths :
Though many, yet they help not ; bright, they light
      not.
They are too late to serve us : and sad things
Are aye too true. We never see the stars

Till we can see nought but them.   So with truth.
And yet if one would look down a deep well,
Even at noon, we might see those same stars
Far fairer than the blinding blue — the truth ;
Probe the profound of thine own nature, man !
And thou may'st see reflected, e'en in life,
The worlds, the Heavens, the ages ; by and **by,**
The coming **come.**   Then welcome, **world-eyed**
        Truth !
But there are other eyes men better love
Than Truth's : for when we have her she is so cold,
And **proud, we** know not what to do with **her.**
We cannot understand her, cannot teach ;
She makes us love her, but she loves not us ;
And quits us as she came and looks back never.
Wherefore we fly to Fiction's warm embrace,
With her **to** relax and bask ourselves at ease ;
And, in her loving and unhindering lap
Voluptuously lulled, we dream at most
On death and truth : she knows them, loves them
        not ;
Therefore we hate them and deny them both.
Call up the dead !
     LUCIFER.   Let rest while rest they may !
For free from **pain** and **from** this world's wear **and**
        tear
It may be **a** relief to them to rot ;
And it must be that at the day of **doom,**
If mortals should take up immortal life,
They will curse me with a **thunder which shall**
        shake
The sun from out the socket of his sphere.
The curse of all created.   Think on it !
     FESTUS.   Those souls thou mean'st whom thou
        hast ruined, damned.
     LUCIFER.   Nor only those ; when once the vir-
        gin bloom
Of soul is soiled — and rudely hath my hand
Swept o'er the swelling clusters of all life —

Little it matters whether crushed or touched
Scarcely : each speaks the spoiler hath been there.
The saved, the lost, shall curse me both alike :
God too shall curse me, and I, I, myself.
That curse is ever greatening — quick with hell ;
The coming consummation of all woe.
    FESTUS.   O man, be happy ! Die and cease for
       ever !
Why wear we not the shroud alway, that robe
Which speaks our rank on earth, our privilege ?
To know I have a deathless soul I would lose it.
    LUCIFER.   Believest thou all I tell thee ?
    FESTUS.   All, I do.
Stringing the stars at random round her head,
Like a pearl network, there she sits — bright night !
I love night more than day — she is so lovely.
But I love night the most because she brings
My love to me in dreams which scarcely lie ;
Oh ! all but truth and lovelier oft than truth !
Let me have dreams like these, sweet Night, for
       ever,
When I shall wake no more ; an endless dream
Of love and holy beauty 'mid the stars.
    LUCIFER.   I see thy heart and I will grant thy
       wish.
I have lied to thee. I have command over spirits.
Whom wilt thou that I call ?
    FESTUS.   Mine Angela !
    LUCIFER.   There is an Angel ever by thine
       hand.
What seest thou ?
    FESTUS.   It is my love ! It is she !
My glory ! spirit ! beauty, let me touch thee.
Nay, do not shrink back : well then I am wrong :
Thou didst not use to shrink from me, my love.
Angela ! dost thou hear me ?   Speak to me.
And thou art there — looking alive and dead.
Thy beauty is then incorruptible.
I thought so, oft as I have looked on thee.

Thou art too much even now for me as once.
I cannot gather what **I raved to say**;
Nor why **I had thee hither.   Stay, sweet sprite!**
Dear art thou to me now, as in that hour
When first Love's wave of feeling, spray-like broke
Into bright utterance, and we said we loved.
Yea, but I must come to thee.   Move no more!
Art thou in death or Heaven or from **the stars?**
Have I done wrong in calling for thee **thus?**
What art thou?   Speak, love; whisper **me as wont**
In the dear times gone bye; or durst thou **not**
Unfold the mystery of thine and mine
Own being?   Was it Death who **hushed thy lips?**
Is his cold finger there still?   **Let me come!**
She is not!

    Lucifer.   **And thou canst not bring** her back.
    Festus.   **I will not, cannot be** without her.
        Call her!
    Lucifer.   **I call on spirits and I** make them
        come;
But they depart according **to their own** will.
Another time and she shall **speak with thee —**
Ere long — and she shall **shew** thee **where she**
    dwells,
And how doth pass her immortality; —
If lengthening decay can so be called.
Can lines finite one way be infinite
Another?   And yet such is deathlessness.
    Festus.   It is hard **to deem that spirits cease,**
        that thought
And feeling flesh-like perish **in the dust.**
Shall we know those again **in a future state**
Whom we have known **and loved on** earth?   Say
        yes!
    Lucifer.   **The mind** hath features as the body
        hath.
    Festus.   **But** is it mind which shall rerise?
    Lucifer.   Man were
Not man without the mind he had in life.

Festus.   Shall all defects of mind and fallacies
Of feeling be immortalized? all needs,
All joys, all sorrows, be again gone through,
Before the final crisis be imposed?
Shall Heaven but be old earth created new?
Or earth, treelike, transplanted into Heaven,
To flourish by the waters of all life,
And we within its shade, as heretofore,
Cropping its fruit, with life-seeds cored at heart?
   Lucifer.   Man's nature, physical and psychical,
Will be together raised, changed, glorified;
And all shall be alike, like God; and all
Unlike each other, and themselves.   The earth
Shall vanish from the thoughts of those she bore,
As have the idols of the olden time
From men's hearts of the present.   All delight
And all desire, shall be with Heavenly things,
And the new nature God bestowed on man.
   Festus.   Then man shall be no more man, but
      an Angel.
   Lucifer.   When he is dead and buried. What
      remains, —
That such an obscure, contradictory, thing
Should be perpetuated anywhere?
   Festus.   Oh! if God hates the flesh, why made
      He it
So beautiful that e'en its semblance maddens?
Am I to credit what I think I have seen?
Or am I suffering some deceit of thine?
   Lucifer.   I am explaining, not deluding.
   Festus.   True
Defining night by darkness, death by dust.
I run the gauntlet of a file of doubts,
Each one of which down hurls me to the ground.
I ask a hundred reasons what they mean,
And every one points gravely to the ground,
With one hand, and to Heaven with the other.
In vain I shut mine eyes.   Truth's burning beam
Forces them open, and when open, blinds them.

Lucifer. Doubly unhappy!

Festus.   I am too unhappy
To die; as some too way-worn cannot sleep.
Planets and suns, that set themselves on fire
By their own rapid self-revolvements, are
But like some hearts. Existence I despise.
The shape of man is wearisome; a bird's,
A worm's — a whirlwind's, I would change with
      aught.
Time! dash thine hour-glass down. Have done
      with this!
The course of Nature seems a course of Death,
And nothingness the sole substantial thing.

Lucifer. Corruption springs from Light: 't is
      the same power
Creates, preserves, destroys: the matter which
It works on, being one ever-changing form, —
The living and the dying and the dead.

Festus. I 'll not believe a thing which I have
      known.
Hell was made hell for me, and I am mad.

Lucifer. True venom churns the froth out of
      the lips;
It works, and works like any water-wheel.
And she then was the maiden of thy heart.
Well, I have promised. Ye shall meet again.

Festus. I loved her for that she was beau-
      tiful;
And that to me she seemed to be all nature
And all varieties of things in one;
Would set at night in clouds of tears, and rise
All light and laughter in the morning: yea,
And that she never schooled within her breast
One thought or feeling, but gave holiday
To all; and that she made all even mine
In the communion of love: and we
Grew like each other for we loved each other —
She, mild and generous as the sun in spring;
And I, like earth all budding out with love.

Lucifer.   And then, love's old end, falsehood
        nothing worse
I hope ?
    Festus.   What's worse than falsehood ? to deny
The god which is within us, and in all
Is love ?   Love hath as many vanities
As charms ; and this, perchance, the chief of both :
To make our young heart's track upon the first,
And snowlike fall of feeling which overspreads
The bosom of the youthful maiden's mind,
More pure and fair than even its outward type.
If one did thus, was it from vanity ?
Or thoughtlessness, or worse ?   Nay, let it pass.
The beautiful are never desolate ;
But some one alway loves them — God or man.
If man abandons, God himself takes them.
And thus it was.   She whom I once loved died.
The lightning loathes its cloud — the soul its clay.
Can I forget that hand I took in mine,
Pale as pale violets ; that eye, where mind
And matter met alike divine ? ah, no !
May God that moment judge me when I do !
Oh ! she was fair : her nature once all spring,
And deadly beauty like a maiden sword ;
Startlingly beautiful.   I see her now !
Whatever thou art thy soul is in my mind ;
Thy shadow hourly lengthens o'er my brain,
And peoples all its pictures with thyself.
Gone, not forgot — passed, not lost — thou shalt
        shine
In Heaven like a bright spot in the sun !
She said she wished to die, and so she died ;
For, cloudlike, she poured out her love, which was
Her life, to freshen this parched heart.   It was thus ·
I said we were to part, but she said nothing.
There was no discord — it was music ceased —
Life's thrilling, bounding, bursting joy.   She sate
Like a house-god, her hands fixed on her knee ;
And her dark hair lay loose and long around her,

Through which her wild bright eye flashed like flint
She spake **not,** moved not, but she looked the **more,**
As if her **eye were action, speech and** feeling.
I felt it all ; **and came and knelt beside** her.
The electric touch solved both **our** souls together.
Then **comes** the feeling which unmakes, undoes ;
Which tears the sealike soul up by the **roots**
And lashes it in **scorn against** the skies.
Twice did I madly swear to God, **hand clenched,**
That not even He nor death should **tear her from me.**
It is the saddest and the sorest sight
One's own love weeping ;— but why **call on God,**
But that the feeling of the boundless **bounds**
All feeling, as the welkin doth the **world ?**
It **is** this which **ones us** with **the** whole **and God.**
Then first we **wept ; then closed** and clung to-
       gether ;
And my heart shook this building of my breast,
Like a live engine booming up and down.
She fell **upon** me like a snow-wreath thawing.
Never were bliss and beauty, love and woe,
Ravelled and twined together into madness,
As in that one wild hour **; to** which all else,
The past, is but **a** picture — that alone
Is real, and for ever there in front ;
Making a black blank on **one** side of life
Like a blind eye.   But after that I left her ;
And only **saw** her once again **alive.**
    Lucifer.   Well, shall we go ?
    Festus.   This moment.   **I am ready.**
Farewell ye dear old walks and **trees ! farewell**
Ye waters !   I have **loved ye well.   In youth**
And childhood it **hath been my life to drift**
Across ye lightly **as** a leaf ; or skim
Your waves in **yon** skiff, swallowlike **; or lie**
Like a loved locket on your sunny bosom.
Could I, like you, by looking in myself
Find mine own Heaven—farewell ! Immortal, come !
The morning peeps her blue **eye** on the east

LUCIFER. Think not so fondly as thy foolish
      race,
Imagining a Heaven from things without ;
The picture on the passing wave call Heaven —
The wavelet, life — the sands beneath it, death ;
Daily more seen till, lo ! the bed is bare.
This fancy fools the world.
FESTUS.   Let us away !

SCENE — *A Mountain — Sunrise.*

FESTUS AND LUCIFER.

FESTUS. Hail beauteous Earth ! Gazing o'er
      thee, I all
Forget the bonds of being ; and I long
To fill thee, as a lover pines to blend
Soul, passion, yea existence, with the fair
Creature he calls his own. I ask for nought
Before or after death but this, — to lie,
And look, and live, and bask, and bless myself
Upon thy broad bright bosom. From thee I
Sprang, and to thee I turn, heart, arm and brain.
Yes, I am all thine own. Thou art the sole
Parent. To rock and river, plain and wood
I cry, ye are my kin. While I, O Earth !
Am but an atom of thee, and a breath,
Passing unseen and unrecorded like
The tiny throb here in my temple's pulse.
Thou art for ever and the sacred bride
Of heaven, — worthy the passion of our God.
O ! full of light, love, grace ! — the grace of all
Who owe to thee their life ; thy Maker's love ;
His face's light. All thine rejoice in thee ;
Thou in thyself for aye ; rolling through air
As seraphs' song out of their trumpet lips
Rolls round the skies of Heaven. See the sun !
God's crest upon His azure shield the Heavens.
Canst thou, a spirit, look upon him ?

LUCIFER.   Ay.
I led him from the void, where he was wrought,
By this right hand, up to the glorious seat
His brightness overshadows; built his throne
On piles of gold; and laid his chambers on
Beams of gold; wrapped a veil of fire around
His face; and bade him reign and burn like me.
There, ever since, sat warming into life
These worlds as in a nest, he has and is.
But fall he must.   I have done, do, nought **else**
From my first thought to this and to my last.
No matter; it is beneath this mind of mine
To reck of aught.   **I bear, have borne** the ill
Of ages, of eternities—and must.
I care **not.**   I shall sway the **world as now,**
Which worse **and worse sinks with me as I** sink,
Till finite souls **evanish as** a vapor;
Till immortality, the proud thing, **perish;**
And God alone be and eternity.
Then will I clap my hands and cry to Him,
I have done! Have **Thy will** now! There is none
        but Thee.
I am the first created being.   **I**
Will be the last to perish and to die.
    FESTUS.   Thou **art a** fit monitor, **methinks, of**
        pleasure.
    LUCIFER.   To the high air **sunshine and cloud**
        are one;
Pleasure and pain to me.   **Thou and the earth**
Alone feel these as different— **for Ye**
Are under them — the **Heavens and I above.**
    FESTUS.   But tell me, **have ye scenes like this** in
        Hell?
    LUCIFER.   Nay, not in Heaven.
    FESTUS.   What is Heaven? not the toys
Of singing, **love and** music? such a place
Were fit for women only.
    LUCIFER.   Heaven is **no** place;
Unless it be a place **with** God, allwhere.

It is the being good — the knowing God —
The consciousness of happiness and power;
With knowledge which no spirit e'er can lose
But doth increase in every state; and aught
It most delights in the full leave to do.
But why consume me with such questions?   Why
Add earth to Hell, in the great chain of worlds
Which God in wrath hath bound about me?
    FESTUS.   Why!
'T was therefore that I closed with thee, great Fiend!
That thou mightst answer all things I proposed,
Or bring me those who would do.
    LUCIFER.   All these things
Thou wilt know sometime, when to see and know
Are one; to see a thing and comprehend
The nature of it essentially; perceive
The reason and the science of its being,
And the relations with the universe
Of all things actual or possible,
Mortal, immortal, spiritual, gross.
This, when the spirit is made free of Heaven,
Is the divine result; proportioned still
To the intelligence as human; for
There are degrees in Heaven as every thing,
By God's will.   Unimaginable space
As full of suns as is earth's sun of atoms,
Faileth to match His boundless variousness;
And ever must do, though a thousand worlds,
As diverse from each other as is thine
From any of thy system's, were elanced
Each minute into life unendingly.
All of yon worlds, and all who dwell in them,
Stand in diverse degrees of bliss and being.
Through the ten thousand times ten thousandth grade
Of blessedness, above this world's and man's
Ability to feel or to conceive,
The soul may pass and yet know nought of Heaven.
More than a dim and miniature reflection
Of its most bright infinity; — for God

Makes to each spirit its peculiar Heaven ; —
And yet is Heaven a bright reality,
As this or any of yon worlds ; a state
Where all is loveliness **and** power **and** love ;
Where all sublimest qualities of **mind,**
Not infinite, are limited alone
By the surrounding Godhood, and where **nought**
But what produceth glory and delight,
To creature and Creator is: where all
Enjoy entire dominion o'er themselves,
Acts, feelings, thoughts, conditions, qualities,
Spirit and **soul** and mind ; **all** under God,
For spirit is soul Deified ; — **while earth,**
To the immortal **vast, God-natured Spirit,**
Is but **a** spell, **which having served to light**
A lamp, is **cast into consuming fire.**
    FESTUS.   **And Hell?** **Is it** naught **but pits** and
        chains and flames ?
    LUCIFER.   **An** ever greatening sense of ill and
        woe,
Aye crushing down the soul, but filling never
Its infinite capacity of pain.
    FESTUS. But human nature is **not infinite,**
And therefore **cannot suffer** endlessly.
    LUCIFER.   **God may create** in time **what shall**
        endure
Unto Eternity. With **Him is no**
Distinction, nor in **that which is of Him.**
    FESTUS. Then **is not soul of God, but man and**
        earth.
Soul when made spirit is of earth no more,
Nor time, **but of Eternity and Heaven.**
'T is but when **in the body, and bent down**
To worldly **ends, that human** souls **become**
Objects of time, **as most are,** till the **hour**
Comes **when the soul of man** shall **be** made one
With God's **spirit ;** and where shall woe be then ?
Where, sin ? where, suffering ? when the mortal
        soul

Shall be Divinized and eternized by
God's very spirit put upon it ?
    LUCIFER.   How
Can souls begotten to predestined doom,
From and before all worlds, be deemed of earth?
    FESTUS.   Things spiritual, as belonging God,
Are known unto Him, and predestined from
Eternity, nor these alone ; but Flesh
Forms not nor does it need the care of Fate.
    LUCIFER. The object of eternal knowledge
          must
Have like existence.
    FESTUS.   Then it cannot be
Bound unto torment ; that would be to bring
Torture on godlike essence.
    LUCIFER.   Hast not heard,
How thine existence here, on earth, is but
The dark and narrow section of a life
Which was with God, long ere the sun was lit,
And shall be yet, when all the bold bright stars
Are dark as death-dust — Immortality
And Wisdom tending thee on either hand,
Thy divine sisters ? But do thou believe
E'en what thou wilt. It matters not to me.
    FESTUS. Is it the nature or the deed of God
To render finite follies infinite,
Or to eternize sin and death in fire ?
For so long as the punishment endures,
The crime lasts. Were it not for thy presence,
Spirit ! I would not deem Hell were.
    LUCIFER.   Let not
My presence pass for more than it is worth,
I pray, nor yet my absence. Trust me, I
Could wish, with thee, that Hell were blotted out
Of utmost space. 'T is man himself aye makes
His own God and his hell. But this is truth.
    FESTUS. The truth is perilous never to the true,
Nor knowledge to the wise ; and to the fool,
And to the false, error and truth alike.

Error is worse than ignorance.   But say : —
How can eternal punishment be due
To temporal offences, to a pulse
Of momentary madness ?
    Lucifer.   Pardon me.
Sin **is** not temporary.   Nothing is,
Of spiritual nature, but hath cause
Immortal and immortal end in all,
As spirits.   Therefore till the soul shall be
By grace redeified, as is the soul,
So is the sin, for **ever** before God.
    Festus.   Sin **is** not **of** the spirit, but of that
Which **blindeth spirit, heart and** brain.
    Lucifer.   **Believe so.**
The **law** of all the worlds is retribution.
    Festus.   **But is it so of God ?**
    Lucifer.   The laws of Heaven
Are not of earth ; there law is liberty.
    Festus.   Thou thundercloud of spirits, darkning
The skies and wrecking earth !   Could I hate men
How I **should** joy with thee, even as an eagle,
Nigh famished, in the fellowship of storms ;
But I still love them.   What will come of men ?
    Lucifer.   Whatever may, perdition is **their**
          meed.
Were Heaven dispeopled for a ministry
To warn them of their ways ; were thou and I
To monish them ; were Heaven, and Earth, and Hell
To preach at once, they still would mock and **jeer**
As now ; but never repent until too late ;
Until the everlasting hour had struck.
    Festus.   **Men** might be better **if we better**
          deemed
Of **them.**   The worst way to improve **the** world
Is to condemn it.   Men may overget
Delusion — not despair.
    Lucifer.   Why love mankind ?
The affections **are** thy system's weaknesses ;
The wasteful outlets of self-maintenance.

Festus. The wild flower's tendril, proof of
    feebleness,
Proves strength; and so we fling our feelings out,
The tendrils of the heart, to bear us up.
O Earth! how drear to think to tear oneself,
Even for an hour, from looks like this of thine;
From features, oh! so fair; to quit for aye
The luxury of thy side. Why, why art thou
Thus glorious, and 't were not to sate the soul,
And chide us for the senseless dream of Heaven?
The still strong stream sweeps onward to its end,
Like one of the great purposes of God;
Or like, may be, a soul like mine to Him.
Along yon deep blue vein upon thy bosom,
Earth, I could float for ever. See it there —
Winding among its green and smiling isles,
Like Charity amidst her children dear;
Or Peace, rejoicing in her olive wreaths,
And gladdening as she glides along the lands.
    Lucifer. And yet all this must end — must
        pass; drop down
Oblivion like a pebble in a pit:
For God shall lay His hand upon the earth,
And crush it up like a red leaf.
    Festus.   Not be?
I cannot root the thought, nor hold it firm.
    Lucifer. This same sweet world which thou
        wouldst fondly deem
Eternal, may be; which I soon shall see
Destruction suck back as the tide a shell.
    Festus. It will not be yet. I'll woo thee,
        world, again,
And revel in thy loveliness and love.
I have a heart with room for every joy:
And since we must part, sometime, while I may,
I'll quaff the nectar in thy flowers, and press
The richest clusters of thy luscious fruit
Into the cup of my desires. I know
My years are numbered not in units yet.

But I cannot live unless I love and **am loved**;
Unless I have the young **and beautiful**
Bound up like pictures in my **book of life.**
It is the intensest **vanity** alone
Which makes us bear with life.   **Some seem to**
          live,
Whose hearts are like those unenlightened stars
Of the first darkness — lifeless, timeless, useless —
With nothing but a cold night air about them;
Not suns — not planets — darkness organized:
Orbs of a desert darkness: with no soul
To light **its** watchfire in the wilderness,
And civilize the solitude **one moment.**
There **are such seemingly; but how or why**
They live **I know not.   This to me is life;**
That if life **be a burden, I will join**
To make it **but** the **burden of a song:**
I hate the world's **coarse thought.   And** this is life
To watch young beauty's **budlike** feelings burst
And load the soul with love; — as that pale flower,
Which opes at eve, spreads sudden on the dark
Its yellow bloom, and sinks the air down with
          sweets.
Let Heaven take all that's good — Hell all **that's**
          foul;
Leave us the lovely! and we will ask no more.
    LUCIFER.   To me **it seems time** all **should end.**
          The sky
Grows gray.   It **is not so** bright **nor blue as once.**
Well I remember, **as it were** yesterday,
When **earth** and **Heaven went happy, hand in**
          hand,
With all the **morning dew of youth** about them;
With the **bright unworldly hearts of** youth and
          truth
And the maiden **bosoms of** the beautiful: —
Ere earth **sinned,** or the pure indignant Heavens
Retreated **high,** nigh God; when earth was all
A creeping mass alive with shapeless things:

And when there were but three things in the
    world —
Monsters, mountains and water : before age
Had thickened the eyes of stars ; and while the sea,
Rejoicing like a ring of saints round God,
Or Heaven on Heaven about some newborn sun,
In its sublime samesoundingness, laughed out
And cried not I ! Like God I never rest.
    Festus. God hath his rest ; **earth hers. Let me**
      have mine.
Yet must I **look** on thee, fair scene, again,
Ere I depart. **The glory** of the world
Is on all hands. In one encircling ken,
I gaze on river, sea, isle, continent,
Mountain, and wood, and wild, and fire-lipped hill,
And **lake, and** golden plain, and sun, and Heaven,
Where the stars brightly die, whose death is day ;
City and port and palace, ships and tents,
Lie massed and mapped before me. All is here.
The elements of the world are at my feet,
Above **me and about** me. Now would I
Be and do somewhat beside that I am.
Canst **thou not give me some** ethereal slave,
Of the pure essence of an element —
Such **as** my bondless **brain hath oft times drawn**
In the divine insanity of dreams —
To stand before **me and obey me, spirit?**
    Lucifer. **Call out, and see if aught arise to**
      thee.
    Festus. Green dewy **Earth,** who standest at my
      feet,
Singing **and** pouring sunshine on thy head,
As näiad native water, speak to me !
I am thy son. Canst thou not now, as once,
Bring forth **some** being dearer, liker to thee
Than is my race, — Titan **or** tiny fay,
Stream-nymph or wood-nymph ? She hath ceased
      to speak,
Like God, except in thunder, **or to look**

Unless in lightning.   Miracles, **with earth,**
Are out of fashion as with Heaven.
   Lucifer.   More's
The pity.   **Call** elsewhere !   Old Earth is **hard**
Of hearing, may be.
   Festus.   I beseech thee, Sea !
Tossing thy wavy locks in sparkling play,
Like to a child awakening with the light
To laughter.   Canst not thou disgulph for me
From thy deep bosom, deep as Heaven is high,
Of all thy sea-gods **one, or** sea-maids ?
   Lucifer.   None !
   Festus.   I half despair.   Fire ! that art slumber-
       ing there,
Like some stern warrior **in his rocky fort,**
After the vast invasion **of the world,**
Hast not some flaming **imp, or messenger**
Of **empyrean** element, **to whom,**
In virtue of his nature, are both known
The secrets of the burning, central, void below,
And yon bright Heaven, **out** of whose aëry fire
Are wrought the forms of angels and the thrones ?
Hast none at hand to do my bidding ?   Come !
Breathe out a spirit for me !   One I ask
That shall be with me always, as a friend,
And not like thee, who despotizest o'er
The heart **thou seek'st to serve.**   I must **be free.**
   Lucifer.   **All finite souls** must **serve ;   their**
      widest sway
Is but the rule of service.   **This** fair earth
Which thou dost boast **so much of,** why, thou **see'st**
'T is but the particolored, scummy dross
Of the original element wherefrom
The **fiery worlds were** framed.
   Festus.   Air ! and thou, Wind !
Which **art the** unseen similitude **of** God
The Spirit, His most meet and mightiest sign ;
The earth with all **her** steadfastness and strength,
Sustaining all, **and bound about** with chains

Of mountains, as is life with mercies, ranging round
With all her sister orbs the whole of Heaven,
Is not so like the unlikenable One
As thou.   Ocean is less divine than thee;
For although all but limitless, it is yet
Visible, many a land not visiting.
But thou art, Lovelike, everywhere; o'er earth,
O'er ocean triumphing, and aye with clouds,
That like the ghost of ocean's billows roll,
Decking or darkening Heaven.   The sun's light
Floweth and ebbeth daily like the tides;
The moon's doth grow or lessen, night by night;
The stirless stars shine forth by fits and hide,
And our companion planets come and go; —
And all are known, their laws and liberties.
But no man can foreset thy coming, none
Reason against thy going; thou art free,
The type impalpable of Spirit, thou.
Thunder is but a momentary thing,
Like a world's death-rattle, and is like death;
And lightning, like the blaze of sin, can blind
Only and slay.   But what are these to thee,
In thine all-present variousness?   Now,
So light as not to wake the snowiest down
Upon the dove's breast, winning her bright way
Calm and sublime as Grace unto the soul,
Towards her far native grove; now, stern and
      strong
As ordnance, overturning tree and tower;
Cooling the white brows of the peaks of fire —
Turning the sea's broad furrows like a plough, —
Fanning the fruitening plains, breathing the sweets
Of meadows, wandering o'er blinding snows,
And sands like sea-beds and the streets of cities,
Where men as garnered grain lie heaped together;
Freshening the cheeks, and mingling oft the locks
Of youth and beauty, 'neath star-speaking eve;
Swelling the pride of canvas, or, in wrath,
Scattering the fleets of nations like dead leaves:

In all, the same o'ermastering sightless force,
Bowing the highest things of earth to earth,
And lifting up the dust unto the stars;
Fatelike, confounding reason, and like God's
Spirit, conferring life upon the world,—
Midst all corruption incorruptible;
Monarch of all the elements! hast thou
No soft Eolian sylph, with sightless wing,
To spare a mortal for an hour?
    LUCIFER.   Peace, peace!
All nature knows that I am with thee here,
And that thou need'st no minor minister.
To thee I personate the world — its powers,
Beliefs, and doubts and practices.
    FESTUS.   Are all
Mine invocations fruitless, then?
    LUCIFER.   They are.
Let us enjoy the world!
    FESTUS.   If 't was God's will
That thou shouldst visit me He shall not send
Temptation to my heart in vain. Sweet world!
We all still cling to thee. Though thou thyself
Passest away, yet men will hanker about thee,
Like mad ones by their moping haunts. Men pass,
Cleaving to things themselves which pass away,
Like leaves on waves. Thus all things pass for
     ever,
Save mind and the mind's meed.
    LUCIFER.   Let us too pass!

SCENE — *Alcove and Garden.*

FESTUS AND CLARA.

FESTUS. What happy things are youth and love
    and sunshine!
How sweet to feel the sun upon the heart!
To know it is lighting up the rosy blood,

And with all joyous feelings, prism-hued,
Making the dark breast shine like a spar grot.
We walk among the sunbeams as with angels.
   CLARA. Yes, there are feelings so serene **and**
      sweet,
Coming and going with a musical lightness,
That they can make amends for their passingness,
And balance God's condition to decay;
As yon light **fleecy** cloudlet floating along,
Like golden **down from some** high angel's wing,
Breaks but relieves and beautifies the blue.
I wonder if ever I could love another.
How I should start to see upon the sward
A shadow not thine own armlinked with mine!
See, here is a garland I have bound for thee.
   FESTUS. Nay, crown thyself; it will suit **thee**
      better, love.
Place wreaths of everlasting flowers on tombs,
And deck with fading beauties forms that fade.
Put it away, — I will no crown save this:
And could the line of dust which here I trace
Upon my brow but warrant dust beneath —
And nothing more — **or** could this bubble frame,
Informed with soul, lashed from the stream of life
By its own impetus, but burst at once,
And vanish part on high and part below,
I would be happy, **nor** would envy **death**.
Could **I, like** Heaven's bolt, earthing quench **my-**
      self,
This moment would I **burn me out a grave.**
Might I but be **as** many years **in dying**
As I have lived — that might **be** some relief.
   CLARA. What canst thou mean?
   FESTUS.   Mean? Is there not a future?
The past, **the** present and the coming, curse each!
The future, curse it!
   CLARA.   Shall we not ever live
And love as now?
   FESTUS.   Ay, live I fear we must.

CLARA.   And love: because we then **are hap-**
          piest.
We shall lack nothing having love: and we,
We must be happy everywhere — we two!
For spiritual life is great and clear,
And self-continuous as the changeless sea,
Rolling the same in every age as now;
Whether o'er mountain tops, where only snow
Dwells, and the sunbeam hurries coldly by;
Or o'er the vales, as now, of some old world
Older than ancient man's.   As is the sea's,
So is the life of spirit, and the kind.
And then with natures raised, refined, **and freed**
From **these poor** forms, **our days shall pass in**
          peace
And love; no thought **of** human littleness
Shall cross **our** high **calm** souls, shining and pure
As the **gold gates of Heaven.**   Like some deep
          lake
Upon a mountain summit they shall rest,
High above cloud and storm of life like this,
All peace and power, and passionless purity;
Or if a thought of other troubled times
Ruffle it for a moment, it shall pass
Like a chance raindrop on its heavenward face.
I love to meditate on bliss to come.
Not that I am unhappy here; but that
The hope of higher bliss may rectify
The lower feeling which we now **enjoy.**
This life, this world is **not enough for** us;
They are nothing to the **measure of our** mind.
For place we must have space; for time we must
          have
Eternity; and for a spirit godhood.
     FESTUS.   Mind means not happiness: power is
          not good.
   CLARA.   True **bliss** is to be found in holy life;
In charity **to** man — **in** love **to** God:
Why should such duties cease, such powers decay?

Are they not worthy of a deathless state —
A boundless scope — a high uplifted life ?
Man, like the air-born eagle who remains
On earth only to feed and sleep and die;
But whose delight is on his lonely wing,
Wide sweeping as a mind, to force the skies
High as the lightfall ere, begirt with clouds,
It dash this nether world — immortal man
Rushes aloft, right upwards, into Heaven.
O faith of Christ, sole honor of the world!

 FESTUS. What know men of religion, save its
  forms ?

 CLARA. True faith nor biddeth nor abideth
  form.

The bended knee, the eye uplift is all
Which man need render; all which God can bear.
What to the faith are forms ? A passing speck,
A crow upon the sky. God's worship is
That only He inspires; and His bright words,
Writ in the red-leaved volume of the heart,
Return to him in prayer, as dew to Heaven.
Our proper good we rarely seek or make ;
Mindless of our immortal powers and their
Immortal end, as is the pearl of its worth,
The rose its scent, the wave its purity.

 FESTUS. Come, we will quit these saddening
  themes. Wilt sing

To me ? for I am gloomy; and I love
Thy singing, sacred as the sound of hymns,
On some bright Sabbath morning, on the moor,
Where all is still save praise; and where hard by
The ripe grain shakes its bright beard in the sun ;
The wild bee hums more solemnly ; the deep sky,
The fresh green grass, the sun, and sunny brook,
All look as if they knew the day, the hour ;
And felt with man the need and joy of thanks.

 CLARA. I cannot sing the lightsome lays of
  love,

Many thou know'st who can ; but none that can

Love thee as I do — for I love thy soul;
And I would save it, Festus!   Listen then:

   Is Heaven a place **where pearly streams**
     Glide over silver sand?
   Like childhood's rosy dazzling dreams
     Of **some far** faery land?
   Is Heaven a clime where **diamond dews**
     Glitter on fadeless flowers?
   And mirth and music **ring aloud**
     From amaranthine **bowers?**

   Ah no; not such, **not such is Heaven!**
     Surpassing far **all these;**
   Such cannot be the **guerdon given**
     Man's **wearied soul to please.**
   For saint and **sinner here below**
     Such **vain to be have** proved:
   And the pure **spirit** will despise
     Whate'er **the sense** hath loved.

   There **we** shall dwell with **Sire and Son,**
     And with the mother-maid,
   And with the Holy Spirit, **one:**
     In glory like arrayed:
   And not to one created **thing**
     Shall **our embrace be given;**
   But all **our joy shall be in God;**
     For only God is Heaven.

  Festus.   **I know that thou dost love me.   I in**
     vain
Strive to love **aught of earth or Heaven but**
     thee.
Thou art my first, last, only love; nor **shall**
Another even tempt my heart.   Like stars,
A thousand sweet and bright and wondrous fair,
A thousand **deathless** miracles of beauty,
They shall ever pass **at** all but eyeless distance,

And never mix with thy love; but be lost
All, meanly in its moonlike lustrousness.
   CLARA. How still the air is! the tree tops stir
      not:
But stand and peer on Heaven's bright face as
      though
It slept and they were loving it: they would not
Have the skies see them move for summers: would
      they?
See that sweet cloud! It is watching us, I am cer-
      tain.
What have we here to make thee stay one second?
Away! thy sisters wait thee in the west,
The blushing bridemaids of the sun and sea.
I would I were like thee, thou little cloud,
Ever to live in Heaven: or seeking earth
To let my spirit down in drops of love:
To sleep with night upon her dewy lap;
And, the next dawn, back with the sun to Heaven,
And so on through eternity, sweet cloud!
I cannot but think that some senseless things
Are happy. Often and often have I watched
A gossamer line sighing itself along
The air, as it seemed; and so thin, thin and bright,
Looking as woven in a loom of light,
That I have envied it, I have, and followed;—
Oft watched the sea-bird's down blown o'er the
      wave,
Now touching it, now spirited aloft,
Now out of sight, now seen,—till in some bright
      fringe
Of streamy foam, as in a cage, at last
A playful death it dies, and mourned its death.
   FESTUS. But thinkest thou the future is a state
More positive than this; or that it can be
Aught but another present, full of cares,
And toils, perhaps, and duties; that the soul
Will ever be more nigh to God than now,
Save as may seem from mind's debility:

Just as the sun, from weakness of the eye,
And the illusions made by matter's forms,
Seems hot and wearied resting on the hill?
It would be well, I think, to live as though
No more were to be looked for; to be good
Because it is best, here; and leave hope and fear
For lives below ourselves.   If earth persuades not
That I owe prayer and praise and love to God,
While all I have He **gives,** will Heaven? **will**
        Hell?
No; neither, **never!**
    CLARA.   I think not all with thee.
Have I not heard thee hint of spirit-friends?
Where are they now?
    FESTUS.   Ah! **close at hand, mayhap.**
I have a might immortal; **and can ken**
With angels.   Neither sky **nor night nor earth**
Hinder **me.**   Through **the forms of** things **I see**
Their essences; and thus, even now, behold —
But **where** I cannot show to thee — far round,
Nature herself — the whole effect of God.
Mind, matter, motion, heat, time, love, and life,
And death and immortality; those chief
And first-born giants all are there; all parts,
All limbs of her their mother; she is all.
    CLARA.   And what does she?
    FESTUS.   Produce: **it is her life.**
The three named last, life, death, deathlessness,
Glide in elliptic path round all things **made —**
For none save God can fill the perfect whole:
And are but to **eternity as** is
The horizon to the **world.**   At certain points
Each seems the other; now, the three are one;
Now, all invisible; **and** now, as first,
Moving in measured round.
    CLARA.   How look these beings?
    FESTUS.   Ah! Life looks gaily and gloomily in
        turns;
With a brow chequered like the sward, by leaves

Between which **the** light glints ; **and she,** careless,
    wears
A wreath of flowers — part faded and part fresh.
And Death is beautiful and sad and still :
She seems too happy ; happier far than life —
In **but one** feeling, apathy : and on
Her chill white brow frosts bright, a braid of snow
    CLARA. And Immortality ?
    FESTUS.   She looks alone ;
As though **she would not know** her sisterhood.
And on her brow a diadem **of** fire,
Matched by the conflagration of her eye,
Outflaming even that eye which in my sleep
Beams close upon me till it bursts **from sheer**
O'erstrainedness of sight, burns.
    CLARA.   What do they ?
    FESTUS. Each strives to win me to herself.
    CLARA.   How ?
    FESTUS.   Death
Opens her sweet white arms and whispers, peace !
Come say thy sorrows in this bosom ! This
Will never close against thee ; **and** my heart,
Though cold, cannot be **colder** much than man's.
Come ! **All** this soon **must end !** and soon the world
Shall **perish leaf by leaf, and land by land ;**
Flower by flower — flood by **flood — and** hill
By hill, away ; Oh ! come, come ! **Let us die.**
    CLARA. Say that **thou** wilt not **die !**
    FESTUS.   Nay, **I love Death.**
But Immortality, with finger spired,
Points to a distant, giant world — and says
There, there is my home ! Live along with me !
    CLARA. **Canst see** that world ?
    FESTUS.   Just — a huge shadowy shape ;
It looks a disembodied **orb —** the ghost
Of some great sphere which God hath stricken dead :
Or like a world which God hath thought — not made.
    CLARA. Follow her, **Festus !** Does she speak
    again ?

FESTUS.   She never speaks but once; and now, in scorn,
Points to this dim, dwarfed, misbegotten sphere.
    CLARA.   Why let her pass?
    FESTUS.   That is the great world-question.
Life would not part with me; and from her brow
Tearing her wreath of passion-flowers, she flung
It round my neck and dared me struggle then.
I never could destroy a flower: and none
But fairest hands like thine can grace with me
The plucking of a rose.   And Life, sweet Life!
Vowed she would crop the world for me and lay it
Herself before my feet even as a flower.
And when I felt that flower contained thyself—
One drop within its nectary kept for me,
I lost all count of those strange sisters three;
And where they be I know not.   But I see
One who is more to me.
    CLARA.   I know not how
Thou hast this power and knowledge.   I but hope
It comes from good hands; if it be not thine
Own force of mind.   It is much less what we do
Than what we think, which fits us for the future.
I wish we had a little world to ourselves;
With none but we two on it.
    FESTUS.   And if God
Gave us a star, what could we do with it
But that we could without it?   Wish it not!
    CLARA. I 'll not wish then for stars; but I could love
Some peaceful spot where we might dwell unknown,
Where home-born joys might nestle round our hearts
As swallows round our roofs,—and blend their sweets
Like dewy-tangled flowerets in one bed.
    FESTUS. The sweetest joy, the wildest woe is love;
The taint of earth, the odor of the skies,

Is in it. Would that I were aught but man!
The death of brutes, the immortality
Of fiend or angel, better seems than all
The doubtful prospects of our painted dust.
And all Morality can teach is — Bear!
And all Religion can inspire is — Hope!
  CLARA. It is enough. Fruition of the fruit
Of the great Tree of Life, **is not for earth.**
Stars are its fruit, its lightest **leaf is** life. ·
The heart hath many sorrows beside **love,**
Yea many as the veins which visit it.
The love of aught on earth is not its chief
Nor ought to be. Inclusive of them all
There is the one main sorrow, life ; — for what
Can spirit, severed from the great one, God,
Feel but a grievous longing to rejoin
Its infinite — its author — and its end?
And yet is life **a** thing to be beloved,
And honored holily, and bravely borne.
A man's life **may** be all ease, and his death
By some dark chance, unthought of agony : —
Or life may be all suffering, and decease
A flower-like sleep ; — or both be full of **woe,**
Or each comparatively painless. Blame
Not God for inequalities like these!
They may be justified. How canst thou know?
They may be only seeming. Canst **thou** judge?
They may be done away with utterly
By loving, fearing, knowing God the Truth.
In all distress of spirit, grief of heart,
Bodily agony, or mental woe,
Rebuffs and vain assumptions of the world,
Or the **poor** spite of weak and wicked souls,
Think **thou** on **God!** Think what he underwent
And did for us as man. Weigh thou thy cross
With Christ's, and judge which were the heavier.
Joy even in thine anguish! — such was His,
But measurelessly more. Thy suffering
Assimilateth thee to Him. Rejoice!

Think upon what thou shalt be! Think on God!
Then ask thyself, what is the world, and all
Its mountainous inequalities? Ah, what!
Are not all equal as dust-atomies?
  Festus. My soul's orb darkens as a sudden star,
      star,
Which having for a time exhausted earth
And half the Heavens of wonder, mortally
Passes for ever, not eclipsed, consumed;—
All but a cloudy vapor darkening there,
The very spot in space it once illumed.
Once to myself I seemed a mount of light;
But now, a pit of night.— No more of this!
Here have I lain all day in this green nook,
Shaded by larch and hornbeam, ash and yew;
A living well and runnel at **my feet,**
And wild flowers, dancing to some delicate air;
An urn-topped column and its ivy **wreath**
Skirting my sight as thus I lie and look
Upon the blue, unchanging, sacred skies:
And thou, too, gentle Clara, by my side,
With lightsome brow and beaming eye, and bright
Long glorious locks, which drop upon thy cheek
Like goldhued cloudflakes on the rosy morn.
Oh! **when** the heart is full of sweets to o'erflowing,
And ringing to the music of its love,
Who but an angel or an hypocrite
Could speak or think of happier states?
  Clara.   Farewell!
Remember what thou saidst about **the stars.**   [*Goes.*
  Festus. Oh! why was woman **made so** fair? or man
      man.
So weak as to see that more than one had beauty?
It is impossible to love but one.
And yet I dare not love thee as I could;
For all that the heart most longs for and deserves,
Passes the soonest and most utterly.
The moral of the world's great fable, life.
All we enjoy seems given to deceive,

Or may be, undeceive us; who cares which?
And when the sum is done, and we have proved it,
Why work it over and over still again?
I am not what I would be.   Hear me, God!
And speak to me in thine invisible likeness
The wind, as once of yore.   Let me be pure
Oh! I wish I was a pure child again,
As ere the clear could trouble me: when life
Was sweet and calm as is a sister's kiss;
And not the wild and whirlwind touch of passion,
Which though it hardly light upon the lip,
With breathless swiftness sucks the soul out of sight
So that we lose it, and all thought of it.
What is this life wherein Thou hast founded me,
But a bright wheel which burns itself away,
Benighting even night with its grim limbs,
When it hath done and fainted into darkness?
Flesh is but fiction, and it flies away;
The gaunt and ghastly thing we bear about us
And which we hate and fear to look upon
Is truth; in death's dark likeness limned — no
          more.

Scene — *Anywhere.*

FESTUS *and* **LUCIFER** *meeting.*

FESTUS. God hath refused me: wilt thou do it
     for me?
Or shall I end with both? remake myself?
   LUCIFER. Now that is the one thing which I
     cannot do.
Am I not open with thee? why choose that?
   FESTUS. Because I will it. Thou art bound to
     obey.
   LUCIFER. The world bears marks of my obe-
     dience.
   FESTUS. Off! I am torn to pieces.   Let me try

And gather **up** myself into a man,
As once **I** was. I have done with thee! **Dost hear?**
   LUCIFER. Thou canst not mean this.
   FESTUS.   **Once for all — I do.**
   LUCIFER. It is **men who are** deceivers — not
      the Devil.
The first and worst of all frauds is to **cheat**
Oneself. All sin is easy after that.
   FESTUS. I feel that we must part: **part now or**
      never;
And I had rather of the two it were **now.**
   LUCIFER. This is my last **walk through my**
      favorite world:
And I had hoped to have enjoyed **it with thee.**
For thee I quitted Hell; for thee **I warped**
And shrivelled up my **soul into a man:**
For thee I shed my shining **wings; for thee**
Put **on** this mask **of flesh,** this mockery
Of **motion, and** this **seeming shape** like thine.
And **by** my woe, I swear that were I now,
For thy false **heart,** to give my spirit spring,
I would **scatter soul** and body both **to Hell,**
And let one burn the other.
   FESTUS.   If thou darest!
Lift but the finger of a thought of ill
Against **me, and** — thou durst not. Mark, **we part.**
   LUCIFER. Well; as thou wilt. **Remember that**
      thy heart
Will shed its pleasures as thine eye its **tears;**
And both leave loathsome furrows.
   FESTUS.   **Thinkest thou**
That I will **have no pleasures without thee,**
Who marrest all thou makest and even more?
   LUCIFER. Thou **canst not; save** indeed some
      poor trite thing
Called moderation, every one can have;
And modesty, God knows, is suffering.
   FESTUS. Now will I prove thee liar for **that**
      word,

And that the very vastest out of Hell.
With perfect condemnation I abjure
My soul; my nature doth abhor itself;
I have a soul to spare   [*Goes.*
    LUCIFER.   A hundred, I.
I have him yet: for he is mine to tempt.
Gold hath the hue of hell flames: but for him
I will lay some brilliant and delicious lure.
Which shall be worth perdition to a seraph.
Most men glide quietly and deeply down:
Some seek the bottom like a cataract.
Now he shall find it, seek it how he will.
None ever went without once taking breath.
It is passion plunges men into mine arms;
But it matters not; Hell burns before them all.
It is by Hell-light they do their chiefest deeds;
And by Hell-light they shine unto each other;
And Hell through life's thick fog glares red and
        round;
And but for Hell they would grope in utter dark.

SCENE — *A Country Town — Market-place — Noon.*

LUCIFER *and* FESTUS.

    LUCIFER. These be the toils and cares of mighty
        men.
Earth's vermin are as fit to fill her thrones
As these high Heaven's bright seats.
    FESTUS.   Men's callings all
Are mean and vain; their wishes more so: oft
The man is bettered by his part or place.
How slight a chance may raise or sink a soul!
    LUCIFER. What men call accident is God's own
        part.
He lets ye work your will — it is His own:
But that ye mean not, know not, do not, He doth.
    FESTUS. What is life worth without a heart to feel

The great and lovely, and the poetry
And sacredness of things? for all things are
Sacred,—the eye of God is on them all,
And hallows all unto it.   It is fine
To stand upon some lofty mountain-thought
And feel the spirit stretch into a view;
To joy in what might be if will and power
For good would work together but one hour.
Yet millions never think a noble thought:
But with brute hate of brightness bay a mind
Which drives the darkness out of them, like
      hounds.
Throw but a false glare round them, and in shoals
They rush upon perdition : that's the race.
What charm is in this world-scene to such minds
Blinded by dust?   What can they do in Heaven
A state of spiritual means and ends?
Thus must I doubt — perpetually doubt.
   LUCIFER.   Who never doubted never half be-
     lieved.
Where doubt there truth is — 't is her shadow.   I
Declare unto thee that the past is not.
I have looked over all life, yet never seen
The age that had been.   Why then fear or dream
About the future?   Nothing but what is, is;
Else God were not the Maker that He seems,
As constant in creating as in being.
Embrace the present!   Let the future pass.
Plague not thyself about a future.   That
Only which comes direct from God, His spirit,
Is deathless.   Nature gravitates without
Effort; and so all mortal natures fall
Deathwards.   All aspiration is a toil;
But inspiration cometh from above,
And is no labor.   The earth's inborn strength
Could never lift her up to yon stars, whence
She fell; nor human soul, by native worth,
Claim Heaven as birthright, more than man may
     call

Cloudland his home.   The soul's inheritance,
Its birth-place, and its death-place, is of earth,
Until God maketh earth and soul anew;
The one like Heaven, the other like Himself.
So shall the new Creation come at once;
Sin, the dead branch upon the tree of Life,
Shall be cut off forever; and all souls
Concluded in God's boundless amnesty.

   FESTUS.   Thou windest and unwindest faith at
      will.
What am I to believe?
   LUCIFER.   Thou mayst believe
But that which thou art forced to.
   FESTUS.   Then I feel
That instinct of immortal life in me,
Which prompts me to provide for it.
   LUCIFER.   Perhaps.
   FESTUS.   Man hath a knowledge of a time to
      come —
His most important knowledge: the weight lies
Nearest the short end; and the world depends
Upon what is to be.   I would deny
The present, if the future.   Oh! there is
A life to come, or all 's a dream.
   LUCIFER.   And all
May be a dream.   Thou seest in thine, men, deeds,
Clear, moving, full of speech and order; then
Why may not all this world be but a dream
Of God's?   Fear not!   Some morning God may
      waken.
   FESTUS.   I would it were.   This life 's a mystery.
The value of a thought cannot be told;
But it is clearly worth a thousand lives
Like many men's.   And yet men love to live
As if mere life were worth their living for.
What but perdition will it be to most?
Life 's more than breath and the quick round of
      blood,
It is a great spirit and a busy heart.

The coward and the small in soul scarce do live.
One generous feeling — one great thought — one
          deed
Of good, ere night, would make life longer seem
Than if each year might number a thousand days, —
Spent as is this by nations of mankind.
We live in deeds, not years; in thoughts, not
          breaths;
In feelings, not in figures on a dial.
We should count time by heart-throbs. He most
          lives
Who thinks most — feels the noblest — acts the
          best.
Life's but a means unto an end — that end,
Beginning, mean and end to all things — God.
The dead have all the glory of the world.
Why will we live and not be glorious?
We never can be deathless till we die.
It is the dead win battles. And the breath
Of those who through the world drive like a wedge,
Tearing earth's empires up, nears death so close
It dims his well-worn scythe. But no! the brave
Die never. Being deathless, they but change
Their country's arms for more — their country's
          heart.
Give then the dead their due; it is they who saved
          us.
The rapid and the deep — the fall, the gulph
Have likenesses in feeling and in life.
And life so varied, hath more loveliness
In one day than a creeping century
Of sameness. But youth loves and lives on change
Till the soul sighs for sameness; which at last
Becomes variety, and takes its place.
Yet some will last to die out thought by thought,
And power by power, and limb of mind by limb,
Like lambs upon a gay device of glass,
Till all of soul that's left be dry and dark;
Till even the burden of some ninety years

Hath crashed into them like a rock; shattered
Their system as if ninety suns had rushed
To ruin earth — or Heaven had rained its stars;
Till they become, like scrolls, unreadable
Through dust and mould. Can they be cleaned
     and read?
Do human spirits wax and wane like moons!
  LUCIFER. The eye dims and the heart gets old
     and slow;
The lithe limb stiffens, and the sun-hued locks
Thin themselves off, or whitely wither; — still
Ages not spirit, even in one point,
Immeasurably small; from orb to orb,
In ever rising radiance, shining like
The sun upon the thousand lands of earth.
Look at the medley, motley throng we meet!
Some smiling — frowning some; their cares and joys
Alike not worth a thought — some sauntering
     slowly
As if destruction never could o'ertake them;
Some hurrying on as fearing judgment swift
Should trip the heels of Death and seize them
     living.
  FESTUS. Grief hallows hearts even while it ages
     heads;
And much hot grief, in youth, forces up life
With power which too soon ripens and which drops.
                  [*A funeral passes.*
Whose funeral is this ye follow, friends?
  LUCIFER. Would ye have grief, let me come!
     I am woe.
  MOURNER. We want no grief: Festus! she
     died of grief.
  FESTUS. Did ye say she died? oh! I knew her
     then.
Set down the body; let me look upon her!
Now, Son of God! what dost Thou now in heaven
While one so beautiful lies earthening here?
I will give up the future for the past;

The winged spirit and the starry home
If Thou wilt let her live, and make me love.
  MOURNER.   **She** was a lock of Heaven which
      Heaven gave earth,
And took again, because unworthy of her.
  FESTUS.   Her **air was an** immortal's; **I have**
      seen
Stars look on **it with** feeling; and her eye,
Wherever she went, it won her way like wine.
Men bowed to it as to the lifted Host.
How could I be so cruel?   Who but I?
And now, corruption, come; sit; feast **thyself!**
This is the choicest banquet thou hast been **at.**
Thou art my happier, only rival: **thou**
Who takest love from **the living** — life **from**
      beauty —
Beauty **from death** — whole ro**bber** of the world!
  MOURNER.   **The moment after** thou desertedst
      her
A cloud came o'er the prospect of her life;
And I foresaw **how** evening would set in,
Early and dark and deadly.   She was true.
  FESTUS.   Did I not love thee too? pure! **perfect**
      thing!
This is a soul **I** see and not **a body.**
Go, beauty, rest for aye; go, starry eyes,
And lips like rosebuds peeping out of snow;
Go, breast love-filled as a boat's sail with **wind,**
Leaping from wave to wave **as leaps a child**
Thoughtless o'er grassy **graves; go, locks,** which
        have
The golden embrownment of **a lion's** eye!
Yet one **more look**; farewell, **thou** well and fair!
All **who but loved** thee shall be deathless.   Nought
Named but with thee can perish.   Thou and Death
Have made each other purer, lovelier, seem,
Like **snow and** moonlight.   Never more for thee
Let eyes be **swollen like** streams with latter rains!
To die were **rapture** having lived with **thee.**

Thy soul hath passed out of a bodily **Heaven**
Into a spiritual. Rest for aye !—
Pure as the dead, **in** life the dead are holy.
I would I **were** among them. Let us pass !
Living is but a habit; **and** I mean
To break myself of it soon.

  LUCIFER.   **Too soon** thou canst not.
Men heed not of the day, how nigh none knows,
Which brings the consummation of the world.
But in my ear **the old machine already**
Begins to grate. **They would not credit warning,**
Or I would up and cry, Repent ! **I will.**
Here is a fair gathering and **I feel moved.**
Mortals, Repent ! the world is nigh **to its end ;**
On its last legs and desperately sick.
See ye not how it reels round all day long ?

  BOYS. Oh! here's a ranter. Come, here's fun.
   Amen !

I know the church service by heart.

  BYSTANDER.   Be off'!
You'll serve the church **by** keeping out of it.

  LUCIFER. **I am a preacher** come to tell ye truth.
I tell ye too there is no time to be lost;
So fold your souls up neatly, while ye may ;
Direct to God in Heaven; **or** some one else
May seize them, seal them, send them — you know
   where.
The world **must end. I weep** to think **of it.**
But you, you laugh! I knew ye would. **I know**
Men never will be wise till **they** are fools
For **ever.** Laugh away! **The time will** come,
When tears of fire are trickling **from** your eyes,
Ye will blame yourselves for having laughed at **me.**
I warn ye, men: prepare ! repent ! be saved !
I warn ye, **not** because **I love, but** know **ye.**
God will dissolve the world, **as** she of old
Her pearl, within His cup and swallow ye
In wrath : although to taste **ye** would be poison,
And death and suicide to aught but God.

Again I warn ye.   **Save** himself who can !
Do ye not oft begin to **seek** salvation ?
You ? you ? and fail, as oft, to find ? Sink **?** Cease !
And **shall I** tell **ye,** brethren, why ye fail
Once and for ever **?** why, there is no past ;
And the future is the fiction of a fiction ;
The present moment is eternity ;
It **is** that ye have sucked corruption from the world
Like milk from your own mothers : it is in
Your soul-blood and your soul-bones.   Earth does
      not
Wean one out of a thousand sons to Heaven.
Beginnings are alike : it is ends which differ.
One drop falls, lasts, and dries up — but **a drop ;**
Another begins a river : and one **thought**
Settles **a** life, an immortality :
And that one thought **ye** will **not take to good.**
Now **I will** tell **ye** just one other truth :
Ye **hate the truth as** snails salt — it dissolves ye,
Body and soul — but **I** don't mind.   So, now :
Up to this moment ye are all, each, damned.
What are ye now ? still damned ! It will be **the**
      same
To-morrow — and the next day — and the next :
Till some fine morning ye will wake in fire.
Ye see I do not mince the truth for ye.
Belike ye think your lives will dribble out
As brooks in summer dry up.   Let us see !
Try : dike them **up :** they **stagnate** — thicken —
      scum.
That would make **life worse than death.**   Well,
      let go !
Where are ye then ? **for life,** like water, will
Find its last level : **what level ?**   The grave.
It **is** but a fall of five feet after all ;
That cannot **hurt ye ;** it is but just enough
To work the **wheel** of life ; so work away !
Ye may think that I **do** not know the terms
And treasures whereupon ye live **so** high.

But I know more than most men, modestly
Speaking. I know I am lost, and ye too. God
Could only save me by destroying me;
So that I have no advantage over you.
And therefore think ye will the rather bear
One of your own state to advise for ye.
Now don't you envy me, good folks, I pray,—
Envy's a coal comes hissing hot from hell.
'T will be such coals will burn ye by the way.
Your other preachers first think they are safe.
Now I say, broadly, I am the worst among ye;
And God knows I have no need to wrong myself,
Nor you. I boast not of it, but as truth:
It is little to be proud of, credit me.
What is salvation? What is safety? **Think!**
Who wants to know? Does any?
   THE CROWD.   All of us.
   LUCIFER. Then I will not tell ye. You shall
      wait until
Some angel come and stir your stagnant souls:
Then plunge into yourselves and rise redeemed.
Come, I'll unroll your hearts and read them to ye.
To say ye live is but to say ye have souls,
That ye have paid for them and mean to play them,
Till some brave pleasure wins the golden stake,
And rakes it up to death as to a bank.
Ye live and die on what your souls will fetch;
And all are of different prices: therefore Hell
Cannot well bargain for mankind in gross;
But each soul must be purchased, one by one.
This it is makes men rate themselves so high:
While truly ye are worth little: but to God
Ye are worth more than to yourselves. By sin
Ye wreak your spite against God — that ye know:
And knowing, will it. But I pray, I beg,
Act with some smack of justice to your Maker,
If not unto yourselves. Do! It is enough
To make the very Devil chide mankind —
Such baseness, such unthankfulness! Why he

Thanks God he is no worse.   You don't do that.
I say be just to God.   Leave off these airs.
Know your place — speak to God — and say, for once,
Go first, Lord ! Take your finger off your eye !
It blocks the universe and God from sight.
Think ye your souls are worth nothing to God ?
Are they so small ? What can be great with God ?
What will ye weigh against the Lord ?   Yourselves ?
Bring out your balance : get in, man by man :
Add earth, heaven, hell, the universe, that 's all.
God puts his finger in the other scale,
And up we bounce, a bubble.   Nought is great
Nor small with God — for none but He can make
The atom indivisible, and none
But He can make a world : He counts the orbs,
He counts the atoms of the universe,
And makes both equal — both are infinite.
Giving God honor, never underrate
Yourselves : after Him ye are every thing.
But mind ! God 's more than every thing ; He is God.
And what of me ? No, us ? no ! I mean the Devil ?
Why see ye not he goes before both you
And God ?   Men say — as proud as Lucifer —
Pray who would not be proud with such a train ?
Hath he not all the honor of the earth ?
Why Mammon sits before a million hearths
Where God is bolted out from every house.
Well might He say He cometh as a thief ;
For He will break your bars and burst your doors
Which slammed against him once, and turn ye out,
Roofless and shivering, 'neath the doom-storm ; Heaven
Shall crack above ye like a bell in fire,
And bury all beneath its shining shards.
He calls : ye hear not.   Lo ! he comes — ye see not.
No ; ye are deaf as a dead adder's ear :
No ; ye are blind as never bat was blind,
With a burning bloodshot blindness of the heart ;

A swimming, swollen senselessness of soul.
Listen! Whom love ye most? Why **him to whom**
Ye in your turn are dearest.   Need I name?
Oh no! **But all are** devils to themselves;
And every man **his own** great foe.   Hell gets
Only the gleanings; earth hath the full wain;
And hell is merry at its harvest home.
But ye are generous to sin and grudge.
The gleaners nothing; ask them, push them in.
Let not an ear, a grain of sin be lost;
Gather it, grind it up; it is our bread:
We should be ashamed to waste the gifts **of God.**
Why is the world so mad? Why runs it **thus**
Raving and howling round the universe?
Because the Devil bit it from the birth!
The fault is all with him.   Fear nothing, friends!
It is fear which beds the far to-come with fire
As the sun does the west: but the sun sets;
Well; still ye tremble — tremble, first at light,
Then darkness.   Tremble! ye dare not believe.
No, cowards! sooner than believe ye would die;
Die **with the black lie** flapping on your lips
Like the **soot-flake upon a** burning bar.
Be merry, happy if ye can: think never
 Of him who slays your souls, nor Him **who saves.**
There is time enough for that when ye are **a-dying**
Keep your old **ways!** It matters not **this once.**
Be brave!   Ye **are** not men **whom** meat **and wine**
Serve **to remind** but of the sacrament;
To whom sweet shapes and tantalizing smiles
Bring up the Devil and the ten commandments —
And so on — **but I** said the **world must end.**
I am sorry; it is such a pleasant world:
With all its faults it is perfect — to a fault:
And you, **of course, end with** it.   Now how long
Will the world take to die?   I know ye place
Great faith upon death-bed repentances;
The suddener the better.   I know ye often
Begin to think of praying **and** repenting;

But second thoughts come and ye are worse than
      ever;
As over new white snow a filthy thaw.
Ye do amaze me verily. How long
Will ye take heart on your own wickedness,
And God's forbearance? Have ye cast it up?
Come now; the year and month, day, hour **and**
      minute,
Sin's golden cycle. Do ye know how long
Exactly Heaven will grant ye? how long God, —
Who when he had slain the world and wasted it,
Hung up His bow in Heaven, as in his hall
A warrior after battle — will yet bear
Your contumely and scorn of His best gifts, —
Man's mockery of man? But never mind !
Some of us are magnificently good,
And hold the head **up high** like **a** giraffe ;
You, in particular, and you — and **you.**
Good men are **here** and there, I know ; but then,—
You must excuse me if I mention this —
My duty **is to** tell it you — the world,
Like a black block of marble, jagged with white,
As with a vein of lightning petrified,
Looks blacker than without such ; looks in truth,
So gross the heathen, gross the Christian too —
Like the original darkness of void **space,**
Hardened. Instead of justice, love and grace,
Each worth to man the mission of **a** God,
Injustice, hate, uncharitableness,
Triequal reign round earth, a Trinity **of Hell.**
Ye think ye never can be bad enough :
And as ye sink in sin, ye rise in hope.
And **let** the worst come to **the** worst, you **say,**
There always will be time to turn ourselves,
And cry for half an hour or so to God:
Salvation, sure, is not so very hard —
It need not take one long ; and half an hour
Is quite as much as we can spare for it.
We have no time for pleasures. Business ! business !

No! ye shall perish sudden and unsaved.
The priest shall, dipping, die. Can man save **man?**
Is water God?   The counsellor, wise fool!
Drop down amid his quirks and sacred lies—
The judge, while dooming unto death some wretch,
Shall meet at once his own death, doom, and judge.
The **doctor, watch** in hand, **and** patient's pulse,
Shall **feel his own heart cease its** beats—and fall:
Professors shall spin out, and students strain
Their **brains no** more **; art, science, toil** shall cease.
The world shall stand still with a rending jar,
As though it struck at sea.   The halls where sit
The heads of nations shall be dumb with death.
The ship shall after **her own** plummet sink,
And sound the sea herself and depths of death.
At the **first** turn Death shall cut off the thief,
And dash the gold bag in his yellow brain.
The gambler, reckoning gains, shall drop a piece;
Stoop down and there see death;—look **up, there**
        God.
The wanton, temporizing with decay,
And qualifying every line which **vice**
Writes **bluntly on the** brow, inviting scorn,
Shall pale through plastered red: and the loose,
        low sot
See clear, for once, through his misty, o'erbrimmed
        eye.
The just, if **there be any, die in prayer.**
Death shall be everywhere among your marts,
And giving bills which no man may decline—
Drafts upon Hell one moment after date.
Then shall your outcries tremble amid the stars :
Terrors shall be about ye like a wind :
And fears come down upon ye like a house.
    FESTUS.   **Yon man** looks frightened.
    LUCIFER.   **Then** it is time to stop.
I hope I have done no good.   He will soon forget
His soul.   **Flesh soaks it up as** sponge does water.
Now wait! I will rub them backwards like a cat;

And you shall see them spit and sparkle up.
Let us suppose a case, friends! You are **men** ;
And there is God! and I will **be the Devil.**
Very **well.** I am the Devil.
    ONE *says.*   I think you are.
You look as if you lived on buttered thunder.
    LUCIFER. Nay, be not wroth. Ye would crucify
        the Devil,
I do believe, if he a moment vexed you.
I know well which ye choose : but choose again!
Time or eternity ? Speak, Hell or Heaven ?
    THE CROWD. **He** 's a mad ranter : **down with**
        him ! —
    FESTUS.   Let him **be** !
    LUCIFER. **Stand** by me, Festus, and I **will by**
        thee.
Why, **God and man!** **this** is the second time
That **I have run for my life.**
    FESTUS.   **Nay,** nay, come back !
They will not harm thee: they would chair thee
    round
The market-place, knew they but whom thou art.
Peace, there my friends ! one minute ; let us pray !
Grant us, oh God ! that in thy holy love
The universal people of the world
May grow more great and happy every day ;
Mightier, wiser, humbler, too, towards Thee.
And that all ranks, all classes, callings, **states**
Of life, so far as such seem right **to** Thee,
May mingle into one, like sister trees,
And so **in one** stem flourish : —**that** all laws
And powers of government be based and used
In good and for the people's sake ; — that each
May feel himself of consequence to all,
And act as though all saw him ; — that the whole,
The mass of every nation may so do
As is most worthy of the next to God ;
For a whole people's souls, each one worth more
Than a mere world of matter, make combined,

A something, godlike — something like to Thee.
We pray thee for the welfare of all men.
Let monarchs who love truth and freedom feel
The happiness of safety and respect
From those they rule, and guardianship from Thee.
Let them remember they are set on thrones
As representatives, not substitutes
Of nations, to implead with God and man.
Let tyrants who hate truth, or fear the free,
Know that to rule in slavery and error,
For the mere ends of personal pomp and power,
Is such a sin as doth deserve a hell
To itself sole.   Let both remember, Lord!
They are but things like-natured with all nations;
That mountains issue out of plains, and not
Plains out of mountains, and so likewise kings
Are of the people, not the people of kings.
And let all feel, the rulers and the ruled,
All classes and all countries, that the world
Is Thy great halidom ; that Thou art King,
Lord! only owner and possessor.   Grant
That nations may now see, it is not kings,
Nor priests they need fear so much as themselves;
That if they keep but true to themselves, and free,
Sober, enlightened, godly — mortal men
Become impassible as air, one great
And indestructible substance as the sea.
Let all on thrones and judgment-seats reflect
How dreadful Thy revenge through nations is
On those who wrong them; but do Thou grant,
        Lord!
That when wrongs are to be redressed, such may
Be done with mildness, speed, and firmness, not
With violence or hate, whereby one wrong
Translates another — both to Thee abhorrent.
The bells of time are ringing changes fast.
Grant, Lord! that each fresh peal may usher in
An era of advancement, that each change
Prove an effectual, lasting, happy gain.

And we beseech Thee, overrule, oh God!
All civil contests to the good of all:
All party and religious difference
To honorable ends, whether secured
Or lost; and let all strife, political
Or social, spring from conscientious aims,
And have a generous self-ennobling end,
Man's good and Thine own glory in view always.
The best may then fail and the worst succeed
Alike with honor.   We beseech Thee, Lord!
For bodily strength, but more especially
For the soul's health and safety. We entreat Thee
In thy great mercy to decrease our wants,
And add autumnal increase to the comforts
Which tend to keep men innocent, and load
Their hearts with thanks to Thee as trees in bear-
      ing : —
The blessings of friends, families, and homes,
And kindnesses of kindred.   And we pray
That men may rule themselves in faith in God,
In charity to each other, and in hope
Of their own souls' salvation : — that the mass,
The millions in all nations may be trained,
From their youth upwards, in a nobler mode,
To loftier and more liberal ends.   We pray
Above all things, Lord! that all men be free
From bondage, whether of the mind or body ; —
The bondage of religious bigotry,
And bald antiquity, servility
Of thought or speech to rank and power; be all
Free as they ought to be in mind and soul
As well as by state-birthright ; — and that Mind,
Time's giant pupil, may right soon attain
Majority, and speak and act for himself!
Incline Thou to our prayers, and grant, oh Lord!
That all may have enough, and some safe mean
Of worldly goods and honors, by degrees,
Take place, if practicable, in the fitness
And fulness of Thy time.   And we beseech Thee,

That Truth no more be gagged, nor conscience
      dungeoned,
Nor science be impeached of godlessness,
Nor faith be circumscribed, which as to Thee,
And the soul's self affairs is infinite;
But that all men may have due liberty
To speak an honest mind, in every land,
Encouragement to study, leave to act
As conscience orders. We entreat Thee, Lord!
For Thy Son's sake to take away reproach
Of all kinds from Thy church, and all temptation
Of pomp or power political, that none
May err in the end for which they were appointed
To any of its orders, low or high;
And no ambition, of a worldly cast,
Leaven the love of souls unto whose care
They feel propelled by Thy most holy spirit.
Be every church established, Lord! in truth.
Let all who preach the word, live by the word,
In moderate estate; and in Thy church, —
One, universal, and invisible
World-wards, yet manifest unto itself,
May it seem good, dear Saviour, in Thy sight,
That orders be distinguished, not by wealth,
But piety and power of teaching souls.
Equalize labor, Lord! and recompense.
Let not a hundred humble pastors starve,
In this or any land of Christendom,
While one or two, impalaced, mitred, throned
And banqueted, burlesque if not blaspheme
The holy penury of the Son of God;
The fastings, the foot-wanderings, and the preach-
      ings
Of Christ and His first followers. Oh that the Son
Might come again! There should be no more war,
No more want, no more sickness; with a touch,
He should cure all diseases, and with a word,
All sin; and with a look to Heaven, a prayer,
Provide bread for a million at a time.

But till that perfect advent grant us, Lord !
That all good institutions, orders, claims,
Charitably proposed, or in the aid
Of Thy divine foundation, may much prosper,
And **more of them** be raised and nobly filled ; —
That **Thy** word may **be** taught throughout all lands,
And **save souls** daily **to** the thrones of Heaven ! —
And we entreat Thee, that all men whom Thou
Hast gifted with great minds may love Thee **well,**
And praise Thee for their powers, and use them most
Humbly and holily, and, lever-like,
Act but in lifting up the mass of mind
About them ; knowing well that **they shall be**
Questioned by thee of deeds the pen **hath done,**
Or caused, or glozed ; inspire them with delight
And power to treat of noble themes and **things,**
Worthily, and **to leave the low and mean** —
Things born of **vice** or **day-lived** fashion, in
Their naked native folly ; — make them know
Fine thoughts are wealth, for the right use of which
Men are and ought to be accountable, —
If **not** to Thee, to those they influence :
Grant this we pray Thee, and that all who read,
Or utter noble thoughts, may make them theirs,
And thank God for them, to the betterment
Of their succeeding life ; — that all who lead
The general sense and taste, too apt, perchance,
To be led, keep in mind the mighty good
They may achieve, and are in conscience, **bound,**
And duty, to attempt unceasingly
To compass.   Grant us, All-maintaining Sire !
That all the great mechanic aids **to toil**
Man's skill hath formed, **found, rendered, — whether** used
In multiplying works of mind, or aught
To **obviate** the thousand wants of life,
May much avail to human welfare now
And in all ages, henceforth and for ever !
Let their effect be, Lord ! to lighten labor,

And give more room to mind, and leave the poor
Some time for self-improvement. Let them not
Be forced to grind the bones out of their arms
For bread, but have some space to think and feel
Like moral and immortal creatures. God!
Have mercy on them till such time shall come;
Look Thou with pity on all lesser crimes,
Thrust on men almost when devoured by want,
Wretchedness, ignorance and outcast life!
Have mercy on the rich, too, who pass by
The means they have at hand to fill their minds
With serviceable knowledge for themselves,
And fellows, and support not the good cause
Of the world's better future! Oh reward
All such who do, with peace of neart and power
For greater good. Have mercy, Lord! on each
And all, for all men need it equally.
May peace and industry and commerce weld
Into one land all nations of the world,
Rewedding those the Deluge once divorced.
Oh! may all help each other in good things,
Mentally, morally, and bodily!
Vouchsafe, kind God! Thy blessing to this isle,
Specially! May our country ever lead
The world, for she is worthiest; and may all
Profit by her example, and adopt
Her course, wherever great, or free, or just.
May all her subject colonies and powers
Have of her freedom freely, as a child
Receiveth of its parents. Let not rights
Be wrested from us to our own reproach,
But granted. We may make the whole world free,
And be as free ourselves as ever, more!
If policy or self-defence call forth
Our forces to the field, let us in Thee
Place, first, our trust, and in Thy name we shall
O'ercome, for we will only wage the right.
Let us not conquer nations for ourselves,
But for Thee, Lord! who hast predestined us

To fight the battles of the future now,
And so have done with war before Thou comest.
Till then, Lord God of armies, let our foes
Have their swords broken and their cannon burst,
And their strong cities levelled; and while we
War faithfully and righteously, improve,
Civilize, christianize the lands we win
From savage or from nature, Thou, oh God!
Wilt aid and hallow conquest, as of old,
Thine own immediate nation's.   But we pray
That all mankind may make one brotherhood,
And love and serve each other; that all wars
And feuds die out of nations, whether those
Whom the sun's hot light darkens, or ourselves
Whom he treats fairly, or the northern tribes
Whom ceaseless snows and starry winters blench,
Savage or civilized, — let every race,
Red, black or white, olive, or tawny-skinned,
Settle in peace and swell the gathering hosts
Of the great Prince of Peace! Oh! may the
    hour
Soon come when all false gods, false creeds, false
    prophets,—
Allowed in Thy good purpose for a time,—
Demolished, the great world shall be at last,
The mercy-seat of God, the heritage
Of Christ, and the possession of the Spirit,
The comforter, the wisdom! shall all be
One land, one home, one friend, one faith, one law
Its ruler God, its practice righteousness,
Its life peace! For the one true faith we pray;
There is but one in Heaven and there shall be
But one on earth, the same which is in Heaven.
Prophecy is more true than history.
Grant us our prayers, we pray, Lord! in the name
And for the sake of Thy Son Jesus Christ,
Our Saviour and Redeemer, who with Thee,
And with the Holy Spirit, reigneth God
Over all worlds, one blessed Trinity!——

THE CROWD.   Amen!
LUCIFER.   Well, friends, we'll sing a hymn; then
            part.
I give it out, and you sing — all of you.

    Oh! Earth is cheating Earth
      From age to age for ever;
  She laughs at faith **and** worth,
    And dreams she **shall die never;**
      Never, never, never!
  And dreams **she** shall die never.

    And Hell is cursing Hell
      From age to age for ever;
  Its groans ring out the knell
    Of souls that may die never;
      Never, never, never!
  Of souls that may **die never.**

    But Heaven is blessing Heaven
      From age to age for ever;
  And **its** thanks to God are given
    For bliss that can die never;
      Never, never, never!
  For bliss that can die never.

My blessing be upon ye **all; now go!**
  FESTUS.   I wonder **what these people make ot**
    thee.
  LUCIFER.   **Ay manner's a** great matter.
  FESTUS.   They **deserve**
All the rebuke thou gavest them and more.
What mountains of delusion **men** have reared!
How every **age** hath bustled **on to** build
Its shadowy mole — its monumental dream!
How faith **and fancy,** in **the** mind of man,
Have spuriously **mingled,** and how much
Shall pass away for aye, as pass before
Yon sun, the Lord ol steadfastness and change,

The visionary landscapes of the skies;—
The golden capes far stretching into Heaven,
The snow-piled cloud-crags, the bright winged isles
Which dot the deep, impassive, ocean air
Like a disbanded rainbow, of all hues,
Fit for translated fairy's Paradise;—
Or as before the eye of musing child,
The faces Fancy forms in clouds and fire
Of glowing angel or of darkening fiend.
Arts, superstition, arms, philosophy,
Have each in turn possessed, betrayed, and mocked
     us.
Yes, vain philosophy, thine hour is come!
Thy lips were lined with the immortal lie,
And dyed with all the look of truth. Men saw,
Believed, embraced, detested, cast thee off.
Those lights, the morn of Truth's immortal day,
As thou didst falsely swear them, have they not
Vanished, the mere auroras of the mind?
And thou didst vow to gather clear again
The fallen waters of humanity;
To smoothe the flaw from out an eye; to piece
A pounded pearl. Thank God! I am a man;
Not a philosopher! Rivers may rot,
Never revive the root of oak firebolted.
Come, let us to the hills! where none but God
Can overlook us; for I hate to breathe
The breaths and think the thoughts of other men,
In close and clouded cities, where the sky
Frowns like an angry Father mournfully.
I love the hills and I love loneliness.
And oh! I love the woods, those natural fanes
Whose very air is holy; and we breathe
Of God; for He doth come in special place,
And, while we worship, He is there for us!
    LUCIFER.   It is time that something should be
       done for the poor.
The sole equality on earth is death;
Now, rich and poor are both dissatisfied.

I am **for** judgment : that will settle both.
Nothing is to be done without **destruction.**
Death is the universal salt of states ;
Blood is the base of all things — law and **war,**
I could **tame** this lion age to follow me.
I should like to macadamize the world ;
The road to Hell wants mending.
  FESTUS.   Come away !

SCENE — *The Surface.*

LUCIFER *and* FESTUS.

LUCIFER. Wilt ride ?
FESTUS.   I 'll have an hour's ride.
LUCIFER. Be mine the steeds ! be me the guide.
Come hither, come hither,
My brave black steed !
And thou, too, his fellow,
Hither with speed!
Though not so fleet
As the steeds of Death,
Your feet are as sure,
Ye have longer breath.
Ye have **drawn the world**
Without wind or bait,
Six thousand years,
And it waxeth late
So take me this once,
And again to my home,
And rest ye and feast ye.
They come, they come.
 FESTUS. Tossing their manes **like**
Pitchy **surge ;** and lashing
Their **tails into a**
Tempest ; **their eyes flashing,**
Like shooting thunderbolts.
 LUCIFER. Come, know your masters, **colts !**
Up, and away !

Festus.   Hurrah! hurrah!
The noblest pace the world e'er saw.
I swear **by** Heaven we'll beat the **sun,**
In the longest heat that ever was **run;**
If we keep **it up** as we have begun.
  Lucifer.   I told thee my steeds
Were a gallant pair.
  Festus.   And **they were not** thine,
They might **be divine.**
  Lucifer.   **Thine is named Ruin;**
And Darkness mine.
  Festus.   Like **all of thy deeds.**
Now that's unfair.
  Lucifer.   A **civiller and gentler beast**
Thou hast never crossed **at least.**
Now, **look around!**
  Festus.   **Why, this is France.**
Nature is here like a living romance.
Look at its vines and streams and skies,
Its glancing feet and dancing eyes!
  Lucifer.   'Tis a strange nation, light yet **strong,**
Fierce of heart and blithe of tongue;
Prone to change; so fond of blood
She wounds herself to quaff her own.
  Festus.   Oh! **it's a** brave and lovely **land;**
And well deserving every good
Which others wish themselves alone,
Could she but herself command.
  Lucifer.   **On! on!** no more delay!
Or we'll not ride **round**
The world all day.
  Festus.   Good horse, get off the ground!
  Lucifer.   Sit firm; and if our horses please,
We will take at once the Pyrenees.
'T was bravely leapt!
  Festus.   **Ay,** this is Spain:
Europe's last land
'T will e'er remain;

Last in the progress of the earth;
The last in liberty;
The last in wealth and worth;
The last in bigotry.
    LUCIFER. Turn thy steed, and slacken rein;
Quick! we must be back again:
O'er the vale hid in the mountain,
O'er the merry forest fountain;
Ruin and Darkness! we must fly
O'er crag and rift,
Swift — swift — swift
As the glance of an eye.
    FESTUS. That is Italy — the grave
And resurrection of the slave.
    LUCIFER. And there lies Greece, whose soul
Men say hath fled.
    FESTUS. Perhaps some God may come,
And raise the dead.
    LUCIFER. Norward now we 'll hold our course.
Thine I think is the bolder horse;
But bear him up with a harder hand!
Rough riding this o'er Swisserland.
    FESTUS. So all have found it who have tried;
High as their Alps the people's pride,
Never to have bowed before
The tyrant or the conqueror.
    LUCIFER. Away, away! before thee lie
The fields and floods of Germany.
    FESTUS. Well I love thee, Father-land!
Sire of Europe, as thou art!
Be free! and crouch no more, but stand!
Thy noblest son will take thy part.
Oh! sooner let the mountains bend
Beneath the clouds, when tempests lour,
Than nations stoop their sky compeering heads
In homage to some petty despot's power!
The worm which suffers mincing into parts,
May sprout forth heads and tails, but grows no
      hearts.

Lucifer.   There lies Austria!   Famous **land**
For fiddlesticks and sword-in-hand.
  Festus.   And Poland, whom truly unhappy **we**
            call.
Unworthy to rise — unwilling **to fall.**
Forge into swords thy feudal **chain!**
Smite e'en the souls of foes in twain!
The fetters have been bound in vain
Round England's arms: and we are free
As the souls of our sires in Heaven which **be.**
That earth should have so few
Men, Fathers, like to you!
  Lucifer.   What **matter who be free or slaves;**
For all there **is** one tyranny, the **grave's;**
Or freedom, may be.   On! on! **haste!**
  Festus.   What land **is yonder wide, white**
            waste?
  Lucifer.   **Ha!** 't is Russia's **gentle realm:**
Whose sceptre is the sword — whose **crown,** the
            helm.
  Festus.   I swear by every atom which exists,
I better **love** this reckless ride
O'er hill and forest, lake and **river** wide;
O'er sunlit plain and through the mountain mists,
Than aught which thou hast given beside.
  Lucifer.   **See** what a long, long track
Of dust and fire behind,
For miles and miles aback!
And shrill and strong,
As we **shoot** along,
Whistles and whirrs,
Like a forest of firs
Falling, the cold north wind.
  Festus.   Look! my way **I** can only read
By the sparks from the hoof **of** my giant steed
  Lucifer.   Where art thou now?
  Festus.   In Tartar land;
I know by the **deserts of** salt and sand.

Nor aim nor end hath a wandering life;
Rest reaps but rest, and strife but strife.
With the nations round
They ne'er have mixed;
For good or ill
They stand all still;
Their bodies but rove,
Their minds are fixed.
And yonder lies old China's wall,
Where gods of gold do men enthrall;
Gods whose gold 's their only worth.
 Lucifer. Well, is not gold the god of
  earth?
Now southward, hey! for Hindostan!
The sun beats down both beast and man.
Insect and herb for life do gasp;
The river reeks and faints the asp.
 Festus. But blithe are we,
And our steeds, I trow;
And the mane of mine
Yet bears the snow
Which fell on us
By Caucasus.
By the four beasts! but this is warm.
 Lucifer. Away! away!
Nor stint nor stay;
We 'll reach the sea before yon storm.
 Festus. Wilt take the sea?
 Lucifer. Ay, that will we!
And swim as we ride,
Our steeds astride;
Come leap, leap off with me!
 Festus. What? shall we leap
Sheer off this steep,
A mile the sea above?
 Lucifer. Leap as to save
From worse than a grave
The maid thou most dost love!

Festus. There is a rapture in the headlong
        leap,
The wedgelike cleaving of the closing deep!
A feeling full of hardihood and power
With which **we** court the **waters that devour.**
Oh! 't is a feeling great, sublime, supreme,
Like the ecstatic influence of a dream,
To speed one's way thus o'er the sliding plain ;
And make a kindred being with the main.
  Lucifer. By Chaos! this is gallant **sport;**
A league at every breath ;
Methinks if I ever have to **die,**
I 'll ride this rate to death.
  Festus. Away, **away upon the** whitening tide,
Like lover hastening **to embrace his bride,**
We hurry faster than the foam **we ride.**
Dashing aside the waves which round us cling,
With strength like that which lifts an eagle's wing
Where the stars dazzle and the angels sing.
  Lucifer. **We scatter** the spray,
And break through **the** billows,
As the wind makes way
Through the leaves of **willows!**
  Festus. In vain they urge **their armies to the**
        fight :
Their surge-crests **crumble 'neath our stroke of**
        might.
We meet and **fear not; mount —** now rise, now
        fall —
And dare, **with full-nerved** arm, the rage of all.
Through anger-swollen **wave** or sparkling spray,
Nothing it recks; **we** hold **our** perilous way
Right onward! till we feel **the** whirling brain
Ring with the maddening music of the main ;
Till the fixed eyeball strives and strains to ken,
Yet loathes to see the shore and haunts of men ;
And the blood, half starting through each ridgy
        vein,
In the unwieldly hand sets **black** with pain.

Then let the tempest cloud on cloud come spread,
And tear the stormy terrors of his head ;
Let the wild sea-bird wheel around my brow,
And shriek — and swoop — and flap her wing **as**
      now !
It gladdens! on! ye boisterous billows, roll!
And keep my body ; ye have ta'en my soul.
Thou element! the type which God hath given,
For eyes and **hearts too earthy, of His** Heaven !
Were Heaven **a mockery, I would never mourn**
While o'er **thy bosom I might still be borne ;**
While yet **to me the power and joy was given**
To fling **my breast on thine, and mingle earth with**
      Heaven.
    LUCIFER.   See yonder! now we quit the main ;
For here 's the Cape, here 's land again, —
And **scour** we must o'er Afric's plain.
    FESTUS.   **Away** ! away ! on either hand
Nor town nor **tower,**
Nor shade nor shower —
Nothing but sun and sand.
    LUCIFER.   See, there they are ! I knew, right
      soon,
We would **light on the mountains of the moon.**
Over them! **over,** nought forbids !
    FESTUS.   Yonder the Nile and the **Pyramids ?**
Hurrah ! by my soul !
At every bound
I see, I feel
The earth rush round.
I see the mountains slide away —
That side night and this side day.
    LUCIFER.   Shall we go to America ?
    FESTUS.   Why, have we time ?
    LUCIFER.   Oh, plenty ;
Be there, **too, ere we** reckon twenty.
Another run, another bound !
And we shall leave this lion ground.
    FESTUS.   The sea again ! the **swift bright sea**

Lucifer.   Hold hard, and follow me !
Well, now we have travelled upon the **waves,**
Wilt travel a time beneath ?
And visit **the** sea-born in their caves;
And **look on the rainbow-tinted wreath**
Of weeds, **beset with pearls, wherewith**
The mermaid **binds** her **long green hair,**
Or rouse the sea-snake from **his lair ?**
  Festus.   Ay, ay ! down let us dive !
  Lucifer.   Look up ! we lack not **stars;**
And every star thou seest 's alive :
A little globe of life — light — love,
Whose every atom **is a** living being;
Each the other's bosom seeing,
Each **enlightening the** other.
  Festus.   **Oh !** how unlike the **world above,**
Where **each** doth mainly, vainly **strive**
To dim or to outshine his brother !
  Lucifer.   **Come on ! come** on !
  Festus.   **Are** those bright spars,
Or eyes of things **which** ne'er forgive,
That seem to play on us, and glare
With rage that we so far should dare
To search the hidden deeps,
Where tide, **the** moonslave, sleeps **?**
Where the wind breathes not, and the wave
Walks **softly as above a** grave ; —
Where coral worms, in countless nations,
Build rocks up from **the sea's foundations;** —
Where the islands strike **their roots**
Far from **the** old mainland ;
And spring like desert-fruits,
Shook off by God's strong hand,
Up from their bed of sand.
Look, listen ! **there is** music in the cave,
Where ocean sleeps, and brightness in the **wave**
The sea-bird makes its pillow, and the star,
Last born of Heaven, its azure mirror ; — far
And wide, the pale, fine, fire of ocean flows,

Softly sublime like lightnings in repose —
Till roused, anon, afar its flaming spray **it throws.**
   Lucifer.   There! now we stand
On the world's-end-land!
Over the hills
Away **we** go!
Through fire, and **snow,**
And rivers, whereto
All others are rills.
   Festus.   Through **the lands of silver,**
The lands of gold;
Through lands untrodden,
And lands untold.
   Lucifer.   By **strait and bay**
We must away;
Through swamp, and plain,
And hurricane;
   Festus.   **And** that dark cloud of slaves
Which **yet may rise;**—
Though nought shall blot the bannered stars
From Freedom's skies.
America! half-brother of the **world!**
With **something good** and bad of every land;
Greater **than thee have** lost their seat —
Greater scarce **none can** stand.
Thy flag now **flouts the skies,**
The highest **under Heaven;**
Save the red cross, **whereto are given**
All victories.
   Lucifer.   Our horses snort and snuff **the sea,**
And pant for where we ought to be.
   Festus.   Well, here we are! **and as** we flew in,
I said, let Darkness follow Ruin!
   Lucifer.   'T was right. Spur on! Come, Dark-
      ness, come!
Think of thy **well-strown stall!**
   Festus.   For me, I care not what's to come,
Nor for the **fate** by which I fall;
But **I** would that I were Ocean's son,

The solitary brave,
Like yon sea-snake, to climb upon
The **crest of** the bounding wave.
Oh ! **happy, if at last I** lie
Within some pearled and coral cave ;
While over head the booming surge
And moaning billow shall chaunt my **dirge ;**
And **the storm-blast, as it** sweepeth by,
Shall, answering, howl to the mermaid's **sigh,**
And the night-wind's mournful minstrelsy,
Their requiem **over** my grave.

    LUCIFER.   Through morn **and midnight, sunset**
        and high noon,
One hour hath ta'en us ; — o'er all land and sea,
O'er opening earthquake and **iceberg, have we**
Swept in swift **safety.**   'T will be over, soon.
Behold the common, narrow sea,
Which, like **a strong man's arm,**
Keeps back **two foes whose lips are white,**
Whose hearts with rage **are** warm.

    FESTUS.   England ! my country, great and **free !**
Heart of **the** world, I leap to thee !
How shall **my** country fight
When her **foes rise against her,**
But with **thine arm, Ò Sea !**
The arm which thou lent'st her ?
Where **shall my country be buried**
When **she shall die ?**
Earth is too scant **for her grave :**
Where shall she **lie ?**
She hath brethren **more than a hundred,**
And they all want **room ;**
They may die **and** may lie where they live —
They shall not **mix** with her doom.
Where but within thine arms,
O sea, O sea ?
Wherein she hath lived and gloried,
Let her **rest be !**
We will **rise and will say to the** sea,

Flow over her !
We will cry to the depths of the deep,
Cover her !
The world hath drawn his sword,
And his red shield drips before him :—
But, my country, rise !
Thou canst never die
While a foe hath life to fly ;
Rise land, and gore him !
   LUCIFER.   Now get on land, and hie along
O'er forest, copse, and glade ;
We have but a league or two more to go
Before our journey 's made ;
With speed that flings the sun into the shade !
   FESTUS.   See the gold sunshine patching,
And streaming and streaking across
The gray-green oaks ; and catching,
By its soft brown beard, the moss.
   LUCIFER.   Ah ! here we get an open plain :
Here we 'll get down.
Away, good steeds ! be off again !
   FESTUS.   We must be near to Town.
I am bound to thee for ever
By the pleasure of this day ;
Henceforth we will never sever,
Come what come may.

SCENE — A Village Feast. Evening.

FESTUS, LUCIFER, and OTHERS.

   FESTUS.   It is getting dark. One has to walk quite close,
To see the pretty faces that we meet.
   LUCIFER.   A disagreeable necessity,
Truly.
   FESTUS.   We 'll rest upon this bridge. I am tired.
Yon tall slim tree ! does it not seem as made

For its place there, a kind of natural maypole ? —
Beyond, the lighted stalls stored with the good
Things of our childhood's world, and behind them,
The shouting showman and the clashing cymbal;
The open-doored cottages and blazing hearth, —
The little **ones** running up with naked feet,
And cake in either hand, to their mother's lap, —
Old and young laughing, schoolboys with **their**
     playthings,
Clowns cracking jokes, and lasses **with sly eyes,**
And the smile settling in their sunflecked **cheeks,**
Like noon upon the mellow apricot ; —
Make **up a** scene I can for once give **in** to.
It must please all, **the** social and the selfish.
Are they not happy ?
    LUCIFER.   Why, it matters not.
They **seem so :** that 's enough.
    FESTUS.   But not the same.
    LUCIFER.   Yet truth and falsehood **meet** in
     seeming, like
The falling leaf and shadow on the pool's face.
And these are joys, like beauty, but skin deep.
    FESTUS. Remove all such and what 's the joy
     of earth ?
'T is they **create the** appetite of life —
Give zest and relish to the lot of millions.
And take the taste **for** them away — what's **left?**
A dry ungainly skeleton of soul.
    LUCIFER. Power is aye above the **soul and joy**
Below **it.** Pleasure men prefer **to power.**
        (*Children at play.*)
    FESTUS. Play away, good **ones!**
    AN OLD MAN.   Pity the poor blind man !
    FESTUS. Here is substantial pity.
    OLD **MAN.**   Heaven reward you !
    FESTUS. Blind **as** the blue skies after sunset
     Blind !
And I am tired of looking on what is.
One might as well see beauty never more,

As look upon it with an empty eye.
I would this world were over.   I am tired.
Nought happens but what happens to one's self;
And all hath happened I have wished, and more.
Our pleasures all pass from us, one by one,
With that relief which sighing gives the heart,
Though each sigh leaves it lower.   It is sad
To think how few our pleasures really are :
And for the which we risk eternal good.
There 's nothing that can satisfy one's self,
Except one's self.   Well, it is very sad,
And by the time we come of age we have felt,
In one degree or other, all that age
Can offer.   We have reaped our field ere noon.
The rest is reproduction ; sowing — reaping —
Losing again.   Toil and gain tire alike.
We cannot live too slowly to be good
And happy, nor too much by line and square.
But youth is burning to forestall its nature,
And will not wait for time to ferry it
Over the stream, but flings itself into
The flood, and perishes.   And yet, why not ?
There is no charm in time as time, nor good.
The long days are no happier than the short ones.
'T is some time now since I was here.   We leave
Our home in youth — no matter to what end ; —
Study — or strife — or pleasure, or what not:
And coming back in few short years, we find
All as we left it, outside ; the old elms,
The house, grass, gates, and latchet's selfsame click.
But lift that latchet, — all is changed as doom :
The servants have forgotten our step, and more
Than half of those who knew us know us not.
Adversity, prosperity, the grave,
Play a round game with friends.   On some the world
Hath shot its evil eye, and they are passed
From honor and remembrance, and a stare
Is all the mention of their names receives ;

And people know no more of them than of
The shapes of clouds at midnight, a year back.
  LUCIFER.   Let us move on to where the dancing
      is ;
We soon shall see how happy they **all are.**
Here is a loving couple quarrelling.
And there, another. It is quite distressing.
See yonder. Two men fighting !
  FESTUS.   **What avail**
These vile exceptions to the rule **of** joy ?
  LUCIFER.   Behold the happiness of **which thou**
    spakest !
The highest hills are **miles** below the **sky,**
And so far is the lightest heart below
True happiness.
  FESTUS.   This **is a snakelike world,**
And always hath its tail **within its mouth,**
As if it ate itself, **and moralled time.**
The world is like **yon children's** merry-go-round ;
What men admire **are** carriages and hobbies,
Which **the** exalted manikins enjoy.
There is a noisy ragged crowd below
Of urchins drives it round, who only **get**   [haps:
The excitement for their pains — best **gain** per-
For **it** is not they who labor that **grow** dizzy
Nor sick — that's for the idle, **proud** above,
Who soon dismount, more **weary of** enjoying
Than those below of working ; **and** but fair.
It is wretchedness or recklessness **alone**
Keeps us alive. Were we happy **we should die.**
Yet what is death ? I like to think on death :
It is but the appearance of an apparition.
One ought to tremble ; but oughts stand for nothing.
I hate the thought of wrinkling up to rest ;
The toothlike aching ruin **of** the body,
With the heart all **out, and** nothing left but **edge.**
Give me the long high bounding feel **of** life,
Which cries, let me but leap unto my grave,
And I'll not mind the when nor where. We never

Care less for life than when enjoying it.
Oh! I should love to die.   What is to die ?
I cannot hold the meaning more than can
An oak's arms clasp the blast that blows on it.
I am made up to die ; for having been
Every **thing,** there is nothing left but nothing
To be again.
    LUCIFER.   Hark ! here is a ballad-singer.
    BALLAD-SINGER.   All of my **own** composing !
    FESTUS.   Yes, Yes— we know.

    SINGER.   **My** gipsy **maid ! my gipsy maid !**
I bless and curse the day
I lost the light of life, and caught
The grief which maketh gray.
Would that the light which blinded me
Had saved me on my way !

My night-haired love ! so sweet she **was,**
So fair and blithe was she ;
Her smile **was** brighter than the moon's,
Her eyes the stars might see.

I met her **by her lane-spread tent,**
Beside a moss-green stone,
And bade **her** make, **not mock, my fate,**
My fortune **was her own.**
Thou art but **yet a boy, she said,**
And I **a** woman grown.

I am a man in love, I cried ;
My heart was early manned ;
She smiled, and only drooped her eyes,
And then let go my hand.
We stood **a** minute : neither spake
What each **must** understand.

I told her, so she would be mine
And follow where I went,

She straight should have a bridal bower
Instead of gipsy tent.

Or would she have me wend with her,
The world between should fall;
For her **I would** fling up faith and friends,
And **name, and** fame, and all.

Her smile so bright froze while I spake,
And ice was in her **eye**;
So near, it seemed ere touch **her heart**
I might have kissed the sky.

I said that if she loved to rule,
Or if she longed **to** reign,
I would make her Queen **of every race**
Which tearlike trode the **world's sad face,**
Or bleed at **every vein.**

She laid her finger **on** her lip,
And pointed to the sky;
There is no God to come, she said:
Dost **thou not fear** to die?

And what is God, I said, to thee?
Thy people worship not.
The good, the happy, and the free,
She said, they need no God.

I looked until **I lost mine eyes;**
I felt **as** though **I were**
In a dark cave, **with one** weak **light —**
The light of life — **with her;**
And that was wasting fast away;
I watched but would not stir.

Again she took my hand in hers,
And read it o'er and **o'er;**
Ah! **eyes so** young, so sweet, I said,
Make as they read love's lore.

She held my hand — I trembled whilst —
For sorely soon I felt
She made the love-cross she foretold,
And all the woe she dealt.

Unhappy I should be, she said,
And young to death be given;
I told her I believed in her,
Not in the stars of Heaven.

Hush! we breathe Heaven, she said, and bowed;
And the stars speak through me.
Let Heaven, I cried, take care of Heaven!
I only care for thee.

She shrank: I looked, and begged a kiss:
I knew she had one for me;
She would deny me none, she said,
But give me none would she.

My gipsy maid! my gipsy maid!
'Tis three long years like this,
Since there I gave and got from thee
That meeting, parting kiss.

I saw the tears start in her eye,
And trickle down her cheek,
Like falling stars across the sky,
Escaping from their Maker's eye:
I saw, but spared to speak.

Go, and forget! she said, and slid
Below her lowly tent.
I will not, cannot — hear me, girl!
She heard not, and I went.

At eve, by sunset, I was there,
The tent was there no more;

The fire which warmed her flickered still —
The fire she sat before.

I stood by it, till through the dark
I saw not where it lay;
And then like that my heart went out
In ashy grief and gray.

My gipsy maid! my gipsy maid!
Oh! let me bless this day;
This day it was I met thee first,
And yet it shall be and is cursed,
For thou hast gone away.

    LUCIFER. Another, please — not quite so gloomy,
        friend.
    GIRL. I wonder if the tale it tells be true.
    SINGER. I dare say — but you want a merrier.
Every man's life has its apocrypha;
Mine has, at least. I have said more than need be.
It happened, too, when I was very young.
We never meet such gipsies when we are old;
And yet we more complain of youth than age.
Now, make a ring, good people. Let me breathe!
                                          [Sings.

Oh! the wee green neuk, the sly green neuk,
   The wee sly neuk for me!
Whare the wheat is wavin' bright and brown,
   And the wind is fresh and free.
Whare I weave wild weeds, and out o' reeds
   Kerve whissles as I lay;
And a douce low voice is murmurin' by
   Through the lee-lang simmer day.
    Oh! the wee green neuk, etc.

And whare a' things luik as though they lo'ed
   To languish in the sun;
And that if they feed the fire they dree,
   They wadna ae pang were gone.
             8

Whare the lift aboon is **still as death,**
　And bright **as** life can be;
While the douce low voice says, na, na, **na!**
　But ye **mauna** luik sae at me.
　　Oh! **the** wee green neuk, etc.

Whare the lang rank bent is saft and cule,
　And freshenin' till the feet;
And the spot is sly, and the spinnie high,
　Whare my luve and I mak seat:
And I teaze her till she rins, and **then**
　I catch her roun' **the tree;**
While the poppies **shak'** their heids and blush·
　Let 'em blush till they drap, **for me!**
　　Oh! the wee green neuk, etc.

　Festus. And **all who know such** feelings **and**
　　such scenes
Will, I am sure, reward you.　Here — take this.
　Others.　And this, and this — too.
　Singer.　Thank **ye** all, good friends!
　Festus.　There's much that hath no merit but
　　its truth,
And no excuse but **nature.**　Nature does
Never wrong: **'t is society which** sins.
Look on the bee **upon the wing among flowers;**
Now brave, **how bright his life!**　Then mark him
　　hived,
Cramped, cringing in his self-built, **social cell.**
Thus is it in the world-hive: most where men
Lie deep in cities as in drifts — death drifts,
Nosing each **other** like a flock of sheep;
Not knowing and not caring whence nor whither
They come or go, so that they fool together.
　Lucifer.　It **is quite fair** to halve these lives and
　　say
This side is **nature's, that** society's,
When both are side-views only of one thing.
　Farmer.　I am glad to see you come among us,
　　sir.

Parson. Why, I have but little comfort in these
        pastimes ;
And any heart, turned Godwards, feels more joy
In one short hour of prayer, than e'er was raised
By all the feasts on earth since their foundation.
But no one will believe us ; as if we
Had never known the vain things of the world,
Nor **lain and** slept in sin's seducing shade,
Listless, until God woke us ; made us feel
We should be up and stirring in the sun ;
For every thing had **to** be done ere night.
What is all this joy and jollity about ?
Grant there may be no sin.   What good is it ?
    Farmer. I can't defend these feasts, **sir, and
        can't blame.**
    Parson. **Good evening, friends! Why, Festus!**
        I rejoice
We **meet again.**   I **have a** young friend here,
A student — who hath staid with us of late.
You would be glad, I know, **to** know each other.
Therefore be known so.
    Festus.   You are a student, sir.
    Student. I profess little ; but it is a title
A man may claim perhaps with modesty.
    Festus. True. All mankind are students. **How**
        to live
And how to die forms the great lesson still.
I know what study is : it is to toil
Hard, through the hours of the sad midnight watch,
At tasks which seem a systematic curse,
And course of bootless penance.   Night by night,
To trace **one's** thought as if on iron leaves ;
And sorrowful as though it were the mode
And date of death we wrote on our own tombs :
Wring **a slight** sleep **out** of **the couch,** and see
The self-same moon, which lit us to our rest,
Her place scarce changed perceptibly in Heaven.
Now light us to renewal of our toils. —
This, to the young mind, wild and all in leaf,

Which knowledge, grafting, paineth. Fruit soon
          comes,
And more than all our troubles pays us powers; `
So that we joy to have endured so much:
That not for nothing have we slaved and slain
Ourselves almost.   And more; it is to strive
To bring the mind up to one's own esteem:
Who but the generous fail?   It is to think,
While thought is standing thick upon the brain
As dew upon the brow—for thought is brain-sweat;
And gathering quick and dark, like storms in
          summer,
Until convulsed, condensed, in lightning sport,
It plays upon the heavens of the mind,—
Opens the hemisphered abysses here,
And we become revealers to ourselves.
      STUDENT. When night hath set her silver lamp
          on high,
Then is the time for study; when Heaven's light
Pours itself on the page, like prophecy
On time, unglooming all its mighty meanings;
It is then we feel the sweet strength of the stars,
And magic of the moon.
      LUCIFER.   It's a bad habit.
      STUDENT. And wisdom dwells in secret and on
          high,
As do the stars.   The sun's diurnal glare
Is·for the daily herd; but for the wise,
The cold pure radiance of the night-born light,
Wherewith is inspiration of the truth.
There was a time when I would never go
To rest before the sun rose; and for that,
Through a like length of time as that now gone,
The world shall speak of me six thousand years
          hence.
      LUCIFER. How know you that the world wont
          end to-morrow?
      PARSON.   I now, an early riser, love to hail
The dreamy struggles of the stars with light,

And the recovering breath of earth, sleep-drowned,
Awakening to the wisdom of the sun,
And life of light within the tent of Heaven : —
To kiss the feet of Morning as she walks
In dewy light along the hills, while they,
All odorous as an angel's fresh-culled crown,
Unveil **to her** their bounteous loveliness.
    STUDENT. I am devote to study.. Worthy **books**
Are not companions — they are solitudes :
We lose ourselves in them and all our cares.
The further back we search the human mind, —
Mean in the mass, but in the instance great —
Which starting first with Deities and stars
And broods of beings earth-born, Heaven-begot,
· And all the bright side of the broad world, **now**
Doats upon dreams and dim atomic truths,
Is all for comfort and no more for glory —
The nobler and more marvellous it shows.
Trifles like these make up the present time ;
The Iliad and the Pyramids the past.
    FESTUS. The future will have glory not the less.
I can conceive a time when the world shall be
Much better visibly, and when, as far
As social life and its relations tend,
Men, morals, manners shall be lifted up
To a pure height we know not of nor dream ; —
When all men's rights and duties shall be clear,
And charitably exercised and borne ;
When education, conscience, and good deeds
Shall have just equal sway, and civil claims ; —
Great crimes shall be cast out, **as** were of old
Devils possessing madmen : — Truth shall reign,
Nature shall be rethroned, and man sublimed.
    STUDENT. Oh ! **then may** Heaven come down
        again to earth ;
And dwell with her, as once, like to a friend.
    LUCIFER. As like each other as a sword and
        scythe.
Oh ! then shall lions mew and lambkins roar !

Festus.   And having studied — what next ?
  Student.   Much I long
To view the capital city of the world.
The mountains, the great cities, and the sea,
Are **each** an era in the life of youth.
    Festus. There to get worldly ways, and thoughts
            and schemes ;
To learn to detect, distrust, despise mankind —
To ken **a** false factitious glare amid much
That shines with seeming saintlike purity —
To gloss misdeeds — to trifle with **great** truths —
To pit the brain against the heart, and **plead**
Wit before wisdom, — these are the **world's ways :**
It learns us to lose that in crowds which we
Must after seek alone — our innocence ;
And when the crowd is gone.
    Student.   Not only that :
There all great things are round one.   Interests,
Mighty and mountainous of estimate,
Are daily heaped or scattered 'neath the eye.
Great deeds, great thoughts, great schemes, **and**
            crimes, and all
Which **is in** purpose, or in practice, great
Of **human** nature — there are common things.
Men make themselves be deathless **as in** spite ;
As if they waged some lineal feud **with time ;**
As though their fathers were immortal, **too,**
And immortality an every-day
Accomplishment.
    Festus. Fie ! fie ! 't is more for this :
Amid gayer people and more wanton ways,
To give a loose to all the lists of youth —
To train your passion flowers high ahead,
And bind them on your brow as others do.
The mornlit revel and the shameless mate —
The tabled hues of darkness and of blood —
The published bosom and the crowning smile —
The cup excessive ; **and** if aught there be
More vain than these or wanton — **that to have —**

Have all but always in intent, effect,
Or fact.   Nay, nay, deny it not : I know.
Youth hath a strange and strong desire to try
All feelings on the heart : it is very wrong,
And dangerous, and deadly : strive against it
 Student. It might be some old sage was warn-
   ing us.
 Festus. Youth might be wise.   We suffer less
   from pains
Than pleasures.
 Student.   I should like to see the world,
And gain that knowledge which is —
 Festus.   Barrener
Than **ice** ; possessing and producing nought
But means and forms of death or vanity.
The world is just as hollow as an eggshell.
It is a surface, not a solid, mind :
And all this boasted knowledge **of the** world
To me seems but to mean acquaintance with
Low things, or evil, or indifferent.
 Farmer.   Much more is said of knowledge than
   it 's worth.
A man may gain all knowledge here, and yet
Be, after death, as much in the dark as I.
 Lucifer. What makes you know of **living**
   after death ?
 Farmer. Why, nothing that I know ; and **there**
   it is, —
But something I am told has told me so.
No angel ever came to me to prove it ;
And all my friends have died, **and** left no ghosts.
 Festus.   All that is good a man may learn from
   himself ;
And much, too, that is **bad.**
 Parson.   Nay, let me speak !
Aught that is good the soul receives of God
When He hath made it His ; and until then
Man cannot know, nor do, nor be, aught good.
Oh ! there is nought on earth worth being known

But God and our own souls — the God we have
Within our hearts ; for it is not the hope,
Nor faith, nor fear, nor notions others have
Of God can serve us, but the sense and soul
We have of Him within us; and, for men,
God loves us men each individually,
And deals with us in order, soul by soul.
    LUCIFER. What are your politics ?
    FARMER.   I have none.
    LUCIFER.   Good.
    FARMER. I have my thoughts. I am no party
       man.
I care for measures more than men, but think
Some little may depend upon the men ;
Something in fires depends upon the grate.
    FIRST BOY. What are your colors ?
    SECOND.   Blue as Heaven.
    THIRD.   And mine
Are yellow as the sun.
    FIRST.   Mine, green as grass.
    SECOND. Green 's forsaken, and yellow 's for-
       sworn,
And blue 's the color that shall be worn.
    STUDENT. As to religion, politics, law, and war,
But little need be said. All are required,
And all are well enough. Of liberty,
And slavery, and tyranny we hear
Much; but the human mind affects extremes.
The heart is in the middle of the system;
And all affections gather round the truth,
The moderated joys and woes of life.
I love my God, my country, kind and kin,
Nor would I see a dog wronged of his bone.
My country! if a wretch should e'er arise,
Out of thy countless sons, who would curtail
Thy freedom, dim thy glory,—while he lives
May all earth's peoples curse him—for of all
Hast thou secured the blessing;—and if one
Exist who would not arm for liberty,

Be he too cursed living, and when dead,
Let him be buried downwards, with his face
Looking to Hell, and o'er his coward **grave**
The hare skulk in **her form.**
 LUCIFER.   Nay, gently, friend.
Curse **nothing, not the** Devil. He's beside you—
For aught **you know.**
  STUDENT.   I neither know nor care.
     (*They pass some card-players.*)
 FESTUS. Kings, queens, knaves, tens would trick
   the world away,
And it were not, now and then, for some brave ace.
 STUDENT. You **see yon** wretched, starved old
   man; his brow
Grooved out with wrinkles, like the brown dry sand
The tide of life is leaving?
 LUCIFER.   Yes, I see him.
 STUDENT. Last week he thought **he** was about
   to die;
So he bade gold be strewn beneath his pillow,
Gold on a chest that he might lie and see,
And gold put in a basin on his bed,
That he might dabble with his fingers in.
He's going now to grope for pence or pins.
He never gave a pin's worth in his life.
What would you do to him?
 LUCIFER.   I would have **him wrought**
Into a living wire, which, beaten out,
Might make a golden network for the **world;**
Then melt him inch by inch and **hell by hell,**
Where is the law of wrath.
 STUDENT.   Oh, charity!
It **is a** thought the Devil might be proud **of**—
Once and away. Misers and spendthrifts may
Torment each other in the world to come.
 FFSTUS. Men look **on** death as lightning, always
   far
Off, or in Heaven. They know not it is in
Themselves, a strong and inward tendency,

The soul of every atom, every hair:
That nature's infinite electric life,
Escaping from each isolated frame,
Up out of earth, or down from Heaven, becomes
To each its proper death, and adds itself
Thus to the great reünion of the whole.
There is a man in mourning! What does he here?
   STUDENT. He has just buried the only friend
      he had,
And now comes hither to enjoy himself.
   FESTUS. Why will we dedicate the dead to God,
And not ourselves, the living? Oft we speak,
With tears of joy and trust, of some dear friend
As surely up in Heaven; while that same soul,
For aught we know, may be shuddering even in
      Hell
To hear his name named; or there may be no
Soul in the case—and the fat icy worm,
Give him a tongue, can tell us all about him.
   STUDENT. Here is music. Stay. That simple
      melody
Comes on the heart like infant innocence —
Pure feeling pure; while yet the new-bodied soul
Is swinging to the motion of the heavens,
And scarce hath caught, as yet, earth's backening
      course.
   FESTUS. The heart is formed as earth was—its
      first age
Formless and void, and fit but for itself;
Then feelings half alive, just organized,
Come next,—then creeping sports and purposes,—
Then animal desires, delights, and loves —
For love is the first and granite-like effect
Of things — the longest and the highest; next
The wild and winged desires, youth's saurian
      schemes,
Which creep and fly by turns; which kill, and eat,
And do disgorge each other: comes at length
The mould of perfect matchless manhood — then

Woman divides the heart, and multiplies it.
The insipidity of innocence
Palls : it is guilty, happy, and **undone.**
A death is laid upon it, and it goes —
Quits **its** green Eden for the sandy **world,**
Where it works out its nature, as it may,
In sweat, smiles, blood, tears, cursings, and what not.
And giant sins possess it ; and it worships
Works of the hand, head, heart—its own or others —
A creature worship, which excludeth God's :
The less thrusts out the greater. Warning comes,
But the heart fears not—feels not ; till at last
Down comes the **flood from** Heaven ; **and that**
     heart,
Broken inwards, earthlike, **to its central** hell ;
Or like **the** bright and burning eye **we** see
Inly, **when** pressed hard backwards **on the** brain,
Ends and begins again — destroyed, is saved.
Every man is **the** first man to himself,
And Eves **are just** as plentiful as apples ;
Nor do **we** fall, **nor are** we saved by proxy.
The Eden we live in is our own heart ;
And the first thing we do, of our free choice,
Is sure and necessary to be sin.   [damned.
   Lucifer. The only right men have is **to be**
What is the good of music, or the beauty ?
Music tells no truths.
   Festus.   Oh ! there is nought so **sweet**
As lying and listening **music from the hands,**
And singing **from** the lips, of one **we love —**
Lips that all others should be turned **to.** Then
The world would **all be love and** song ; Heaven's
     harps
And orbs join in : the whole be harmony —
Distinct, yet blended — blending all in one
Long and delicious tremble like a chord.
But to Thee, God ! all being is a harp,
Whereon Thou makest mightiest melody.
Hast ever been in love ?

STUDENT. I never was.
FESTUS. 'T is love which mostly **destinates our**
    life.
What makes the world in after life I know **not,**
For our horizon alters as we age:
Power can only make up for the lack of love —
Power of some sort. The mind at one time grows
So fast, it fails; and then its stretch is more
Than its strength; but, as it opes, love fills it up,
Like to the stamen in the flower of life,
Till for the time we well-nigh grow all love;
And soon we feel the want of one kind heart
To love what's well, and to forgive what's ill,
In us, — that heart we play for at all risks.
    STUDENT. How can the heart which lies em-
        bodied deep,
In blood and bone, set like a ruby eye
Into the breast, be made a toy for beauty,
And, vane-like, blown about by every wanton
        sigh?
How can the soul, the rich star-travelled stranger,
Who here sojourneth only for a purchase,
Risk all the riches of his years of toil,
And his God-vouched inheritance of Heaven,
For one light momentary taste of love?   [sport—
    FESTUS. It is so; and when once you know the
The crowded pack of passions in full cry —
The sweet deceits, the tempting obstacles —
The smile, the sigh, the tear, and the embrace —
All the delights of love at last in one,
With kisses close as stars in the milky way,
In at the death you cry, though 't were your own!
    STUDENT. Upon my soul, most sound morality!
Nothing is thought of virtue, then, nor judgment?
    FESTUS. Oh! every thing is thought of — but
        not then,
And — judgment — no! it is nowhere in the field.
    STUDENT. Slow-paced and late arriving, still
        it comes.

I cannot understand this love ; I hear
Of its idolatry, not its respect.
   FESTUS. Respect is what we owe ; love what
      we give.
And men would mostly rather give than pay.
Morality's the right rule for the world,
Nor could society cohere without
Virtue ; and there are those whose spirits walk
Abreast of angels and the future, here.
Respect and love thou such.
   LUCIFER.   Of course you wish
Women to love you rather than love them.
It is better. Now, you say you are a student.
All things take study; what more than the face —
Whether your own, or hers you look and long at ?
There are many ways to one end : here is one : —
You are good-looking; but that matters little :
It only pleases them. To please yourself
Your face may be as ugly as the ——. Well, well ;
But you must cultivate yourself : it will pay you.
Study a dimple ; work hard at a smile :
The things most delicate require most pains.
Practise the upward — now the sidelong glance —
Now the long passionful unwinking gaze,
Which beats itself at last, and sees air only.
Be restless, and distress yourself for her.
Take up her hand — press it, and pore on it —
Let it drop — snatch it again as though you had
Let slip so much of honor or of Heaven.
Swear — vow by all means — never miss an oath :
If broken, why it only spoils itself ;
It is a broken oath and not an whole one.
Frown — toss about — let her lips be for a time :
But steal a kiss at last like fire from Heaven.
Weep if you can, and call the tears heat-drops.
Droop your head — sigh deep — play the fool, in
      short,
One hour, and she will play the fool for ever.
Mind ! it is folly to tell women truth ;

They would rather live on lies sc they be sweet.
Never be long in one mind to one love.
You change your practice with your subject.   All
Differ.   But yet, who knows one woman well
By heart, knows all.   It is my experience;
And I advise on good authority.
So thank me for my lecture on delusion.
  FESTUS.   Time laughs at love.   It is a hateful
          sight,
That bald old gray-beard jeering the boy, Love.
But as to women: that game has two sides.
Passion is from affection; and there is nought
So maddening and so lowering as to have
The worse in passion.   Think, when one by one,
Pride, love, and jealousy, and fifty more
Great feelings column up to force a heart.
And all are beaten back — all fail — all fall:
The tower intact: but risk it: we must learn.
To know the world, be wise and be a fool.
The heart will have its swing — the world its way:
Who seeks to stop them, only throws himself down.
We must take as we find: go as they go,
Or stand aside.   Let the world have the wall.
How do you think, pray, to get through the world?
  STUDENT.   I mean not to get through the world
          at all,
But over it.
  FESTUS.   Aspiring!   You will find
The world is all up-hill when we would do;
All down-hill when we suffer.   Nay, it will part
Like the Red Sea, so that the poor may pass.
We make our compliments to wretchedness,
And hope the poor want nothing, and are well.
But I mean, what profession will you choose?
Surely you will do something for a name.
  STUDENT.   Names are of much more conse-
          quence than things.   [friend
  FESTUS.   Well; here's our honest, all-exhorting
The parson — here the doctor.   I am sure

The Devil may act as moderator there,
And do mankind some service.
    LUCIFER.   In his **way.**
    STUDENT.   But **I care** neither for **men's souls**
        nor bodies.
    FESTUS. What say you to the law ? are you **am-**
        bitious ?
    STUDENT. **Nor do I mind for other people's**
        business.
I have no heart for their predicaments :
I am for myself. I measure every thing
By, what is it to me ? from which I find
I have but little in common with **the mass,**
Except my meals and so forth ; dress and **sleep.**
I have that within me I can live upon :
Spider-like, spin my place **out anywhere.**
    FESTUS. To none of all the arts and sciences, —
Astronomy nor entomology,
Nor gunnery, for instance, then you feel
Attracted heartily and mentally ?
    STUDENT. Why **no ; there** are so many rise
        and fall,
One knows not which to choose. **As for the stars,**
I never look on them without dismay.
Earth has outrun them in our modern mind,
By worlds of odds. Enough for us, it seems,
And our cold calculators **to** jot down
Their revolutions, distances, and squares ; —
And the bright laws which stars and spirits **rule,**
Are all laid out and buried grave on grave.
The fourfold worlds and elemental spheres,
Which in concentric circles, like the ring
That the magician stands in, from **on** high
Give spiritual calling to our earth,
And lord it over her, yet in such wise,
That still by them we may conjoin our souls
Unto the starry spirits of all worlds ;
Beyond the changeful mansions of the moon,
Beyond the burning heart of heaven, where dwell

The governors of nature and the **blest,**
All knowing spirits and celestial,
And divine demons ; are all gone — extinct.
There is no danger now of knowing aught
Which ought not to be known. No more of that ! —
And you, ye planetary sons of light !
From **him** who hovereth, moth-like, round the sun
To six-mooned Uranus, Light's loftiest round.
Your aspects, dignities, ascendancies,
Your partile quartiles, and your plastic trines,
And all your Heavenly houses and effects,
Shall meet no more devout expounders here.
You too, ye juried signs, earth's sunny path
Upon her wheeling orbit, all farewell !
Your exaltations and triplicities,
Fiery, airy, and the rest ; your falls,
And detriments, and governments, and gifts,
Are all abolished. Henceforth ye shall shine
In vain to man. Diurnal, cardinal,
Nocturnal, equinoctial, hot or dry,
Earthy, or moist, or feminine, or fixed,
Luxurious, violent, bicorporate,
Masculine, barren, and commanding, cold,
Fruitful or watery, or what not, now
It matters nothing. The joy of Jupiter,
The exaltation of the Dragon's **head,**
The **sun's** triplicity and glorious
Day house on high, the moon's dim **detriment,**
And all the starry inclusions of all signs —
Shall rise, and rule, and pass, and no one know
That there are spirit-rulers of all worlds,
Which fraternize with earth, and, though unknown,
Hold in **the** shining voices of the stars
Communion on high, ever and everywhere. —
The mystic charm of numbers, and the sole
Oneness which is in all, of **nature's** great
Triadic principle, **in** all things seen ;
In man thus, as composed of thrice **three** forms
Intrinsic ; first, corporeally, **blood,**

Body, and bones; next, intellectively,
Imagination, judgment, memory;
And thirdly, spiritually, mind and soul,
And spirit, which unites with God the whole
Being, and comes from and returns to Him, —
Allures **no** more man's mind debased.   Thus, **too,**
Of alchemy; the golden starry stone,
Invisible, the principle of life,
The quintessence of all the elements,
Is still unbought;— still flows the stream of pearl
Beneath the magic mountain; still the scent
As of a thousand amaranthine wreaths, **which lures**
All life unto its sweetness, **floats** around
Mistlike, the shining bath where Luna laves,
Or Sol, bright brother **of that mooned maid,**
Triumphs in light; — the spiritual sun,
The Heavenly Earth smaragdine, **and the fire-**
Spirit of life, the live land still exist,
Immortally, internally unseen. —
Still breathes the Paradisal air around
The universal whole; **the** watery fire,
Destructive, yet impalpable to sense,
The initial and conclusion of the world,
Yea, **the** beginning and the end of Death,
The **secret** which is shared 'tween God and **man,**
And **which** is nature **only,** wholly, still
In Heavenly gloom incomprehensible
Wait the Deific **will**; yea, still the light
Whereto all elements contribute, burns
About us and within us, world and soul; —
The primal sperm **and matter** of the world,
Whose centre is the **limit of** all things, —
The snowy gold, the star and spirit seed
Which is to render rich and deathless all, —
The self-begot, self-wedded, and self-born,
Which the wind carries in its womb, all have,
And few receive; the spirit of the earth,
The water of immortal life still lives: —
The universal solvent of disease

Still bounds through nature's veins; and still, in
    fine,
The secrets only to be told by fire
Starry or beamless, central and extreme,
Burn to be born.   And other natures may
Use them, and do.   In Demogorgon's hall
Still sits the universal mystery
Throned in itself and ministered unto
By its own members: — Man, alas! alone,
The recreant spirit of the universe,
Contemns the operations of the light;
Loves surface-knowledge; calls the crimes of crowds
Virtue: adores the useful vices; licks
The gory dust from off the feet of war,
And swears it food for gods, though fit for fiends
Only: — reversing just the Devil's state
When first he entered on this orb of man's, —
A fallen angel's form, a reptile's soul.
    LUCIFER.   Oh! this is libellous to man and fiend
And brute together.
    STUDENT.   All are art and part
Of the same mystic treason.   But enough; —
The most material, immaterial
Departments of pure wisdom are despised.
For well we know that, properly prepared,
Souls self-adapted knowledge to receive
Are by the truth desired, illumined; man's
Spirit, extolled, dilated, clarified,
By holy meditation and divine
Lore, fits him to convene with purer powers
Which do unseen surround us aye and gladden
In human good and exaltation; thus
The face of Heaven is not more clear to one,
Than to another outwardly; but one
By strong intention of his soul perceives,
Attracts, unites himself to essences
And elemental spirits of wider range
And more beneficent nature, by whose aid
Occasion, circumstance, futurity ·

Impress on him their image, and impart
Their secrets to his soul; thus chance and ot
Are sacred things; thus dreams are verities.
But oh! alas for all earth's loftier lore,
And spiritual sympathy of worlds!—
There shall be **no** more magic nor cabala,
Nor Rosicrucian nor Alchymic lore,
Nor fairy fantasies; no more hobgoblins,
Nor ghosts, nor imps, nor demons.   Conjurors,
Enchanters, witches, wizards, shall all die
Hopeless and heirless; their divining arts
Supernal or infernal — dead with them.
And so 't will doubtless be with other things
In time; **therefore** I will **commit my brain**
To **none of them.**

FESTUS.   Perchance 't were wiser not.
Man's heart hath not half uttered itself yet,
And much remains **to do** as well as say.
The heart is some time ere it finds its focus.
And when it does, with the whole light of nature
Strained through it to a hair's breadth, it but burns
The things beneath it, which it lights to death.
Well, farewell, Mr. Student.   May you never
Regret those hours which make the mind, if they
Unmake the body; for the sooner we
Are fit to be all mind, the better.   Blest
Is he whose heart is the home of the great dead,
And their great thoughts.   Who can mistake great
          thoughts?
They seize upon **the mind — arrest, and** search,
And shake it **— bow the tall soul as by** wind —
Rush over it like **rivers over reeds,**
Which quaver in **the current —** turn us cold,
And pale, and voiceless; leaving **in** the brain
A rocking **and** a ringing,— glorious
But momentary, madness might it last,
And close the soul with Heaven as with a seal!
In lieu of all these things whose loss thou mournest,
If earnestly or not I know not, use

The great and good and true which ever live,
And are all common to pure eyes and true.
Upon the summit of each mountain-thought
Worship thou God; for Deity is seen
From every elevation of the soul.
Study the Light; attempt the high; seek out
The soul's bright path; and since the soul is fire
Of heat intelligential, turn it aye
To the all-Fatherly source of light and life;
Piety purifies the soul to see
Perpetual apparitions of all grace
And power, which to the sight of those who dwell
In ignorant sin are never known.   Obey
Thy genius, for a minister it is
Unto the throne of Fate.   Draw to thy soul,
And centralize the rays which are around
Of the Divinity.   Keep thy spirit pure
From worldly taint by the repellant strength
Of virtue.   Think on noble thoughts and deeds,
Ever.   Count o'er the rosary of truth;
And practice precepts which are proven wise.
It matters not then what thou fearest.   Walk
Boldly and wisely in that light thou hast; —
There is a hand above will help thee on.
I am an omnist, and believe in all
Religions, — fragments of one golden world
Yet to be relit in its place in Heaven —
For all are relatively true and false,
As evidence and earnest of the heart
To those who practice, or have faith in them.
The absolutely true religion is
In Heaven only, yea in Deity.
But foremost of all studies, let me not
Forget to bid thee learn Christ's faith by heart.
Study its truths, and practice its behests:
They are the purest, sweetest, peacefullest,
Of all immortal reasons or records:
They will be with thee when all else have gone.
Mind, body, passion, all wear out — not faith,

Nor truth.   Keep thy heart cool, or rule its heat
To fixed ends : waste it not upon itself.
Not all the agony of all the damned,
Fused in one pang, vies with that earthquake throb
Which wakens it from waste to let us see
The world rolled by for aye ; and that we must
Wait an eternity for our next **chance,**
Whether it **be in** Heaven or elsewhere.
   STUDENT.   Sir,
I will remember this most grave advice,
And think of you with all respect.
   FESTUS.   Well, mind!
The worst **men often give the** best **advice.**
Our deeds **are sometimes better** than our **thoughts.**
Commend me, friend, to every one you meet :
I am an universal favorite.
Old men admire me deeply for my beauty,
Young women for my genius and strict virtue,
And young men for my modesty and wisdom.
All turn to me,.whenever I speak, full-faced,
As planets to the sun, or owls to a rushlight.
Farewell !
   STUDENT.   I hope to meet again.
   FESTUS.   And **I.** —
Yonder 's a woman singing.   **Let us** hear **her.**

   SINGER.   In the gray church **tower**
     Were the clear bells ringing
When a maiden sat in her lonely bower
     Sadly and lowly singing,
And thus she sang, that maiden fair,
Of the soft **blue** eyes and the long light hair ·

This hand hath oft been held by one
     Who now is far away ;
And here I sit and sigh alone   ·
     Through all the weary day.
Oh, when will he I love return !
Oh, when shall I forget to **mourn !**

Along the dark and dizzy path
    Ambition madly runs,
'T is there they say his course he hath,
    And therefore love he shuns.
Oh, fame and honor bind his brow,
For so he would be with me now!

In the gray church tower
    Were the clear bells ringing,
When a bounding step in that lonely bower
    Broke on the maiden singing;
She turned, she saw; oh, happy fair!
For her love who loved her so well was there!

LUCIFER.   And we might trust these youths and
        maidens fair,
The world was made for nothing but love, love!
Now I think it was made but to be burned.
    FESTUS.   And if I love not now, while woman is
All bosom to the young, when shall I love?
Who ever paused on passion's fiery wheel?
Or trembling by the side of her he loved
Whose lightest touch brings all but madness, ever
Stopped coldly short to reckon up his pulse?
The car comes — and we lie — and let it come;
It crushes — kills — what then?   It is joy to die.
Enough shall not fool me.   I fling the foil
Away.   Let me but look on aught which casts
The shadow of a pleasure, and here I bare
A breast which would embrace a bride of fire.
Pleasure — we part not!   No!   It were easier
To wring God's lightnings from the grasp of God.
I must be mad; but so is all the world.
Folly.   It matters not.   What is the world
To me?   Nought.   I am all things to myself.
If my heart thundered, would the world rock?
        Well —
Then let the mad world fight its shadow down;
There soon will be nor sun, nor world, nor shadow.
And thou, my blood, my bright red running soul —

Rejoice thou, like a river, in thy rapids!
Rejoice — thou wilt never pale with age, nor **thin** ;
But in thy full dark beauty, vein by vein,
Fold by fold, serpent-like, encircling me
Like **a** stag, sunstruck, top **thy** bounds and die.
Throb, bubble, sparkle, laugh and leap along !
Make **merry** while the holidays shall last.
Heart ! I could tear thee out, thou fool ! thou **fool !**
And strip thee into shreds upon the wind :
What have I done that thou shouldst serve **me**
    thus ?
  LUCIFER.   Let us away.   We have **had enough**
    of this.
  FESTUS.   The night is glooming on **us. It is the**
    hour
When lovers will speak lowly, for the **sake**
Of being nigh each other ; and when **love**
Shoots up the eye like morning on the east,
Making amends for the long northern night
They passed ere **either** knew the other loved.
It is the hour of hearts, when all hearts feel
As they could love to mad death, finding aught
To give back fire ; for love, like nature, is
War — sweet war ! **Arms** ! To arms ! so they be
    thine,
Woman ! Old people may say what they please —
The heart of age is like an emptied wine-cup,
Its life lies **in a** heel-tap — how can they judge ?
'T were a waste of time **to** ask how they **wasted**
    theirs.
But while the **blood is bright,** breath **sweet, skin**
    smooth,
And limbs all made to minister delight —
Ere **yet we** have shed our locks like trees **their**
    leaves,
And **we** stand staring bare into the air —
He i- a fool **who** is not for love and beauty.
I speak unto the young, for I am of them,
And alway shall be.   What are years to me ?

Traitors! that vice-like fang the hand ye lick:
Ye fall like small birds beaten by a storm
Against a dead wall, dead. I pity ye.
Oh! that such mean things should raise hope or
    fear;
Those Titans of the heart, that fight at Heaven
And sleep by fits on fire; whose slightest stir's
An earthquake. I am bound and blest to youth!
Oh! give me to the young — the fair — the free —
The brave, who would breast a rushing, burning
    world
Which came between them and their heart's de-
    light.
None but the brave and beautiful can love.
Oh, for the young heart like a fountain playing!
Flinging its bright, fresh feelings up to the skies
It loves and strives to reach — strives, loves in
    vain;
It is of earth, and never meant for Heaven.
Let us love both, and die. The sphinx-like heart,
Consistent in its inconsistency,
Loathes life the moment that life's riddle is read:
The knot of our existence is untied,
And we lie loose and useless. Life is had;
And then we sigh, and say, can this be all?
It is not what we thought — it is very well —
But we want something more — there is but death.
And when we have said, and seen, and done, and
    had,
Enjoyed and suffered, all we have wished and
    feared —
From fame to ruin, and from love to loathing —
There can come but one more change — try it —
    death.
Oh! it is great to feel we care for nothing —
That hope, nor love, nor fear, nor aught of earth
Can check the royal lavishment of life;
But like a streamer strown upon the wind,
We fling our souls to fate and to the future.

And to die young is youth's divinest gift, —
To pass from one world fresh into another,
Ere change hath lost the charm of **soft** regret,
And feel the immortal impulse from within
Which makes the coming, life — cry, alway, on !
And follow **it** while strong — is Heaven's last
     mercy.
There is a fire-fly in the southern clime
Which shineth only when upon the wing ;
So is it with the mind : when once we rest,
We darken.   On ! said God unto the **soul**
As to the earth, for ever.   On it goes,
A rejoicing native of **the infinite** —
As a bird of air — an **orb of heaven.**

Scene — *The* centre.

Festus *and* Lucifer.

Lucifer.   Behold us in the fire-crypts of the
     world !
Through seas and buried mountains tomblike tracts,
Fit to receive the skeleton of Death
When he is dead — through earthquakes, **and the**
     bones
Of earthquake-swallowed cities, have we wormed
Down to the ever-burning forge of fire,
Whereon in awful and omnipotent ease
Nature, **the** delegate of God, brings forth
Her everlasting elements, and breathes
Around that fluent heat of life which clothes
Itself in lightnings, wandering through the air,
And pierces to the **last** and loftiest pore
Of Earth's snow-mantled mountains. **In** these yaults
Are hid the archives of the universe ;
And here, the ashes of all ages gone,
Each finally inurned.   These pillars stand,
Earth's testimony to eternity.

FESTUS.   All that is solid now was fluid once;
Water, or air, or fire, or some one
Permanent, permeating, element;
As in this focal, world-evolving fire
Like what I see around — the vacuous power
Whereon the world is based, e'en as wherein
It rolls, I must believe.
      LUCIFER.   The original
Of all things is one thing.   Creation is
One whole.   The differences a mortal sees
Are diverse only to the finite mind.
      FESTUS.   This marble-walled immensity o'er-
            roofed
With pendant mountains glittering, awes my soul.
God's hand hath scooped the hollow of this world;
Yea, none but his could; and I stand in it,
Like a forgotten atom of the light,
Some star hath lost upon its lightning flight.
      LUCIFER.   Here mayst thou lay thy hand on
            nature's heart,
And feel its thousand yeared throbbings cease.
High overhead, and deep beneath our feet,
The sea's broad thunder booms, scarce heard;
            around,
The arches, like uplifted continents
Of starry matter, burning inwardly,
Stand; and, hard by, earth's gleaming axle sleeps,
All moving, all unmoved.
      FESTUS.   Age here on age
Lie heaped like withered leaves.   And must it
            end?
      LUCIFER.   God worketh slowly: and a thousand
            years
He takes to lift his hand off.   Layer on layer
He made earth, fashioned it and hardened it
Into the great, bright, useful thing it is;
Its seas, life-crowded, and soul-hallowed lands
He girded with the girdle of the sun,
That sets its bosom glowing like Love's own

Breathless embrace, close-clinging as for life ; —
Veined it with gold, and dusted it with gems,
Lined it with fire, and round its heart-fire bowed
Rock-ribs unbreakable ; until at last
Earth took her shining station as a star,
In Heaven's dark hall, high up the crowd of
    worlds.
All this and thus did God ; and yet it ends.
The ball He rolled and rounded, melts away
E'en now to its constituent atomics.
   Festus.   It is enough. Though here were
     posited
All secrets of existence, natural
Or supernatural, dwell not here would I,
Though 't were to drain profoundest fountains. No
I love it not, the science nor the scene.
I long to know again the fresh green earth,
The breathing breeze, the sea and sacred stars.
These recollections crowd upon my soul,
As constellations on the evening skies,
And will not be forgotten. Let us leave !
   Lucifer.   Aught that reminds the exile of his
     home
Is surely pleasant. I, friend, am content.
   Festus. I cannot be content with less than
     Heaven.
O Heaven, I love thee ever ! sole and whole,
Living and comprehensive of all life ;
Thee, agy world, thee, universal Heaven,
And heavenly universe ! thee, sacred seat
Of intellective Time, the throned stars
And old oracular night ; — by night or day,
To me thou canst not but be beautiful,
Boundless, all-central, universal sphere !
Whether the sun all-light thee, or the moon,
Embayed in clouds, mid starry islands round,
With mighty beauty inundate the air ; —
Or when one star, like a great drop of light,
From her full flowing urn hangs tremulous, —

Yea, like a tear from her the eye of night,
Let fall o'er nature's volume **as** she reads : —
Or, when in radiant thousands, each **star** reigns
In imparticipable royalty,
Leaderless, uncontrasted with the light
Wherein their **light** is lost, the sons of fire,
Arch element of the Heavens ; — when **storm and
      cloud**
Debar the mortal **vision of the eye**
From wandering o'er **thy threshold,** — **more and
      more**
I love thee, thinking **on the** splendid **calm**
Which bounds the deadly fever of **these days** —
The higher, holier, spiritual Heaven.
And when this world, within whose heartstrings
      now
I feel myself encoiled, shall be resolved,
Thee I shall be permitted still, perchance,
To love and live in endlessly.
      LUCIFER.   **All here**
Thou seest hath **holden** fellowship **with** gods ;
With eldest **Time and** primal matter, space,
And stars, and air, and **all-inherent** fire,
The watery deep and chaos, night, the all,
And the **interior immortality,**
And first-begotten Love. **These rocks retain**
Their caverned footsteps printed **in pure fire.**
Those **were** the times, the **ancient youth of** earth,
The elemental years, when earth and **Heaven**
Made one in holy bridals, — royal gods ·
Their bright immortal issue : when men's minds
Were vast as continents, **and** not as now
Minute and indistinguishable plots,
With here and there acres of untilled brains ; when
      lived
The great original, broad-eyed, sunken race,
Whose wisdom, **like** these sea-sustaining rocks,
Hath formed the base of **the** world's fluctuous
      lore : —

When, too, by mountainous travail, human might
Sought to possess the everlasting Heavens,
And incommunicable, by the right
Of self-acquirement and high kindred with
Celestial virtues ; — when the mortal powers —
Forecounsel, wisdom, and experience,
Teachers of all arts, founders of all good,
With Godhood strove, and gloriously failed —
In failure half successful ; as these scenes,
Fire-fountains, and volcano-utterances,
Earth-heavings, island vomitings, evince.
   Festus. The world hath made such comet-like
      advance
Lately on science, we may almost hope,
Before we die of sheer decay, to learn
Something about our infancy. But me
This troubles not. Were all earth's mountain
      chains
To utter fire at once, what a grand show
Of pyrotechny for our neighbor moon !
Let us ascend ; but not through the charred throat
Of an extinct volcano.
   Lucifer.   This way — down.
So shalt thou thread the world at once.
   Festus.   Haste, haste.

Scene — *A ruined* **Temple.**

Festus and Lucifer.

   Festus. Here will I worship solely.
   Lucifer.   'T is a fane
Once sacred to the Sun.
   Festus.   It matters not
What false god here hath falsely been adored,
Or what life-hating rites these walls have viewed.
The truly holy soul, which hath received
The unattainable, can hallow hell.
Now to the only true and Triune God

These walls shall echo praise, **if never yet.**
Bring me a morsel **of** the fire **without ;**
For I will make a sacred offering
To God, as though the High Priest of the world.
He lacks not consecration at best hands
Whom Thou hast hallowed, Lord, by choice ; **and
      these,**
The elements I offer, Thou hast made
Holy, **by making them.**
    LUCIFER.   **Lo ! here is fire.**
I will await thee **in the air.**
    FESTUS.   Withdraw !
Thine, Lord ! are all the elements and worlds ; —
The sun is Thy bright servant, and the moon
Thy servant's servant ; — the round rushing earth,
The lifeful air, the thousand winged winds,
The Heaven-kinned fire, the continental clouds,
The sea broad breasted, and the tranced lake,
The rich arterial rivers, and the hills
Which wave their woody tresses in the breeze,
In grateful undulation, all are Thine ; —
Thine are the snow-robed mountains circling earth
As the white spirits God **the** Saviour's throne ; —
Thine the bright secrets, central in all orbs,
And rudimental mysteries of life.
The sun-starred night, the **ever-maiden morn,**
The all-prevailing day, consummate eve,
Confess them Thine through the perpetual world : —
All art hath wrought from earth, or **science** lured
From truth, like flame out of the fire cloud, are
Thine ; — Thine the glory, all belongs **to** Thee,
Finite, indefinite, and infinite,
As mountains to a world, **as** worlds to Heaven.
The high doomed **city and** the toilful town
And early hamlet, — **all that** live or die,
That flourish or decay, **that** change, or stand
Before **Thy** face, unchanged, exist for Thee,
Or are not at Thy bidding ; **Thine, all** souls ;
Atom and world, **the universe is Thine !** —

Thou canst as easily turn Thy kindest eye
From comprehending the bright Infinite,
To this crushed temple, where the wild flower decks
Its earthquake-rifted walls, and the birds build
In corners of its columned capitals, —
And to this crumbling heart I offer here,
As trust Thine own Eternity.   Behold !
Accept, I pray Thee, Lord ! this sacrifice ;
These elemental offerings simple, pure,
Which in the name of man I make to Thee,
Formless, save prostrate soul and kneeling heart —
In token of Thy perfect monarchy
And all comprising mercy.   These are they !
A flowery turf, a branch, a burning coal,
A cup of water and an empty bowl ;
This air-filled bowl is typic of the world
Thou fillest with Thy spirit, and the soul,
Receptive of Thy life-conferring truth ; —
This the symbolic element wherefrom
We are to be reborn, wherein made pure ;
Those whom Thou choosest are to be redeemed
Out of the mighty multitudes of men ;
Yet all as of one nature be redeemed.
This coal, torn flaming from the earth, proclaims
Thy sin-consuming mercy as of earth ;
And may our souls ever aspire to Thee,
As these pale flames unto the stars ; this turf
Is as the earthy nature and abode
We would subject to Thee ; and lieth here,
The representative of every star
And world-extended matter ! Lord ! this branch,
Which waveth high o'er all, oh, let it sign
Thine own Eternal Son's humanity,
Which was on earth, yet ever lives in Heaven,
Redemptive of all Being.   Golden Branch !
Which, in the eld-time, seer's and sybil's words,
Full of dark central thought and mystic truth,
Foretold should overspread the spirit world,
And with its fruit heal every wound of Death,—

Tree of eternal life, Thee **all adore.**
Accept this prayer, O Saviour ! **that if men**
Can nothing do but sin, Thou mayst forgive
The creature crime, and bring back all to Thee.
Thou art the one who made the universe ;
Yet didst Thou walk **on** earth ; Thou **brakest bread**
And drankest wine with men, betokening so
Thine **own** complete, **Divine Humanity.**
May all obey Thy **words and do Thy will !**
We praise Thee God, **our father ; whoso would**
Be saved, let him believe in Thee Triune.
Thou doest all things rightly ; all are best,
Sorrow, or joy, or power, or suffering.
Providing, therefore, all things that must be
And ought to be, as Thou dost and hast done,
From the beginning even to the end,
This heart let cease from prayer, these **lips** from praise,
Save that which life shall offer pauselessly.
Now go I forth again **refreshed,** consoled,
Upon my time-enduring pilgrimage.
Ho ! Lucifer !

LUCIFER.   I wait thee.
FESTUS.   Whither next ?
LUCIFER.   As thou wilt, apposite or opposite.
'Tis light translateth night ; 'tis inspiration
Expounds experience ; 'tis the west explains
The east : 'tis time unfolds Eternity.

SCENE — *A Metropolis — Public Place.*

FESTUS *and* LUCIFER.

FESTUS.   What can be done here ?
LUCIFER.   Oh ! a thousand things,
As well as elsewhere.
FESTUS.   True ; it is a place

Where passion, occupation, or reflection,
May find fit food or field ; but suits not me.
My burden is the spirit, and my life
Is henceforth solely spiritual.
    Lucifer.   Well; —
At the occurrent season, **too,** it shall
Be satisfied. **It** might be even **now,**
From things about **us.** But **look,** here comes **a**
       man
Thou knowest well.
    Festus.   **I do.   Stop, friend ! of late**
I have not seen **thee.   Whither** goest thou now?
    Friend.   I am **upon** my business, **and** in **haste.**
·   Festus.   Business **! I** thought thou **wast a sim-**
      ple schemer.
   Friend.   Mayhap I am.
    Festus.   **There** is **a visionary**
Business, as well as visionary faith.
    Friend.   **I have** been, all life, living in a mine,
Lancing the world for gold.   I have not yet
Fingered the right vein.   Oh ! I often wish
The **time** would come again, which science prates of,
When earth's bright veins ran ruddy, virgin gold.
    Festus.   When **the** world's gold melts, all **the**
      poorer metals,
All things less pure, less precious, all **beside,**
Will vanish ; nought be left but gems **and gold.**
If all were rich, gold would be penniless.
    Lucifer.   I have **a secret I** would fain **impart**
To one who **would make** right use **of it. Now, mark !**
Chemists say **there** are fifty **elements,**
And more ; — wouldst know **a ready recipe**
For riches ? —
    Friend.   That indeed **l** would, good sir.
    Lucifer.   Get then these fifty earths, or **ele-**
      ments,
Or what not.   Mix them up together.   Put
All to the question.   Tease them well with fire,
Vapor, and trituration — every way ;
       10

Add the right quantity of lunar rays;
Boil them, and let them cool, and **watch what** comes.
   Friend.   Thrice greatest **Hermes! but** it must
      be; yes!
I'll go and get them; good day,—instantly. [*Goes.*
   Lucifer.   He 'll be astonished, probably.
   Festus.   He will,
In any issue **of the experiment.**
Perhaps the **nostrum may explode and** blow him
Body **and soul to atoms and to —**
   Lucifer.   Nonsense!
   Festus.   **There needs no satire on men's rage**
      for gold;
Their nature is the best one, **and excuse.**
And now what next?
   Lucifer.   Why let us take our ease
Beside this feathery fountain.   It is cool
And pleasant, and the people passing by,
Fit subjects for two moralists like us.
Here we **can speculate** on policy,
On social manners, fashions, and the news.
Now the political **aspect of the** world,
At present, **is most cheerful.**   To begin,
Like charity, **at home.   Out** of all wrongs
The most **atrocious, the most** righteous ends
Are happiest **wrought.**
   Festus.   It ofttimes chances so.
   Lucifer.   Take of the **blood of martyrs, tears**
      of slaves,
The groans of prisoned patriots, and **the sweat**
Wrung from **the** bones of Famine, like parts.   **Add**
Vapor of orphan's sigh, and wail of all
Whom war hath spoiled, or law first fanged, then
      gorged; —
The stifled breath **of man's** free natural thought, —
The tyrant's lies; **the curses** of the proud;
The usurpations of the lawful heir,
The treasonous rebellions of the wise,
The poor man's patient prayers; and **let all these**

Simmer, some centuries, o'er the slow red fire
Of human wrath ; and there results, at last,
A glorious constitution, and a grand
Totality **of** nothings ; — as we see. —

       [Soldiers pass ; Music, etc.

Man is a military animal,
Glories in gunpowder, and loves parade ;
Prefers them **to** all things.
 Festus.   Of recipes,
Enough ! Life **'s but a** sword's length, at the **best.**
  Lucifer. War, war, still war ! from **age to**
   age, old Time
Hath washed his hands **in the heart's blood of**
   Earth.
  Festus. Yet fields **of death! ye are earth's**
   purest pride ;
For what is life to freedom ? War **must be**
While **men** are what they are ; while they have bad
Passions **to** be roused up ; while ruled by men ;
While all the powers and treasures of a land
Are at the beck of the ambitious crowd ;
While injuries can be inflicted, or
Insults be offered ; yea, while rights are **worth**
Maintaining, freedom keeping, **or** life having,
So long the sword shall shine ; so long shall war
Continue, and the need for war remain.
  Lucifer. And yet all war shall **cease.**
  Festus.   ·   It **must and shall.**
Some news seems stirring ; what, I **know** not yet.
  Lucifer. Nor I. I heard that **one** of Saturn's
   moons
Had flown upon his face and blinded **him.**
'T was also said, in circles I frequent
At times, his outer ring was falling off.
If I should find, I 'll keep it. It might fit
A **little** finger such as mine, I think.
Poor Saturn ! much I doubt he is breaking up.
But for these news, I know not what they be.
Some one perhaps has lit on a new vein

Of stars in Heaven : or cracked one with his teeth,
To look inside it, or made out at last
The circulation of the light ; or what
Think'st thou ?
    FESTUS.   I know not.   Ask !
    LUCIFER.   Sir, what's the news ?
    PASSER-BY.   The news are good news, being
        none at all.
    LUCIFER.   Your goodness, Sir, I deem of like
        extent.
We heard the great Bear was confined of twins.
    STRANGER.   'T is not unlikely stars do propagate.
    FESTUS.   And so much for civility and news.
This city is one of the world's social poles,
Round which events revolve : here, dial-like,
Time makes no movement but is registered.
    LUCIFER.   Yon gaudy equipage ! hast ever seen
A drowning dragon-fly floating down a brook,
Topping the sunny ripples as they rise,
Till in some ambushed eddy it is sucked down
By something underneath.   Thus with the rich ; —
Their gilding makes their death conspicuous.
    FESTUS.   Some men are nobly rich, some nobly
        poor,
Some the reverse.   Rank makes no difference.
    LUCIFER.   The poor may die in swarms un-
        heeded.   They
But swell the mass of columned ciphers.   Oh,
Ye poor, ye wretched, ye bowed down by woe !
Thank God for something, though it were but this.
He fire, ye ashes !
    FESTUS.   Thou art surely mad.
    LUCIFER.   I meant to moralize.   I cannot see
A crowd, and not think on the fate of man —
Clinging to error as a dormant bat
To a dead bough.   Well, 'tis his own affair.
    FESTUS.   All homilies on the sorts and lot of
        men
Are vain and wearisome.   I want to know

No more of human nature.   As it is,
I honor it and hate it.   Let that do.
   LUCIFER.   Here is a statue to some mighty **man**
Who beat his name on the drum of the world's ear
Till it was stupefied, and, I suppose,
Not knowing what it was about, reared **up**
This marble mockery of mortality,
Which shall outlive the memory of the man
And all like him who water earth with blood,
And sow **with** bones, or any good **he** did,
As eagles outlive gnats.   But never mind !
Why carp at insect sins, or crumb-like crimes ?
The world, the great imposture, still succeeds ;
Still, in Titanic immortality,
Writhes 'neath the burning mountain of its sins.
   FESTUS.   There**'s** an old **adage about sin and
          some one.**
The world is not exactly what I thought it,
But pretty nearly so ; and after all,
'T is not so bad as good men make it out,
Nor such a hopeless wretch.
   LUCIFER.   For all the world
Not I would slander it.   Dear world, thou art
Of all things under Heaven by me most loved,
The most consistent, the least fallible.
Believe me ever thine affectionate
Lucifer.   P. S. Sweet, remember me !
   FESTUS.   Wilt go to the cathedral ?
   LUCIFER.   No, indeed ;
I have just confessed.
   FESTUS.   **W**ell, **to the** concert, then ?
   LUCIFER.   **Some** fifteen hundred thousand mil-
          lion years
Have passed since last **I heard a chorus.**
   FESTUS.   Good !
   LUCIFER.   In sooth, I cannot calculate the time
There are no eras in Eternity.
No ages.   Time is as the body, and
Eternity the spirit of existence.

FESTUS.   That would I learn and prove.
LUCIFER.   The finite soul
Can never learn the Infinite, nor be
Informed by it, unaided.
FESTUS.   Be it so.
What shall **we do?**
LUCIFER.   I put myself in your hands.
FESTUS.   Wilt go on 'Change?
LUCIFER.   I rarely speculate.
Steady receipts are **mostly to** my **taste.**
Besides, I spurn the system.   Take **my arm.**
FESTUS.   But something must **be done to pass**
      the time.
LUCIFER.   True; let us pass, then, all time.
FESTUS.   I shall **be**
Most happy; only show me how.
LUCIFER.   **Why, thus.**
I have the power to make thy spirit free
Of its poor frame of flesh, yet not by death,—
And reunite them afterwards!   Wilt thou
Intrust thyself to me?
FESTUS.   In God I trust,
And in His word of safety.   Have thy will.
Where shall it be effected?
LUCIFER.   Here and now.
Recline thou calmly **on yon** marble slab,
As though asleep.   The world will miss **thee not;**
Its complement is perfect.   I will mind
That no impertinent meddler troubles there
Thy trancéd frame.   The brain shall cease its life-
Engrossing business, and the living blood,
The wine of life which maketh drunk the soul,
Sleep in the sacred vessels of the heart.
Three steps the sun hath taken from his throne,
Already, downwards, and ere he hath gone,
Who calmeth tempests with his mighty light,
We will return; and till then the bright rain
Of yonder fountain fails not.

FESTUS.   Thus be it !
Come ! we are wasting moments here that now
Belong, of right, to immortality,
And to another **world.**
   LUCIFER.   Prepare ! —
   FESTUS.   **And thou ?**
   LUCIFER.   I vanish altogether.
   FESTUS.   **Excellent !**
   LUCIFER.   Body and **spirit part !** —

SCENE — *Air.*

LUCIFER *and* FESTUS.

   FESTUS.   Where, where am **I ?**
   LUCIFER.   We **are in space and time,** just **as we**
       were
Some half a second since ; where wouldst thou **be ?**
   FESTUS.   I would be in Eternity **and Heaven ;**
The spirit and the blessed spirit, of
Existence.
   LUCIFER.   And thou shalt be, and shalt pass
All secondary nature ; all the rules
And the results of time : upon thy spirit
These things shall act no more ; their hands shall be
Withered upon thee, as the ray of life
Returns to that it came from : they shall cease
In thee, like lightning in the deadening sea.
But **not** now ; we have worlds to go through, **first.**
When spirit hath deposited its earth,
And brightly, freely flows, self-purified
In its own action, acted **on** by God,
It holds the starry transcript of **the** skies
Booklike within its bosom, evermore.
But thine even now, exhausted, not exhaled,
Bears the design of earthly discontent,
Not sacred satisfaction.   Unto him
Whose soul is saved, all things are clear as stars,
And, to the chosen, safety : — to none else.

Nor **cold** insurgent heart, nor **menial** mind
Can compass this: it is the way of **God**:
The **starry** path of Heaven which **none** can tread
But **spirits** high as Heaven, which He hath raised;
Who **were** of Him before all worlds, and **are**
Beloved **and** saved for ever while they live.
Thou of the world art yet, with motives, means,
And ends as others.

  Festus.   **I will no more of** it.
  Lucifer. **Oh, dream it not!** Thou knowest
    not the depth
Of nature's dark abyss, thyself, **nor God.**
Light over-strong, and darkness over-long,
Blind equally the eye. Thou mayst **yet** rise
And fall **as** often as the sea.
  Festus.   How comes it,
Being **a** spirit, that I see **not all**
As spirit should?
  Lucifer. **Thou** lackest life and death.
The **life of Heaven and** the death of earth.
Then wouldst thou see in harmony with God,
Creation's strife.
  Festus. Death alters not the spirit!
  Lucifer. Death must be undergone ere understood,
    stood,
One world is as another. Rest we here!—

Scene— Another and a better World.

Festus and Lucifer.

  Festus. **What a** sweet world! Which is this,
  Lucifer?
  Lucifer. **This is the star of** evening and of
    beauty.
  Festus. Otherwise **Venus.** I will stay here.
  Lucifer.   Nay:
It is but a visit.

FESTUS. Let us **look** about us.
It is Heaven, it must be; aught so beautiful
Must, I am sure, have feeling. Cannot worlds **live ?**
Least things have **life.** Why not **the** greatest, too ?
An atom is **a** world, **a** world **an atom**
Seen relatively: Death **an act of Life.**
   LUCIFER. This is a **world** where **every** loveliest
     thing
Lasts longest; where decay lifts never **head**
Above the grossest forms, and matter here
Is all transparent substance; the flower **fades not,**
The beautiful die never, here: Death **lies**
A dreaming — **he** has nought **to do** — the babe
Plays with his **darts.** Nought **dies but what should
die.**
Here are no earthquakes, storms, nor plagues; no
Hell
At heart; no floating flood **on high. The soil**
Is ever fresh and fragrant as a rose —
The skies, like one wide rainbow, stand on gold —
The clouds are light as rose leaves — and the dew,
'T is of **the** tears which stars weep, sweet with joy—
The air **is** softer than a loved one's sigh —
The ground is glowing with all priceless ore,
And glistening with gems like a bride's bosom —
The **trees** have silver stems and emerald leaves —
The fountains bubble nectar — and the **hills**
Are half alive **with light.** Yet it **is not Heaven.**
   FESTUS. **Oh, how this** world **should pity man's:**
     I love
To walk **earth's woods when the storm bends** his
     bow,
And volleys all his arrows **off at once;**
And when the dead brown **branch** comes crashing
     close
To my feet, to tread it down, because I feel
Decay my foe: and not to triumph's worse
Than not **to win.** It is **wrong to** think on earth;
But **terror hath** a beauty **even** as mildness;

And I have felt more pleasure far on earth;
When, like a lion or a day of battle,
The storm rose, roared, shook out his shaggy mane,
And leaped abroad on the world, and lay down red
Licking himself to sleep as it got light;
And in the cataract-like tread of a crowd,
And its irresistible rush, flooding the green
As though it came to doom, than e'er I can
Feel in his færy orb of shade and shine.
I love earth!
    LUCIFER.   Thou art mad to dote on earth
When with this sphere of beauty.
    FESTUS.   It is the blush
Of being; surely, too, a maiden world,
Unmarred by thee.   Touch it not, Lucifer!
    LUCIFER.   It is too bright to tarnish.
    FESTUS.   Didst thou fail?
    LUCIFER. I cannot fail. With me success is
          nature.
I am the cause, means, consequence of ill.
Thou canst not yet enjoy a sensuous world—
Refined though ne'er so little o'er thine own,
And yet wouldst enter Heaven. Valhalla's halls,
And sculls o'erbrimmed with mead, Elysian plains—
Eden, where life was toilless, and gave man
All things to live with, nothing to live for;—
The Moslem's bowers of love, and streams of wine,
And palaces of purest adamant,
Where dark-eyed houris, with their young white
       arms,
The ever virgin, woo and welcome ye,—
The Chaldee's orbs of gold, where dwells the pri-
       mal Light,
Were all too pure for thee; yet shalt thou be
Surely in Heaven, ere Death unlock the heart.
I said that I would show thee marvels here;
For here dwell many angels—many souls
Who have run pure through earth, or been made
       pure

By their salvation since.   It is a mart
Where all the holy spirits of the world
Perform sweet interchange, and purchase truth
With truth, and love with love.   Hither came He,
The Son — the Saviour of the universe;
Not in the stable-state He went to earth —
A servant unto slaves; but as a God,
Carrying His kingdom with Him, and His Heaven.
   FESTUS.   Lo, here are spirits! and all seem to love
Each other.
   LUCIFER.   He hath only half a heart
Who loves not all.
   FESTUS.   Speak for me to some angel.
See, here is one, a very soul of beauty:
It is the muse.   I know her by the lyre
Hung on her arm, and eye like fount of fire.
   MUSE.   Mortal, approach! I am the holy Muse,
Whom all the great and bright of spirit choose —
'T is I who breathe my soul into the lips
Of those great lights whom death nor time eclipse:
'T is I who wing the loving heart with song,
And set its sighs to music on the tongue:
It is I who watch, and, with sweet dreams, reward
The starry slumbers of the youthful bard;
For I love every thing that is sweet and bright.
And but this morn, with the first wink of light
A sunbeam left the sun, and, as it sped,
I followed, watched, and listened what it said:
Wherefore, with all this brightness am I given
From sun to earth?   Am I not fit for Heaven?
From God I came o. ne; and, though worlds have
       passed,
Ages, and dooms, yet I am light to the last.
Whatever God hath once bent to His will
Is sacred; so the world's to be loved still.
What of this swift, this bright, but downward being,
Too burning to be borne — too brief for seeing?
What is my aim — mine end?   I would not die
In dust, or water, or an idiot's eye:

I would not cease in blood, nor end in fire,
Nor light the loveless to their low desire:
No; let me perish on the poet's page,
Where he kisses from his beauty's brow all age;
Spelling it fair for aye, and wrinkle scorning,
As when first that brow brake on him like a morning.
But yet I cannot quit this line I tread,
Though it lead and leave me to the eyeless dead:
It is mine errand: 't is for this I come,
And live, and die, and go down to my doom.
This is my fate — right and bright to speed on.
God is His own God: fate and fall are one.
Straight from the sun I go, like life from God,
Which hits, now on a heaven, now on a clod.
But, spite of all, the world's air warps our way,
And crops the roses off the cheek of day;
As some false friend, who holds our fall in trust,
Oils our decline, and hands us to the dust.
Where are the sunbeams gone of the young green
      earth?
Search dust and night: our death makes clear our
      birth —
It said — and saw earth; and one moment more
Fell bright beside a vine-shadowed cottage door:
In it came — glanced upon a glowing page,
Where, youth forestalling and foreshortening age —
Weak with the work of thought, a boyish bard,
Sate suing night and stars for his reward.
The sunbeam swerved and grew, a breathing dim,
For the first time, as it lit and looked on him:
His forehead faded — pale h' lip and dry —
Hollow his cheek — and fever fed his eye.
Clouds lay about his brain, as on a hill,
Quick with the thunder thought, and lightning will
His clenched hand shook from its more than mid-
      night clasp,
Till his pen fluttered like a winged asp,
Save that no deadly poison blacked its lips:
'T was his to life-enlighten, not eclipse;

Nor would he shade one atom of another,
To have a sun his slave, **a god** his brother.
The young moon laid **her down as one who dies,**
Knowing that death **can be no** sacrifice,
For that the sun, her god, through nature's night
Shall make her bosom to grow great with light.
Still he sate, though his lamp sunk ; and he strained
His eyes **to** work the nightness which remained.
Vain pain ! **he could** not make the light he wanted,
And soon thought's wizard **ring** gets disenchanted.
When earth was dayed — was **morrowed** — the first
    ray
Perched on his pen, **and diamonded its way ; — -**
The sunray that I watched ; **which, proud to mark**
The line it loved as deathless, **there died dark —**
Died in **the** only **path** it would have trod,
Were there as many **ways as worlds** to God, —
There, in the eye of **God** again **to burn,**
As all man's glory **unto** God's must turn.
And so may sunbeams **ever** guide his pen,
And God his heart, who lights the morn of men ;
For this life is but Being's first faint ray ;
And sun on sun, and heaven on heaven, make up
    God's day.
And were there suns in day **as** stars in night,
They would show but like one ray from out his full-
    sphered **light ;**
As but one **momentary** gleam **would fly ;**
Or, as years, **the arrows of eternity.**
    Festus. Poets are all who love — who feel
    great **truths —**
And tell them ; **and the truth of truths** is love.
There was a **time —** oh, I remember well !
When, like a sea-shell with its seaborn strain,
My **soul aye** rang with music of the lyre ;
And my heart shed its lore as leaves their **dew —**
A honey dew, and throve on what it shed.
All things I loved ; but song I loved in chief.
Imagination is the air of mind ;

Judgment its earth, and memory its main;
Passion its fire.   I was at home in Heaven:
Swiftlike I lived above: once touching earth,
The meanest thing might master me: long wings
But baffled.   Still and still I harped on song.
Oh! to create within the mind is bliss;
And, shaping forth the lofty thought, or lovely,
We seek not, need not Heaven: and when the
          thought —
Cloudy and shapeless, first forms on the mind,
Slow darkening into some gigantic make,
How the heart shakes with pride and fear, as heaven
Quakes under its own thunder: or as might,
Of old, the mortal mother of a god,
When first she saw him lessening up the skies.
And I began the toil divine of verse,
Which like a burning-bush, doth guest a god.
But this was only wing-flapping — not flight;
The pawing of the courser ere he win;
Till, by degrees, from wrestling with my soul,
I gathered strength to keep the fleet thoughts fast,
And made them bless me.   Yes, there was a time
When tomes of ancient song held eye and heart —
Were the sole lore I recked of: the great bards
Of Greece, of Rome, and mine own master land,
And they who in the holy book are deathless, —
Men who have vulgarized sublimity,
And brought up truth for the nations; parted it,
As soldiers lotted once the garb of God, —
Men who have forged gods — uttered — made them
          pass:
In whose words, to be read with many a heaving
Of the heart, is a power, like wind in rain —
Sons of the sons of God, who, in olden days,
Did leave their passionless Heaven for earth and
          woman,
Brought an immortal to a mortal breast;
And, like a rainbow clasping the sweet earth,
And melting in the covenant of love,

Left here a bright precipitate of soul,
Which lives for ever through the lines of men,
Flashing, by fits, **like fire** from an enemy's front —
Whose thoughts like **bars** of sunshine in shut rooms
Mid gloom, **all** glory, win the world to light —
Who make their very follies like their souls;
And, like the young moon with a ragged edge,
Still, in their imperfection, beautiful —
Whose weaknesses are **lovely** as their strengths,
Like the white nebulous matter between **stars,**
Which, if not light, at least is likest light, —
Men whom we build our love round like an arch
Of triumph, as they pass us on their way
To glory and to immortality ;
Men whose **great thoughts** possess **us like a passion**
Through every limb and the **whole heart; whose**
          words
Haunt us as eagles haunt the mountain air;
Thoughts which command all coming times and
          minds,
As from a tower a warden, — fix themselves
Deep in the heart as meteor stones in earth,
Dropped from some higher sphere ; the words of
          gods,
And fragments of the undeemed tongues of Heaven
Men who walk up to fame as to a friend
Or their own **house,** which from **the wrongful heir**
They have wrested, from the **world's hard hand and**
          gripe, —
Men who, like **Death, all bone, but all unarmed,**
Have ta'en the **giant world by the throat, and thrown**
          him ;   .
And made him swear to maintain their name and
          fame
At peril of his life — who shed great thoughts
·**As easily as** an oak looseneth its golden leaves
In **a** kindly largess to the soil it grew on —
Whose rich dark ivy thoughts, sunned o'er with love,
Flourish around the deathless stems of their names —

Whose names are ever on **the** world's broad tongue,
Like sound upon the falling of a force —
Whose words, if winged, are with angels' wings —
Who play **upon** the heart as on a harp,
And make **our** eyes bright as we speak of them —
Whose hearts **have a** look southwards, and **are** open
To **the** whole noon of **nature,** — **these** I have waked
And wept o'er, night by night; oft pondering thus:
Homer is gone; and where is **Jove**? and where
The rival cities seven?   His song outlives
Time, tower, and god — all that then **was save** Heaven.
  MUSE.   Yea, but the poor perfections of **thine** earth
Shall **be** as little as nothing to **thee here.**
  FESTUS. God must be happy, who **aye makes;** and since
Mind's **first of** things, who makes from mind is blest
O'er men.   **Thus** saith the bard to his work: — I am
Thy **god, and** bid thee live as my God me:
I **live** or die with thee, soul of my soul!
Thou cam'st and went'st, sunlike, from morn to eve:
And **smiledst** fire upon my heaving heart,
Like **the sun** in the sea, till it arose
And **dashed** about its house all might and mirth,
Like ocean's tongue in Staffa's stormy cave.
Thou art a weakly reed to lean upon;
But, like that reed the false one filched from Heaven
Full of immortal fire — immortal as
The breath of God's lips — every breath a soul.
  MUSE. Mortal! **the** muse is with thee: leave her not.
  FESTUS. **Once** my ambition **to** another end
Stirred, stretched itself, but slept again.   I rose
And dashed on earth the harp, mine other heart,
Which, ringing, brake; its discord ruinous
Harmony still; and coldly I **rejoiced**
No other joy I had, wormlike, **to feed**

Upon my ripe resolve.   It might not be:
The more I strove against, the more I loved it.
   LUCIFER.   Come, let us walk along.   So say **fare-**
     well.
   FESTUS. **I will not.**
   MUSE.   **No**; my greeting is forever
   LUCIFER. **Well, well,** come on !
   FESTUS.   **Oh!** show me that **sweet** soul
Thou brought'st to me the first night that we met.
She must be here, where all are good and fair :
And thou didst promise me.
   LUCIFER.   **Is** that not she
Walking alone, up-looking to thine earth ?
For, lo ! it shineth through the mid-day air.
   FESTUS. It is ! **it is** !
   LUCIFER.   Well, **I will come again.**
                      [Goes.

   FESTUS. Knowest thou me, mine own immortal
     love ?
How shall I call thee ? Say, what mayest thou be
   ANGELA. **I am** a spirit, Festus ; and I love
Thy spirit, and shall love, when once like mine,
More than we ever did or can even now.
Pure spirits are of Heaven, all heavenly.
Yet marvel not to meet me in this guise,
All radiant like a diamond as it is.
We wander in what way we will through **all**
Or any of these worlds, and wheresoe'er
We are, there Heaven is, here, and there too, God.
   FESTUS. Thou dost remember **me** ?
   ANGELA.   **Ay,** every thought
And look of love which thou **hast lent to** me,
Comes daily through my **memory as stars**
Wear through **the** dark.
   FESTUS.   And thou art happy, love ?
   ANGELA. Yes: I am happy when I can do good
   FESTUS. To be good is to do good.   Who dwell
     here ?
Are they all deathless — happy ?

ANGELA.   All are not!
Some err, though rarely — slightly.   Spirits sin
Only in thought; and they are of a race
Higher **than** thine — have fewer wants **and less**
Temptations — **many more** joys — greater powers.
They need no **civil** sway : each rules himself —
Obeys himself: **all** live, too, as they choose,
And they choose nought but good.   They who have
        come
From earth, **or** other orb, use the same powers,
Passions, and purposes, they **had e'er death;**
Although enlarged and freed, **to** nobler **ends,**
With better means.   Here the hard warrior **whets**
The sword of truth, and steels his soul against sin.
The **fierce** and lawless wills which trooped it over
His breast — the speared desires **that overran**
The fairest fields of virtue, sleep **and** lie
Like a slain host 'neath snow; he dyes his hands
Deep in the blood of evil passions.   Mind !
• **There is no passion evil in** itself ;
In Heaven we shall enjoy all to right ends.
There sit the perfect women, perfect men; —
Minds which control themselves, hearts which in-
        dulge
Designs of wondrous goodness, **but so** far
Only, as soul extolled to bliss and power
Most high, sees fit for each, divinely.   Here,
The statesman makes new laws for growing worlds,
Through their forefated ages.   Here, the sage
Masters all mysteries, more and more, from day
To day, watching **the** thoughts of men and angels
Through moral microscopes ; or hails afar,
By **some** vast intellectual instrument,
The mighty spirits, good or bad, which range
The space **of** mind ; some spreading death and woe
On far-off worlds — some great with good and life.
And here the poet, like that wall of fire
In ancient song, surrounds the universe :
Lighting himself, where'er he soars or dives,

With his own bright brain — this is the poet's
        heaven.
Here he may realize each form or scene
He e'er on earth imagined; or bid dreams
Stand fast, and faery palaces appear.
Here he has Heaven to hear him; to the which
He sings, with manlike voice and song, the love
Which lent him his whole strength, as is the wont
Of all great spirits and good throughout the world.
Oh! happiest of the happy is the bard!
Here, too, some pluck the branch of peace where‧
        with
To greet a suffering saint, and show his flood
Of woe hath sunken: this I love to do.
My love, we shall be happy here.
   FESTUS.   Shall I
Ever come here?
   ANGELA. Thou mayest. I will pray for thee,
And watch thee.
   FESTUS. Thou wilt have, then, need to weep.
This heart must run its orbit. Pardon thou
Its many sad deflections. It will return
To thee and to the primal goal of Heaven.
   ANGELA. Practise thy spirit to great thoughts
        and things,
That thou mayst start, when here, from vantage
        ground,
We can foretell the future of ourselves,
And fateful only to himself is each.
   FESTUS. I do not fear to die; for, though I
        change
The mode of being, I shall ever be.
World after world will fall at my right hand;
The glorious future be the past despised:
All now that seemeth bright will soon seem dim,
And darker grow, like earth, as we approach it;
While I shall stand upon yon heaven which now
Hangs over me. If aught can make me seek
Other to be than that lost soul I fear me,

It is, that thou lovest me.   Heaven were not Heaven
Without thee.
    Lucifer.   I am here now.   Art thou ready ?
Let us go.
    Angela.   Well — farewell.   It makes me grieve
To bid a loved one back to yon false world —
To give up even a mortal unto death.
Thou wilt forget me soon, or seek to do.
    Festus.   When I forget that the stars shine in
        air —
When I forget that beauty is in stars —
When I forget that love with beauty is —
Will I forget thee : till then, all things else.
Thy love to me was perfect from the first,
Even as the rainbow in its native skies :
It did not grow : let meaner things mature.
    Angela.   The rainbow dies in Heaven, and not
        on earth ;
But love can never die ; from world to world,
Up the high wheel of heaven, it lives for aye.
Remember that I wait thee, hoping, here.
Life is the brief disunion of that nature
Which hath been one and same in Heaven ere now,
And shall be yet again, renewed by Death.
Come to me when thou diest !
    Festus.   I will, I will.
    Angela.   Then, in each other's arms, we will
        waft through space,
Spirit in spirit, one ! or we will dwell
Among these immortal groves ; or watch new worlds,
As, like the great thoughts of a Maker-mind,
They are rounded out of chaos : and we will
Be oft on earth with those we love, and help them ;
For God hath made it lawful for good souls
To make souls good ; and saints to help the saintly
That thou right soon mayst fold unto thy heart
The blissful consciousness of separate
Oneness with God, in Him in whom alone
The saved are deathless, shal' become, for thee,

My earliest, earnest, and most constant prayer.
Oh! what is dear to creatures of **the** earth?
Life, love, light, liberty! **But** dearer far
Than all — and oh! an universe more divine —
The gift, which God endows his chosen **with,**
Of His own uncreated glory, — His
Before all worlds, all ages, and reserved
Till after all for those He loves and saves.
As when the eye first views some Andean **chain**
Of shadowy rolling mountains, based **on air,**
Height upon height, aspiring to the last,
Even to Heaven, in sunny snow sheen, **up**
Stretching like angel's pinions, **nor can tell**
Which be the loftiest nor the **loveliest;**
As when an army, wakening **with the sun,**
Starts to its feet all hope, spear after spear
And line on line reundulating light,
While night's dull **watchfires** reek themselves away,
So feels the spirit when it first receives
The bright and mountainous mysteries **of** God,
Containing Heaven, moving themselves towards **us,**
In their **free** greatness, as by ships **at sea**
Come icebergs, pure and pointed as a star
Afar off glittering, of invisible
Depth, and dissolving in the light above.
   Festus. My prayer shall be **that thy prayer be**
      fulfilled.
I must **to** earth again. **Farewell, sweet soul!**
   Angela. Farewell! **I love thee, and** will **oft**
      be with **thee.** [love
   Lucifer. I **like earth** more than this: **I** rather
A splendid failing than a petty good;
Even as the thunderbolt, whose course is down-
      wards,
Is nobler far than any fire which soars.
   Festus. I am determined to be good again —
Again? When was I otherwise than ill?
Does not sin pour from my soul like dew from earth,
And, vaporing up before the face of God,

Congregate there in clouds between Heaven and
    me ? .
What wonder that I lack delight of life?
For it is thus — when amid the world's delights,
How warm so'er we feel a moment among them —
We find ourselves, when the hot blast hath blown,
Prostrate, and weak, and wretched, even as I am.
I wish that I could leap from off this star,
And dash my soul to atoms like a glass.
    LUCIFER. I have done nothing for thee yet.
        Thou shalt
See Heaven, and Hell, and all the sights of space,
When'er thou choosest.
    FESTUS.   Not then now.
    LUCIFER.   Up! rise!
    FESTUS. No; I'll be good: and will see none
      of them.
Earth draws us like a loadstone. We are coming.

SCENE— *A Large Party and Entertainment.*

FESTUS, LADIES, *and* OTHERS.

    FESTUS. My Helen! let us rest awhile,
For most I love thy calmer smile;
We'll not be missed from this gay throng,
They dance so eagerly and long;
And were one half to go away,
I'll bet the rest would scarce perceive it.
    HELEN. With thee I either go or stay,
Prepared, the same, to like or leave it.
These two, perhaps, will take our places.
They seem to stand with longing faces.
    FESTUS. Then sit we, love, and sip with me,
And I will teach thyself to thee.
Thy nature is so pure and fine,
'T is most like wine;
Thy blood, which blushes through each vein,
Rosy champagne;

And the fair skin which o'er it grows,
Bright as its snows.
Thy wit, which thou dost work so well,
Is like cool moselle ;
Like madeira, bright and warm,
Is thy smile's charm ;
Claret's glory hath thine eye,
Or mine must lie ;
But nought can like thy lips possess
Deliciousness ;
And now that thou 'rt divinely merry,
I 'll kiss and call thee sparkling sherry.   [me
    HELEN. I sometimes dream that thou wilt leave
Without thy love, even me, lonely ;
And oft I think, though oft it grieve me,
That I am not thy one love only :
But I shall always love thee till
This heart, like earth in death, stand still.
    FESTUS.   I love thee, and will leave thee
        never,
Until my soul leave life for ever.
If earth can from her children run,
And leave the seasons — leave the sun, —
If yonder stars can leave the sky,
Bright truants from their home in heaven —
Immortals who deserve to die,
Were death not too good to be given, —
If Heaven can leave and live from God,
And man tread off his cradle clod —
If God can leave the world He sowed,
Right in the heart of space to fade —
Soul, earth, star, Heaven, man, world, and God
May part — not I from thee, sweet maid.
Ah! see again my favorite dance,
See the wavelike line advance ;
And now in circles break,
Like raindrops on a lake :
Now it opens, now it closes,
Like a wreath dropping into roses.

HELEN. It is a lovely scene,
Fair as aught on earth ;
And we feel, when it hath been,
At heart a dearth ;
As from the breaking up of some bright dream —
The failing of a fountain's spray-topt stream.
WILL. Ladies — your leave — we 'll choose a
Queen
To rule this fair and festive scene.
CHARLES. And it were best to choose by lot,
So none can hold herself forgot.
[*They draw lots: it falls to Helen.*
FESTUS. I knew, my love, how this would be ;
I knew that Fate must favor thee.
ALL. Lady fair! we throne thee Queen !
Be thy sway as thou hast been —
Light, and lovely, and serene.
FESTUS. Here — wear this wreath ! No ruder
crown
Should deck that dazzling brow ;
Or ask yon halo from the moon —
'T would well beseem thee now.
I crown thee, love ; I crown thee, love ;
I crown thee Queen of me !
And oh ! but I am a happy land,
And a loyal land to thee.
I crown thee, love ; I crown thee, love ;
Thou art Queen in thine own right !
Feel ! my heart is as full as a town of joy :
Look ! I 've crowded mine eyes with light.
I crown thee, love ; I crown thee, love ;
Thou art Queen by right divine !
And thy love shall set neither night nor day
O'er this subject heart of mine.
I crown thee, love ; I crown thee, love ;
Thou art Queen by the right of the strong !
And thou didst but win where thou mightst have
slain,
Or have bounden in thraldom long.

I crown thee, love; I crown thee, love;
Thou art my Queen for aye!
As the moon doth Queen the night, my love;
As the night doth crown the day;
I crown thee, love; I crown thee, love;
Queen of the brave and free!
For I'm brave to all beauty but thine, my love;
And free to all beauty by thee.
   HELEN. Here in this court of pleasure, blest to
      reign,
If not the loveliest, where all are fair,
We still, one hour, our royalty retain,
To out-queen all in kindness and in care.
Love, beauty, honor, bravery, and wit—
Was ever Queen served by such noble slaves?
The peerage of the heart—for Heaven's court fit:
We'll dream no more that earth hath ills or
      graves.
With mirth, and melody, and love we reign:
Begin we, then, our sweet and pleasurous sway:
And here, though light, so strong is beauty's chain,
That none shall know how blindly they obey.
We have but to lay on one light command—
That all shall do the most what best they love;
And Pleasure hath her punishments at hand,
For all who will not pleasure's rule approve.
But no! there's none of us can disobey,
Since, by our one command, we free ye thus;
And, as our powers must on your pleasures stay—
Support—and you will reign along with us.
   FESTUS. Ha! Lucifer! How now?
   LUCIFER. I come in sooth to keep my vow.
   FESTUS. Thy vow?
   LUCIFER.   To revel in earth's pleasures,
And tire down mirth in her own measures.
   FESTUS. Go thy ways: I shrink and tremble
To think how deep thou canst dissemble;
For who would dream that in yon breast
The heart of Hell was burning?

Or deem that strange and listless guest
Some-priceless spirit earning?
I hear, from every footstep, rise
A trampled spirit's smothered cries.
    CHARLES.   Fest, engage fair Marian's hand.
    FESTUS.   Pass me; she is free no less
Than I, who by my queen will stand —
May it please her loveliness!
    HELEN.   Festus, we know the love, and see,
Which was with Marian and thee.
    FESTUS.   I will not dance to-night again,
Though bid by all the Queens that reign.
    HELEN.   What, Festus! treason and disloyalty
Already to our gentle royalty?
    FESTUS.   No — I was wrong — but to forgive
Be thy sublime prerogative!
    HELEN.   Most amply, then, I pardon thee;
In proof whereof, come, dance with me.   [*A dance.*
    LAURENCE.   How sweetly Marian sweeps along;
Her step is music, and her voice is song.
Silver sandalled foot! how blest
To bear the breathing heaven above,
Which on thee, Atlas-like, doth rest,
And round thee move.
Ah! that sweet little foot; I swear
I could kneel down and kiss it there.
I should not mind if she were Pope;
I would change my faith.
    CHARLES.   Works, too, we hope.
    LAURENCE.   Ah! smile on me again with that
           sweet smile,
Which could from Heaven my soul to thee beguile
As I mine eye would turn from awful skies
To hail the child of sun and storm arise;
Or, from eve's holy azure, to the star
Which beams and becks the spirit from afar;
For fair as yon star-wreath which high doth shine,
And worthy but to deck a brow like thine;
Pure as the light from orbs which ne'er

Hath blessed us yet in this far sphere;
As eyes of seraphs lift alone
Through ages on the holy throne;
So bright, so fair, so free from guile,
And freshening to my heart thy smile;
Ay, passing all things here, and all above,
To me, thy look of beauty, truth and love.
    HARRY.   Thy friend hath led his lady out.
    FESTUS.   He looks most wickedly devout.
    FANNY. When introduced, he said he knew her,
And had been long devoted to her.
    EMMA.   Indeed — but he is too gallant,
And serves me far more than I want.
He vows that he could worship me —
Why — look! he is now upon his knee!
    LUCIFER.   I quaff to thee this cup of wine,
And would, though men had nought but brine —
E'en the brine of their own tears,
To cool those lying lips of theirs;
And were it all one molten pearl,
I would drain it to thee, girl;
Ay, though each drop were worth of gold
Too many pieces to be sold;
And though, for each I drank to thee,
Fate add an age of misery:
For thou canst conjure up my spirit
To aught immortals may inherit;
To good or evil, woe or weal —
To all that fiends or angels feel;
And wert thou to perdition given,
I'd join thee in the scorn of Heaven!
    EMMA.   Oh fie! to only think of such a fate!
    LUCIFER.   Better than not to think on 't till too
        late.
They 'd not believe me, Festus, if I told them,
That Hell, and all its hosts, this hour behold them.
    FESTUS.   Scarcely — that Devil here again!
But though my heart burst in the strain,
I will be happy, might and main!

So wreathe my **brow** with flowers,
And pour me **purple** wine,
And make **the** merry hours
Dance, dance, with glee like thine.
While thus enraptured, I and thou,
Love crowns the heart, as flowers the **brow**.
The rosy garland twine
Around the noble bowl,
Like laughing loves that shine
Upon the generous soul;
Be mine, dear maid, the loves, and thou
Shalt ever bosom them as now.
Then plunge the blushing wreath
Deep in the ruddy wine;
As the love of thee till death
Is deep in heart of mine.
While both are blooming on my **brow**,
I cannot be **more** blest than now.
    Lucifer.   **Thou talk'st of** hearts, in style to me,
        quite **fresh.**
The human heart's about a pound of flesh.
    Festus.   Forgive him, love, and aught he says.
    Helen.   What is that trickling down thy face?
    Festus.   Oh, love, that is only wine
From the wreath which thou didst twine;
And, casting in the bowl, I bound,
For coolness' sake, my temples round.
    Helen.   I thought 't was a thorn **which was**
        tearing thy brow;
And if it were only a rose-thorn was tearing,
Why, **whether of** gold or of roses, as now,
A **crown, if it hurt** us, is **hardly** worth wearing.
    Lucy.   **From what fair** maid hadst thou that
        flower?
It came not from **my** wreath **nor me.**
    Charles.   Love lives in thee **as in a flower,**
And sure this must have dropped **from thee** —
From thy lip, or from thy cheek:
See, **its** sister blushes speak.

Nay, never harm the harmless rose,
Though given by a stranger maid :
'T is sad enough to feel that flower
Feels it must fade.
And trouble not the transient love,
Though **by** another's side I sigh ;
It is enough to feel the flame
Flicker and die.
And thou to me art flame and flower
Of rosier body, brighter breath :
But softer, warmer than the **truth** —
As sleep than death.
   Festus. **The** dead of night : earth seems but
      seeming —
The soul seems **but a** something dreaming.
The bird is dreaming, in its nest,
Of song, and sky, and loved one's breast ;
The lap-dog dreams, as round he lies,
In moonshine of his mistress' eyes :
The **steed is** dreaming, **in** his stall,
Of one long breathless leap and fall :
The hawk hath dreamt him thrice of wings
Wide as the skies he may not cleave ;
But waking, feels them clipt, and clings
Mad to the perch 't were mad to leave :
The child is dreaming of its toys —
The murderer of calm home joys ;
The weak are dreaming endless fears —
The proud **of how** their pride appears :
The poor enthusiast who dies,
Of his life dreams the sacrifice —
Sees, as enthusiast only can,
The **truth** that made him more than man ;
And hears, once more, **in** visioned **trance,**
That voice commanding to advance,
Where wealth is gained — love, wisdom won,
Or **deeds** of danger dared and done.
The mother dreameth of her child —
The maid of **him** who hath beguiled —

The youth of her he loves too well;
The good of **God** — the ill of Hell, —
Who live of **death** — **of life** who die —
The dead of immortality.
The earth is dreaming back her youth;
Hell never dreams, for woe is truth;
And Heaven is dreaming o'er her prime,
Long ere the morning stars of time;
And dream of Heaven **alone can I,**
My lovely one, when thou art **nigh.**
   HELEN.   Let some one sing. Love, mirth and
      song,
The graces of this life of ours,
Go ever **hand in hand** along,
And **ask alike each other's** powers.

   LUCY *sings.*   For every leaf **the loveliest flower**
    Which Beauty **sighs** for from her **bower** —
    For **every star a drop** of dew —
    For **every sun a sky of blue** —
    For **every heart a heart as true.**

    For every tear by pity shed
    Upon a **fellow-sufferer's head,**
    Oh ! be a crown of glory given;
    Such crowns as saints to gain **have striven** —
    Such crowns as seraphs wear **in Heaven.**

    For all who toil at honest fame,
    A proud, a pure, **a** deathless name;
    For all who love, who loving bless,
    Be life one long, kind, close caress —
    Be life all love, all happiness.

   LUCIFER.   Tell me what's the chiefest pleas-
      ure
In this world's high **heaped measure ?**
   ALL. **Power** — beauty — love — wealth — wine !
   LUCIFER.   All different **votes!**

FANNY.   Come, Frederic — thine ?
What may thy joy-judgment be ?
        FREDERIC.   I scarce know how to answer thee ;
Each, apart, too soon will tire ;
All together slake desire.
So ask not of me the one chief joy of earth,
For that I 'm unable to say ;
But here is a wreath which will lose its chief worth,
If ye pluck but one flower away.
Then these are the joys that should never dispart —
The joys which are dearest to me :
As the song, and the dance, and the laugh of the
        heart,
Thou, girl, and the goblet be.
        LUCIFER.   Oh, excellent ! the truth is clear —
The one opinion, too, I love to hear.
        HELEN.   Is this a Queen's fate — to be left
        alone ?
I wish another had the throne.
Festus ! why art thou not here,
Beside thy liege and lady dear ?
        FESTUS.   My thoughts are happier oft than I,
For they are ever, love, with thee ;
And thine, I know, as frequent fly
O'er all that severs us, to me ;
Like rays of stars that meet in space,
And mingle in a bright embrace.
Never load thy locks with flowers,
For thy cheek hath a richer flush ;
And than wine, or the sunset hour,
Or the ripe yew-berry's blush.
Never braid thy brow with lights,
Like the sun, on its golden way
To the neck and the locks of night,
From the forehead fair of day.
Never star thy hand with stones,
For, for every dead light there,
Is a living glory gone,
Than the brilliant far more fair.

Nay, nay; wear thy buds, braids, **gems**!
Let the lovely never part;
Thou alone canst rival them,
Or in nature, or **in art.**
Be **not** sad; — **thou** shalt not be:
Why wilt mourn, love, when with me?
One tear that in thine eye doth start
Could wash all purpose from my heart,
But that of loving thee;
If I could ever think to wrong
A love so river-like, deep, pure, and long.
   HELEN. I cast mine eyes around, and **feel**
There is a blessing wanting;
Too **soon our** hearts the truth reveal,
That joy is disenchanting.
   FESTUS. I am a wizard, love; and **I**
A new enchantment will supply;
And the charm of thine own smile
.Shall thine own heart of grief **beguile.**
Smile — I do command thee **rise**
From the bright depths **of those eyes!**
By the bloom wherein **thou dwellest,**
As in a rose-leaved **nest;**
By the pleasure which **thou tellest,**
And **the bosom** which thou **swellest,**
I bid **thee rise** from rest;
By the rapture which thou causest,
And the bliss while e'er thou pausest,
Obey my high behest!
   HELEN. Dread magician! Cease thy spell;
It hath **wrought** both quick and well.
   FESTUS. Ah! thou hast dissolved the **charm!**
Ah! thou hast outstepped **the** ring!
Who shall answer for the harm
Beauty on herself will bring?
Come, I will conjure up again that smile —
The scarce departed spirit. There it is!
Settling and hovering round thy lips the while,
Like some bright angel o'er the gates of bliss.

And I could sit and set that rose-bright smile,
Until it seem to grow immortal there —
A something abstract even of all beauty,
As though 't were in the eye or in the air.
Ah! never may a heavier shadow rest
Than thine own ringlets' on that brow so fair;
Nor sob, nor sorrow, shake the perfect breast
Which looks for love, as doth for death despair.
And now the smile, the sigh, the blush, the
    tear —
Lo! all the elements of love **are here.**
Oh, weep not — wither not the soul
Made saturate with bliss;
I would not have one briny tear
Embitter Beauty's kiss.
Nay, weep not, fear not! woe nor wrath
Can touch a soul like thine,
More than the lightning's blinding path
May strike the stars divine.
Sing, then, while thy lover sips,
And hear the truth that wine discloses;
Music lives within thy lips
Like a nightingale in roses.

Helen *sings.*   **Oh! love is like the rose,**
    And a month it may not **see,**
    Ere **it** withers where it grows —
    Rosalie!

    I loved thee from afar;
    Oh! **my heart** was lift to thee
    Like a **glass up to** a star —
    Rosalie!

    Thine eye was glassed in mine
    As the moon is in the sea,
    And its shine was on the brine —
    Rosalie!

The rose hath lost its red,
And the star is in the sea,
And the briny tear is shed —
Rosalie!

FESTUS.   What the stars are to the night, my
   love,
What its pearls are to the sea, —
What the dew is to the day, my love,
Thy beauty is to me.
   HELEN.   I am but here the under-queen of
      beauty,
For yonder hangs the likeness of the goddess;
And so to worship her is our first duty.
The heavenly minds of old first taught the heavenly
      bodies
Were to be worshipped; and the idolatry
Holds to this hour; though, Beauty! but of thine.
I am thy priestess, and will worship thee,
With all this brave and lovely train of mine;
Lo! we all kneel to thee before thy pictured shrine.
Yes — there, thou goddess of the heart,
Immortal beauty, there!
Thou glory of Jove's free-love skies,
E'en like thyself too fair,
Too bright, too sweet for mortal eyes,
For earthly hearts too strong;
Thy golden girdle lift'st and drawest
The heavens and earth along.
Oh! thou art as the cloudless moon,
Undimmed and unarrayed;
No robe hast thou, no crown save yon —
Goddess! thy long locks' soft and sunbright braid.
And there's thy son, Love — beauty's child —
World-known for strangest powers —
Boy-god! thy place is blest o'er all!
Smil'st thou at thoughts of ours?
And there, by thy luxurious side,
The Queen of Heaven and Jove

Stands; and the deep delirious draught
Drinks, from thy looks, of love,
And lips, which oft have kissed **away**
The thunders from **his brow**
Who ruled, **men say, the world of worlds,**
As God our **God rules now.**
And thou art yet as great **o'er this**
As erst o'er olden sky;
Of all Heaven's darkened deities
The last live light **on** high.
God after God hath left thee lone,
Which lived on human breath;
When prayers were breathed to them **no more,**
The false ones pined to **death.**
But in the service of young-hearts
To loveliness and **love;**
Live thou shalt while yon wandering world
Named unto thee shall move.
No fabled dream art **thou :** all god,
Our souls acknowledge **thee;**
For what would life from **love be worth,**
Or love from beauty be ?
Come, universal beauty, then,
Thou apple of God's **eye,**
To **and** through **which all things were made —**
Things deathless — things that die.
Oh! lighten — live before us **there —**
Leap in yon **lovely form,**
And give a **soul.   She comes! it breathes —**
So bright — **so sweet — so warm.**
Our sacrifice **is over: let us rise!**
For we have worshipped acceptably here;
And let our glowing hearts and glimmering eyes,
O'erstrained with gazing on thy light too near,
Prove that our worship, Goddess, was sincere!
   FESTUS.   I read that we are answered.   The
      soft air
Doubles its sweetness; and the fainting flowers,
Down hanging **on** the walls in wreaths so fair,

Bud forth afresh, as in their birth-day bowers,
Dew-laden, as oppressed with love **and** shame,
The rose-bud drops upon the lily's breast;
Brighter the wine, the lamps have softer flame,
Thy **kiss** flows freer than the grape first pressed.

WILL.   **A dance, a** dance!
HELEN.   Let us remain!
FESTUS.   We **will** not tempt your sport again.
HELEN.   Behold where Marian sits alone,
The **dance** all sweeping round,
Like to some goddess hewn in stone,
With blooming garlands bound.
FESTUS.   Tell me, Marian, what those eyes
Can discover in the skies? —
Those eyes, that look, so bright, so sweet their
        hue,
As they had gained from gazing on that view,
The high and starry beauty of their blue.
MARIAN.   For earth my soul hath lost all love,
But Heaven still loves and watches o'er me;
Why should I not, then, look above,
And pass, and pity all before me?
FESTUS.   Oh! **if yon worlds** that shine o'er this,
Have more of joy — of passion **less** —
I would not change earth's chequered **bliss**
For thrice the joys those orbs possess;
Which seem so strange their nature is,
Faint with excess of happiness.
MARIAN.   Thy heart with others hath its rest,
And it shall wake with me;
And if within another breast
Thy heart hath made itself **a nest,**
Mine is no more for thee.
Heart-breaker, go! I **cannot choose**
But love thee, and **thy love refuse;**
And if my brow **grow lined while young,**
And youth fly cheated from my cheek,
'T is, that there lies below my tongue
A word I will not **speak;**

For I would rather die than deem
Thou art not the glory thou didst **seem.**
But if engirt by flood or fire,
Who would live that could expire?
Who would not dream, **and dreaming die,**
If to wake were **misery?**
    FESTUS. Whose woes **are like to my woes?**
        What is **madness?**
The mind, exalted to a sense of ill,
Soon sinks beyond it into utter **sadness,**
And sees its grief before it like a **hill.**
Oh! I have suffered till my brain **became**
Distinct with woe, as is the skeleton leaf
Whose green hath fretted off its fibrous frame,
And bare to our immortality of grief.
    MARIAN. Like **the** light line **that laughter**
        leaves
One moment on a bright young brow;
So truth is lost ere love **believes**
There can be aught save **truth below.**
    FESTUS. But as the **eye** aye brightlier beams
For every fall **the** lid lets on **it,**
So oft the fond heart happier dreams
For the soft cheats love puts upon **it.**
    MARIAN. **I never** dreamed of wretchedness;
I thought to love meant but **to bless.**
    FESTUS. **It once** was bliss to me **to watch**
Thy passing smile, and sit and catch
The sweet contagion of **thy breath —**
For love is catching — **from** such teeth;
Delicate little pearl-white wedges,
All transparent **at the edges.**
    MARIAN. False flatterer, cease!
    FESTUS.   It is my **fate**
To love, and make who love me hate.
    MARIAN. No! 'tis to sue — to gain — deceive—
To **tire of** — to neglect — and **leave:**
The desolation of the soul
Is what I **feel —**

A sense of lostness that leaves death
But little to reveal ;
For death is nothing but the thought
Of something being again nought.
   HELEN. Cease, lady, cease those aching sighs,
Which shake the tear-drops from thine eyes,
As morning wind, with wing fresh wet,
Shakes dew out of the violet.
Forgive me, if the love once thine
Hath changed itself unsought to me ;
I did not tempt it from thy heart,
I nothing knew of thee ;
And soon, perchance, 't will be my part
As thou now art, to be.
   MARIAN. I blame no heart, no love, no fate,
And I have nothing to forgive ;
I wish for nought, repent of nought,
Dislike nought but to live.
   HELEN. Nay, sing; it will relieve thy heart.
   MARIAN. I cannot sing a mirthful strain ;
And feel too much to act my part
E'en of an ebbing vein.
   FESTUS. Our hearts are not in our own hands
Why wilt thou make me say
I cannot love as once I loved ?
   MARIAN. Hear !— 't is for this I stay —
To say we part — for ever part:
But oh ! how wide the line
Between thy Marian's bursting heart
And that proud heart of thine.
And thou wilt wander here and there,
Ever the gay and free ;
To other maids wilt fondly swear,
As thou hast sworn to me ;
And I — oh! I shall but retire
Into my grief alone ;
And kindle there the hidden fire,
That burns, that wastes unknown.

And love and life shall find their tomb
In that sepulchral flame : —
Be happy — none shall know for whom —
I will not dream thy **name.**
   FESTUS. As sings the swan with parting breath,
So **I to thee;**
While **love is leaving** — worse than life —
Forewarningly.
Speak not, nor think thou, any ill of me,
If thou wouldst **not die** soon and wretchedly.
I cannot waver **on** my path
To shun fair lady's love or wrath.
Nor condescend the world **to** undeceive
Which doth delight **in error and believe.**
Thus then farewell, **dear lady, ere I go:**
And dearly **have I earned my lightest woe.**

   Oh! if we e'er **have loved, lady,**
    We must forego it now;
Though sore the heart **be** moved, **lady,**
   · When bound to break its vow.
    I 'll always think on thee,
And thou sometimes — on whom, lady ?
   And yet those thoughts must be
Like flowers flung on the tomb, lady,
Then think that I am blest, lady,
   Though aye for thee I sigh;
In peace and beauty rest, lady,
   Nor **mourn and mourn** as I.

From **one** we love **to part, lady,**
   Is harder than **to die** ;
I see it by thy heart, lady,
   I feel it by thine eye.
   Thy lightest look can tell
Thy heaviest thought to me, lady;
   Oh! **I** have loved **thee** well,
   But well seems ill with thee, lady

Though sore the heart be moved, lady,
　When bound to break its vow —
Yet if we ever loved, lady,
　We must forego it now. —

LUCIFER.　Come, I must separate you two,
Such wretchedness will never do.
The little cloud of grief which just appears,
If left to spread, will drown us all in tears.
　EMMA.　Oblige us, pray, then, with a song.
　CHARLES.　I am sure he has a singing face.
　WILL.　At church I heard him loud and long.
　LUCIFER. Pardon — but you are doubly wrong.
　HELEN.　Obey, I beg.　Here — give him place.
　LUCIFER.　I have not sung for ages, mind;
So you must take me as you find.
This is a song supposed of one —
A fallen spirit — name unknown —
Fettered upon his fiery throne —
Calling on his once angel-love,
Who still remaineth true above.　　　　　　[Sings.

Thou hast more music in thy voice
　Than to the spheres is given,
And more temptations on thy lips
　Than lost the angels Heaven.
Thou hast more brightness in thine eyes
　Than all the stars which burn,
More dazzling art thou than the throne
　We fallen dared to spurn.

Go search through Heaven — the sweetest smile
　That lightens there is thine;
And through Hell's burning darkness breaks
　No frown so fell as mine.
One smile — 't will light, one tear — 't will cool;
　These will be more to me
Than all the wealth of all the worlds,
　Or boundless power could be.

HELEN.   Entreat him, pray, to sing again.
LUCIFER.   Any thing any one desires.
FESTUS.   Your loveliness hath but to deign
To will, **and** he 'll do all that will requires.

LUCIFER *sings.*   **Oh!** many a cloud
    Hath lift its wing,
    And many a leaf
    Hath clad the spring;
    But there shall be thrice
    The leaf and cloud,
    And thrice shall the world
    Have worn her shroud,
    Ere there 's any like thee,
    But where thou wilt **be.**

    Oh! many a storm
    Hath drenched the sun,
    And many a stream
    To sea hath run;
    But there shall be thrice
    The storm and stream,
    Ere there 's any like thee,
    But in angel's dream;
    Or in look, or in love,
    But in Heaven above.

LUCY.   What **is love?   Oh! I wonder so;**
Do tell me — who pretends to know?
FRANK.   **Ask** not of me, love, what is love?
Ask what is good of God above —
Ask of the great sun what is light —
Ask what is darkness of the night —
Ask sin of what may be forgiven —
Ask what is happiness of Heaven —
Ask what is folly of the crowd —
Ask what is fashion of the shroud —
Ask what is sweetness of thy kiss —
Ask of thyself what **beauty** is;

And, if they each should answer, I!
Let me, too, join them with a sigh.
Oh! let me pray my life may prove,
When thus, with thee, that I am love.
   FESTUS.   I cannot love as I have loved,
And yet I know not why;
It is the one great woe of life
To feel all feeling die;
And one by one the heartstrings snap,
As age comes on so chill;
And hope seems left that hope may cease,
And all will soon be still.
And the strong passions, like to storms,
Soon rage themselves to rest,
Or leave a desolated calm —
A worn and wasted breast;
A heart that like the Geyser spring,
Amidst its bosomed snows,
May shrink, not rest — but with its blood
Boils even in repose.
And yet the things one might have loved
Remain as they have been, —
Truth ever lovely, and one heart
Still sacred and serene;
But lower, less, and grosser things
Eclipse the world-like mind,
And leave their cold dark shadow where
Most to the light inclined.
And then it ends as it began,
The orbit of our race,
In pains and tears, and fears of life,
And the new dwelling-place.
From life to death — from death to life,
We hurry round to God,
And leave behind us nothing but
The path that we have trod.
   HELEN.   In vain I try to lure thy heart
From grief to mirth.

It were as easy to ward off
Night from the earth.
   FESTUS.   Fill! I'll drink it till I die —
Helen's lip and Helen's eye!
An eye which outsparkles
The beads of the wine,
With a hue which outdarkles
The deeps where they shine.
Come! with that lightly flushing brow,
And darkly splendid eye,
And white and wavy arms which now,
Like snow-wreaths on the dark brown bough,
So softly on me lie.
Come! let us love, while love we may,
Ere youth's bright sands be run;
The hour is nigh when every soul
Which 'scapeth evil's dread control,
Nor drains the furies' fiery bowl,
Shall into Heaven for aye,
And love its God alone.   [the hours
   HELEN.   Now let me leave my throne; and if
Have measured every moment by a kiss,
As I do think, since first ye gave these flowers,
It was to teach us how to dial bliss.
Farewell, dear crown, thy mistress will not wear,
Save when she sitteth royally alone.
Farewell, too, throne! not quickly wilt thou bear
A happier form, if fairer than mine own.
   WILL.   The ladies leave us!
   LUCIFER.   Oh! by all means let them
But say, for Heaven itself, we'll not forget them;
Say we will pledge them to the top of breath,
As loud as thunder, and as deep as death.
   FESTUS *apart.*   Where is thy grave, my love?
I want to weep.
High as thou art this earth above,
My woe is deep;
And my heart is cold as is thy grave,
Where I can neither soothe nor save.

Whate'er I **say,** or do, or see,
I think and feel alone to thee.
Oh! can it — can it be forgiven,
That I forget thou art in Heaven?
Thou wilt forgive **me** this, and **more:**
Love spends his all, and still hath store.
Thou wilt forgive, if beauty's **wile**
Should win, perforce, one glance **from me;**
When they, whose art it is to smile,
Can never smile my heart from **thee;**
And if with them I chance **to be,**
And give mine ear up to their singing,
It, wind-like, only wakes **the sea,**
In **all** its mad monotony,
Of memory forth thy music ringing.
Thou wilt forgive, if now and then
I link with hands less loved than thine,
Whose gold-like touch makes kings of men,
But wakes **no will in** blood of mine;
And if with them **I toss** the **wine,**
And set my soul in **love's ripe riot,**
It echoes not — this desert **shrine,**
Where still thy love from **Heaven doth shine,**
Moon-like, **across some ruin's quiet.**
Thou wilt forgive me, if my feet
Should **move** to music with the **fair,**
When, at each turn, **I** burn to **meet**
Thy stream-like step and airy air;
And if, before some beauty there,
Mine eye may forge one glance of **gladness,**
It is but the ripple of despair,
That shows the bed is all but bare,
And nought scarce left but **stony** sadness.
Thou wilt forgive, if e'er **my heart**
Err from the orbit of its love;
When even **the** bliss-bright stars **will start**
Earthwards, some lower sphere **to prove.**
Thou wilt forgive, if soft white **arms**
Embrace, by fits, this breast of **mine;**

When, while amid their pillowy charms,
My heart can kiss no heart but thine;
And if these lips but rarely pine
In the pale abstinence of sorrow,
It is, that nightly I divine,
As I this world-sick soul recline,
I shall be with thee ere the morrow.
Thou wilt forgive, if once with thee
I limned the outline of a Heaven;
But go and tell our God, from me,
He must forgive what He hath given;
And, if we be by passion driven
To love, and all its natural madness,
Tell Him, that man by love hath thriven,
And that by love he shall be shriven;
For God is love where love is gladness.
Thou wilt forgive, if clay-bound mind
Can scarce discover that thou art;
But wait! I feel the outward wind
Rush fresh into my fluttering heart.
Perchance thy spirit stays in yon mild star
In peace, and flame-like purity, and prayer;
And, oh! when mine shall fly from earth afar,
I will pray God that it may join thine there:
'T were doubling Heaven, that Heaven with thee
    to share.
And, while thou leadest music and her lyre,
Like a sunbeam holden by its golden hair,
May I, too, mingling with the immortal choir,
Love thee, and worship God! what more may soul
    desire?
Enough for me! but, if there be
More, it shall be left for thee.
  WALTER. If any thing I love in chief,
It is that flowery rich relief
That wine doth chase on mortal metal
Before good wine begins to settle;
But all seem smilingly, serenely dull,
And melancholy as the moon at full.

Quenched by their company they seem,
Like sparks of fire in clouds of steam.
   CHARLES.   They who mourn the lack of wit,
Show, at least, no more of it.
   FESTUS.   I cannot bear to be alone,
I hate to mix with men;
To me there's torture in the tone
Which bids me talk again.
Like silly nestlings, warned in vain,
My heart's young joys have flown;
While singing to them, even then,
They left me one by one.
I envy every soul that dies
Out of this world of care:
I envy e'en the lifeless skies,
That they enshrine thee there.
And would I were the bright blue air
Which doth insphere thine eyes,
That thou mightst meet me everywhere,
And feel these faithful sighs.
E'en as the bubble that is mixed
Of air and wine right red,
So my heart's love is shared betwixt
The living and the dead.
If on her breast I lay my head,
My heart on thine is fixed:—
Wilt thou I loose, as I have said,
Or keep the soul thou seek'st?
From me thou canst not pass away
While I have soul or sight;—
I see thee on my waking way,
And in my dreams thee bright;
I see thee in the dead of night,
And the full life of day;
I know thee by a sudden light;
It is thy soul, I say.
If yonder stars be filled with forms
Of breathing clay like ours,

Perchance the space that spreads between
Is for a spirit's powers;
And loving as we two have **loved**
In spirit and in heart,
Whether **to space or** star removed,
God will **not bid us part.**
   Frank. **As to this seat—its late** and fair **pos-**
     sessor
Should, ere **she** went, have chosen her successor.
   Festus. **In** right of her who sat thereon
I think I might demand the throne;
I rather choose **to** let it be.
   All. George shall be King of the company!
   George. My loving subjects! **I shall** first pro-
     mulge
A few good rules **by which** to indulge;
They are good, according to my thinking,
And shall be held the laws **of** drinking.
First—each man shall do what he **chooses,**
Provided that he ne'er refuses,
But shall be sworn, by stand and stopper,
To drink as much as I think proper.
   Will. Stay!—all of you who think, with me,
This law should pass,
Will please to signify the same
By emptying their glass.
   Walter. Filling again and emptying, **and so**
     on,
At each **law — pari** passu, as we go **on.**
   George. Secondly — no man shall **be held as**
     mellow
Who can distinguish blue from yellow.
Thirdly — no man shall miss his turn nor toast,
Nor yet give more than two at once, at most.
Fourthly — if one at table should fall under,
There let him lie — so much extinguished thun-
     der.
Fifthly — let all, in such case, who still stay,
Like living lightnings, but the brighter play.

Sixthly, **and** last but one — mind this, there shan't
Be aught said that is not irrelevant.
Seventhly — if any **of** these edicts should not
Be **kept,** it shall **be** good **to** plead, I would not.
　CHARLES.　Oh, let the royal law
Be **writ** in rosy wine !
And read and kept
At every feast
Where wit and mirth combine.
　FESTUS.　How sweetly shine the steadfast stars,
Each eyeing, sister-like, the earth ;
And softly chiding scenes like this,
Of senseless and profaning mirth.
　LUCIFER.　Thou art ever prating of the stars
Like an old soldier of his scars ;
Thou shouldst have been a starling, friend,
And not an earthling : end !
　FESTUS.　**And** could I speak as many times
Of each as there are stars in Heaven,
I could not utter half the thoughts —
The sweet thoughts one to me **hath given.**
The holy quiet of the skies
May waken well the **blush of shame,**
Whene'er we think that thither lies
The Heaven we heed not — ought not **name.**
Oh, Heaven ! let down thy cloudy lids,
And close thy thousand **eyes** ;
For each, in burning glances, bids
The wicked fool be wise.
　LUCIFER.　I can interpret well the stars.
　CHARLES.　Indeed ! they need interpreters.
　LUCIFER.　Then thus, in their eternal tongue
And musical thunders, all have sung.
To every **ear which ear hath given,**
From birth to **death, this note of Heaven.**
Deathlings ! **on earth drink, laugh, and love !**
Ye may n't hereafter — **under or above.**
Yes, this the tale they all have told,
Since first they made old Chaos shrink —

Since first they flocked creation's fold,
And filled all air like flakes of gold
Which drop yon **royal** drink :
For as the moon **doth madmen rule,**
It is, that near **and few they are;**
And **so in Heaven each single star**
Doth **sway some reasonable fool,**
Whether on earth **or other sphere;**
For what's above **is what is here.**
Moons and madmen **only change;**
What can truth **or stars derange ?**

   EDWARD.   **Brave stars, bright monitors of joy!**
Right well ye time your hours of warning;
For, sooth to say, the eve's employ
Doth wax less lovely towards the morning.
So push the **goblet gaily round —**
Drink deep of its wealth — drink on!
Our earthly joy **too soon doth cloy,**
Our life is all but gone ;
And, not enjoy yon glorious **cup,**
And all the sweets which lie,
Like pearls, within its purple well —
Who would not hate to die ?

   WILL.   And who, without the cheering **glance**
Of woman's witching eye,
Could stand against the storms of **fate,**
Or cankering care defy ?
It adds **fresh** brightness **to the bowl;**
Then **why will men repine ?**
Content we 'll **live with Heaven's best gifts —**
With woman, and with **wine.**

   HARRY.   **Cups** while they sparkle —
Maids while they sigh;
Bright eyes will darkle —
Lips grow dry.
Cheek while the dew-drops
Water its rose ;
Life's fount hath few drops
Dear as those.

Arms while they tighten —
Hearts as they heave:
Love **cannot** brighten
Life's **dark eve.**
   GEORGE.   Oh ; the wine is like life ;
And the sparkles that play
By the lips of the bowl
Are the loves of the day.
Then kiss the bright bubble
That breaks in its rise ;
Oh ! love is a trouble,
As light when it dies.
   CHARLES.   Let the young be glad ! **though cares**
     in crowds
Leave scarce a break of blue,
Yet hope gives wings to morning clouds ;
And while their shade the **sky** enshrouds —
By love and wine, which through them shine —
They are turned to a golden hue.
Then give us wine, for we ought to shine
In the hour of dark and dew.

   FESTUS.   **Well** might **the** thoughtful race of old
    With ivy twine the **head**
Of him they hailed **their** god of **wine,** —
    Thank God ! **the lie is** dead :
For ivy climbs the crumbling hall
    To decorate decay ;
And spreads its dark deceitful pall
    To hide what wastes away.

And wine will circle round the brain
    As ivy o'er the brow,
Till what could once see far as stars
    Is dark as Death's eye now.
Then dash the cup down ! 'tis not worth
    A soul's great sacrifice :
The wine will sink into the earth,
    The soul, the soul — must rise.

CHARLES. A toast!

FREDERIC. Here's beauty's fairest flower —
The maiden of our own birth-land!

HARRY. Pale face! — Oh for one **happy hour**
To hold **my** splendid Spaniard's hand!

FESTUS. Why differ on which is the fairest form,
When all are the same the heart to warm?
Although by different charms they strike,
Their power is equal and alike.
Ye bigots **of** beauty! behold I stand forth,
And drink to the lovely all **over the earth.**
Come, fill to the girl by the Tagus' waves!
Wherever she lives there's a land of slaves.
And here's to the Scot! with her deep blue eye,
Like the far off lochs 'neath her hill-propt sky.
To her of the green Isle! whose tyrants deform
The land, where she beams like the bow in the storm.
To the Norman! so noble, and stately and tall;
Whose charms, ever changing, can please as they
     pall:
Two bowls in **a** breath! here's to each and to all!
Come fill to the English! whose eloquent brow
Says, pleasure is passing, but coming, and now;
Oh! her eyes o'er the wine are like stars o'er the sea,
And her face is the face of all Heaven **to me.**
And here's to the Spaniard! that warm, blooming
     maid,
With her step superb, and **her black locks' braid.**
To her of dear Paris! with soul-spending glance,
Whose feet, **as she's sleeping,** look dreaming a
     dance.
To the maiden whose lip like a rose-leaf is curled,
And her eye like the star-flag **above it** unfurled!
Here's **to** beauty, young beauty, **all over the** world! —

WILL. Hurrah! a glorious toast;
'T would warm a ghost.

FESTUS. It moves not me. I cannot drink
The toast I have given.
There! — Earth may pledge it, and she will —

Herself and her beauty to Heaven.
Drink **to the dead** — **youth's** feelings vain !
Drink **to the heart** — the battered wreck,
Hurled from all passion's stormy main !
Though aye the billows o'er it break,
The ruin rots, nor rides again.
    CHARLES.   Friend of my heart ! **away with** care,
And sing, and dance, and laugh :
To love, and to the favorite fair,
The wine-cup **ever quaff.**
Oh, drink to the lovely ! whatever they are,
Though fair **as** snow — as light;
For whether or falling, or fixed the star,
They **both** are heavenly bright.
Out upon Care ! he shall not stay
Within **a** heart like thine ;
There's nought in Heaven or earth can weigh
Down youth, and love, and wine.
Then drink with the merry ! though we must die,
Like beauty's tear we 'll fall;
We have lived in the light of **a** loved one's eye,
And to **live, love, and** die **is all.**
    FESTUS.   **Vain is the world and all it boasts :**
How brief Love's pleasure's **date !**
We turn the bowl **and all forget**
The bias of our fate.
    GEORGE.   How goes **the** enemy ?
    LUCIFER.   What can he mean ?
    FESTUS.   He asks the hour.
    LUCIFER.   Aha ! then I
Advise, if Time **thy foe** hath been,
Be quick ! shake hands, man, with Eternity.

SCENE — *A Church-yard.*

FESTUS *and* LUCIFER *beside a Grave.*

    FESTUS.   Let years crowd on, and age bow down
My body to the **earth which gave,**

As yon gray, worn out, crumbling stone
Dips o'er the grave!
What, though for me no music thrill,
Nor mirth delight, nor beauty move;
Though the heart stiffen and wax still,
And make no love;
Still, deep, and bright, like river gold,
Imbedded here thy love shall lie —
Sun-grains, that with the sands are rolled,
Of memory.
Shall that soul never burst the tomb,
Draped in long robes of living light?
Or, worm-like, alway eat the gloom
And dust of night?

    LUCIFER.   Oh! life in sporting on earth lies,
Till death share up the rich green sod;
But if the spirit lives or dies,
Why try ye God?
What should it never smile nor sigh
From cheeks or lips but those beneath?
Doth love not weigh the world's vast lie?
Doth life not death?

    FESTUS.   I ask why man should suffer death?
    LUCIFER.   Answer — what right to life hath
        he?
God gives and takes away your breath:
What more have ye?
Breath is your life, and life your soul;
Ye have it warm from His kind hands:
Then yield it back to the great Whole
When He demands.
Why, deathling, wilt thou long for Heaven?
Why seek a bright but blinding way?
Go, thank thy God that He hath given
Night upon day:
Go, thank thy God that thou hast lived,
And ask no more: 't is all He gave:
'T is all there needs to be believed —
God and the grave.

FESTUS.   For Thee, God, will I save my heart
For Thee **my nature's** honor keep;
Then, soul and body, all or part —
Rest, **wake,** or sleep!

SCENE — *Space.*

FESTUS *and* **LUCIFER.**

FESTUS.   Listen!   I hear the **harmonies of**
        Heaven,
From sphere to sphere and from the boundless
        round
Reëchoing bliss to those serenest heights
Where angels sit and strike their emulous harps
Wreathed round with flowers and diamonded with
        dew;
Such dew as gemmed the everduring blooms
Of Eden winterless, **or** as all night
The tree of Life wept from its every leaf
Unwithering.   And now methinks I hear
The music of the murmur of the stream
Which **through** the Bridal City of the **Lord**
Floweth all **life for ever;** and the brèath
Through the star-shading branches of that Tree
Transplanted now to Heaven, but once on earth,
Whose fruit is for all Beings — breathed of God.
Oh! **breathe** on me, inspiring spirit-breath!
Oh! **flow to** me, ye heart-reviving waves;
Freshen the faded soul that droops and dies.
    LUCIFER.   The **universe** is but **the** gate of
        Heaven.
Lo! from **this** highest **orb, the** crown of space
And footstool unto Heaven, we can look up
And gain **a** glimpse of glory unconceived.
    FESTUS.   See how yon angels stretch their shin-
        ing arms,

Wave their star-haunting wings which gleam **like**
    glass,
And locks that look like Morning's when she comes
Triumphant in the East.   Is this their joy
O'er some world penitent?
    LUCIFER.   **Lo**! there it rides;
Blest to discharge on Heaven's all peaceful shores
Its long accumulated load of life,
Its deathless freight,—pilgrims of time **and space.**
Yon guilty orb of hesitating light
Slow looming, there, on its dark path, goes up
At the forewritten hour, as do all worlds
To God, to judgment; and the earthquake groans
Which rend its adamantine breast forebode
Its agonizing **doom.**
    FESTUS.   **And** doth not Heaven
Grieve with the lost as gladden with the saved?
    LUCIFER.   How many immortals mourn **at the**
    decree
Of righteous wisdom, which alone to them
Is bliss sufficient, being infinite?
    FESTUS.   If God hath made all, He alone it is
Who hath to answer for all.
    LUCIFER.   He hath made.
To secondary natures **it seems** just
That justice should **be** realized, **and there**
Is one example extant in the skies.
    FESTUS.   But wherefore did **it not repent in**
    Time?
    LUCIFER.   What **unto us is** Time, stands before
    God
Eternity.   Repentance is the grief
For and effectual abstinence from sin,
Which secondary natures without God
Cannot attain to.
    FESTUS.   Cloudy and clear by turns
Thy words as Heaven.   I know not what to think
Nor how to act.
    LUCIFER.   It is natural; **and** none

Can aim or hit but as appointed them.
There is but one great sinner, Human nature,
Predict of every world and predicate:
The wicked one, the Enemy of God,
To be destroyed in the eternal fire
Of His wrath, even thus in Deity —
In whom as they begin must all things end.
God loveth only His own spirit, so
All that is base shall perish.   From the first
These things were fixed, and are and aye shall be
Consummating, and are revealed as writ
In words always fulfilled and burning truth
Under the buried basements of the skies,
Which after overthrown shall reappear.
The unenlightened mind sees Deity
In all things, but the spiritual soul
All things in God.   Now, ere we higher rise,
Look downwards from this coping of the world;
And know that down to the profoundest depth
Of utter space, where not an atom mars
The void invisible, it were easier far
To cast a line and calculate its rate,
Or pierce all space, nor cross the path of light,
Than fathom man's dark heart or sound his soul.

SCENE — *Heaven*.

LUCIFER *and* FESTUS, *entering*.

THE ARCHANGELS.   Infinite God!   Thy will is
  done.
  The world's last sand is all but run:
  The night is feeding on the sun.
LUCIFER.   All-being God!   I come to Thee
  again,
Nor come alone.   Mortality is here.
Thou bad'st me do my will, and I have dared
To do it.   I have brought him up to Heaven.

GOD.

Thou canst not do what is not willed to **be**.
Suns are made up of **atoms, Heaven of souls;**
And souls and suns are **but the atoms of**
The body I, God, dwell in.   **What wilt thou.**
With him who **is** here with **thee ?**
   Lucifer.   **Show him God.**

God.

No being, upon **part of whom the curse**
Of death rests — were **it only on his shadow,**
Can look on God **and live.**
   Lucifer.   **Look, Festus, look.**
  Festus.   **Eternal fountain of the Infinite,**
On whose life-tide the stars seem strown **like**
       bubbles,
Forgive **me that an atomie of being**
Hath sought to see **its Maker face to face.**
I have **seen** all Thy **works and wonders,** passed
From **star to** star, from **space to space,** and feel
That to see all which **can** be seen is nothing,
And not to look on Thee the Invisible.
The spirits **that** I met all seemed to say,
As on they sped upon their starward **course,**
And slackened their lightning **wings one moment**
       o'er me,
I could not look **on God whate'er I was.** .
And Thou **didst give this spirit at my side**
Power to **make me more than them immortal.**
So when we **had winged through Thy wide world**
     of things,
And seen stars **made and saved, destroyed and**
     judged,
I said — and **trembled lest** Thou shouldst not hear
     me,
And make Thyself right ready to forgive,
I will see God, before **I** die, in Heaven.
Forgive me, Lord !

God.

        Rise, mortal ! look on me.

FESTUS. Oh! I see nothing but like dazzling
    darkness.
LUCIFER.   I **knew** how it would be. I am
    away.
FESTUS.   I am **Thy creature,** God! oh, slay me
    not,
But let some angel **take** me, **or I die.**
GENIUS.   **Come** hither, Festus.
FESTUS.   Who art thou?
GENIUS.   **I am**
One who hath **aye been** by thee from thy birth,
Thy guardian angel, thy good genius.
FESTUS.   I knew thee not till now.
GENIUS.   I am never seen
In the earth's low thick **light, but** here in Heaven,
And in the air which God breathes, I am clear.
I tell to God each night thy thoughts and deeds;
And watching o'er thee both on earth and here,
Pray unto Him for thee and intercede.
FESTUS.   And **this is Heaven.** Lead on. **Will**
    God forgive
That I did **long to see Him?**
GENIUS.   **It is** the strain
Of all **high** spirits **towards Him.** Thou couldst not
Even if thou **wouldst, behold God; masked in**
    dust,
Thine eye did light on darkness; but when dead,
And the dust shaken off the shining essence,
God shall glow through thee as through living
    glass,
And every thought and **atom of** thy being
Shall guest **His** glory, be overbright with God.
Hadst thou **not been by** faith immortalized
For the instant, then thine eye had been **thy death.**
Come, I will show thee **Heaven** and all **angels.**
Lo! the recording angel.
FESTUS.   Him I see
High-seated, and the pen within his **hand**
Plumed like a storm-portending **cloud which curves**

Half over Heaven, and swift, in use divine,
As is a warrior's spear!
   GENIUS.   **The** book wherein
Are writ the records **of** the **universe,**
Lies like a world laid open at his feet.
And there, **the** Book **of** Life which holds the
      names,
Formed out in starry brilliants, of God's sons,—
The spirit-names which angels learn by heart,
Of worlds beforehand.   Wilt thou see thine own **?**
  FESTUS.   My **name is** written **in the** Book **of**
      Life.
It is enough.   That constellated word
Is more to me and clearer than all stars,
Henceforward and **for aye.**
   GENIUS.   Raise still thine eyes!
Thy gleaming **throne!** hewn from that mount of
      light
Which was before created light or night
Never created, Heaven's eternal base,
Whereon God's throne is 'stablished.   Sit on it!
  FESTUS.   Nay, I will forestall nothing more **than**
      sight.
  GENIUS.   Turn, then, **and view yon streams**
      where spirits sport,
Quaffing immortal life, preparing aye
For higher and intenser Being still.
These are the upper fountains **of the Heavens,**
The emanations of **Eternity;**
By **washing them** in **which they** purify
Their eyes to penetrate the **essential** light
In all things hidden, seen **alone by** eyes
Fire-spirited, etherially clear,
Which like the fabled stone, conceived of fire,
Son of the sun, transmutes all seen to soul.
And such the bliss and power reserved for man **;**
Yet but the surface-shadow canst thou see,
The substance is to be.   Behold yon **group**
Of spirits blest! **in** their divinest **eyes**

The spirit speaks, and shows that in their own
All doubt and want hath ceased, as death hath
    ceased.
Hither **they** come, rejoicing, marvelling.
    FESTUS.   How all with kindly wonder **look on**
      me!
Mayhap I tell of **earth to their** pure **sense.**
Some seem **as** if they knew me. I know **none.**
But how claim kinship with **the** glorified
Unless with them like-glorified! Yet, yes —
It is — **it must be ;** — that angelic spirit! —
My **heart** outruns me — mother! see thy son.
    ANGEL.   Child, how art thou here?
    FESTUS.   God hath let me come.
    ANGEL.   Hast thou not come unbidden and un-
      prepared?
    FESTUS.   Forgive **me,** if **it** be so. I am come.
And I have ever said there are two who will
Forgive me aught I **do** — **my** God and thou!
    ANGEL.   I do! may **He!**
    FESTUS.   Dear **mother, thou art** blessed ; -
And I am blessed, too, in knowing thee.
    ANGEL.   Son of my hopes on **earth** and prayers
      in Heaven!
The love of God! oh, **it is** infinite
Even as our imperfection. Promise, child,
That thou wilt love Him more and more for this,
And for His boundless kindness thus towards me.
Now, my son, hear me! for the hours of Heaven
Are **not as those** of earth; **and all is all**
But lost that is not given **unto** God. -
Oft have I seen with joy thy thoughts of Heaven,
And holy hopes, which track the soul with light,
Rise from dead doubts within thy troubled breast,
As souls **of drowned** bodies from the **sea,**
Upwards **to God,** and marked them so received,
That oh! **my soul** hath overflowed with **rapture**
As now thine eye **with tears.** But oh! **my son**
Beloved! fear thou **ever for** thy soul;

It yet hath to be saved.   Nought perfect stands
But that which is in Heaven.   God is all-kind ;
And long time hath he made **thee think** of Him ;
Think on Him yet in time.   **Ere I left earth,**
With the last breath **which air would spare for me,**
With the last look **which light would** bless **me**
     with,
I prayed thou mightst be happy and be wise —
And half the prayer I brought myself **to God** —
And lo ! thou **art unhappy** and **unwise.**
    FESTUS.   Blessed one ! I rejoice that thou art
       clear,
And all **who have cared for me, of my misdeeds.**
Thy spirit **was on those who nurtured me.**
All word and **practice that could be of** good,
Was given me ; so that my **sin is** splendid.
Yes ! if **I have sinned, I** have **sinned** sublimely ;
And **I am glad I suffer** for my faults.
I would not if I might, be bad and happy.
    ANGEL.   God laughs at ill **by man** made, and
      allows it.
The **vaunt** of mountainous evil and the power
To challenge Heaven from a molehill, child !
    FESTUS.   God **hath** made **but few better hearts**
      than mine,
However much **it fail in the wise ways**
Of the world, as **living in the dull, dark streets**
Of forms and follies **wherein men build themselves.**
    ANGEL.   The goodness of **the heart is shown in**
      deeds
Of peacefulness **and kindness.   Hand and** heart
Are one thing **with the good as thou shouldst** be.
The splendor of **corruption hath no power**
Nor vital essence ; **and content in sin**
Shows apathy, not satisfied **control.**
Do my words trouble thee ?   Then treasure them.
Pain overgot gives peace as death does Heaven.
All things that speak of Heaven speak of peace.
Peace hath more might than **war.**   High brows are
      calm.

Great thoughts are still as stars; and truths, like suns,
    Stir not; though many systems tend round them.
Mind's step is still as death's; and all great things
Which cannot be controlled, whose end is good.
Behold yon throne! there, Love, Faith, Hope, are one!
There, judgment, righteousness, and mercy make
One and the same thing. God's salvation is
His vengeance, and his wrath glory, as on earth
Destruction restoration to the pure.
Humanity is perfected in Heaven.
    FESTUS. I did not make myself, nor plan my soul.
I am no angel nursed in the lap of light,
Nor fed on milk immortal of the stars,
Nor golden fruit grown in the summery suns.
How am I answerable for my heart?
It is my master, and is free with me,
As fixed with fate, even as a star which moves,
Yet moveth only on a certain course
In certain mode; — its liberties are laws,
Its laws tyrannic; I cannot hinder it,
It cannot hinder God. All that we do
Or bear is settled from eternity;
Whereof is no beginning, midst, nor end.
To act, is ours; quite sure, whate'er we do,
Whether it be for our own good or ill,
Or others' ill or good, it is for God's
Glory — the same and always: it is ordered.
The soul is but an organ, and it hath
No power of good and evil in itself,
More than the eye hath power of light or dark.
God fitted it for good; and evil is
Good in another way we are not skilled in.
The good we do is of His own good will, —
The ill, of His own letting. Doth not nature —
All light in life, shine, marsh-like, too, in death?
Yea, wandering fires wait even on rottenness

Like a stray gleam of thought in an idiot's brain.
And thus I look on souls that seem decaying
In sin, and flying off by elements.
All may not live again ; but all which do
Must change perpetually e'en in Heaven ;
And not by death to death, but life to life.
   ANGEL. **No!** step by step, and throne by **throne,**
     we rise
Continually towards the infinite,
And ever nearer — never near — to God.
   FESTUS. Yet merit or demerit none **I see** ·
In nature, human or material,
In passions or affections good or bad.
We only know that God's best purposes
Are oftenest brought about by dreadest **sins.**
Is thunder evil or is dew divine ?
Does virtue lie in sunshine, sin in storm ?
Is not each natural, each needful, best ?
How **know we what** is evil from what good ?
Wrath and revenge God claimeth as His own.
And yet men speculate on right and wrong
As **upon** day and night, forgetting both
Have **but one** cause, and that the same — God'**y**
     will,
Originally, ultimately **Him.**
All right is right divine. A worm hath rights
A king cannot despoil **him** of, nor sin ;
Yet wrongs are **things** necessitate, like **wants,**
And **oft** are **well permitted to** best **ends.**
A double error sometimes sets us right.
In **man there is no rule of** right and wrong
Inherent as mere man. Why, conscience is
The basest thing of all. **Its** life **is** passed
In justifying and condemning sin ;
Accomplice, traitor, judge, and headsman, too,
But conscience knows its business and performs.
Nothing is lost in nature ; and no soul,
Though buried in the centre of all sin,
Is lost to God ; but there it works His will

And burns comfortably.   The weakest things
Are to be made the examples of His might;
The most defective, of His perfect grace,
Whene'er He thinketh well.   Oh! every thing
To me seems good and lovely and immortal;
The whole is beautiful; and I can see
Nought wrong in man nor nature, nought not meant
As from His hands it comes who fashions all,
All holy as His word.   The world is but
A revelation.   He breathes Himself upon us
Before our birth, as o'er the formless void
He moveth at first, and we are all inspired
With His spirit.   All things are God or of God.
For the whole world is in the mind of God
What a thought is in ours.   Why boast we then
Of aught?   All that is good belongs to God;
And good and God are all things, or shall be.
　　ANGEL.   There lacks in souls like thine unsaved,
　　　　unraised,
The light within — the light of perfectness —
Such as there is in Heaven.   The soul hath sunk
And perished like a light-house in the sea;
It is for God to raise it and rebuild.
　　GENIUS.   And his, thy son's, He will raise.   Since
　　　　with me,
I have shown him infinite wonders: we have oped
And scanned the golden scroll of Fate, wherein
Are writ, in God's own hand, all things which
　　　　happen.
There we have seen the record of his being —
His long temptation, sin, and suffering.
　　FESTUS.   And hear it, oh beloved and blessed
　　　　one!
Mine own salvation!
　　ANGEL.　　　　　　　God is great in love;
Infinite in His nature, power, and grace;
Creating, and redeeming, and destroying —
Infinite infinitely.   But in love —
Oh! it is the truth transcendent over all —

When thus to one poor spirit He gives His hand,
He seems to impart His own unboundedness
Of bliss.   We seem to **be hardly worth** destroying,
And much less saving ; **yet He loveth** each
As though all were His equal.
   Festus.   I know **all**
I have to go through henceforth, — all the **doubts**,
Passions of life, and woes ; but knowing them
Hinders them not ; **I bear** obeyingly ;.
And pine no more, as once when I looked **back**
And saw how life had balked, and foiled, and **fooled**
       me.
Fresh as a spouting **spring upon the hills**
My heart leaped out **to life ; it little thought**
Of all the vile **cares that would rill into it,**
And the low places it would **have to** go through, —
The drains, the **crossings, and the** mill-work after.
God hath **endowed me with a soul** that scorns life —
An **element over and above** the world's :
But **the price** one pays for pride is mountain-high,
There is a curse beyond the rack of death —
A woe, wherein God hath put out His strength —
A pain, past all **the** mad wretchedness we feel,
When the sacred secret hath flown out of **us,**
And the heart broken **open** by **deep** care, —
The curse of **a high spirit** famishing,
Because all **earth but sickens it.**
   Angel.   **Go, child !**
Fulfil thy fate !   Be — do — bear — and thank
      God !
To **me** it **seems as I had lived all ages**
Since I left earth ; **and thou art yet scarce man.**
   Festus.   **It was not, mother, that I** knew thy
      face ;
The luminous eclipse that **is on it now,**
Though it was fair on earth, **would have made it**
      strange
Even to one who knew as well as he loved thee ;
And if these time-tired eyes ever imaged thine,

It was but for a moment, and the sight
Passed; and my life was broken like a line
At the first word — but my heart cried out in me.
    ANGEL.   I knew thee well.   And now to earth
        again !
Go, son ! and say to all who once were mine —
I love them, and expect them.
    FESTUS.   Blessed one !
I will.
    ANGEL.   I charge thee, Genius, bear him safely.
    GENIUS.   Through light, and night, and all the
        powers of air,
I have a passport.
    ANGEL.   God be with thee, child !
    GENIUS.   Come !
    FESTUS.   I feel happier, better, nobler now.
See where she sits, and smiles, and points me out
To those who sit along with her.   Who are
The two ?
    GENIUS.   One is the mother of mankind,
And one the mother of the Man who saved
Mankind ; and she, thine own, the mother of
The last man of mankind — for thou art he.
    FESTUS.   Am I ?   It is enough : I have seen
        God.
    GENIUS.   God and His great idea, the universe,
Are over and above us.   Be the one
Worshipped, the other reverently proved.
Wilt sojourn for a time among the worlds,
And test their natures ?
    FESTUS.   Gladly.
    GENIUS.   Seek we, then,
All rareness and variety these worlds
Can offer, ere we reach thine orb.   Descend !
Now is the age of worlds.

Scene — *A Visit.*

FESTUS *and* HELEN.

HELEN.   Come **to the light, love !   Le me look**
      on thee !
Let me make sure I have thee.   Is it thou ?
Is this thy hand ?   Are these thy velvet lips, —
Thy lips so lovable ?   Nay, speak not yet !
For oft as I have dreamed of thee, it **was**
Thy speaking woke **me.   I** will dream no more.
Am I alive ?   And **do I really** look
Upon these soft and **sea-blue eyes of thine,**
Wherein I half believe **I** can espy
The riches of **the sea** ?   These dark rolled locks !
Oh God ! art **Thou not glad, too,** he **is** here ! —
Where hast **thou been so** long ?   Never to hear,
Never to **see, nor see one** who had seen thee —
Come, now, confess **it was** not kind to treat
Me in this manner.
      FESTUS.   I confess, my love,
But I have been where neither tongue, nor pen,
Nor hand could give thee token where I was ;
And seen, but 't is enough !   I see thee now.
I would rather look upon **thy** shadow there,
Than Heaven's bright **thrones** for ever.
      HELEN.   **Where** hast **been ?**
      FESTUS.   Say, **am I altered** ?
      HELEN.   Nowise.
      FESTUS.   It is well.
Then in the resurrection we may know
Each other.   I have been among the worlds,
Angels and spirits bodiless.
      HELEN.   Great God !
Can it be so ?
      FESTUS.   **It** is : — and that **both** here
And elsewhere.   When the stars come, thou shalt see

The track I travelled through the light of night;
Where I have been, and whence my visitors.
   HELEN.   And thou hast been with angels all the
      while,
And still dost love me?
   FESTUS.   Constantly as now.
But for the time I did devote my soul
To their divine society, I knew
Thou wouldst forgive, yet dared not trust myself
To see thee, or to pen one word, for fear
Thy love should overpower the plan conceived,
And acting, in my mind, of visiting
The spirits in their space-embosomed homes.
   HELEN.   Forgive thee! 'tis a deed which merits
      love.
And should I not be proud, too, who can say,
For me he left all angels?
   FESTUS.   I forethought
So thou wouldst say; but with an offering
Came I provided, even with a trophy
Of love angelic, given me for thee;
For angel bosoms know no jealousy.
   HELEN.   Show me.
   FESTUS.   It is of jewels I received
From one who snatched them from the richest
      wreck
Of matter ever made, the holiest
And most resplendent.
   HELEN.   Why, what could it be?
Jewels are baubles only; whether pearls
From the sea's lightless depths, or diamonds
Culled from the mountain's crown, or chrysolith,
Cat's eye, or moonstone, toys are they at best.
Jewels are not of all things in my sight
Most precious.
   FESTUS.   Nor in mine. It is in the use
Of which they may be made their value lies;
In the pure thoughts of beauty they call up,
And qualities they emblem. So in that

Thou wearest there, thy cross; — **to me** it is
Suggestive of bright thoughts and hopes in Him
Whose one great sacrifice availeth all,
Living and dead, **through** all Eternity.
Not to the **wanderer over southern** seas
Rises the constellation **of** the **Cross**
More lovelily o'er sky and **calm blue** wave,
Than does **to** me that bright one on thy breast.
As diamonds are purest of all things,
And but embodied light which **fire consumes**
And renders back to air, **that nought remains,** —
And as the cross is symbol **of our creed,**
So let that ornament signify **to thee**
The faith of Christ, **all purity, all light,**
Through fervency **resolving into Heaven.**
Each hath his cross, **fair lady, on his heart.**
Never may thine be heavier or darker
Than that now on thy breast, so light and bright,
Rising and falling with its bosom-swell.
    HELEN. I thank thee for that **wish, and for the**
       love
Which prompts **it** — the immeasurable love
I know is mine, **and** I with none would share.
Forgive me ; I have not yet felt my wings.
Now have I not been patient ? Let **me see**
My promised present.
    FESTUS.   **Look, then —they are here ;**
Bracelets **of chrysoprase.**
    HELEN.   **Most beautiful !**
    FESTUS. **Come, let me clasp them,** dearest, **on**
       thine arms ;
For these of those are worthy, and are named
In the foundation stones of the bright city,
Which is to be for the immortal saved,
Their last and blest abode ; and such their hue,
The golden green of paradisal plains
Which lie about it boundlessly, and more
Intensely tinted with the burning beauty
Of God's eye, which alone doth light that land,

Than our earth's cold grass-garment with the sun;
Though even in the bright, hot, blue-skied East,
Where he doth live the life of light and Heaven;
Where, o'er the mountains, at midday is seen
The morning star, and the moon tans at night
The cheek of careless sleeper.　Take them, love.
There are no nobler earthly ornaments
Than jewels of the city of the saved.
　　HELEN.　But how are these of that bright city?　I
Am eager for their history.
　　FESTUS.　　　　　　　　　　They are
Thereof prophetically, and have been —
What I will show thee presently, when I
Relate the story of the angel who
Gave them to me.
　　HELEN.　　　　　Well; I will wait till then,
Or any time thou choosest: 'tis enough
That I believe thee always; — but would know,
If not in me too curious to ask,
How came about these miracles?　Hast thou raised
The fiend of fiends, and made a compact dark,
Sealed with thy blood, symbolic of the soul,
Whereby all power is given thee for a time,
All means, all knowledge, to make more secure
Thy spirit's dread perdition at the end?
I of such awful stories oft have heard,
And the unlawful lore which ruins souls.
Myself have charms, foresee events in dreams;
Can prophesy, prognosticate, know well
The secret ties between many magic herbs
And mortal feelings, nor condemn myself
For knowing what is innocent; but thou!
Thy helps are mightier far and more obscure.
Was it with wand and circle, book and scull,
With rites forbid and backward-jabbered prayers,
In cross-roads or in churchyard, at full moon,
And by instruction of the ghostly dead,
That thou hast wrought these wonders, and attained
Such high transcendent powers and secrets?　Speak!

Or is man's mastery over spirits not
Of such a vile and vulgar consequence ?
  FESTUS. Were not my heart as guiltless of all
      mirth
As is the oracle of an extinct god
Of its priest-prompted answer, I might smile
To list such askings. Mind's command o'er mind,
Spirit's o'er spirit, is the clear effect
And natural action of an inward gift,
Given of God, whereby the incarnate soul
Hath power to pass free out of earth and death
To immortality and Heaven, and mate
With beings of a kind, condition, lot,
All diverse from his own. This mastery
Means but communion, the power to quit
Life's little globule here, and coalesce
With the great mass about us. For the rest,
To raise the Devil were an infant's task
To that of raising man. Why, every one
Conjures the Fiend from Hell into himself
When passion chokes or blinds him. Sin is Hell.
  HELEN. How dost thou bring a spirit to thee,
      Festus ?
  FESTUS. It is my will which makes it visible.
  HELEN. What are those like whom thou hast
      seen ?
  FESTUS.   They come,
The denizens of other worlds, arrayed
In diverse form and feature, mostly lovely ;
In limb and wing ethereal finer far
Than an ephemeris' pinion ; others, armed
With gleaming plumes, that might o'ercome an air
Of adamantine denseness, pranked with fire.
All are of different offices and strengths,
Powers, orders, tendencies, in like degrees
As men, with even more variety ;
Of different glories, duties, and delights.
Even as the light of meteor, satellite,
Planet and comet, sun, star, nebula,

Differ, and nature also, so do theirs.
With them is neither need, nor sex, nor age,
Nor generation, growth, decay, nor death;
Or none whom I have known; there may be such.
Mature they are created and complete,
Or seem to be.   Perfect from God they come.
Yet have they different degrees of beauty,
Even as strength and holy excellence.
Some seem of milder and more feminine
Nature than others, Beauty's proper sex,
Shown but by softer qualities of soul,
More lovable than awful, more devote
To deeds of individual piety,
And grace, than mighty missions fit to task
Sublimest spirits, or the toil intense
Of cultivating nations of their kind;
Or working out from the problem of the world
The great results of God, — result, sum, cause.
These ofttimes charged with delegated powers,
Formative or destructive; those, in chief,
Ordained to better and to beautify
Existence as it is; with careful love
To tend upon particular worlds or souls;
Warning and training whom they love, to tread
The soft and blossom-bordered, silvery paths,
Which lead and lure the soul to Paradise,
Making the feet shine which do walk on them;
While each doth God's great will alike, and both
With their whole nature's fulness love His works.
To love them lifts the soul to Heaven.

   HELEN.   Let me, then!
Whence come they?

   FESTUS.   Many of them come from orbs
Wherein the rudest matter is more worth
And fair than queenly gem; the dullest dust
Beneath their feet is rosy diamond : —
Others, direct from Heaven; but all in high
And serious love towards those to whom they come.
None but the blest are free to visit where

They choose.   The lost are slaves for ever; here
Never but on their Master's merciless
Business, nor elsewhere.   Still, **sometimes with
these**
Dark spirits have I held communion,
And in their soul's deep shadow, as **within**
A mountain cavern of the moon, conversed
With them, and **wormed** from them the gnawing
truth
Of **their extreme perdition;** marking oft
Nature revealed **by** torture, as a leaf
Unfolds itself in fire and writhes the while,
Burning, **yet unconsumed.   Others there are**
Come garlanded with flowers unwithering,
Or crowned with sunny jewels, clad in light,
And girded with the lightning, in their hands
Wands of **pure rays or** arrowy starbeams; **some**
Bright as **the sun self-lit,** in **stature** tall,
Strong, straight and splendid as the golden reed
Whereby **the** height, and length, and breath, **and**
depth,
Of the descendant city of the skies,
In which God sometime shall make glad with man,
Were measured by the angel; (the same reed
Wherewith our Lord **was** mocked, that angel found
Close by the Cross and took; God made it gold,
And now it makes the sceptre of His Son
Over all worlds; **the** sole bright rule of Heaven,
The measure **of immortal life, the** scale
Of power, **love, bliss, and** glory infinite) :—
Some gorgeous and gigantic, who with wings
Wide as the wings of armies in the field
Drawn out for death, sweep **over** Heaven, **and**
eyes
Deep, dark as sea-worn caverns, with a torch
At **the** end, far back, glaring.   Some with wings
Like an unfainting rainbow, studded round
With stones of every hue and excellence,
Writ **o'er** with mystic **words which** none may **read,**

But those to whom their spiritual state
Gives correlative meaning, fit thereto.
Some of these visit me in my dreams; with some
Have I made one in visions, in their own
Abodes of brightness, blessedness, and power:
And know moreover I shall joy with them,
Ere long their sacred guest, through ages yet
To come, in worlds not now perhaps create,
As they have been mine here: and some of them
In unimaginable splendors I
Have walked with through their winged worlds of
        light,
Double and triple particolored suns,
And systems circling each the other, clad
In tints of light and air, whereto this earth
Hath nothing like, and man no knowledge of: —
Orbs heaped with mountains, to the . which ours
        are
Mere grave-mounds, and their skies flowered with
        stars,
Violet, rose or pearl-hued, or soft blue,
Golden or green, the light now blended, now
Alternate; many moons and planets, full,
Crescent, or gibbous-faced, illumining
In periodic and intricate beauty,
At once those strange and most felicitous skies.

  HELEN. How I should love to visit other worlds,
Or see an angel!
    FESTUS.   Wilt thou now?
    HELEN.   I dare not.
Not now at least. I am not in the mood.
Ere I behold a spirit I would pray.
  FESTUS. Light as a leaf thy step, or arrowy
Footing of breeze upon a waveless pool;
Sudden and soft, too, like a waft of light,
The beautiful immortals come to me;
Oh, ever lovely, ever welcome they!
  HELEN. But why art thou, of all men, favored
        thus?

To say there is a mystery in this,
Or aught, is only to confess God.   Speak!
   Festus.   It is God's will **that** I possess **this**
      power,
Thus to **attract** great spirits **to mine** own,
As **steel** magnetically charged draws steel;
Himself the magnet of the universe,
Round whom all spirits tremble, and towards whom
All tend.
   Helen.   If **as thou sayest, it is good :—**
May it be an immortal **good to thee.**
   Festus.   There is no **keeping** back the **power**
     we have.
He hath no power **who hath not power to use.**
Some of these bodies **whom I** speak **of are**
Pure spirits, other bodies soulical:
For spirit is to soul as wind **to air.**
They give me all I **seek, and at** a wish
Would furnish treasures, thrones, or palaces;
But all these things have I eschewed, and chosen
Command of mind alone, and of the **world**
Unbodied **and** all-lovely.
   Helen.   **Is not this**
Pleasure too much for mortal **to be good?**
   Festus.   All pleasure **is with Thee, God! else-**
     where, **none.**
Not silver-ceiled **hall nor golden** throne,
Set thick **with priceless gems, as** Heaven **with stars,**
Or the high **heart of youth with its bright hopes; —**
Nor marble **gleaming like the white moonlight,**
As 't were **an apparition of** a palace
Inlaid with light as is a waterfall; —
Not rainbow-pinions colored **like** yon cloud,
The sun's broad banner o'er **his** western tent,
Can match the bright imaginings of a child
Upon the glories of his coming years;
How equal, then, the full-assured faith
Of him to whom the Saviour hath vouchsafed
The Heaven **of His** bosom?   What can tempt

In its performance equal to that promise?
My soul stands fast to Heaven as doth a star;
And only God can move it who moves all.
There are **who might have** soared to **what I**
		spurned;
And like to heavenly orders human souls;
Some fitted most for contemplation, some
For action, these for thrones, **and** those for wheels.
    HELEN.   Tell me **what they** discourse upon,
		these angels?
     FESTUS. **They speak of what is past or coming,**
		less
Of present things **or** actions. Some say **most**
About the future, others of the gone,
The dim traditions of Eternity,
Or Time's first golden moments. One there was —
From whose sweet lips elapsed as from a well,
Continuously, truths which made my soul
As they sank in it, fertile with rich thoughts —
Spake to **me** oft of Heaven, and our talk
Was of divine things always — angels, Heaven,
Salvation, immortality, and **God;**
The different states of **spirits and the kinds**
Of **Being in all** orbs, **or physical,**
Or **intellectual.** I never **tired**
Preferring questions, **but at each response**
My soul drew back, sealike, **into its depths**
To urge another charge on him. **This** spirit
Came to me daily for a long, long **time,**
Whene'er I prayed his presence. **Many a world**
He knew right well which man's eye **never yet**
Hath marked, **nor** ever may mark while on earth;
Yet grew **his** knowledge every time he came.
His thoughts **all** great and solemn and serene,
Like the immensest features of an orb,
Whose eyes **are** blue seas, and whose clear broad
		brow,
Some cultured continent, came ever round
From **truth to** truth — day bringing as they came.

He was to me an all-explaining spirit,
Teaching divine things by analogy
With mortal and material.   Thus of God,
He showed, as the three primal rays make one
Sole beam of Light, so the three Persons make
One God; neither without the other is.
However bright or beautiful itself
The theme he touched, he made it more so by
His own light, like a fire-fly on a flower.
And one of all I knew the most of, yet
The least can say of him ; for full oft
Our thoughts drown speech, like to a foaming force,
Which thunders down the echo it creates.
Yet must I somewhat tell of him.   He was
The spirit evil of the universe,
Impersonate.   Oh, strange and wild to know!
Perdition and destruction dwelt in him,
Like to a pair of eagles in one nest.
Hollow and wasteful as a whirlwind was
His soul; his heart as earthquake, and engulphed
World upon world.   In him they disappeared
As might a morsel in a lion's maw,
The world which met him rolled aside to let him
Pass on his piercing path.   His eyeballs burned
Revolving lightnings like a world on fire ;
Their very night was fatal as the shade
Of Death's dark valley.   And his space-spread
        wings —
Wide as the wings of Darkness when she rose
Scowling, and backing upwards, as the sun,
Giant of Light, first donned his burning crown,
Gladdening all Heaven with his inaugural smile, —
Were stained with the blood of many a starry world:
Yea, I have seen him seize upon an orb,
And cast it careless into worldless space,
As I might cast a pebble in the sea.
His might upon this earth was wondrous most.
He stood a match for mountains.   Ocean's depths
He clove unto their rock-bed, as a sword,

Through blood and muscle to the central bone,
With one swoop of his arm.   His brow was pale —
Pale as the life-blood of the undying worm
Which writhes around its frame of vital fire.
His voice blew like the desolating gust
Which strips the trees, and strews the earth with
      death.
His words were ever like a wheel of fire,
Rolling and burning this way now, now that:
Now whirling forth a blinding beam, now soft
And deep 'as Heaven's own luminous blue — and
      now
Like to a conqueror's chariot wheel they came,
Sodden with blood and slow, revolving death:
And every tone fell on the ear and heart,
Heavy and harsh and startling, like the first
Handful of mould cast on the coffined dead,
As though he claimed them his.
      LUCIFER *entering.*   Dost recognize
The portrait, lady?
      HELEN.   Festus! who is this?
What portrait? —
      FESTUS. `Wherefore comest thou?   Did I not
Claim privacy one evening?
      LUCIFER.   Why, indeed —
I simply called, as I was on my way
To Jupiter — and he 's a mouthful, mind ; —
To keep the proverbs, too, in countenance.
Any commands for our planetary friends?
I go.   Make my excuses!   *Goes.*
      FESTUS.   A mistake,
Dearest; but rectified. [*Apart.*]   And he is gone!
Hell hath its own again.   Some sorrow chills
Ever the spirit, like a cloudlet nursed
In the star-giant's bosom.
      HELEN.   Tell me, love,
More of these angels!
      FESTUS.   There was one I loved
Of those immortals, of a lofty air,

Dimly divine and sad, and side by side
Him whom I spake of first she oft would stand
With her fair form — shadow illuminate —
Like to the dark moon in the young one's arms.
She never murmured at the doom which made
The sorrow that contained her, as the air
Infolds the orb whereon we dwell, but spake
Of God's will alway as most good and wise.
She had but little pleasure; but her all,
Such as it was, was in devising plans
Of bliss to come, or in the tales of Time
And the sweet early earth.   She was, in truth,
Our earth's own angel.   Ofttimes would she dwell
With long and luminous sweetness on her theme,
Unwearying, unpausing, as a world.
The sun would rise and set; the soul-like moon,
In passive beauty and receptive light, —
Absorbing inspiration from the sun,
As doth from God His prophet ceaselessly —
She too would rise and set; and the far stars,
The third estate of Light, complete the round
Of the divine day; — still our angel spake,
And still I listened to the eloquent tongue
Which e'en on earth retained the tone of Heaven.
The shadow of a cloud upon a lake,
O'er which the wind hath all day held his breath,
Is not more calm and fair than her dear face —
So sweetly sad and so consolingly,
When she spake even on the end of earth.
Save that her eye grew darker, and her brow
Brighter with thought, as with galactic light
Mid Heaven when clearest, — at such times, not I
Had known that earth were dearer unto her
Than other of the visitants divine,
Which hallow oft mine hours; — save, too, that
        then,
As though to touch but on that topic had,
Torpedo-like, numbed thought, she would straight
        cease

All converse suddenly, and kneel and seem
Inwardly praying with much power, — rise,
And vanish into Heaven.   My mind is full
Of stories she hath told me of our world.
No word an angel utters lose I ever.
One I will tell thee now.
    HELEN.   Do! let me hear!
Thy talk is the **sweet extract** of all **speech,**
And **holds** mine ear in **blissful slavery.**
    FESTUS.   'Twas on **a lovely summer** afternoon,
Close by the grassy marge **of** a deep **tarn,**
Nigh halfway up a mountain, that we **stood,**
I and the angel, when she told me this.
Above us rose the gray rocks, by our side
Forests of pines, and the bright breaking wavelets
Came crowding, dancing to the brink, like thoughts
Unto our lips.   Before us shone the sun.
The angel waved her hand ere she began,
As bidding earth **be** still.   The birds ceased sing-
       ing
And the trees breathing, **and the** lake smoothed
       down
Each shining wrinkle, and the wind drew off.
Time leaned him o'er his scythe **and,** listening,
       wept.
The circling world reined in her lightning pace
A moment; Ocean hushed his snow-maned **steeds,**
And **a** cloud hid the sun, as does the face
A meditative hand: then spake she thus: —
Scarce had the sweet **song** of the morning stars,
Which rang through **space** at the first sign of life
Our earth gave, springing from the lap of God
On to her orbit, when from Heaven
Came down **a** white-winged **host; and in** the east,
Where Eden's Pleasance **was,** first furled their
       wings,
Alighting like **to** snowflakes.   **There they** built,
Out of the riches of the soil **around,**
A house to God.   There were the ruby rocks,

And there, in blocks, the quarried diamonds lay;
Opal and emerald mountain, amethyst,
Sapphire and chrysoprase, and jacinth stood
With **the** still action of a star, all light,
Like sea-based icebergs, blinding.   These, with
        tools
Tempered in Heaven, **the band** angelic wrought,
And raised, and fitted, having first laid down
The deep foundations of the holy dome
On bright and beaten gold; and all the **while**
A song of glory hovered round the work
Like rainbow round a fountain.   Day and **night**
Went **on** the hallowed labor till 't was done.
And yet but thrice the sun set, and but thrice
The moon arose; so quick is work divine.
Tower, and roof, and pinnacle, without,
Were solid diamond.   Within, the dome
Was eyeblue sapphire, **sown** with gold-bright stars
And clustering constellations; the wide floor
All emerald, earthlike, veined with gold and silver,
Marble and mineral of every hue
And marvellous quality, the meanest thing,
Where all things were magnificent, was gold, —
The plainest.   The high altar there was shaped
Out of one ruby heartlike.   Columned round
With alabaster pure was all.   And now
So high and bright **it** shone in the midday light,
It could be seen from Heaven.   Upon their thrones
The sun-eyed angels hailed it, and there **rose**
A hurricane of blissfulness in Heaven,
Which **echoed for** a thousand years.   One **dark,**
One solitary **and** foreseeing thought,
Passed, like a planet's transit o'er the sun,
Across the brow of God; but soon he smiled
Towards earth, and that smile did consecrate
The temple to Himself.   And they who built
Bowed themselves down and worshipped in its
        walls.
High on the front were writ these words — to God

The heavenly built this for the earthly ones,
That in his worship both might mix on earth,
As afterward they hoped to do in Heaven.
Had man stood good in Eden this had been :
He fell and Eden vanished.   The bright place
Reared by the angels of all precious things,
For the joint worship of the sons of earth
And Heaven, fell with him, on the very day
He should have met God and His angels there —
The very day he disobeyed and joined
The host of death black-bannered.   Eden fell;
The groves and grounds, which God the Lord's
        own feet
Had hallowed ; the all-hued and odorous bowers
Where angels wandered, wishing them in Heaven ;
The trees of life and knowledge — trees of death
And madness, as they proved to man — all fell ;
And that bright fane fell first.   No death-doomed
        eye
Gazed on its glory.   Earthquakes gulped it down.
The Temple of the Angels, vast enough
To hold all nations worshipping at once,
Lay in its grave ; the cherubs' flaming swords
The sole sad torches of its funeral.
Till at the flood, when the world's giant heart
Burst like a shell, it scattered east and west,
And far and wide, among less noble ruins,
The fragments of that angel-builded fane,
Which was in Eden, and of which all stones
That now are precious, were ; and still shall be,
Gathered again unto a happier end,
In the pure City of the Son of God,
And temple yet to be rebuilt in Zion ;
Which, though once overthrown, and once again
Torn down to its foundations, in the quick
Of earth, shall soul-like yet re-rise from ruin —
High, holy, happy, stainless as a star,
Imperishable as eternity.
— The angel ended ; and the winds, waves, clouds,

The sun, the woods, the merry birds went on
As theretofore, in brightness, strength and music.
One scarce could think that earth at all had fallen,
To look upon her beauty.   If the brand
Of sin were on her brow, it was surely hid
In natural art from every eye but God's.
All things seemed innocence and happiness.
I was all thanks.   And look! the angel said,
Take these, and give to one thou lovest best:
Mine own hands saved from them the shining ruin
Whereof I have late told thee; and she gave
What now are greenly glowing on thine arms.
Ere I could answer, she was up, star-high!
Winging her way through Heaven!

HELEN.   How shall I thank thee
Enough, or that kind angel who hath made
The gift to me dear doubly?   I shall be
Afraid almost to wear them, but would not
Part with them for the treasures of all worlds.
How show my thanks?

FESTUS.   Love me as now, dear beauty!
Present or absent always, and 't will be
More than enough of recompense for me.

HELEN.   Hast met that angel late-while?

FESTUS.   I have not.
Yet oft methinks I see her, catch a glimpse
Of her sun-circling pinions or bright feet,
Which fitter seem for rainbows than for earth,
Or Heaven's triumphal arch, more firm and pure
Than the world's whitest marble;—see her seated
       oft
On some high snowy cloud-cliff, harp in hand,
Singing the sun to sleep as down he lays
His head of glory on the rocking deep:
And so sing thou to me.

HELEN.   There, rest thyself. [*Sings.*

     Oh! not the diamond starry bright
        Can so delight my view,

As doth the moonstone's changing light
  And gleamy glowing hue;
Now **blue as** Heaven, and then **anon**
  As golden as the **sun,**
It hath a charm in every change —
  In brightening, darkening, one.

And so **with** beauty, **so with love,**
  And everlasting mind;
It takes a tint from Heaven **above,**
  And shines as **it** 's inclined;
Or from the sun, or towards the **sun,**
  With blind or brilliant eye,
And only lights as it reflects
  The life-light of the sky.

He sleeps! The fate of many a gracious moral
This, to be stranded **on a** drowsy ear.

Scene — *Home.* **Festus,** *and* **Helen** *at her*
Piano. — *Dusk.*

Helen. I cannot live **away** from thee. How
  can
A flower live **without its root?**
Festus. I, too,
Must love **or die.**
Helen. But I must have. Attend!
I am to say and do **just** as I please;
I may command thee, may I? that I **will.**
Festus. I love to be enslaved. Oh! I would
  rather
Obey thee, beauty! than rule **men by** millions.
Helen. Near, as afar, I will have love the
  same —
With a bright sameness, **like this diamond,**
Which, wherever the **light** be, shines like **bright.**
And thou shalt say all sorts of pretty things
To **me;** mind, **to me** only: write love-songs

About me, and I will sing them to myself;
Perhaps to thee, sometime, as it were now,
If I should happen to be very kind.

    FESTUS.   Sing now!

    HELEN.   No!

    FESTUS.   Tyrant! I will banish thee.

    HELEN. Nay, if to sing and play would please
        thee, I
Would die to music. It was very wrong
To say I would deny thee any thing;
But be not angry with me : for though God
Forgave me, I could ne'er forgive myself,
If I brought sorrow to thee, could I love?

    FESTUS. As thou art empress of my bosom, No!

    HELEN. Nought fear I but an unkind word
        from thee.
Dark death may frighten children, Hell the wretch
Who feels that he deserves it ; but for me,
I know I cannot do nor say aught worthy
Of the pure pain a frown of thine can cause,
Or a cold, careless look. No! never frown.
If I do wrong, forgive me, or I die ;
And thou wilt then be wretcheder than I ; —
The unforgiving than the unforgiven.

    FESTUS. I do absolve thee, beauty, of all faults,
Past, present, or to come.

    HELEN.   Well, that will do.
What was I saying ? I love this instrument,
It speaks, it thinks — nay, I could kiss it : look !
There are three things I love half killingly ; —
Thee lastly, and this next, and myself first.

    FESTUS. Thou art a silly, tiresome thing, and yet
I never weary of thee ; but could gaze,
Sick with excess and not satiety,
Upon thy countenance, with the serious joy
With which we eye and eye the unbounded space
Which is the visible attribute of God,
Who makes all things within Himself ; and thus
It is the Heaven we hope for, and can find

No point from which to take its altitude;
For the Infinite is upwards, and above
The highest thing created — upwards aye:
So I could, thinking on thy face, believe
An infinite expression, heightening still
The longer that I thought, and leaving thee,
Coming to thee, or being with thee, — love!
 HELEN. I am so happy when with thee.
 FESTUS.   And I.
They tell us virtue lies in self-denial.
My virtue is indulgence. I was born
To gratify myself unboundedly,
So that I wronged none else. These arms were
   given me
To clasp the beautiful, and cleave the wave;
These limbs to leap and wander where I will;
These eyes to look on every thing without
Effort; these ears to list my loved one's voice;
These lips to be divinized by her kiss:
And every sense, pulse, passion, power, to be
Swoln into sunny ripeness.
 HELEN.   Virtue is one
With nature, or 't is nothing: it is love.
 FESTUS. I come fresh from thee every time we
   meet,
Steeped in the still sweet dew of thy soft beauty,
Like earth at day-dawn, lifting up her head
Out of her sleep, starwatched, to face the sun —
So I, to front the world, on leaving thee.
Oh! there is inspiration in thy look;
Poesie, prophecy. Come hither, love;
The evening air is sweet.
 HELEN.   It comes on us
Fresher and clearer through these dewy vine-
   leaves,
Fit for the forehead of the young wine-god.
 FESTUS. A large, red egg of light the moon lies
   like
On the dark moor-hill, and now, rising slow,

Beams on the clear flood, smilingly intent,
Like a fair face, which **loves** to look on itself,
Saying —' there is **no** wonder that **men love me,**
For I am beautiful!'— **as I** heard thee.
    HELEN. **It was not right to overhear** me that.
    FESTUS. **'T was very wrong to do** what I could
        not help ;
But vanity speaks **out.**
    HELEN.   Well, **I don't mind ;**
I never knew **that I was as I am**
Till **others told me.**
    FESTUS.   Now were **soon enough.**
    HELEN. **Ah, nothing** comes **to us too soon but**
        sorrow.
    FESTUS. For all were happiness, if all **might live**
Long, **or** die soon, enough : for even **us.**
    HELEN. Dost not remember, when, **the other eve,**
Thy friend the student **called,** there was **a tale**
Upon **thy tongue** he interrupted ?
    FESTUS.   Was there ?—
    HELEN. **A** tale out **of the poets,** about love,
And **happiness,** and sorrow, and such things.
    FESTUS. But I forget such things when thou art
        by.
Besides, I asked **him here again, to-night,**
Here, at this hour ; **and he is punctual.**
    HELEN. In **truth, then, I despair of** hearing it.
He keeps **his word** relentlessly. **With not**
More pride an **Indian** shows his **foeman's scalp**
Than he **his watch for** punctuality.
    FESTUS. **But tales** of love **are far more readily**
Made than remembered.
    HELEN.   Tell-tale, **make** one, then.
    FESTUS. **Love is** the art of hearts and hear. of
        arts.
Conjunctive looks and interjectional sighs
Are its vocabulary's greater half.
Well, then, my story says, there was **a pair**
Of lovers, once —

HELEN.   Once! nay, how singular!
FESTUS.   But where they lived, indeed, I quite
          forget;—
Say anywhere—say here: **their** names were—I
Forget those, too; say any one's, say ours.
    HELEN.   Most probable, most pertinent, so far!
    FESTUS.   **The** lady **was,** of course, most beautiful
And made her lover do just **as she** pleased;
And consequently he did very **wrong.**
They met, sang, walked, **talked folly, just as all**
Such couples do, adored **each other; thought,**
Spoke, wrote, dreamed of and for **nought on earth**
Except themselves; and so on.
    HELEN.   Pray proceed!—
    FESTUS.   That's all;
    HELEN.   **Oh,** no!
    FESTUS.   Well, thus the tale **ends;** stay!
No, I cannot remember nor invent.
    HELEN.   **Do think!**
    FESTUS.   **I can't.**
    HELEN.   **Oh then, I** don't like that
'Tis not in earnest.
    FESTUS.   Well, **in earnest, then.**
She did **but look** upon **him, and his blood**
Blushed deeper even from **his inmost** heart;
For at each glance of those sweet eyes a soul
Looked forth as from the azure gates of **Heaven;**
She laid her finger on him, and he felt
As might a formless mass of marble feel
While feature after feature of a god
Were being wrought from **out** of it.   She spake,   ·
And his love-wildered and idolatrous soul
Clung to the airy music of her words,
Like a bird **on** a bough, high swaying in the wind.
He looked upon **her** beauty **and** forgot,
As in a sense of drowning, all things else;
And right and wrong seemed one, seemed nothing;
          she
Was beauty, and that beauty every thing.

He looked upon her as the sun on earth:
Until, like him, he gazed himself away
From Heaven so doing! till he even wept,—
Wept on her bosom as a storm-charged cloud
Weeps itself out upon a hill, and cried—
I, too, could look on thee until I wept,—
Blind me with kisses! let me look no longer;
Or change the action of thy loveliness,
Lest long same-seemingness should send me mad!—
Blind me with kisses; I would ruin sight
To give its virtue **to** thy lips, whereon
I would die now, or ever live; and she,
Soft as a feather-footed cloud **on** Heaven,
While her sad face grew bright **like** night with stars,
Would **turn** her brow to his, and both be happy;—
Numbered among the constellations they!—
Then as tired wanderer, snow-blinded, sinks
And swoons upon the swelling drift, and dies,
So on her dazzling bosom would he lay
His famished **lips,** and end their travels there,
Oh, happy they! not he would go to Heaven,
Not, though he might that moment.

    HELEN.   **Nor I now.**
    FESTUS.   Helen, my love!
    HELEN.   Yes, I am here.
    FESTUS.   It has
Been such a day as **that, thou** knowest, when first
I said I loved thee; **that long,** sunny day
We passed upon the waters—heeding nought,
Seeing nought but each other.
    HELEN.   **I remember.**
The only wise thing that I ever did—
The only good, was to love thee, and therefore
I would have no one else as wise as I.
Didst thou not say that student would be here?
    FESTUS.   I think I hear him every minute come.
    HELEN.   It is not kind. We should be more alone.
There was **a** time thou wouldst have no one else.
    FESTUS.   Am **I** not with thee all day?

HELEN.   Yes, I know;
But often and often thou art thinking not
Of me.   •
    FESTUS.   My good child!—
    HELEN.   Well, I know thou lovest me;
And so I cannot bear thee to think, speak,
Or be with any but me.
    FESTUS.   Then I will not.
    HELEN.   Oh, thou wouldst promise me the clock
        round.   Now,
Promise me this — that I shall never die,
And I 'll believe thee when I am dead — not till.
But let it pass.   I am at peace with thee;
And pardon thee, and give thee leave to live.
    FESTUS.   Magnanimous!
    HELEN.   ʼ When earth, and Heaven, and all
Things seem so bright and lovely for our sakes,
It is a sin not to be happy.   See,
The moon is up, it is the dawn of night.
Stands by her side one bold, bright, steady star —
Star of her heart, and heir to all her light,
Whereon she looks so proudly mild and calm,
As though she were the mother of that star,
And knew he was a chief sun in his sphere,
But by her side, in the great strife of lights
To shine to God, he had filially failed,
And hid his arrows and his bow of beams.
Mother of stars! the Heavens look up to thee.
They shine the brighter but to hide thy waning ·
They wait and wane for thee to enlarge thy beauty ,
They give thee all their glory night by night;
Their number makes not less thy loneliness
Nor loveliness.
    FESTUS.   Heaven's beauty grows on us;
And when the elder worlds have ta'en their seats,
Come the divine ones, gathering one by one,   ·
And family by family, with still
And holy air, into the house of God —
The house of light He hath builded for Himself—

And worship Him in silence and in sadness,
Immortal and immovable.   And there,
Night after night, they meet to worship God.
For us this witness of the worlds is given,
That we may add ourselves to their great glory,
And worship with them.   They are there for lights
To light us on our way through Heaven to God;
And we, too, have the power of light in us.
Ye stars, how bright ye shine to night; mayhap
Ye are the resurrection of the worlds, —
Glorified globes of light !   Shall ours be like ye ?
Nay, but it is ! this wild, dark earth of ours,
Whose face is furrowed like a losing gamester's,
Is shining round, and bright, and smooth in air,
Millions of miles off.   Not a single path
Of thought I tread, but that it leads to God.
And when her time is out, and earth again
Hath travailed with the divine dust of man,
Then the world's womb shall open, and her sons
Be born again, all glorified immortals.
And she, their mother, purified by fire,
Shall sit her down in Heaven, a bride of God,
And handmaid of the ever-being One.
Our earth is learning all accomplishments
To fit her for her bridehood.
   HELEN.   He is here.
   FESTUS.   Welcome.
   STUDENT.   I thought the night was beautiful,
But find the in-door scene still lovelier.
   HELEN.   Ah! all is beautiful where beauty is.
   STUDENT.   Night hath made many bards; she
       is so lovely.
For it is beauty maketh poesie,
As from the dancing eye comes tears of light.
Night hath made many bards; she is so lovely.
And they have praised her to her starry face
So long, that she hath blushed and left them, often.
When first and last we met, we talked on studies :
Poetry only I confess is mine,

And is the only thing I think or read of: —
Feeding my soul upon the soft, and sweet,
And delicate imaginings of song;
For as nightingales do upon glowworms feed,
So poets live upon the living light
Of nature and of beauty; they love light.
    FESTUS.   But poetry is not confined to books.
For the creative spirit which thou seekest
Is in thee, and about thee; yea, it hath
God's everywhereness.
    STUDENT.   Truly. It was for this
I sought to know thy thoughts, and hear the course
Thou wouldst lay out for one who longs to win
A name among the nations.
    FESTUS.   First of all,
Care not about the name, but bind thyself,
Body and soul, to nature, hiddenly.
Lo, the great march of stars from earth to earth,
Through Heaven. The earth speaks inwardly
      alone.
Let no man know thy business, save some friend, —
A man of mind, above the run of men;
For it is with all men and with all things.
The bard must have a kind, courageous heart, .
And natural chivalry to aid the weak.
He must believe the best of every thing;
Love all below, and worship all above.
All animals are living hieroglyphs.
The dashing dog, and stealthy-stepping cat, [more
Hawk, bull, and all that breathe, mean something
To the true eye than their shapes show; for all
Were made in love, and made to be beloved.
Thus must he think as to earth's lower life,
Who seeks to win the world to thought and love,
As doth the bard, whose habit is all kindness
To every thing.
    HELEN.   I love to hear of such. ·
Could we but think with the intensity
We love with, we might do great things, I think.

FESTUS. Kindness is wisdom. There is **none** in life
But needs it and may learn; eye-reasoning man,
And spirit unassisted, unobscured.
STUDENT. Go on, I pray. I came to be informed.
Thou knowest my ambition, and I joy
To feel thou feedest it with purest food.
FESTUS. I cannot tell thee all I feel; and **know**
But little save myself, and am not ashamed
To say, that I have studied my own life,
And know it is like to a tear-blistered letter,
Which holdeth fruit **and** proof of **deeper** feeling
Than the poor pen can utter, or the eye
Discover; and that often my heart's thoughts
Will rise and shake my breast, **as** madmen shake
The stanchions of their dungeons, and howl **out.**
HELEN. But thou **wast** telling **us** of poesie,
And the kind nature-hearted bards.
FESTUS. **I was.**
I **knew** one **once** — he was a friend of mine;
I **knew him well**; his mind, habits, and works,
Taste, temper, temperament, and every thing;
Yet with as kind a heart as ever beat,
He was no sooner made than marred. Though young,
He wrote amid the ruins of his heart;
They were his throne and theme; — like some **lone** king,
Who tells the **story of the land he lost,**
And how **he lost it.**
STUDENT. Tell **us more of him.**
HELEN. **Nay,** but **it** saddens thee.
FESTUS. 'Tis like enough;
We slip away like shadows into shade;
We end, and make **no** mark we had begun;
We come to nothing, like a pure intent.
When we have hoped, sought, striven, and lost our aim,
Then the truth fronts us, beaming out of darkness,

Like a white brow, through its overshadowing
        hair—
As though the day were overcast, my Helen!
But I was speaking of my friend. He was
Quick, generous, simple, obstinate in end,
High-hearted from his youth; his spirit rose
In many a glittering fold and gleamy crest,
Hydra-like to its hinderance; mastering all,
Save one thing — love, and that out-hearted him.
Nor did he think enough, till it was over,
How bright a thing he was breaking, or he would
Surely have shunned it, nor have let his life
Be pulled to pieces like a rose by a child;
And his heart's passions made him oft do that
Which made him writhe to think on what he had
        done,
And thin his blood by weeping at a night.
If madness wrought the sin, the sin wrought mad-
        ness,
And made a round of ruin. It is sad
To see the light of beauty wane away,
Know eyes are dimming, bosom shrivelling, feet
Losing their spring, and limbs their lily roundness;
But it is worse to feel our heart-spring gone,
To lose hope, care not for the coming thing,
And feel all things go to decay with us,
As 'twere our life's eleventh month : and yet
All this he went through young.
    HELEN.   Poor soul! I should
Have loved him for his sorrows.
    FESTUS.   It is not love
Brings sorrow, but love's objects.
    STUDENT.   Then he loved.
    FESTUS. I said so. I have seen him when he
        hath had
A letter from his lady dear, he blessed
The paper that her hand had travelled over,
And her eye looked on, and would think he saw
Gleams of that light she lavished from her eyes

Wandering amid the **words of** love there traced,
Like glowworms among **beds** of flowers.   He seemed
To bear with being but because she loved him,
She was the sheath wherein his soul had rest,
As hath a **sword** from **war:** and he at night
Would solemnly and singularly curse
Each minute that he had not thought of **her.**
  HELEN. **Now that was** like a lover! **and she**
    loved
Him, and him **only.**
  FESTUS.   **Well, perhaps it was so.**
But he could **not restrain his heart, but loved**
In that voluptuous purity of taste
Which dwells on beauty coldly, and yet kindly,
As **night-dew,** whensoe'er he met with beauty.
  HELEN.   **It** was a pity, that inconstancy —
If she he loved were but as good **and** fair
As he **was worthy of.**
  STUDENT.   It was **his way.**
  FESTUS.   There **is a** dark and bright to every
    thing;
To every thing but beauty such as thine,
And that is all bright. If a fault in him,
'T was one which made him do the sweetest wrongs
Man ever did.   And yet a whisper went
That **he did** wrong: and if **that** whisper **had**
Echo in **him or** not, it **mattered** little;
Or right **or** wrong, he were **alike unhappy.**
Ah me! **ah me!** that there **should be so much**
To call **up love, so** little **to delight!**
The best enjoyment **is half** disappointment
To that we mean **or would** have in this world.
And there were many strange and sudden lights
Beckoned him towards **them;** they were wreckers,
    lights:
But he shunned these, and righted when she rose,
Moon of his life, that ebbed and flowed with her.
A sea of sorrow struck him, but he held
On; dashed all sorrow from him as a bark

Spray from her bow bounding; he lifted **up**
His head, and the deep ate his shadow merely.
   HELÈN.   A poet not in love is out at sea;
He must have a lay-figure.
   FESTUS.   I meant not
To screen, but to describe this friend of mine.
   HELEN.   Describe the lady, too; of course she was
Above all **praise and all** comparison.
   FESTUS. **Why, true.** Her **heart was all hu-
      manity,**
Her soul all **God's**; in spirit **and in** form,
Like fair. **Her** cheek had the pale pearly pink
Of seashells, the world's sweetest tint, as though
She lived, one half might deem, on roses sopped
In silver dew; she spake as with the voice
Of spheral harmony which greets the soul
When at the hour of death the saved one knows
His sister angels near; **her eye** was as
The golden pane the setting **sun** doth just
Imblaze; which shows, till Heaven comes down
      again,
All other lights but grades **of** gloom; her dark,
Long, rolling locks **were as** a stream the slave
Might search for **gold, and** searching **find.**
   HELEN.   **Enough!—**
I have her picture perfect;—quite **enough.**
   STUDENT.   What were his griefs?
   FESTUS.   He who hath most of heart
Knows most of sorrow; not a thing he saw
Nor did, but was to him, at times, a woe;
At times indifferent, at times **a** joy.
Folly and sin and memory **make** a curse
Wherewith the future **fires may** vie in vain
The sorrows of the soul are graver still.
   STUDENT. **Where and when did he** study? Did
    . he mix
Much with the world, or was he a recluse?
   FESTUS. He had no times of study, and **no
    place;**

All places and all times to him were one.
His soul was like the wind-harp, which he loved,
And sounded only when the spirit blew.
Sometimes **in** feasts and follies, for he **went**
Life-like through all **things; and his** thoughts **then**
    rose
Like sparkles in the bright wine, brighter still.
Sometimes in dreams, and then the shining words
Would **wake** him in the dark before his face.
All things talked thoughts to him.   The sea **went**
    mad,
And the wind whined as 't were in pain, to show
Each one his meaning ; and the awful sun
Thundered his thoughts into **him** ; and at night
The stars would whisper theirs, the moon sigh hers.
The spirit speaks all tongues and understands;
Both God's and angel's, man's and all dumb things,
Down to an insect's inarticulate hum
And an inaudible organ.   And it was
The spirit spake to him of every thing;
And with the moony eyes like those we see,
Thousands on thousands, crowding air in dreams,
Looked into him its mighty meanings, till
He felt the power fulfil him, as a cloud
In every fibre feels the forming wind.
He spake the world's one tongue ; in earth **and**
    Heaven
There is but one, it is the word **of truth.**
To him **the eye** let out **its hidden** meaning ;
And young and old made their hearts over to **him** ;
And thoughts were told to him as unto none
Save one who heareth said and unsaid, **all.**
And his heart held these as **a** grate its gleeds,
Where others warm them.
   Student.   I would I had known him.
   Festus.   All things were inspiration unto him ;
Wood, wold, hill, field, sea, city, solitude,
And crowds, and streets, and man where'er he was;
And the blue eye of God which is above us ;

Brook-bounded pine spinnies, where spirits flit;
And haunted pits the rustic hurries by,
Where cold wet ghosts sit ringing jingling bells;
Old orchards' leaf-roofed aisles, and red cheeked
    load;
And the blood-colored tears which yew trees weep
O'er churchyard graves, like murderers remorseful.
The dark green rings where fairies sit and sup,
Crushing the violet dew in the acorn cup:
Whe e by his new-made bride the bride-groom sips,
The white moon shimmering on their longing lips;
The large o'erloaded wealthy-looking wains
Quietly swaggering home through leafy lanes,
Leaving on all low branches as they come,
Straws for the birds, ears of the harvest home.
Summer's warm soil or winter's cruel sky,
Clear, cold, and icy-blue, like a sea-eagle's eye;
All things to Him bare thoughts of minstrelsy.
He drew his light from that he was amidst,
As doth a lamp from air which hath itself
Matter of light, although it show it not.   His
Was but the power to light what might be lit.
He met a muse in every lovely maid;
And learned a song from every lip he loved.
But his heart ripened most 'neath southern eyes,
Which sunned their sweets into him all day long:
For fortune called him southwards, towards the sun.
    HELEN.   Did he love music?
    FESTUS.   The only music he
Or learned or listened to was from the lips
Of her he loved, and that he learned by heart.
Albeit, she would try to teach him tunes,
And put his fingers on the keys; but he
Could only see her eyes, and hear her voice,
And feel her touch.
    HELEN.   Why, he was much like thee.
    FESTUS.   We had some points in common.
    STUDENT.   Was he proud?
    FESTUS.   Lowliness is the base of every virtue

And he who goes the lowest, builds the safest.
My God keeps all his pity for the proud.
   STUDENT.   Was he world-wise ?
   FESTUS.   The only wonder **is**
He **knew so** much, leading the life **he** did.
   STUDENT.   Yet it **may seem less strange when**
        we think back,
That we, in **the** dark chamber of the heart,
Sitting alone, see the world tabled **to** us ;
And the world wonders how recluses know
So much, and most of all, how we **know them.**
It is they who paint themselves upon **our hearts**
In their own lights and **darknesses, not we.**
One stream of light **is to us from above,**
And that is that we see by, light of **God.**
   FESTUS. We **do** not make **our thoughts ; they**
       grow in us
Like grain in **wood : the growth is of the skies,**
Which are of nature, nature is of God.
The world is full **of** glorious likenesses.
The poet's power is to sort these out,
And **to make** music from the common strings
With which the world is strung : to make the **dumb**
Earth utter heavenly harmony, and draw
Life clear, and sweet, and harmless as spring water,
Welling its way through flowers. Without faith,
Illimitable faith, strong **as a state's**
In its **own might,** in God, **no bard can be.**
All things **are signs of** other **and of nature.**
It is at night **we see heaven moveth,** and
A **darkness** thick with suns. **The** thoughts we think
Subsist the **same** in God as stars in Heaven.
And as these specks of light will prove great worlds
When we approach them sometime free from flesh,
So, too, our thoughts will become magnified
To mindlike things immortal. And as space
Is but a property **of** God, wherein
Is laid all matter, **other** attributes
May be the infinite **homes** of mind and soul.

And thoughts rise from our souls, as from the sea
The clouds sublimed in Heaven.   The cloud is cold,
Although ablaze with lightning — though it shine
At all points like a constellation ; so
We live not to ourselves, our work is life ;
In bright and ceaseless labor as a star
Which shineth unto all worlds but itself.
    HELEN.   And were this friend and bard of whom
        thou speakest,
And she whom he did love, happy together ?
    FESTUS. True love is ever tragic, grievous, grave.
Bards and their beauties are like double stars,
One in their bright effect.
    HELEN.   Whose light is love.
    STUDENT.   Or is it poesie thou meanest ?
    FESTUS.   Both:
For love is poesie — it doth create :
From fading features, dim soul, doubtful heart, ·
And this world's wretched happiness, a life
Which is as near to Heaven as are the stars.
They parted ; and she named Heaven's judgment·
        seat
As their next place of meeting : and 't was kept
By her, at least, so far that nowhere else
Could it be made until the day of doom.   [sinks
    HELEN. So soon men's passion passes ! yea, it
Like foam into the troubled wave which bore it.
Merciful God ! let me entreat Thy mercy !
I have seen all the woes of men — pain, death,
Remorse, and worldly ruin ; they are little
Weighed with the woe of woman when forsaken
By him she loved and trusted.   Hear, too, thou !
Lady of Heaven, Mother of God and man,
Who made the world His brother, one with God —
Maid-mother ! mould of God, who wrought in thee
By model as He doth in the world's womb,
So that the universe is great with God —
Thou in whom God did deify Himself,
Betaking him into mortality,

As in Thy Son He took it into Him,
And from the temporal and eternal made
Of the soul-world one same and ever **God**!
Oh! for the sake of thine own womanhood,
Pray away aught of evil from her soul,
And take her out of anguish unto thee,
Always, as **thou** didst this **one**!
  Festus.   Who **doth not**
Believe that that **he** loveth cannot die?
There is no mote **of** death **in** thine eye's beams
To hint of dust, or darkness, or decay;
Eclipse upon eclipse, and death on death;
No! immortality sits mirrored **there**
Like a fair face long looking on itself;
Yet thou shalt lie in death's angelic garb
As in a dream of dress, my beautiful!
The worm shall trail across thine unsunned sweets,
And fatten him on that men pined to death for;
Yea, have a further knowledge of thy beauties
Than **ever** did thy best-loved lover dream of.
  Helen. It is unkind to think of me in this wise.
Surely the stars must feel that they are bright,
In beauty, number, nature infinite;
And the strong sense we have of God **in us**
Makes me believe my soul can **never** cease.
The temples perish, but the God still lives.
  Festus. It is therefore that I love thee; **for that
when**
The fiery perfection of the world,
The sun, shall be **a** shadow **and burnt out,**
There is **an impulse** to eternity
Raised by this moment's love.
  Student.   I pray it may!
Time is the crescent shape to bounded eye
Of what is ever perfect unto God.
The bosom heaves to Heaven and to the stars;
Our very hearts throb upwards, our eyes look;
Our aspirations always are divine:
Yet is it in **the** gloom of soul we see

Most of the God about us, as at night.
For then the soul, like the mother-maid of Christ,
Is overshadowed by the Holy Spirit;
And in creative darkness doth conceive
Its humanized Divinity of life.

    FESTUS.   Think then God shows his face to us no less
In spiritual darkness than in light.

    HELEN. But of thy friend? I would hear more of him.
Perhaps much happiness in friendship made
Amends for his love's sorrows.

    FESTUS.   Ask me not.

    HELEN. But loved he never after? Came there none
To roll the stone from his sepulchral heart,
And sit in it an angel?

    FESTUS.   Ah, my life!
My more than life, my immortality!
Both man and womankind belie their nature
When they are not kind: and thy words are kind,
And beautiful, and loving like thyself;
Thine eye and thy tongue's tone, and all that speak
Thy soul, are like it. There's a something in
The shape of harps as though they had been made
By music: beauty's the effect of soul,
And he of whom thou askest loved again.
Couldst thou have loved one who was unlike men?
Whose heart was wrinkled long before his brow?
Who would have cursed himself if he had dared
Tempt God to ratify his curse in fire:
And yet with whom to look on beauty was
A need, a thirst, a passion?

    HELEN.   Yes, I think
I could have loved him: but, no — not unless
He was like thee; unless he had been thee.
Tell me, what was it rendered him so wretched
At heart?

    FESTUS. I will not tell thee.

STUDENT.   But tell me
How and on what he wrote, this friend of thine ?
   FESTUS. Love, mirth, **woe**, pleasure, was in turn
         his theme,
And the great good which beauty does the soul;
And the God-made necessity of things.
And like that noble knight in olden tale,
Who changed his armor's hue **at each** fresh **charge**
By virtue of his lady-love's strange **ring,**
So that none knew him save his private page
And she who cried, God **save** him, every time
He brake spears with the **brave** till **he quelled all—**
So he applied him to all themes **that came;**
Loving the most to breast **the rapid deeps**
Where others had been **drowned, and heeding**
         nought
Where danger might **not fill the** place **of fame.**
And 'mid the magic circle **of** those sounds,
His **lyre rayed** out, spell-bound himself he stood,
Like **a stilled** storm.   It is no task for suns
To **shine.   He knew** himself a bard ordained,
More **than** inspired, of God, inspirited :—
Making himself like an electric rod   .
A lure for lightning feelings; and his **words**
Felt like the things that fall **in thunder, which**
The mind, when in a **dark, hot, cloudful state,**
Doth make metallic, meteoric, **ball-like.**
He spake to spirits with **a spirit tongue,**
Who came compelled by **wizard word of truth,**
And rayed them **round him from the ends of**
         Heaven.
For as be all bards, **he was born of** beauty,
And with a natural **fitness to draw** down
All tones and shades of beauty to his soul,
Even as the rainbow-tinted shell, which lies
Miles deep at bottom of the sea, hath all
Colors of skies and flowers, and gems, and plumes,
And all by Nature which doth reproduce
Like loveliness in seeming opposites.

Our life is like the wizard's charmed ring:
Death's heads, and loathsome things fill up the
    ground ;
But spirits wing about, and wait **on us,**
While yet the hour of enchantment **is.**
And while we keep in, we are safe, and can
Force **them** to do our bidding.   And he raised
The rebel in himself, **and in** his **mind**
Walked **with** him through the world.
    STUDENT.   **He wrote of this ?**
    FESTUS. **He wrote a poem.**
    STUDENT.   What was said **of it ?**
    FESTUS. Oh, much was said — much more **than**
    understood ;
One said that he was mad; another, wise ;
Another, wisely mad.   The **book is there.**
Judge thou among them.
    STUDENT.   Well, but, who said what ?
    FESTUS. **Some said that** he blasphemed ; and
    these men lied
To all eternity, unless **such men**
Be saved, when God shall **rase** that lie from life,
And from His own eternal memory :
But still the word is lied ; though it **were writ**
In honey dew upon a lily leaf,
With quill of nightingale, like love **letters**
From Oberon sent to the bright Titania,
Fairest of all the fays — for that he used
The name of God as spirits use it, barely,
Yet surely more sublime in nakedness,
Statue-like, **than in a whole tongue** of dress.
Thou knowest, God ! **that to** the full of worship
All things are worshipful ; and Thy **great** name,
In all its awful brevity, **hath nought**
Unholy breeding in it, **but doth bless**
Rather the tongue **that utters it ;** for me,
I ask no higher office than to fling
My spirit at Thy feet, and cry Thy name,
God ! through eternity.   The man who sees

Irreverence in that name, must have been used
To take that name in vain, and the same man
Would see obscenity in pure white statues.
Call all things by their names. Hell, **call** thou
    hell;
Archangel, call archangel; and God, **God.**
  STUDENT. **And** what said **he** of such?
  FESTUS.   He held his peace
A season, as a **tree** its sap till spring,
Preparing to unfold itself, and let
All rigor do its worst, which only served
To harden him, though nothing nesh at **first.**
And then he said at last, **what, at the first,**
He deemed would have been seen by other **men,**
By men, at least, above low-water mark,
Who take it, they lead others; **that it** is they
Who set their shoulders to the stalled world's wheel,
And give it a hitch forwards.
  HELEN.   There were some
Encouraged him with good will, surely?
  FESTUS.   Many.
The kind, the noble, and the able cheered him;
The lovely, likewise: others knew he nought of.
And yet he loved not praise, nor sighed for fame.
Men's praise begets an awe of one's own **self**
Within us, till we fear our heart, lest it,
Magician-like, show more than we can bear.
Nor was he fameless; but obscurity
Hath many a **sacred** use. The clouds **which** hide
The mental mountains rising nighest Heaven,
Are full of finest lightning, and a **breath**
Can give those gathered shadows fearful life,
And launch their light in thunder o'er the world.
  STUDENT. And thought he well of that he
    wrote?
  FESTUS.   Perchance.
Perchance we suffer, and perchance succeed.
Perchance he would his tongue had perished ere
It uttered half he **said, from** childhood up

To manhood, and so on; for much I heard
From him required expiation, much
Soul sacrifice and penance for heart-deeds
Which passion had accomplished; yea, perchance,
He wished, how vain! that fruitful heart and breast
Had withered like a witch's ere he had trained
The parasites of feeling that he did
About it; and perchance, for all I know,
He would his brain had died ere it conceived
One half the thought-seeds that took life in it,
And in his soul's dark sanctuary dwelt.
Yet his blue eye's dark ball grew greater with
Delight, and darker, as he viewed the things
He made; not monsters outside of the fane,
Grinning and howling, but seraphic forms—
Embodied thoughts of worship, wisdom, love,
Joining their fire-tipped wings across the shrine
Where his heart's relics lay, and where were wrought
Immortal miracles upon men's minds.

    STUDENT. Take up the book, and, if thou under-
       · standest,
Unfold it to me.
    FESTUS.   What I can, I will.
Well I remember me of thee, poor book!
But there is consolation e'en for thee.
Fair hands have turned thee over, and bright eyes
Sprinkled their sparkles o'er thee with their prayers.
The poet's pen is the true divining rod
Which trembles towards the inner founts of feel-
       ing;
Bringing to light and use, else hid from all,
The many sweet, clear sources which we have
Of good and beauty in our own deep bosoms;
And marks the variations of all mind
As does the needle an air-investing storm's.

    STUDENT. How does the book begin, go on, and
       end?
    FESTUS. It has a plan, but no plot. Life hath
       none.

HELEN. Tell us, love; we will listen and not
   speak.
I wish I understood it, for I know
You would rather hear me than yourselves talk.
  STUDENT.   Surely.
I'd give up half the organs in my head,
Besides all undiscovered faculties,
To list to such a lecturer; and then
Have quite enough, perhaps, to comprehend.
  HELEN. 'T were needless that, to one half-
   witted now.
  FESTUS. There is a porch, wherefrom is some-
   thing seen
Of the main dome beyond. Though shadows cross
Each other's path, yet let us go through it.
And lo! an opening scene in Heaven, wherein
The foredoom of all things, spirit and matter,
Is shown, and the permission of temptation;
The angelic worship of the Trinity,
By God's name uttered thrice; the joys and powers
Of souls o'erblest, and the sweet offices
Of warden-angel told; and the complete
Well-fixed necessity and end of all things.
From Heaven we come to earth, and so do souls.
For next succeeds a soft and sunset scene,
Wherein is shown the collapsed, empty state
In which all worldly pleasures leave us; youth's
Though natural, fitful, unavailing, struggle
Against a great temptation come unlooked for:
And that to sin is to curse God in deed.
The soul long used to truth still keeps its strength,
Though plunged upon a sudden mid the false;
As hands, thrust into a dark room, retain
Their sunlent light a season. So with this.
The lines have under meanings, and the scene
Of self-forgetfulness and indecision
Breaks off, not ends. A starry, stirless night
Follows, which shadows out youth's barren long-
   ings

For goodness, greatness, marvels, mysteries.
Whence comes this **dream of** immortality,
And the resurgent **essence ?**   Let us think !
What mean we by **the dead ?**   **The dead** have
        life,
The changed; and, if they come, it is to show
Their change is for the better.   The bait takes.
Man and his foe shake hands **upon** their bargain.
The youth sets out for joy, **and 'neath the** care
Of his good enemy, begins **his course.**
The next scene seems to promise **fair; for sure**
If that there be one scene **in** life, **wherefrom**
Evil is absent, it is pure early **love.**
    HELEN.   Alas ! when beauty pleads the cause
            of virtue
The chief temptation to embrace it's wanting.
    FESTUS.   A man in love sees wonders.   But not
            love
Makes the soul happy: **so the youth** gets hope-
            less.
To this comes on a stern **and** stormy quarrel
'Tween the two foe friends — Youth demanding
            what
Cannot be; and **the other** withholding safe
And easy grants.   They part and meet, **as though**
Nothing had happened, in the next **scene :   none**
Know how we reconcile ourselves to **evil.**
But there they are, together, aiding each
The other, and abusing others.
    HELEN.   I
Was waiting for an eloquential pause
In this mysterious, allegorical,
Mythical, theological, odd story.
So now, then, I shall ask myself to sing;
And granting I **agree to** my **request,**
I think you ought **to thank me.**
    STUDENT.   That we will.
But not just now.

HELEN.   Oh! yes, now; yes, this moment.
I 'm in the humor.
  STUDENT.   We are not.
  FESTUS.   Yes, let her!
  HELEN.   What **shall I** sing?
  FESTUS.   Sing something merry, love.
  HELEN.   **I won't: I 'll** sing the dullest thing I
     know,
One of thine own songs.
  STUDENT.   What a compliment!
  FESTUS.   Sing what thou lik'st, then.
  HELEN.   No; what thou lik'st.
  STUDENT.   **Well,**
Something about love, and it can't be wrong.
     For love the sunny world supplies
     With laughing lips and happy eyes.
  FESTUS.   And 't will be sooner over.
  STUDENT.   And so better.

     HELEN.   Like an island in a river,
       Art thou, my love, to me;
     And I journey by thee ever
       With a gentle ecstasy.
    I arise to fall before thee;
      I come to kiss thy **feet**;
    To adorn thee and adore thee,
      Mine **only one! my sweet!**

     And thy love hath power upon me,
       Like a dream upon **a** brain;
    For the loveliness which won me,
      With the love, too, doth remain.
    And my life it beautifieth,
      Though love be but a shade,
    Known of only ere it dieth,
      By the darkness it hath made.

Was that addressed to me?
  STUDENT.   Well, now resume.

Festus. Trial alone of ill and folly gives
Clear proofs of the world's vanities; but little
Good comes of sermons, prophecies, or warnings.
Though from the steps of an old **gray** market
      cross,
The devil is holding forth to the faithless. There
A social prayer is offered up, too. This
Is followed by a bird's-eye view of earth,
A stirring-up of the dust of all the nations.
Then comes a village feast; a kind of home
Unto the traveller — where, **with the world,**
We mix in private, talking divers things;
A country merry-making, where all speak
According to their sorts, and the occasion.
Deeper than ever leadline went, **behold**
We search the rayless central sun within.
We penetrate **all mysteries,** but **are**
Unfitted long **to dwell in the recess**
Of our own nature, **and** we long for light.
True aspiration riseth from research.
Next, by **the** o'erthrown altar of a fane,
Foundation-shattered, like the ripened heart,
We find ourselves in worship. Let us hope
The spirit, form, and offering, **grateful** all.
In one of Earth's **head cities, after this,**
We **tower-like rise, and with an eminent eye**
Glance round society, insatiate;—
The high unknown as yet unrealized.
In less time than the twinkling of a star,
Insphered in air, the arch-fiend and the youth,
Like twilight and midnight, discourse and rise.
Thence to another planet, for the book,
Stream-like, doth steal the images of stars,
And trembles at its boldness, where we meet
The spirit of the first night of temptation;
And mix with many of those lofty musings
Which sow in us the seeds of higher kind
And brighter being. Heavenly poesie,
Which shines among the powers of our mind,

As that bright star she dwells in, mid the worlds
Which make the system of the sun, is there too.
But these high things are lost, and drowned, and
    dimmed,
Like a blue eye in tears, that trickle from it
Like angels leaving Heaven on their errands
Of love, behind them, in the scene succeeding ; —
A scene of song, and dance, and mirth, and wine,
And damsels, in whose lily skin the blue
Veins branch themselves in hidden luxury,
Hues of the heaven they seem to have vanished
    from.
    HELEN. Moonlight and music, and kisses, and
        wine,
And beauty, which must be, for rhyme-sake, divine.
    FESTUS. Mere joys ; but saddened and sublimed
        at close
By sweet remembrance of immortal ones
Once loved, aye hallowed. Still, in scenes like this,
Youth lingers longest, drawing out his time
As a gold-beater does his wire, until
'T would reach round the earth.
    STUDENT.   And be of no use then.
    FESTUS. Blame not the bard for showing this,
        but mind
He wrote of youth as passionate genius,
Its flights and follies — both its sensual ends
And common places. To behold an eagle
Batting the sunny ceiling of the world
With his dark wings, one well might deem his heart
On heaven ; but, no ! it is fixed on flesh and blood,
And soon his talons tell it. Pass we on !
A brief and solemn parley o'er a grave
Follows, in which youth vows to trust in God,
Be the end what it may. A prescient view
Of what is true repentance to the soul,
Spirit-informed, expands ; and over all
The spiritual harmonies of Heaven
By the raised soul are heard, and God's great rule

To creatures justified. And next we find
Ourselves in Heaven. Even man's deadly life
Can be there, by God's leave. Once brought to
        God,
The soul's foredoom is set before it brightly,
And Heaven's designs are seen to be brought to
        bear,
A lightning revelation of the Heavens,
And what is in them. Let it not be said
He sought his God in the self-slayer's way,
Whose highest aim was but to worship in
All humbleness; for he was called thereto,
To show the holy God, in three scenes, first
And last in Threelihood, and midst in One:
Although less hard to shape the wide-winged wind
O'er the bright heights of air. He will forgive:
For we, this moment, and all living souls —
All matter, are as much within his presence,
And known through, like a glass film in the sun,
As we can ever be. Through sundry worlds
The mortal wends, returning, and relates
To her he loves — and joyously, they greet,
As boat by breeze and billow backed by tide —
His bright experience of celestial homes;
Where spiritual natures, kind and high,
Light-born, which can divine immortal things,
Abide embosomed in Eternity.
Something he tells, too, of the friendly fiend,
Something of ancient ages, infant Earth.
To this succeeds a scene explaining much,
Of retrospective and prospective cast,
Between the bard, his beauty and his friend.
Our story ties us here to earth again,
And sea all aged. Evil is in love;
And ever those who are unhappiest have
Their hearts' desire the oftenest, but in dreams.
Dreams are mind-clouds, high and unshapen beauties,
Or but God-shaped, like mountains, which contain
Much and rich matter; often not for us,

But for another.   Dreams are rudiments
Of the great state to come.   We dream what **is**
About to happen to us.
    HELEN.   What may be
The dream in this **case?**
    FESTUS.   It is one of death.
    HELEN.   Of death! is that all? Well, I too have
        had,
What every one hath once, at least, in life —
A vision of the region of the dead;
It was the land of shadows: yea, the land
Itself was but a shadow, and the race
Which seemed therein were voices, forms of forms,
And echoes of themselves.   And there was nought,
Of substance seemed, save one thing in the midst,
A great red sepulchre — a granite grave;
And at the bottom lay a skeleton,
From whose decaying jaws the shades were born;
Making its only sign of life, its dying
Continually.   Some were bright, some dark.
Those that **were** bright, went upwards heavenly.
They which were dark, grew darker and remained.
A land of change, yet did the half things nothing
That **I** could see; but passed stilly on,
Taking no note of other, mate or child;
For all had lost their love **when** they put off
The beauty of the body.   **And·as** I
Looked on, the grave before me backed away.
And **I** began to dream it was a dream;
And I rushed after it: when the earth quaked,
Opened and shut, like the eye of one in fits;
It shut to with a shout.   The grave was gone.
And in the stead there stood a gleedlike throne,
Which all the shadows shook to see, and swooned
For fiends were standing, loaded with long chains
The links whereof were fire, waiting the word
To bind and cast the shadows into hell;
For Death the second sat upon that throne,
Which set on fire the air, not to be breathed.

17

And as he lifted up his arm to speak,
Fear preyed upon all souls, like fire **on paper,**
And mine **among the rest,** and I awoke.
   STUDENT. By Hades! 't was most awful.
   FESTUS.   And when **love**
Merges in creature-worship, let us mind :
We know not what it is we love : perhaps
It is incarnate evil. **In the time**
It takes **to turn a leaf,** we are in Heaven;
Making our way among the wheeling worlds,
Millions of suns, half infinite each, and **space**
For ever shone into, for ever dark,
As God is, to and by created mind,
Upheld by the companion spirit. There
The nature **of** the all in one, and whence
Evil; the fixed impossibility
Of creatures' perfectness, until made one
With God; and the necessity **of ill**
As yet, are things all touched upon and proven.
The next scene shows us hell, in the mad mock
Of mortal revelry — the quelling truth
That all life's sinful follies run **to** hell;
That lies, debauches, murders never die,
But live in hell forever; **make, are hell.**
And truth is there too. **Hell is its own moral.**
Perdition certain to the unrepentant;
Redemption on a like scale with creation;
And all creation needing it, and having.
What follows is of earth, and setteth forth
God's mercy, and the mystery of sin;
And a great gathering of the worlds round God,
Told by the youth to his truthful, trustful, love;
Who, light **and lowly** as a little glowworm,
Sheddeth her beauty round her like a rose,
Sweet-smelling dew upon the ground it grows on.
And then **a rest in** light, as though 'tween earth
And Heaven **there** were a mediate spirit point,
A bright effect **original** of God,
Enlightening all ways, inwardly and round.

Then comes a scene of passion, brought about
By the bad spirit's means for his own ends,
Whom we know not when come, so dark we grow;
Making it but a blind for the next scene,
Laid by the lonely seashore, as before,
Where the **great** waves come in frothed, like **a horse**
Put to **his** heart-burst speed, sobbing up hill,
Wherein he works his victim's death, to clear
His **way,** and keep his **name of** murderer;
As **he in other** parts **makes** good **his** titles,
Deceiver, liar, tempter, and accuser;
Hater of **man,** and, **most of all,** of **God.**
In the next **scene we** picture back our **life,**
Contrasting the pure joys of earlier **years,**
With **the** unsatedness of **current sin;**
And the sad feel that **love's** own heart turns sick
Like **a** bad pearl; but that the feeling still
Is adamantine, though the splendid thing
Whereon it writes its record, is **of** all
Frailest; and though earth shows to good and bad,
The same blind kindness, beautiful to see,
Wherewith **our** lovely mother loveth us,
The **world in** vain unbosometh her beauty,
We **have** no lust to live; for things may be
Corrupted into beauty; **and** that love,
Where all the passions **blend, as** hues in white,
Tires at the last, **as day would, if all day**
And no night.   **So despair of heart increases.**
The last lure — **power** — is proffered, taken.   **All**
Hangs on **the** last desire, whatever it be.
A scene of prescient solitude and soul
Commune with heaven, repentance, prayer, faith,
Which are all things inspired alone of God,
Who signifies salvation, follows this.
In the next scene, we feel the end draw nigh.
A change is wrought on earth as great as that
In its first ages, when the elements
Less gross and palpable than air, were changed
To mountainous and adamantine mass,

Now 'neath the feet of nations;— figuring forth
The fateful mind which is to govern all,
Controlling the great evil; for it is mind
Which shall rule and be ruled, and not the body,
In the last age of human sway on earth;—
Ambition ruined by its own success;
Aims lost, power useless: love, pure love, the last
Of mortal things that nestles in the heart.
There is a love which acts to death, and through
　　　death,
And may come white, and bright, and pure, like
　　　paper,
From refuse, or from clearest things at first;
It is beyond the accidents of life.
For things we make no count of have in them
The seeds of life, use, beauty, like the cores
Of apples that we fling away;— nought now
Is left but trust in God, who tries the heart
And saves it, at the last, from its own ruin —
The parting spirit fluttering like a flag,
Half from its earthly staff. The death-change
　　　comes.
Death is another life. We bow our heads
At going out, we think, and enter straight
Another golden chamber of the king's,
Larger than this we leave, and lovelier.
And then in shadowy glimpses, disconnect,
The story, flower-like, closes thus its leaves.
The will of God is all in all. He makes,
Destroys, remakes, for His own pleasure, all.
After inferior nature is subdued,
The evil is confined. All elements
Conglobe themselves from chaos, purified.
The rebegotten world is born again.
The body and the soul cease; spirit lives:
And gloriously falsified are all
Earth's caverned prophecies of bodyhood.
Spirits rise up, and rule, and link with Heaven;—
The soul state is searched into; dormant Death,

Evil, and all the dark gods of the heart,
And the idolatrous passions, ruined, chained,
And worshipless, are seen; **and** there, the Word,
Heard and obeyed;— next comes the truth divine,
Redintegrative;— Evil's last and worst
Endeavor, vanquished — by Almighty good.
The last scene shows the final doom of earth,
Soul's judgment, and salvation of the youth,
As was fore-fixed on from and in the first:
The universe expurgated of evil,
And hell for aye abolished; all create,
Redeemed, their God all love, themselves all bliss.
We may say that **the** sun **is** dead **and** gone
For ever; and may swear he will rise no more;
The skies **may** put on mourning for their God,
And earth heap ashes on her head: but who
Shall keep the sun back, when he thinks to rise?
Where is the chain shall bind him? Where the cell
Shall hold him? Hell, he would burn down to
       embers;
And would **lift** up **the** world with a lever of light
Out of his way: yet, know ye, 'twere thrice less
To do thrice this, than keep **the** soul from **God.**
O'er earth, and cloud, and sky, and star, and **Heaven,**
It dwells with God uprisen as a prayer.
The spirit speaks of God in Heaven's **own tongue,**
No mystery to those **who love,** but **learned,**
As is our mother tongue, from him, **the parent;**
By whom created, **fashioned, flesh and spirit,**
All forms and feelings of all **kinds of beauty**
Are burned into our heart-clay, pattern-like.
Much, too, is writ, elsewhere and here, not yet
Made clear, **nor** can be till **earth come** of age;
Like the unfinished rudiments **of** light
Which **gather** time by time into a star.
Thus have I shown the meaning of the book,
And the most truthful likeness of a mind,
Which hath as yet been limned; the mind of youth
In strengths and failings, in its overcomings,

And in its short comings; the kingly ends,
The universalizing heart of youth;
Its love of power, heed not how had, although
With surety of self-ruin at the end.
Every thing urged against it proves its truth
And faithfulness to nature.　Some cried out
'T was inconsistent; so 't was meant to be.
Such is the very stamp of youth and nature;
And the continual losing sight of its aims,
And the desertion of its most expressed
And dearest rules and object, this is youth.
 Student.　I look on life as keeping me from
  God,
Stars, Heaven, and angels' bosoms.　I lay ill;
And the dark, hot blood throbbing through and
  through me;
They bled me, and I swooned; and as I died,
Or seemed to die, a soft, sweet sadness fell
With a voluptuous weakness on my soul,
That made me feel all happy.　But my heart
Would live, and rose, and wrestled with the soul,
Which stretched its wings and strained its strength
  in vain,
Twining around it as a snake an eagle.
My eyes unclosed again, and I looked up,
And saw the sweet, blue twilight, and one star,
One only star, in Heaven; and then I wished
That I had died and gone to it; and straight
Was glad I lived again, to love once more.
And so our souls turned round upon themselves
Like orbs upon their axles; what was night
Is day; what day, night.　God will guide us on,
Body and soul, through life and death, to judg-
  ment.
 Festus.　Earth hath her deserts mixed with
  fruitful plains; •
The word of God is barren in some parts;
A rose is not all flower, but hath much
Which is of lower beauty, yet like needful

And he who in great makings doth like **these,**
Doth only that which is most natural.
Like life, too, it is boundlessly unequal,
Now soaring, and now grovelling: at one time
All harmony, and then again all harshness,
With an ever-changing style of thought and speech.
The work is still consistent with itself:
As one part often bears upon another,
Lifting it to the light, where most it **needs.**
The thoughts we have of men **are** bold as men ;
Our thoughts of God are thin **and** fleet as ghosts ;
But it was not his meaning **to** draw **men,**
Such as he heard they **were in the old world**
And sometimes mixed **with ; he blessed God he
knew**
But **little** of the world, **that** little **good ;**
While some sighed out **that** little was **its all.**
So for **the** persons and **the scenes he drew,**
Oft in a dim and dreamy imagery
Shapen, half-shapen, mis-shapen, unshapen,
They are the shadowy **creatures** which youth
dreams
Live in the world embodied, but are not,
Save in the mind's, which is the mightier **one.**
They are the names of things which we **believe in,**
Ideas not embodied, alas, not!
And the sad fate which many **of those meet**
Whom the youth **loves and quits, means nought so
ill**
As the betrayer's sin, salvationless
Almost : it is **but** desertion, not betrayal;
And forced on him according to a promise,
Made at the first unto **him,** and to be
Wrought out in brief **time ;** and the same fair souls
Saved, stand for our desires made pure in Heaven.
Let **us work** out our natures ; we can do
No wrong in them, they are divine, eterne :
I follow my attraction, and obey
Nature, as earth does, circling round her source

Of life and light, and keeping true in Heaven,
Though not perfect in round, which nothing is.
'T was the heart-book of love, well nigh all grief.
For the heart leaves its likeness best in that
O'erwhelming sorrow which burns up and buries,
Like to the eloquent impression left
In lava, of Pompeian maiden's bosom.
All passions, and all pleasures, and all powers
Of man's heart, are brought in, and mind and frame
He made this work the business of his life;
It was his mission; and was laid on him.
He was a laborer on the ways of God,
And had his hire in peace and power to work.
He wrote it not in the contempt of rule,
And not in hate; but in the self-made rule
That there was none to him, but to himself
He was his sole rule, and had right to be.
The faults are faults of nature, and prove art
Man's nature, that a thing of art, like it,
Should be so pure in kind.

    HELEN.   I do believe
The world is a forged thing, and hath not got
The die of God upon it. It will not pass
In Heaven, I tell ye.

    STUDENT.   How shouldst thou know anght
Of Heaven, unless by contrast?

    FESTUS.   Pray now, cease;
Ye two are jarring ever, though as with
The bickering beauty of two swords, whose strife,
Though deadly, maketh music, I could listen,
Did not each stab, whichever way, pain me.

    HELEN. Oh, I could stand and rend myself with rage
To think I am so weak, that all are so;
Mere minims in the music made from us —
While I would be a hand to sweep from end
To end, from infinite to infinite,
The world's great chord. The beautiful of old

Had but to say some god had been with them,
And their worst fault **was** hallowed to their **best**
    deed.
That was to live.   Could we uproot the past,
Which grows **and** throws its chilling shade o'er us,
Lengthening every hour and darkening it;
Or could we plant the future where we would,
And make it flourish, that, too, were to live.
But it is not **more true** that what is, is,
Than that **what is** not, is **not.**   It is enough
To bear **the ever** present, as **we** do.
The city **of** the **past** is laid in ruins;
Its echo-echoing walls at a whisper fall :
The coming is not yet built; nor as yet
Its deep foundations laid ; but seems, at once,
Like the air city, goodly and well watered,
Which the dry **wind** doth dream of on the sands
Where he dies away with his wanderings :
While we enjoy the hope thereof, and perish ;
Not seeing that the desert present is
Our end.
    FESTUS.   The brightest natures oft have darkest
End, as fire smoke.
    STUDENT.   I will read the book in the hope
Of learning somewhat **from** it.
    FESTUS.   Thou may'st learn
A hearty thanksgiving for blessings here,
And proud prediction of a state to come,
Of love, and life, and power unlimited;
And uttered in a sound and homely tongue,
Fit **to** be used by all who think while speaking.
With here and there some old, hard, uncouth **words,**
Which have withal a quaint and meaning richness,
As stones make more the power of the soil.
The world hath said its say for and against;
And **after praise** and blame cometh the truth.
Living **men look** on all who live askance.
Were he **a cold,** gray ghost, **he** would have honor;
And though **as man** he must **have** mixed with men,

Yet the true bard doth make himself ghost-like ;
He lives apart from men ; he wakes and walks
By nights; he puts himself into the world
Above him ; and he is what but few see.
He knows, too, to the old hid treasure, truth :
And the world wonders, shortly, how some one
Hath come so rich of soul; it little dreams
Of the poor ghost that made him.   Yet he comes
To none save of his own blood, and lets pass
Many a generation till his like
Turns up ; moreover, this same genius
Comes, ghost-like, to those only who are lonely
In life and in desire ; never to crowds :
And it can make its way through every thing,
And is never happy till it tells its secret ;
But pale and pressed down with the inward weight
Of unborn works, it sickens nigh to death,
Often ; but who like happy at a birth ?

   STUDENT.   Say what a poet ought to do and be.
   FESTUS.   Though it may scarce become me,
        knowing little,
Yet what I have thought out upon that theme,
And deem true, I will tell thee.
   HELEN.   Now I know
You two will talk of nothing else all night ;
So I will to my music.   Sweet! I come.
Art thou not glad to see me ?   What a time
Since I have touched thine eloquent white fingers.
Hast thou forgot me ?   Mind, now ?   Know'st thou
        not
My greeting ?   Ah ! I love thee.   Talk away !
Never mind me ; I shall not you.
   STUDENT.   Agreed !
   HELEN.   By the sweet muse of music, I could
        swear
I do believe it smiles upon me ; see it
Full of unuttered music, like a bird ;
Rich in invisible treasures, like a bud
Of unborn sweets, and thick about the heart

With ripe and rosy beauty — full **to trembling.**
I love it like a sister.   Hark ! — its **tones ;**
They melt the soul within one like a **sword,**
Albeit sheathed, **by lightning.**   Talk **to me,**
Lovely one ! **Answer me, thou beauty !**
    STUDENT.   Hear her
    FESTUS.   Experience and imagination are
Mother and sire of song — the harp and hand.
The bard's aim **is to** give us thoughts : his **art.**
Lieth in giving them as bright **as may** be.
And **even** when **their looks are earthy,** still
If opened, like geoids, **they may** be found
Full of all sparkling, **sparry** loveliness.
They should be **wrought, not cast ; like** tempered
        steel,
Burned and **cooled, burned** again, and cooled again.
A thought is like **a ray of** light — complex
In **nature,** simple only **in** effect.
Words are the motes **of thought,** and nothing
        more.
Words are like sea-shells on the shore ; they show
Where the **mind** ends, and not how far **it** has
        been.
Let every thought, **too,** soldier-like, be stripped,
And roughly looked **over.   The** dress of words,
Like to the Roman **girl's enticing** garb,
Should let the play **of limb be seen through it,**
And the round, rising **form.   A** mist of **words,**
Like halos **round** the **moon, though they** enlarge
The seeming **size** of thoughts, **make the** light less
Doubly.   **It is the** thought writ **down we** want,
Not its effect — **not** likenesses **of** likenesses.
And such descriptions are not, more than gloves
Instead of hands **to** shake, enough for **us.**
    STUDENT.   **But is the** power — **is poesy inborn,**
Or is it to be gained by art **or toil ?**
    FESTUS.   It is underived, except from God ; but
        where
Strongest, asks most of human **care and aid.**

Great bards toil much and most ; **but** most at first,
Ere they **can** learn **to** concentrate the soul
For hours upon a thought to carry it.
    STUDENT.   Why, I have sat for hours and never
        moved,
Saving my hands, **clock-like, in** writing round
Day after day of thought, **and** lapse of life.
    FESTUS.   **Many** make books, few poems, which
        may do
Well for their gains, but they do nought for truth,
Nor man, true bard's main aim.   Perish **the** books,
But the creations live.   Some steal a thought,
And clip it round the edge, and challenge him
Whose 't was to swear to it.   To serve things thus
Is **as** foul witches **to cut up** old **moons**
Into new stars.   Some **never** rise above
A pretty fault, like faulty dahlias;
And of whose best things **it is** kindly said,
The thought is fair ; but, to be perfect, wants
A little heightening, like a pretty face
With a low forehead.   **Do** thou more than such,
Or else do nothing.   And **in** poetry,
There is a poet-worship, **one** of other
Which is idolatry, and **not the** true
Love-service **of** the **soul to God,** which hath
Alone of His inbreathing, and **is** rendered
Unto Him, from the first, without man's mean,
By those whom He makes worthy of His worship;
Who kneel at once to Him, and at no shrine,
Save in the world's wide **ear,** do they confess
    them
Of faults **which are all truths ; and** through which
    ear
As the world says them **over to** itself,
He heareth and absolveth ; **for** the bard
Speaks but what all feel more **or** less within
The heart's heart, and the sin confessed is done
Away with, and forever.
    STUDENT.   What of style ?

Festus.   There is no style is good but nature's
        style.
And the great ancients' writings, beside ours,
Look like illuminated manuscripts
Before plain press print; all had different minds,
And followed only their own bents: for this
Nor copied that, nor that the other; each
Is finished in his writing, each is best
For his own mind, and that **it was** upon;
And all have lived, are living, and shall live;
But these have died, are dying, and shall die;
Yea, copyists shall die, spark out and out.
Minds which combine and make alone **can tell**
The bearings and workings of all things
In and upon each other.   All the parts
Of nature meet and **fit**: wit, wisdom, worth,
Goodness and greatness; to sublimity
Beauty arises, like a planet world,
Laboring slowly, seemingly, up Heaven;
But with **an** infinite pace to some immortal eyes.
And he who **means** to be a great bard, must
Measure himself against pure mind, and fling
His soul into a stream of thought, as will
A swimmer hurl himself into the water.
But never swimmer on the stream, nor bird
On wind, feels half **so** strong, or swift, or glad,
As bard borne high on his mind above himself;
As though he should begin a lay **like this,**
Where spiritual element is all;
Thought chafing **thought,** as bough **bough, till all**
        burn,
Like the star-written prophecies **of Heaven.**
The shattered shadow of eternity
Upon the troubled world, even as the sun
Shows brokenly on wavy waters, time;
All time is but a second to the dead.
The smoke **of** the great burning of the world
Had trailed across the skies for many an age,
And was fast wearing into air away,

When a saint stood before the throne, and cried —
Blessed be Thou, Lord God of all the worlds
That have been, and that are, and are to be !
For Thy destruction is like infinite
With Thy creation, just and wise in both :
Give me a world; and God said, Be it so :
And the world was: and then go on to show
How this new orb was made, and where it shone ; ·
Who ruled, abode, worshipped and loved therein ;
Their natures, duties, hopes: let it be pure,
Wise, holy, beautiful ; if not to be
Without it, made so by constraint of God —
Kindly forced good : we have had enough of sin
And folly here to wish for and love change.
Let him show God as going thither mildly,
Father-like, blessing all and cursing none ;
And that there never will be need for them
That He shall come in glory new to Himself,
With light to which the lightning shall be shadow,
And the sun sadness ; borne upon a car
With wheels of burning worlds, within whose rims
Whole hells burn, and beneath whose course the stars
Dry up like dew-drops.   But of this enough ;   ·
I mean that he must weigh himself as he
Will be weighed after by posterity ;
After us all are critics, to a man.
Write to the mind and heart, and let the ear
Glean after what it can.   The voice of great
Or graceful thoughts is sweeter far than all
Word-music ; and great thoughts, like great deeds, need
No trumpet.   Never be in haste in writing.
Let that thou utterest be of nature's flow,
Not art's ; a fountain's, not a pump's.   But once
Begun, work thou all things into thy work ;
And set thyself about it, as the sea
About earth, lashing at it day and night.
And leave the stamp of thine own soul in it

As thorough as the fossil flower in clay.
The theme shall start and struggle in thy breast,
Like to a spirit in its tomb at rising,
Rending the stones, and crying, Resurrection!
   STUDENT.   What theme remains?
   .FESTUS.   Thyself, thy race, thy love,
The faithless and the full of faith in God;
Thy race's destiny, thy sacred love.
Every believer is God's miracle.
Nothing will stand whose staple is not love;
The love of God, or man, or lovely woman;
The first is scarcely touched, the next scarce felt,
The third is desecrated; lift it up;
Redeem it, hallow it, blend the three in one
Great holy work. It shall be read in Heaven
By all the saved of sinners of all time;
Preachers shall point to it, and tell their wards
It is a handful of eternal truth;
Make ye a heartful of it: men shall will
That it be buried with them in their hands:
The young, the gay, the innocent, the brave,
The fair, with soul and body both all love,
Shall run to it with joy; and the old man,
Still hearty in decline, whose happy life
Hath blossomed downwards, like the purple bell-
     flower,
Closing the book, shall utter lowlily —
Death, thou art infinite, it is life is little.
Believe thou art inspired, and thou art.
Look at the bard and others; never heed
The petty hints of envy. If a fault
It be in bard to deem himself inspired,
'T is one which hath had many followers
Before him. He is wont to make, unite,
Believe; the world to part, and doubt, and narrow.
That he believes, he utters. What the world
Utters, it trusts not. But the time may come
When all, along with those who seek to raise
Men's minds, and have enough of pain, without

Suffering from envy, may be God-inspired
To utter truth, and feel like love for men.
Poets are henceforth the world's teachers.   Still
The world is all in sects, which makes one loathe it.
   STUDENT.   The men of **mind** are mountains,
         and their heads
Are sunned long ere the **rest of earth.**   I would
Be **one** such.
   FESTUS.   **It is** well.   **Burn to be great.**
Pay not thy praise to lofty **things alone.**
The plains are everlasting **as the hills.**
The bard cannot have two pursuits: aught **else**
Comes on the mind with the like shock **as though**
Two worlds had gone to war and met in air.
And now that thou hast heard thus much from **one**
Not wont to seek, nor give, nor take advice,
Remember, whatsoe'er thou **art** as **man,**
Suffer the world, entreat it and forgive.
They who forgive most shall be most forgiven.
Dear Helen, I will tell thee what I love
Next to thee — poesy.
   HELEN.   ·   Can any thing
Be even second to me in thy love?
Doth it **not** distance **all things?**
   FESTUS.   To say sooth,
I once loved many things **ere** I met with thee,
My one blue break of beauty in the **clouds;**
Bending thyself to me as Heaven to earth.   ·
   HELEN.   My love is like the moon, seems **now**
        to grow,
And now to lessen; but it is only so
Because thou canst not see it all at once.   ·
It knows nor **day,** nor **morrow,** like the sun;
Unchangeable **as space it shall still be**
When yon **bright** suns, **which are** themselves but
        sands
In the great glass of Time, shall be run out.
   FESTUS.   Man is but half man without woman;
        and

As do idolaters their heavenless gods,
We deify the things which **we** adore.
   Helen.   Our life is comely as **a whole ; nay,**
     more,
Like rich brown ringlets, with odd hairs all gold.
We women **have** four seasons, like the year,
Our spring **is in our** lightsome girlish days,
When the heart laughs within **us** for sheer **joy** ;
Ere yet we know what love is **or** the ill
Of being loved by those whom we **love not.**
Summer is when **we** love and are **beloved,**
And seems short; from its very splendor seems
To pass the quickest; crowned with flowers it **flies.**
Autumn, when some young thing **with** tiny **hands,**
And rosy cheeks, and flossy tendrilled locks,
Is wantoning about **us day** and **night.**
And winter is **when these** we **love have** perished ;
For the heart **ices then.**   And **the** next spring
Is in another **world, if one there be.**
Some **miss one season, some another;** ·this
Shall **have them early, and that late ; and yet**
The year wear round with all **as best it may.**
There is no **rule** for it ; **but** in **the main**
It is as I have said.
   Festus.   My **life** with **thee**
Is like a song, and the sweet music **thou,**
Which doth accompany it.
   Student.   Say, did thy friend
Write aught **beside the work** thou tellest of ?
   Festus.   **Nothing,**
After that, like the burning peak, **he fell**
Into himself, and was missing ever **after.**
   Student. If not a secret, pray **who was he ?**
   Festus.   **L**

SCENE — *Garden and Bower by the Sea.*

LUCIFER *and* ELISSA.

LUCIFER.   Night comes, world-jewelled, as my
              bride should be.
The stars rush forth in myriads as to wage
War with the lines of Darkness ; and the moon,
Pale ghost of Night, comes haunting the cold earth
After the sun's red sea-death — quietless.
Immortal Night ! I love thee.   Thou and I
Are of one seed — the eldest blood of God.
He makes ; we mar together all things — all
But our own selves.   Love makes thee cold and
              tremble,
And me all fire.   Do off that starry robe ;
Catch me up to thee.   Let us love, and die,
And weld our souls together, Night !   But here
Cometh mine earthly.   My Elissa ! welcome.   ·

ELISSA.   Is't not a lovely, nay, a heavenly eve ?
LUCIFER.   Thy presence only makes it so to me.
The moments thou art with me are like stars
Peering through my dark life.
ELISSA.   Nay, speak not so,
Or I shall weep, and thou wilt turn away
From woman's tears : yet are they woman's wealth.
LUCIFER.   Then keep thy treasures, lady !   I
              would not have
The world, if prized at one sad tear of thine.
One tear of beauty can outweigh a world
Even of sin and sorrow, heavy as this ;
But beauty cannot sin and should not weep,
For she is mortal.   Oh ! let deathless things
Alone weep.   Why should aught that dies be sad ?
ELISSA.   The noble mind is oft too generous,
And, by protecting, weakens lesser ones ;
And tears must come of feeling though they
              quench
As oft the light which love lit in the eye.

LUCIFER.   And thy love ever hangs **about my**
    heart
Like the pure pearl-wreath which enrings thy **brow.**
I meant not to be mournful.   Tell me, now,
How thou hast **passed** the hours since last we met ?
    ELISSA.   **I have** stayed **the** livelong day within
    this bower ;
It was here that thou didst promise me **to come —**
Watching from wanton morn to repentant eve,
The self-same roses ope and close ; untired,
Listening the **same** bird's first and latest songs —
And still thou camest not.   To the mind which **waits**
Upon one hour, the others are but **slaves.**
The week hath but oné **day — the day one hour —**
That hour of the heart — **that lord of time.**
    LUCIFER.   Sweet **one!   I raced with light and**
    passed the laggard
To meet thee — or, I mean I could **have** done —
Yea, have outsped the very dart of Death —
So much I sought ; and were I living light
From God, with leave to range the world, and choose
Another brow than His whereon to beam —
To mark what **even** an angel could but covet —
A something lovelier than Heaven's loveliness —
To thee I straight would dart, **unheeding all**
The lives of other worlds, **even those who name**
Themselves thy kind ; **for oft my mind o'ersoars**
The stars ; and pondering **upon what may be**
Of their chief lording natures, man's seems worst —
The darkest, meanest, which, through all these·
    worlds,
Drags what is deathless, may be, **down** to dust.
    ELISSA.   Speak not so bitterly **of** human kind **;**
I know that thou dost love it.   Hast not heard
Of those great spirits, who, the greater grow,
The better we are able them to prize ?
Great minds can never cease ; **yet** have **they not**
A separate estate of deathlessness :
The future is a remnant of **their** life :

Our time is part of theirs, not theirs of ours :
They know the thoughts of ages long before.
It is not the weak mind feels the great mind's might;
None but the great can test it.   Does the oak
Or reed feel the strong storm most ?   Oh ! unsay
What thou hast said of man ; nor deem me wrong.
Mind cannot mind despise — it is itself.
Mind must love mind : the great and good are friends;
And he is but half great who is not good.
And, oh ! humanity is the fairest flower
Blooming in earthly breasts : so sweet and pure,
That it might freshen even the fadeless wreaths
Twined round the golden harps of those in Heaven.
   LUCIFER.   For thy sake I will love even man,
      or aught.
Spirit were I, and a mere mortal thou,
For thy sake I would even seek to die ;
That, dead, or living, I might still be with thee.
But no ! I 'll deem thee deathless — mind and make,
And worthier of some spirit's love than mine;
Yea, of the first-born of God's sons, could he
In that sweet shade thy beauty casts o'er all,
One moment lay and cool his burning soul;
Or might the ark of his wide flood-like woe
But rest upon that mount of peace and bliss —
Thy heart imbosomed in all beauteousness.
Nay, lady ! shrink not.   Thinkest thou I am he ?
   ELISSA.   Thou art too noble, far.   I oft have
      wished,
Ere I knew thee, I had some spirit's love ;
But thou art more like what I sought than man,
And a forbidden quest, it seems ; for thou
Hast more of awe than love about thee, like
The mystery of dreams which we can feel,
But cannot touch.
   LUCIFER.   Nay, think not so !   It is wrong.
Come, let us sit in this thy favorite bower,
And I will hear thee sing.   I love that voice,
Dipping more softly on the subject ear

Than that calm kiss the willow gives the wave —
A soft rich tone, a rainbow of sweet sounds,
Just spanning the soothed sense. Come, nay me
    not.
  Elissa. Do thou lead out some lay; I'll fol-
    low thine.
  Lucifer. Well, I agree. It will spare me
    much of shame
In coming after thee. My song is said
Of Lucifer, the star. See there he shines. [*Sings.*

I am Lucifer, the star:
  Oh! think on me,
As I lighten from afar
  The Heavens and thee!
In town, or tower,
Or this fair bower,
  Oh! think on me;
Though a wandering star,
As the loveliest are,
  I love but thee.

Lady! When I brightest beam,
  Love! look on me!
I am not what I may seem
  To the world or thee;
But fain would love
With thee above,
  Where thou wilt be.
But if love be a dream,
As the world doth deem,
  What is 't to me?

  Elissa. Could we but deem the stars had
    hearts, and loved,
They would seem happier, holier, even than now;
And ah! why not? they are so beautiful;
And love is part and union in itself
Of all that is in nature brilliant, pure —

Of all in feeling sacred and sublime.
Surely the stars are images of love :
The sunbeam and the starbeam doth bring love.
The sky, the sea, the rainbow, and the stream
And dark blue hill, where all the loveliness
Of earth and Heaven, in sweet ecstatic strife,
Seem mingling hues which might immortal be,
If length of life by height of beauty went:
All seem but made for love — love made for all :
We do become all heart with those we love :
It is nature's self — it-is everywhere — it is here.
   Lucifer. To me there is but one place in the
      world,
And that where thou art ; for where'er I be,
Thy love doth seek its way into my heart,
As will a bird into her secret nest ;
Then sit and sing ; sweet wing of beauty, sing.
   Elissa. Bright one ! who dwellest in the hap-
      py skies,
Rejoicing in thy light as does the brave,
In his keen, flashing sword, and his strong arm's
Swift swoop, canst thou from among the sons of
      men,
Single out those who love thee as do I
Thee from thy fellow glories ? If so, star,
Turn hither thy bright front ; I love thee, friend.
Thou hast no deeds of darkness. All thou dost
Is to us light and beauty : yea, thou art
A globe all glory ; thou who at the first
Didst answer to the angels which in Heaven
Sang the bright birth of earth, and even now,
As star by star is born, dost sing the same
With countless hosts in infinite delight, •
Be unto me a moment ! Write thy bright
Light on my heart before the sun shall rise
And vanquish sight. Thou art the prophecy
Of light which He fulfils. Speak, shining star,
Drop from thy golden lips the truths of Heaven ;
First of all stars and favorite of the skies,

Apostle of the sun — thou upon whom
His mantle resteth — speak, prophetic beauty !
Speak, shining star out of the heights of Heaven,
Beautiful being, speak to God for man !
Is it because of beauty thou wast chosen
To be the sign of sin ?   For surely sin
Must be surpassing lovely when for her
Men forfeit God's reward of deathless bliss
And life divine ; or, is it that such beauty,
Sometimes, before the truth, and sometimes after,
As is a moral or a prophecy,
Is ever warning ?   Why wast thou accorded
To the great Evil ?   Is it because thou art
Of all the sun's bright servants nearest earth ?
And shall we then forget that Christ hath said
He is thyself, the light-bringer of Heaven ?
Star of the morning ! unto us thou art
The presage of a day of power.   Like thee
Let us rejoice in life, then, and proclaim
A glory coming greater than our own.
All ages are but stars to that which comes,
Sunlike. Oh ! speak, star ! Lift thou up thy voice
Out of yon radiant ranks, and I on earth,
As thou in Heaven, will bless the Lord God ever.
Hear, Lucifer, thou star ! I answer thee.   [*Sings.*

Oh ! ask me not to look and love,
   But bid me worship thee ;
For thou art earthly things above,
   As far as angels be :
Then whether in the eve or morn
Thou dost the maiden skies adorn,
   Oh ! let me worship thee !

I am but as this drop of dew ;
   Oh ! let me worship thee !
Thy light, thy strength, is ever new,
   Even as the angels' be ,

> And as this dew-drop, till it dies,
> Bosoms the golden stars and skies,
> Oh! let me worship thee!

But, dearest, why that dark look?
LUCIFER.   Let it not
Cloud thine even with its shadow: but the ground
Of all great thoughts is sadness; and I mused
Upon past happiness.   Well — be it past!
Did Lucifer, as I do, gaze on thee,
The flame of woe would flicker in his breast,
And straight die out — the brightness of thy beauty
Quenching it as the sun doth earthly fire.
    ELISSA.   Nay, look not on me so intensely sad.
    LUCIFER.   Forgive me: it was an agony of bliss.
I love thee, and am full of happiness.
My bosom bounds beneath thy smile as doth
The sea's unto the moon, his mighty mistress;
Lying and looking up to her, and saying —
Lovely! lovely! lovely! lady of the Heavens!
Oh! when the thoughts of other joyous days —
Perchance, if such may be, of happier times —
Are falling gently on the memory
Like autumn leaves distained with dusky gold,
Yet softly as a snowflake; and the smile
Of kindliness, like thine, is beaming on me —
Oh! pardon, if I lose myself, nor know
Whether I be with Heaven or thee.
    ELISSA.   Use not
Such ardent phrase, nor mix the claim of aught
On earth with thoughts more than with hopes of
        Heaven.
    LUCIFER.   Hopes, lady! I have none.
    ELISSA.   Thou must have.   All
Have hopes, however wretched they may be,
Or blest.   It is hope which lifts the lark so high —
Hope of a lighter air and bluer sky:
And the poor hack which drops down on the
        flints —

Upon whose eye the dust is settling —
He hopes to die.   No being is which hath
Not love and hope.
    Lucifer.   Yes — **one** !   The ancient Ill,
Dwelling and damned through all which is; that
       spirit
Whose heart is hate — who is the **foe** of God —
The foe of all.
    Elissa.   How knowest thou such doth **live** ?
Love is the happy privilege of mind —
Love is the reason of all living things.
A Trinity there seems of principles,
Which represent and rule created life —
The love of self, our fellows, and our God.
In all throughout one common feeling reigns :
Each doth maintain and is maintained by the other ;
All are compatible — **all** needful ; one
To life — to virtue one — and one **to** bliss ;
Which thus together **make** the power, the end,
And the perfection **of created** Being.
From these three principles doth every deed,
Desire, and will, and reasoning, good or bad, come ;
To these they all determine — sum and scheme :
The three are one in centre and **in** round ;
Wrapping the world of life as do the skies
Our world.   Hail ! air of love, by which **we live !**
How **sweet,** how fragrant ! Spirit, though **unseen** —
Void of gross sign — is scarce a simple essence,
Immortal, immaterial, though **it be.**
One only simple **essence** liveth — **God** —
Creator, uncreate.   The brutes beneath,
The angels high above us, with ourselves,
Are but compounded things of mind and form.
In all things animate is therefore cored
An elemental sameness of existence ;
For **God,** being Love, in love created all,
As **He** contains the whole, and penetrates.
Seraphs love God, and angels love **the** good :
We love **each** other ; and these **lower** lives,

Which walk the earth in thousand diverse shapes,
According to their reason, love us too :
The most intelligent affect us most.
Nay, man's chief wisdom 's love — the love of God.
The new religion — final perfect, pure —
Was that of Christ and love.   His great command —
His all-sufficing precept — was't not love ?
Truly to love ourselves we must love God —
To love God we must all His creatures love —
To love His creatures, both ourselves and Him.
Thus love is all that 's wise, fair, good, and happy.
        LUCIFER.   How knowest thou God doth live ?
            Why did He not,
With that creating hand which sprinkled stars
On space's bosom, bidding her breathe and wake
From the long death-like trance in which she lay, —
With that same hand which scattered o'er the sky,
As this small dust I strew upon the wind,
Yon countless orbs, aye fixing each on Him
Its flaming eye, which winks and blenches oft
Beneath His glance, — with the finger of that hand
Which spangled o'er infinity with suns,
And wrapped it round about Him as a robe, —
Why did He not write out his own great name
In spheres of fire, that Heaven might alway tell
To every creature, God ?   If not, then why
Should I believe when I behold around me
Nought scarce, save ill and woe ?
        ELISSA.   God surely lives
Without God all things are in tunnel darkness.
Let there be God, and all are sun — all God.
And to the just soul, in a future state,
Defect's dark mist, thick-spreading o'er this vale,
Shall dim the eye no more, nor bound survey ;
And evil, now which boweth being down
As dew the grass, shall only fit all life
For fresher growth and for intenser day,
Where God shall dry all tears as the sun dew.
        LUCIFER.   Oh! lady, I am wretched.

ELISSA.   Say not so.
With thee I could not deem myself unhappy.
Hark to the sea!   It sounds like the near hum
Of a great city.
      LUCIFER.   Say, the city earth;
For such these orbs are in the realms of space.
    ELISSA.   I dreamed once that the night came
            down to me ;
In figure, oh! too like thine own for truth,
And looked into me with his thousand eyes,
And that made me unhappy; but it passed,
And I half wished it back.   Mind hath its earth
And Heaven.   The many petty, common thoughts
On which we daily tread, as it were, make one,
And above which few look ; the other is
That high and welkin-like infinity —
The brighter, upper half of the mind's world,
Thick with great sun-like and constellate thoughts;
And in the night of mind, which is our sleep,
These thoughts shine out in dreams.   Dreams
            double life ;
They are the heart's bright shadow on life's flood ;
And even the step from death to deathlessness —
From this earth's gross existence unto Heaven —
Can scarce be more than from the harsh hot day
To sleep's soft scenes, the moonlight of the mind.
The wave is never weary of the wind,
But in mountainous playfulness leaps to it
Always ; but mind gets weary of the world,
And glooms itself in sleep, like a sweet smile,
Line by line, settling into proper sadness ;
For sleep seems part of our immortality :
And why should any thing that dies be sad ?
Last night I dreamed I walked within a hall —
The inside of the world.   Long shroud-like lights
Lit up its lift-like dome and pale, wide walls,
Horizon-like ; and every one was there :
It was the house of Death, and Death was there.
We could not see him, but he was a feeling :

We knew he was around us — heard us — eyed us;
But where wast thou ?   I never met thee once.
And all was still as nothing ; or as God,
Deep judging, when the thought of making first
Quickened and stirred within Him ; and He made
All Heaven at one thought as at a glance.
Noise was there none ; and yet there was a sound
Which seemed to be half like silence, half like
          sound.
All crept about still as the cold wet worms,
Which slid among our feet, we could not scape from.
Round me were ruined fragments of dead gods —
Those shadows of the mystery of One —
And the red worms, too, flourished over these,
For marble is a shadow weighed with mind ;
Each being, as men of old believed, distinct
In form, and place, and power.   But Oh ! not all
The gathered gods of Eld could shine like ours,
No more than all yon stars could make a sun.
But truly then men lived in moral night,
'Neath a dim starlight of religious truth.
I felt my spirit's spring gush out more clear,
Gazing on these : they beautified my mind
As rocks and flowers reflected do a well.
Mind makes itself like that it lives amidst,
And on ; and thus, among dreams, imaginings,
And scenes of awe, and purity, and power,
Grows sternly sweet and calm — all beautiful
With god-like coldness and unconsciousness
Of mortal passion, mental toil ; until,
Like to the marble model of a god,
It doth assume a firm and dazzling form,
Scarcely less incorruptible than that
It emblems : and so grew, methought, my mind.
Matter hath many qualities ; mind, one :
It is irresistible : pure power — pure god.
While wandering on I met what seemed myself :
Was it not strange that we should meet, and there ?
But all is strange in dreaming, as in death,

And waking, as in life : nought is not strange.
Methought that I was happy, because dead.
All hurried to and fro ; and many cried
To each other — Can I do thee any good ?
But no one heeded : nothing could avail :
The world was **one** great grave.   I looked, and saw
Time on his two **great** wings — one, night — one,
        day —
Fly, moth-like, right into the flickering sun ;
So that the sun went out, and they both perished.
And one gat up and spake — a holy man —
Exhorting them ; but each and all cried out —
Go to ! — it helps not — means not : we **are dead.**
Death spake no word methought, but me **he made**
Speak for him : and I dreamed that I was Death ;
Then, that Death only lived : all things were mixed ;
Up and down shooting, like the brain's fierce dance
In a delirium, when we are apt to die.
Hell is my heir ; what kin to me is Heaven ?
Bring out **your hearts** before me.   Give your limbs
To whom ye **list or** love.   My son, Decay
Will take them : give them him.   I want your hearts,
That I may take them up to God.   There came
These words among us, but we knew not whence ;
It was as if the air spake.   And there **rose**
Out of the earth a giant thing, all **earth** ;
His eye was earthy, and **his arm was earthy :**
He had no heart.   He **but said, I am Decay ;**
And, as he spake, he **crumbled into earth,**
And there **was** nothing **of** him.   But **we all**
Lifted our **faces** up at the word, God,
And spied a dark star high above in **the** midst
Of others, numberless as are the dead.
And all plucked out their hearts, and held them in
Their right hands.   Many tried **to** pick out specks
And stains, but could **not : each gave** up his heart.
And something — all things — nothing — it **was**
        Death,
Said, as before, from air — Let us to God !

And straight we rose, leaving behind the raw
Worms and dead gods, all of us — soared and soared
Right upwards, till the star I told thee of
Looked like a moon — the moon became a sun:
The sun — there came a hand between the sun and
     us,
And its five fingers made five nights in air.
God tore the glory from the sun's broad brow,
And flung the flaming scalp off flat to Hell.
I saw Him do it; and it passed close by us.
And then I heard a long, cold, skeleton scream,
Like a trumpet whining through a catacomb,
Which made the sides of that great grave shake in.
I saw the world and vision of the dead
Dim itself off — and all was life! I woke,
And felt the high sun blazoning on my brow
His own almighty mockery of woe,
And fierce and infinite laugh at things which cease.
Hell hath its light — and Heaven; he burns with
     both.
And my dream broke, like life from the last limb —
Quivering; so loth I felt to let it go,
Just as I thought I had caught sight of Heaven.
It came to nought, as dreams of Heaven on earth .
Do always.
    LUCIFER.   It is time we part again.
    ELISSA.   Farewell, then, gentle stars!   To-
      night, farewell!
For we all part at once.   It is thus the bright
Visions and joys of youth break up — but they
For ever.   When ye shine again I will
Be with ye; for I love ye next to him.
To all, adieu!   When shall I see thee next?
    LUCIFER.   Lady, I know not.
    ELISSA.   Say!
    LUCIFER.   Never! perchance.
    ELISSA.   There is but one immortal in the world
Who need say — never!
    LUCIFER.   What if I were he ?

Elissa.   But thou art **not he; and thou shalt**
    not say it.
Stars rise and set—rise, set, and rise again
In their sublime-like beauty through all time.
Why should **not we,** too, ever meet, like them?
    Lucifer.   **I see no** beauty — feel no love — **all**
      things
Are unlovely.
    Elissa.   O earth! be deaf; **and Heaven!**
Shut thy blue eye.   He doth blaspheme the **world.**
Dost not love me?
    Lucifer.   Love **thee?** Ay! Earth and **Heaven**
Together could **not make** a love like mine.
    Elissa.   When **wilt thou come again? To-**
      morrow?
    Lucifer.   Well.
And **then I cross yon sea ere I return;**
For **I have matters in another land.**
Fear **not.**
    Elissa.   **When** will our parting days be over?
    Lucifer.   **Oh!** soon—soon!   Think **of** me
      love, on the waters!
Be happy! and, for me, I love few things **more**
Than at night to ride upon the broad-backed **bil-**
      low,
Seaing along and plunging on his precipitous **path;**
While the red moon is westering low **away,**
And the mad waves are **fighting for the stars,**
Like men for — what they **know not.**
    Elissa.   Scorner!
    Lucifer.   Saint!
    Elissa.   The world **hath** much that's **great;**
    and **but one sea,**
Which is her spirit; **and to** her it stands
As the mad monarch passion **to** the heart—
Fathomless, overwhelming, which receives
The rivers of all feeling; in whose depths
Lie wrecked the riches of all **nature.**   God,
When He did **make thee, moved** upon thee then,

And left His impress there, the same even now
As when the last wave leapt from Chaos. — Hark!
Nay, there is some one coming.
    FESTUS *entering.*   It is I.
I said we should be sure to meet thee here:
For I have brought one who would speak with thee.
    LUCIFER.   Thanks! **and where** is he?
    FESTUS. ·   **Yonder.** He would not
Come up so far as this.
    LUCIFER.   Who is it?
    FESTUS.   **I know not**
Who he may be, or what; but I can guess.
    LUCIFER. Remain a moment, love, till I return.
    ELISSA. Nay — let me leave!
    LUCIFER.   Not **yet**: do not dislike **him.**
He is a friend, and — more another time.
    FESTUS. I am sorry, **lady, to** have caused this
       parting.
I fear I am unwelcome.
    ELISSA.   We were parting.
    FESTUS. Then am I doubly sorry; for I **know**
It is the **saddest** and the sacredest
Moment of all with those who love.
    ELISSA.   He is coming!
So I forgive **thee.**
    LUCIFER.   I must leave thee, **love:**
I know not for how long; it rests with **thee**
If it seem long at all. Eternity
Might pass, and I not know it in thy love.
    ELISSA. If **to** believe that I do love thee **always**
May make time **fly the fleeter** —
    LUCIFER.   I 'll believe it —
Trust me. I leave this lady in thy charge,
Festus. Be kind — wait on her — may he, love?
    ELISSA. **Thou knowest.** I receive him **as thy**
       friend
Whenever he come.
    FESTUS.   I ask no higher title
Than friend of the lovely and the generous.

Elissa.   Farewell!

Festus.   Lady! I will not forget my trust.
[*Apart*] The **breeze** which curls the lake's bright
        lip but **lifts**
A purer, deeper, water to the light;
The ruffling of the wild bird's wing but wakes
A warmer beauty and a downier depth.
That startled shrink, that faintest blossom-blush
Of constancy alarmed!— **Love! if** thou **hast**
One weapon in that shining armory,
The quiver on thy shoulder, where thou keep'st
Each arrowy eye-beam feathered with a sigh;—
If from that bow, shaped so like Beauty's lip,
Strung with a string **of** pearls, thou wilt **twang**
        forth
But one dart, fair into the mark I mean, —
Do it, and I will worship thee for ever:
Yea, I will give thee glory and a name
Known, sunlike, in all nations.   Heart, **be** still!

Lucifer. This parting over—

Elissa.   Yes, this one — **and then?**

Lucifer.   Why, then another, may be.

Elissa.   No—no **more.**
I 'll be unhappy if thou tell'st me so.

Lucifer.   Well, then — no more.

Elissa.   But when wilt thou come **back?**

Lucifer.   Almost before thou wishest.   **He will**
        know.

Elissa.   I **shall** be always asking **him.**   Fare-
        well!   [*Goes.*

Lucifer.   **Shine on, ye stars!** and light her to
        her **rest;**
Scarce are ye worthy for her handmaidens.
Why, Hell would laugh to learn I had been in love.
I have affairs in Hell.   Wilt go with me?

Festus.   Yes, **in a** month or two:— not **just**
        this minute.

Lucifer.   I shall be there and back again ere
        then.

FESTUS. Meanwhile I can amuse myself: so, go!
But sometime I would fain behold thy home,
And pass the gates of fire.
LUCIFER.   And so thou shalt.
My home is everywhere where spirit is.
All things are as I meant them.   Fare thee well.
                                        [*Goes.*

FESTUS. The strongest passion which I have is
            honor:
I would I had none: it is in my way.

SCENE — *Everywhere.*

LUCIFER *and* FESTUS.

FESTUS. Why, earth is in the very midst of
            Heaven!
And space, though void of things, feels full of God.
Hath space no limit?
LUCIFER.   None to thee.   Yet, if
Infinite, it would equal God; and that
To think of is most vain.
FESTUS.   And yet if not
Infinite how can God exist therein?
LUCIFER.   I say not.
FESTUS.   No.   So soon when placed beside
The infinite, the poor immortal fails.
LUCIFER.   Space is God's space: Eternity is
            His
Eternity; His, Heaven.   He only holds
Perfections which are but the impossible
To other beings.
FESTUS.   We are things of time.
LUCIFER.   With God time is not. Unto Him all is
Present Eternity.   Worlds, beings, years,
With all their natures, powers, and events,
The range whereof when making He ordains,
Unfold themselves like flowers.   He foresees
Not, but sees all at once.   Time must not be

Contrasted with Eternity : 't is not
A second of the everlasting year.
Perfections, although infinite with God,
Are all identical ; as much of Him —
And holy is His mercy, merciful
His wisdom, wise His love, and kind his **wrath** —
As form, extension, parts, are requisites
Of matter.   Spirit hath no parts.   It is
One substance, whole and indivisible,
Whatever else.   Souls see each other clear
At one glance, as two drops of rain in air
Might look into each **other,** had they life.
Death does away disguise.   Even here I **feel**
Among these mighty things, **that, as I am,**
I am akin to God ; — that I am part
Of the use universal, and can grasp
Some portion of that reason in the which
The whole is ruled **and** founded ; — that I have
A **spirit nobler** in its **cause** and end,
Lovelier in order, greater in its powers,
Than **all these** bright immensities — how swift !
And **doth** creation's tide for ever flow,
Nor **ebb** with like destruction ?   World on world,
Are they for ever heaping up, and still
The mighty measure never full ?
    Lucifer.   **To act**
Is power's habit ; **alway to create,**
God's ; which, thus ever causing worlds, to **Him**
Nought cumbrous more than new down to a **wing,**
Aye multiplies at once my power and pain.
I have seen many frames of being pass.
This generation of the universe
Will soon be gathered to its grave.   These worlds,
Which bear its sky-pall, soon will follow thine.
I, both.   All things **must** die.
    Festus.   What are ye orbs ?
The words of God — **the** Scriptures of the skies ?
For words with Him cannot be passing, nor
Less real, **vast,** or glorious, than yourselves.

The world is a great poem, and the worlds
The words it is writ in, and we souls the thoughts.
Ye cannot die.
    LUCIFER.   Think **not** on death. Here **all**
Is life, light, beauty. Harp not so on death.
    FESTUS. **I cannot** help me, spirit! Chide **no**
        more.
As who dare gaze the sun, doth after see
Betwixt him and else a dark sun in his eye;
So **I**, once having braved my burning **doom**,
See nought beside — or that in every **thing**.
Hark, what is that I hear?
    LUCIFER.   An angel weeping —
Earth's guardian angel. She is ever weeping.
    FESTUS. See where she **flies**, spirit-torn, **round**
      the heavens,
Like a fore-feel of **madness** about the brain.

    ANGEL OF EARTH. Stars, stars!
        Stop your bright cars!
        Stint your breath —
        Repent ere worse —
        Think of the death
        Of the universe.
        Fear doom, and fear,
        The fate of your kin-sphere.
        As a corse in the tomb,
        Earth! thou art laid in doom:
        The worm is at thy heart.
        I see all things part: —
        The bright air thicken,
        Thunder-stricken:
        Birds from the sky
        Shower like leaves:
        Streamlets stop
        Like ice on leaves:
        The sun go blind:
        Swoon the wind
        On the high hill top —

Swoon and die:
Earth rear off her cities
As a horse his rider;
And still, with each death-strain,
Her heart-wound tear wider:
The lion roar and die
With his eye-balls on the sky:
The eagle scream
And drop like a beam:
Men crowd and cry,
Out on this deathful dream!
A·low dull sound —
'Tis the march of many bones
Under ground;
Up! and they fling,
Like a fly's wing,
Off them the gray grave-stones;
They sit in their biers —
Father and mother,
Man and wife,
Sister and brother,
As in life;
Lady and lover —
Love all over.
Their flesh re-appears —
Their hearts beat —
Their eyes have tears:
Woe! woe!
Do they speak?
Stir? No!
Tongues were too weak,
Save to repeat
Woe!
But they smile
In a while;
For to wipe from His word
The dust of years,
He comes! he comes! the Lord,
Man-God, reappears;

> To bless, and to save
> From death and the grave —
> To redeem and deliver
> For ever and ever!
> The dead rise —
> Death dies.
> Go, Time, and sink
> Thy great thoughts in the sea!
> And quench thy red link!
> Let him flutter to rest
> On thy God-nursing breast,
> Eternity!
> Mother Eternity!
> What is for me?

FESTUS.   Poor angel! · Ah! it is the good who
    suffer.
Look! like a cloud, she has wept herself away.
What of this world we view, and all yon worlds?
If God made not all things from nothing, how
Is He creator?   Something must exist
If otherwise, eternal with Himself;
And all things had not origin in Him.
    LUCIFER.   He made all things of Him.   The
    visible world
Is as the Christ of nature; God the maker
In matter made self-manifest through time.
All things are formed of all things — all of God.
The world is made of wonders.   Every day
Is born a new creation.   Every orb
Hath its revealed word; and every race
Of Being hath its judgment, or shall have.
    FESTUS.   Are all these worlds, then, stocked
    with souls like man's —
Free, fallible, and sinful?
    LUCIFER.   Ay, they are.
All creature-minds, like man's, are fallible.
The seraph who in Heaven highest stands
May fall to ruin deepest.   God is mind —

Pure, perfect, sinless.   Man imperfect is —
Momently sinning.   Evil then results
From imperfection.   The idea of good
Is owned in imperfection's lowest form.
God would not, could not, make aught wholly **ill,**
Nor **aught not like to** err.   Man never was
Perfect nor pure, **or** he would be **so** now.
Thy nature hath some excellences — these
Oft thwarted by low lusts and wicked wills.
What then ?   They are necessitate in kind,
As change in nature, or as shade to light.
No darkness hath the sun — no weakness God :
These only be the faulty qualities
Of secondary natures — planets, men.
God hath no attributes unless To Be
Be one : 't would mix Him with the things He hath
        made.
God is all God, as life is that **which lives.**
I am a mighty spirit, and **yet I**
Am but to God what lightning **is** to light :
Lightning slays **one** thing — light makes all things
        live.
Bear, then, thy necessary ills with grace ;
No positive estate or principle
Is Evil — debtor wholly for its form
And measure to defect — defect to good.
Good's the sole positive principle in the **world ;**
It is only thus, that **what** God makes, He **loves** —
And must : the others are **but** off-shoots.   **Ill**
Is limited.   One cannot **form a** scheme
For universal evil ; not even **I.**
   Festus.   **Can** imperfection **from perfection**
        come ?
Can God make aught defective ?
   Lucifer.   How aught else ?
There are but three proportions **in** all things —
The greater — equal — less.   God could not **make**
A God above Himself, nor equal with —
By nature and necessity the Highest ;

So, if He make, it must be lesser minds
Little and less from angels down to men,
Whose natures are imperfect, as His own
Must be all-perfect. These two states are not,
Except as whole unto its parts, opposed ;
And evil is itself no ill unless
Creation be.
> FESTUS.   Is God the cause of evil ?
> LUCIFER.   So far as evil comes from imperfec-
> tion,
And imperfection from the things He hath made,
And what He hath made from His will to make.
> FESTUS.   Oh ! let me rest, be it but a moment's
> pause !
This endless light-like journey wearies me.
Remember still my spirit toils in dust —
A dark, close cloud.
> LUCIFER.   Alight, then, on this orb.
I am not wearied : I will watch by thee.
He sleeps — he dreams. How far men see in
> dreams !
In dreams they can accomplish worlds of things:
The heart then suffers a fusion of all feeling
Back to its youthful hours of innocence,
And nakedness, and paradise ; ere yet
The world had wound a perishing garb around it ;
While yet its God came down and spake to it.
Such and so great are dreams. My might, my
> being
To him is but a dream's. And could a state
To come fill up their dream-stretched minds, they
> might
Be gods. And may it not be so ? Then man
Is worth my ruining. What does he dream ?
With all the sway his spirit now exerts
O'er time, space, thought, it is but a shadowy
> sway,
Light as a mountain shadow on a lake.
Mine is the mountain's self. A touch would shake

To nought whatever his soul now feels or acts;
But not a world-quake could touch aught of mine
Thus much we differ.   I will **not envy man.**
Power alone makes being **bearable.**
And yet this dream-power is mind-power — real :
All things are real : fiction cannot be.
A thought is real as the world — a dream
True as all God doth know — with whom all is
  true.
The deep, dense sleep of half-dead exhaustedness !
Would I could feel it.   Ah ! **he wakes** at last.
 FESTUS.   Oh ! I have **dreamed a dream** so
  beautiful !
Methought I **lay** as **it were here ;** and, lo !
A spirit came and **gave me wings of light,**
Which thrice I **waved delighted.   Up we flew**
Sheer through **the shining air, far past** the sun's
Broad blazing **disk, — past where the** great great
  snake
Binds in his **bright** coil half **the host of** Heaven, —
Past thee, **Orion ! who,** with arm uplift,
Threatening the **throne** of God, dost ever stand
Sublimely impious; and thy mighty mace
Whirling **on** high, down from its glorious seat
Drops, crushed and shattered, many a **shining**
  world.
And so **the brave** and beautiful **of old**
Believed thou **wast a giant made of worlds** :
And they **were right, if thus** they bodied **out**
The immortal **mind; for it hath** starlike beauty,
And worldlike **might; and is as** high above
The things it scorns, **and will** make war with God,
Though He gave **it** earth and Heaven, and arms
  to win
Them both **; and,** spite of lust and pride, to earn
  them.
And now **thy** soul informs yon **hundred stars,**
As mine my limbs — well, 'tis **a noble end.**
What now to thee be mortal maid **or goddess ?**

Look! she who fled thee once, **now** loves and longs
To clasp thee to her **cold and** beamy breast.
Pine moon! thou art as far below him now,
As **once she was** above thee, thou of the world-belt!
And she **who** had thee, and who knew thee god,
Died of **her** boast, and lies in her own dust.
And she who loved thee, the young blushy Morning,
Who caught **thee** in her arms, and bore thee off
Far o'er the lashing seas **to a** lonely **isle,**
Where she might pleasure longer **and in secret—**
That love undid thee; and **it is so now:**
Whether **the** beauty **seek,** or flee, **or** have,
'Tis **a like** ill — this beauty doubly mortal.
What though the moon with madness slew thee there,
Let me believe it was within the arms
That loved thee even **in** the stroke of death,
And that there snapped the lightning link of life.
Kill, but not conquer, man nor mind may gods.
Thou image of the Almighty error, man!
Banished and banned to Heaven, by a weak world,
Which makes the minds, it cannot master gods.
And thou, **the first and greatest** of half-gods,
Which they in olden time did star together
To an **idolatrous immortality;**
Who nationalized the Heavens, **and gave all stars**
Unto **the** spirits **of** the good and **brave,**
Forestalling God by ages — wondrous **men!**   .
And if— beguiled by wine, and the low wiles
Thou wouldst not creep to meet, and a drunken
         sleep,
Like **to** high **noon** in the midst **of all his might,**
Close by the **brink of** immortality —
The deep dominions **of thy** sea-sire, thou
Didst lose **thy** light by kings who hate the great,
Thou only hadst to stand up to the sun,
And gain again thine eyes.   So the great king,
The world, the tyrant we elect, in vain
Puts out **the** eyes of mind: it looks to God,
And reaps its light again.   Wherefore, revenge!

Oùt with the sword! the world will run before thee,
Orion! belted giant of the skies!
Thou with the treble strain **of** godhood in thee!
March! there is nought **to** hinder thee in Hea-
    ven:—
Past that great **sickle saved** for one day's work,
When He **who sowed shall** reap Creation's field;—
Past those **high diademed** orbs which show to man
His crown to come;—up through the starry strings
Of that high harp close by the feet of God,
Which He, methought, took up **and** struck, **till**
    Heaven,
In **love's** immortal **madness, rang and reeled;**
The stars fell **on their faces; and, far off,**
The wild world **halted—shook his burning mane—**
Then, like a **fresh-blown trumpet blast, went on,**
Or like a god gone **mad. On, on we flew,**
I and the spirit, **far beyond all things**
Of measure, motion, time, and aught create;
Where the stars stood on the edge of the first noth-
    ing,
And looked each other in the face and fled,—
Past even the last long starless void, to God;
Whom straight I heard, methought, commanding
    thus:
Immortal! I am God. **Hie** back to earth,
And say to all, that **God doth** say — Love God!
    LUCIFER. God **visits men** a dreaming: I, **awake.**
    FESTUS. And **my dream** changed **to one of**
        general doom.
Wilt hear it?
    LUCIFER. **Ay,** say on! **It is** but **a dream.**
    FESTUS. **God** made **all mind** and **motion cease;**
        and, lo!
The whole was death and peace. **An** endless time
Obtained, in which the power of **all** made failed.
God bade the worlds to judgment, and they came—
Pale, trembling, corpse-like. To **the** souls therein
Then spake the Maker: **Deathless** spirits, rise!

And straight they thronged around the throne. His arm
The Almighty then uplift, and smote the worlds
Once, and they fell in fragments like to spray,
And vanished in their native void. He shook
The stars from Heaven like rain-drops from a
            bough;
Like tears they poured adown creation's face.
Spirit and space were all things. Matter, death,
And time, left even not a wake to tell
Where once their track o'er being. God's own light
Undarkened and unhindered by a sun,
Glowed forth alone in glory. And through all
A clear and tremulous sense of God prevailed,
Like to the blush of love upon the cheek,
Or the full feeling lightening through the eye,
Or the quick music in the chords of harps.
God judged all creatures unto bliss or woe,
According to their deeds, and faith, and His
Own will: and straight the saved upraised a voice
Which seemed to emulate eternity
In its triumphant over-blessedness.
The lost leapt up and cursed God to His face —
A curse might make the sun turn cold to hear;
And thee, in all thy burning glory, tremble,
In front of all thine angels, like a chord.
Rage writhed each brow into a changeless scowl.
Madly they mocked at God, and dared His eye,
Safe in their curse of deathlessness. To Hell
They hied like storms; and, cursing all things, each
Soul wrapped him in his shroud of fire for aye,
With one long, loud howl, which seemed to deafen
            Heaven —
And then I woke.
    LUCIFER.   A wild, fantastic dream
A mere mirage of mind! Come, let us leave:
We have seen enough of this world.
    FESTUS.   Lift me up, then
World upon world, how they come rolling on!

But none that I see are so fair as earth :
There is so much to love **that is** purely earth.
Now I could wander all day in the wood,
Where nature, **like a sibyl,** writes **the** fate
Of all that live **on her** red forest **leaves :**
And have no other aim than wandering
Within that wood, and wind my arms around
Its gray, gaunt trunks, and think and feel to them ;
While the wind, sinking, moans over the earth
Like a giant over some dead captive dame,
Whom death had saved **from** madness and **his**
        love ;—
Could tramp across the brown **and** springy moor,
And over the purple ling, and never tire ;—
Could look upon the ripple **of** a river,
Or on a tree's long shadow down a hill,
For a whole summer's day, wishing the sun
Would drink **my** soul up **to** him as he draws
Dew from the earth.   These things are in my
        mind,
And suns and systems cannot drive them out.
Dost ravage all these worlds ?
    Lucifer.   Ay, all mine **own.**
Where spirit is, there evil ; and the world
Is full of me as ocean is of brine.
    Festus.   God is all **perfect** ; **man⁻ imperfect.**
        Thou ?
    Lucifer.   **I am the imperfection of the whole —**
The pitch profoundest **of the fallible.**
Myself the all of evil **which** exists —
The ocean heaped into a single surge.
    Festus.   O God ! why **wouldst** Thou make the
        universe ?   •
    Lucifer.   Child ! **quench** yon suns ; strip death
        of its decay ;
Men **of their** follies — Hell of all its woe !
These, if thou didst, thou couldst not banish me.
I am the shadow which Creation casts
From God's own light. — But here we are, at Hell.

Hark to the thunderous roaring of its fires!
Yet ere we further pass — stop! dost thou shrink?
  FESTUS.   At nought — not I!   Come on, fiend!
      follow me!

SCENE — *Hell.*

LUCIFER *and* FESTUS *entering.*

  LUCIFER. Behold my world! Man's science counts it not
Upon the brightest sky. He never knows
How near it comes to him; but, swathed in clouds,
As though in plumed and palled state, it steals
Hearselike and thieflike round the universe,
For ever rolling and returning not —
Robbing all worlds of many an angel soul —
With its light hidden in its breast, which burns
With all concentrate and superfluent woe.
Nor sun nor moon illume it, and to those
Which dwell in it, not live, the starry skies
Have told no time since first they entered there.
Worlds have been built, and to their central base
Ruined and razed to the last atom; they
Of neither know, nor can — unconscious, save
To agony — nought knowing even of God
But His omnipotence to execute
Torture on those He hath in wrath endowed
With Heaven's own immortality, to make
Them feel what woe the Almighty can inflict,
And the all-feeble suffer, and not be
Annihilated as they would. Be sure
That this is Hell. The blood which hath embrued
Earth's breast, since first men met in war, may hope
Yet to be formed again and reascend,
Each drop its individual vein : the foam-bubble,
Sun-drawn out of the sea into the clouds,

To scale the cataract down which it fell,
Or seek its primal source in earth's hot heart ;
But for the lost to rise **to or** regain
Heaven, or to hope it, **is** impossible.
    FESTUS.   Are all these angels then, or men, **or**
       both ?
Or mortals of all worlds ?
    LUCIFER.   Immortals, all.
    FESTUS.   **What numbers !**
    LUCIFER.   **All** are spirits fallen through **sin**
At various periods of eternity ;
And not by one offence, **to** one **same doom,**
And **at** one moment, did they down from **Heaven**
Like to the rapid droppings of a shower ; —
No ! each distinct as thunder-peals, they fell ;
Save those that fell with me. With me began
Sin even in Heaven ; with me but sin remains.
Once I alone was Hell. Behold my fruits !
    FESTUS. What do yon fiends ! some 'mong
       them look like mortals :
Their hearts **shine** through them like live coals
       through **ashes.**
They look like madmen gone delirious.
Oh ! horror ! let me hence !
    LUCIFER.   **Nay, hear.**
    FESTUS.   **I hear**
A strain incongruous as a merry dirge,
Or sacramental bacchanal might be.
    LUCIFER. Men are they **not, but devils at the**
       best ;
And I would have thee mark **them.**
    FESTUS.   I attend.

    FIENDS. Fill the bowl ! it burns but blackly·
    Fill **it** up with living fire :
Drunkard ! hadst thou sipped as slackly
    As thou pourest — pour it higher !
Then thou hadst ne'er with me been bound
    In Hell to dwell ;

But let the burning health **go round** —
  Drunkard ! — to Hell !

Fill ! it drinks but cold and leadly ;
  Fill it up with bubbling fire :
Drink ! 'tis nothing half so deadly
  As thy soul when living, Liar !
Or thou hadst ne'er **with me** been **bound**
  In Hell to dwell ;
  But let the burning health go round —
  Liar ! — to Hell !

Fill ! it boils but sick and sadly ;
  Fill ! **some** more immortal fire :
Murderer ! drain it quickly, madly,
  As **the** stab thou gav'st thy sire !
Or thou hadst ne'er with me **been bound**
  In Hell to dwell ;
  But let the burning health **go round** —
  Murderer ! — **to** Hell !

FESTUS.   Nay, let me quit ! now know I what
  Hell is.
What are **they** — drunkards, liars, murderers ?
  LUCIFER.   **Can wine destroy the soul ? or Hell's**
  fierce flames
Feed upon holy water, wherewith **Priest**
Baptizeth sinless babe ?   Can liar make
God lie ? or cheat his neighbor **of** his soul ?
No ! God's salvation waiteth **not** on man's
Weak will nor ministry ; nor **man's** perdition
Upon his brother's **hatred or neglect.**
Can murderer slay the soul ? or suicide
Drug immortality ?   Their sin is great,
And is eternally condemned of God ;
But of their nature, the which Death destroys,
Their own as well as victim's recompense.
When Time hath overcome the ruin **wrought**
Upon their hearts who loved the dead, that **they**

Who suffered most have most forgiven ill, —
Shall the dead slay the living ceaselessly? —
Shall God, who is all Love, reverse, reserve,
Here **in** Hell, ages afterwards, those crimes?
And **because** man hath sinned a **moment, crown**
All crime **in** instituting punishment
Unending for an instantaneous wrong?
Shall that be justice? It were more **than ven-**
  geance.
Yet such the Deity men fable, such
The Hell whereto **they** doom themselves.
 Festus.   **No more**
The world is all-sufficient for itself;
And Hell and Heaven are not the equivalents
Of earth's iniquities and righteousness.
 Lucifer. Can those who are idolaters **defraud**
God of His worship? **who** adore the world,
Gold, **or as** savages, the stars and Heaven,
And Elements of Earth? None worship Him,
But **with and in** His spirit. Nought attains
His love **but that** proceedeth from **it** first.
His praise is everlasting in all **worlds**
And **starry ages of** eternity.
Can they who covet the world's worthiest goods,
Wealth, honor, power, knowledge, rank, or aught
Merit eternal **torment** for **a sin**
Wherewith is bound the world's prosperity
And human glory? Nought eternal is
But that which **is of** God. All **pain** and **woe**
Are therefore finite. **Can** the robber steal
From God **or Heaven a thing, or** from **the soul?**
Or the deflowerer **desecrate** and undo
The **espousals of the** spirit **with its** Lord?
How weak **is** virtue, then, and **vice,** how vain!
How wretched human righteousness — and sin,
How despicable to the soul assured,
Since neither hath a recompense. The **one**
By Him destroyed who **can** alone unmake
That He hath **made; the** other perfected,

United, Deified in God the Son
With His own nature.   Infinite Universe!
Thou hast no like, no second favorite
To mortal man of God's.
　　FESTUS.　　　　　　　What mean the words
Of yonder fiendish chant, there?
　　LUCIFER.　　　　　　　　Words and shapes
Are equally as soon assumed by spirits.
What mean my words to thee?
　　FESTUS.　　　　　　In sooth, I know not.
I am constrained to hear them.
　　LUCIFER.　　　　　　　As for these!—
It is a fire of soul in which they burn,
And by which they are purified from sin —
Rid of the grossness which had gathered round
　　　them,
And burned again into their virgin brightness.
All things work round like worlds.   The orb of Hell
Hath yet its place in Heaven as thine and all.
But, as a spiritual quality,
As spirit is the substance of all matter—
Hidden or open, heatlike doth inhere
In all existence — or for good or ill.
Look at yon' spirit.
　　FESTUS.　　　　What was it brought thee hither?
　　SPIRIT.　I was an angel once, ages agone;
But doing good and glorifying not
God, who empowered me, He sent me here
To fire the proud spot from my heart.
　　FESTUS.　　　　　　　　And when
Wilt thou do this, and own thou hast wronged God?
　　SPIRIT.　I do repent me, and confess it now.
I will not ask God now to let me be
What once I was; but might I only sit
A footstool for some other worthier far
Who owneth now my throne, I should be happy —
Far happier than I was in my proud prayers,
That God would give me worlds on worlds to
　　　govern,

And in receiving all their prayers and blessings.
O God! remember me!   O save me!
  Festus.   See!
I do believe there is an angel coming
This way from Heaven.
  Spirit.   He comes to me — to me!
  Angel.   Hail, sufferer!
  Spirit.   Sinner.
  Angel.   God hath bade me bring thee
Away to Heaven; thy throne is kept for thee;
And all the hosts of Heaven are on the wing
To welcome thee again.
  Spirit.   I dare not come:
I am not worthy Heaven.
  Angel.   But God will make thee.
  Festus.   Spirit — farewell! and may we meet
     again
In better time and place.
  Spirit.   Glory to God!
I go — farewell! — and I will speak of thee.
But, oh! repent!   Be humble, and despair not.
             [Angel and Spirit rise.
  Lucifer.   Oh! think, when all are judged,
     what hosts of souls
Will then be mine at last! — what wings of fire!
Deemest thou yet as mortal?
  Festus.   This is not
As thou didst speak of Hell, nor as I judged.
  Lucifer.   Hell is the wrath of God — His hate
     of sin.
God hates man's nature; be it said of his
As of all beings!
  Festus.   How hate that he hath made?
  Lucifer.   The infinite opposition of Perfection
To imperfection leaves nor choice nor mean.
Thus the demeanor of thy world grieved God,
Till its destruction pleased Him, and its name
Was struck out of the starry scroll; thus all
Creation worketh infinite grief in Time.

When human nature is most perfect, then
Its fall is nearest, as of ripest fruit.
Man's pleasure in the world — to both of which
His nature is made fit — is not of God,
Save theirs on whom His spirit He bestows,
As in a twilight between earth and Heaven,
A promissory Being unfulfilled —
But still how glorious to the stone-blind world.
This is in time, but in eternity,
He raises, remakes, adds to all He made
His own immortalizing love and grace,
Which keeps them ever pure as is the sea,
And incorruptible in godly will.
The bliss of God and man originates,
Unites, and ends in self — in Deity :
To whom is neither motive — good — nor end
Greater or less, or other than Himself.

    FESTUS.   But how can the Creator glory find
In Hell, or creature, good — if God be Love,
Or man a being salvable ? Oh, say !
But who comes hither ?

    LUCIFER.   It is the Son of God ! —
Omnipotent ! before whose steadfast feet
The thrones of Heaven, which hoped to have o'er-
      thrown thine,
But now all strengthless, hopeless, Godless here,
Rose once and ebbed forever, even these
Deep in their fiery abyss of woe
Unbent, unbettered will again rush forth
In all the might of madness and despair,
To prove their hatred of Thee and Thy love.
Salvation is the scorn of Angels here.
What dost Thou here, not having sinned ?

    SON OF GOD.   For men
I bore with death — for fiends I bear with sin ;
And death and sin are each the pain I pay   [save
For the love which brought me down from Heaven to
Both men and devils ; and the Father makes
And orders every instant what is best.

Festus.   This is **God's truth**; Hell feels **a mo-**
    ment cool.   [His love, —
  Son of God.   **Hell is** His justice — Heaven is
Earth His long-suffering: all the world is but
A quality of God; therefore come I
To temper these — to give to justice, mercy;
And **to** long-suffering, longer.   Heaven is mine
By birthright.   Lo! I am the heir of God:
He hath given all things to me.   I have made
The earth mine own, and all yon **countless** worlds,
And all the souls therein; yea, soul by soul,
And world by world, have I redeemed **them all** —
One by one through eternity, or given
The means **of** their salvation: why not, **then,**
Hell?
  Festus.   Every spirit is to be redeemed.
  Son of God.   Mortal! it has: the best and worst
    need one
And same salvation.   There is nothing final
In all this world but God; therefore these souls
Whom I see here, **and** pity for their woes —
But for their **evil** more — these need not be
Inhelled **for** ever; for although once, twice, thrice,
On earth or here they may have put God from
    them —
Disowned **His** prophets — mocked **His angels** —
    slain
His Son in his mortality — and stormed
His curses back to Him; yet God is such,
That He can pity still; and I can suffer
For them, and save them.   Father! I fear not,
But by Thy might I can save Hell from Hell.
Fiends! hear ye me!   Why will ye burn for ever?
Look!   I am **here all** water: come and drink,
And bathe in me! baptize your burning souls
In the pure well of life — the spring of God.
I come to save all souls who will be saved.
Come, ye immortal fallen! rise again!
There is a resurrection for the dead,

And for the second dead.   And though ye died,
And fell, and fell again, and again died —
There is a life to come, a rise for all, —
A life to come for ever, and a rise
Perpetual as the spring is in the year.
    A FIEND.   Thou Son of God! what wilt thou
       here with us?
Have we not Hell enough without Thy presence?
Remorse, and always strife, and hate of all,
I see around me : is it not enough?
Why wilt Thou double it with Thy mild eyes?
    SON OF GOD.   Spirit! I come to save thee.
    FIEND.   How can that be?
    SON OF GOD.   Repent!   God will forgive thee
       then; and I
Will save thee; and the Holy One shall hallow.
Repent thou, for thy judgment is at hand;
But if thou slurrest over these means and times,
Which have been given thee for repentance here —
Tremble!   This Hell is nothing to thy next.
Believest thou I can save thee?
    FIEND.   Son of God!
I do believe it.   Let me worship.
    SON OF GOD.   Come!
Come to me!   Lo! I will but touch thy brow,
And make thee bright as morning is in Heaven.
    SPIRIT.   Angel of light I am again!   Look here!
This — this is to be saved!
    LUCIFER.   I like it not.
    SON OF GOD.   Hear! ye immortals dead! this I
       can do.
Repent! and be all angels.
    SPIRIT.   Oh, believe!
He is God.   Worship Him!   He comes to save us.
    LUCIFER.   Stand thou beside me : I will speak to
       them;
Or they will sure believe Him.   Hell! oh Hell!
Powers of perdition! thrones of darkness! — hear!
Wrath, ruin, torment! — hear me!   It is I!

Thanks, fiends !   I know ye hate me well, and may :
I tempted, ruined, damned ye every one.
Were ye not proud, now, to be conquered by me ?
But wherefore so supine ?   **Am** I your lord ?
Me do ye doubt ? or dare ye Him believe ?
What is an **angel dressed** in shiny white ?
Can I not make ye angels ?   Ay ! and more :
I cannot make ye less — nor ye yourselves —
Nor God — nor Son of God.   But hark to **me** !
Be still, ye thunderblasts and hills of fire !
Hell doth out-din itself. — Hell-hearted slaves !
What are ye that I thus should toil for ye ?
Who hardly earn the fire that burns ye up ?
Power I have proffered, but ye have refused :
Nothing is for ye but your fiery fate.
Kingdoms I have prepared, and ye have spurned.
Slaves ! slaves ! ye are too much at **ease** !   Ye leave
Me single in the work of woe.   I, sole,
Go forth to sow destruction : I, alone,
Reap ruin.   Had ye been as I, ere now
The universe had been all Hell ; and, for
A pit, each fiend had had a world to rule.   *
Rise !   Yet we 'll play all hell against all Heaven.
Up ! up ! and then at once we will battle God ;
And hurling each his orb against the throne,
Strange if we will not scatter it like sand.
To reign is nothing half like to dethrone !
Dethrone ! and each is greater then than God.
And will ye, then, give **up your** hopes of Heaven,
And entrance as young conquerors fresh from spoil,
And choice of thrones won by your death-red hands,
For pitiful repentance, like him yonder ?
Forbid it ! all the prowess, pride, and pain
Of Hell that we have borne with ! do ye not ?
Meanwhile man's world is straight to be destroyed.
Be glad ! be glad !   Earth's sons may soon be here.
And here, as earnest of the truth I tell,
Behold this earthling standing by my side !
Speak to them, **Festus.**

FESTUS.   Nay, I dread them.
LUCIFER.   Speak !
Great spirits ! he scarce is worthy to address ye,
In that I cannot say he yet is damned.
      FESTUS.   But I am here ; what recks it how or
            why ?
Ye care not, and I know not.   It is fate :
The will of God and him who sets me here ;
And which I question not.   It must be good,
Whether decreed that I be saved or lost.
But I have poor pretensions for this place ;
And none, I hope, have worse that are to come.
For I have never mocked the word of God,
Nor torn it into fuel for my scorn :
Nor doubted, saving tremblingly, His being : —
His love to man — His right to be adored, —
Never have hated, never wronged my race, —
Deluded nor rejoiced in their delusion ;
Never have beckoned off the good from good —
Never have mocked nor scattered hopes — nor e'er
Have wasted hearts, nor desolated hearths ;
And if I have once, twice, as who hath not ?
Toyed with temptation, yet even he will say
Who standeth there, that I have never given
Up to his burning dalliance my soul.
And yet he is my friend, the Evil one.
And why is wondrous ; judge ye wherefore too.
I have no malice, envy, nor revenge ;
None of those petty passions which bad hearts
Scourge red into themselves — for passions are
Sufferings — and which to nourish is his want ;
Wherein doth lie his power : these I have not.
And, save enjoying earth, I have done never
Aught that he could take part in.   But he came
From God he said, to give ; and I believed ; —
Great spirits lie not — doubt not.
      LUCIFER.   He says truth.
But it is not for him nor you to know
The reason of my doings : it is the thing

Unfeared and unforethought which tempts, **betrays.**
It is I who bait the world to do its will.
As to this mortal, God hath sanctioned all
That I have done, or may do to the end;
Which I have nought to do with.   Son of God!
Go on redeeming!— I will go **on** damning.
God! go on making!— I will go on marring.
Go on believing, **man!**— I go **on** tempting.
Saint! angel! cherub! seraph! and archangel!
Go ye on blessing!— I will go on cursing!
I now retrack my course to earth; therein
To work out what remaineth of the fate
Of this man, **and await his world's** destruction.
What next may **hap I care not.**
    Festus.   **Let** us hence!
    Lucifer.   Where is **He?**
    Festus.   There — see! many do believe.
Orb of perdition! thou, too, shalt die out,
And thy red-sheeted flames shall fail for **aye.**
Thy palpitating piles of ruin, hot
With ever-active agony, and quick
With soul immortal, down whose midnight heights
The wrath of God in cataracts of fire
Precipitates itself unceasingly,
Shall **rush** into destruction as a steed
Rushes into the battle, there to die.
Thy quivering hills of black and bloody hue,
Death-breathing, shall collapse **like** lifeless lungs,
And end in air and ashes.   Thou shalt be
Dashed from creation spark-like from a hand
Scarless: pass like a rolled syllable
Of midnight thunder from the coming day.
The river of all life, which flows through Heaven,
Shall **yet** reach thee **and** overflood thy flames!—
Thou shalt no more **vex** God nor man; nor all
The seekings of the soul shall hunt thee out.
Thy day is sometime **over.**   Be it soon!
And thou the lost world which the world hath lost!

SCENE. — *Colonnade and Lawn.*

FESTUS *and* CLARA.

CLARA.   What is it thou wilt tell me?
FESTUS.   I have seen
What ne'er again may be, nor e'er till now hath
      been.
CLARA.   Where didst thou see — and what?
FESTUS.   In space.   He took me there,
Of whom I oft have told thee.   Midst in air
Was God.   I 'll tell thee that he told the spheres;
For the great family of the universe
Round Him were gathered as a fire : but we
Held back; and, saving God, none did us see.
Though round his throne in sunny halo rolls
A ceaseless, countless throng of sainted souls.
CLARA.   Say on, love!   Let me hear.
FESTUS.   A sound, then, first
I heard as of a pent-up flood just burst :
It was the rush of God's world-winnowing wing;
Which bowed the orbs as flowers are bowed by
          breath of spring.
And then a voice I heard, a voice sublime —
To which the hoarded thunders of all time
Pealing earth's death knell shall a whisper be —
Saying these words — Where will ye worship me?
Ay, where shall be your Maker's holy place?
The Heaven of Heavens is poor before His face.
How shall ye mete my temple, ye who die?
Look! can ye span your God's infinity?
Hear, mighty universe, thy Maker's voice!
Let all thy myriad, myriad worlds rejoice!
Lo! I, your Maker, do amid ye come,
To choose my worship and to name my home.
This heard each sphere; and all throughout the sky
Came crowding round.   Our earth was rolling by,
When God said to it — Rest! and fast it stood.
With voice like winds through some wide olden
          wood,

Thus spake the One again : Behold, **O** Earth !
Thy parent, God ! it is **I who** gave thee birth.
With all **my** love I **did** thee **once** endow ;
With **all my mercy** — and thou hast them now.
But hear my words ! thou never lovedst me well,
Nor fearedst **my** wrath : dreadst thou no longer
     Hell ?
Dream'st **thou that** guilt **shall always mock** those
     fires ?
That deathless death which Hell **for aye expires ?**
Should all creation its rebellion raise,
I speak, and this broad universe doth blaze —
Pass like a dew-drop **'neath** mine angry rays —
Blaze like the fat in **sacrificial** flame :
And that burned offering, when I come **to claim,**
Its scorching, quenchless mass, all, **I** will pour
Upon thy naked soul : — canst thou endure ?
He spake ; and, **as the** fear-fraught words flew past,
Earth fluttered **like a dead leaf** in their blast.
Am not I God ? Answer me ! Hope not thou,
Impenitent, to ward my righteous blow.
Yet, come again ! my proffered mercy hear !
Rejoice and sing ! sweet music in thine ear
And peace I speak : seek but to be forgiven :
Repent ! and thou shalt meet thy God in Heaven.
Go ! Cleanse thy brow **from** blood, **thy heart from**
     crime,   .
And on thy Saviour call while yet **is time !**
Now to this universe of pride **and sin**
I speak, ere yet I call mine angels in.
Draw nigh, ye worlds ! — and, lo ! their light did
     seem
Before His eye paled to a pearl's dull beam.
Attend ! said God — o'er all He lift his hand. —
Where will ye set my tent ? where shall **my temple**
     stand ?
And all were dumb. Distracting silence spread
Throughou that host **as** each were stricken dead.
I made ye. I endowed ye. Ye are mine.

Then trembled out each orb: Thine, God! for ever
   Thine!
All that ye have, within myself have I;
God, am complete; full inexhaustibly.
I dwell within myself, and ye in me,
Not in yourselves; I have infinity.
The every thing in all things is my **throne;**
Your might is my might, and your **wealth mine** own:
'Tis by my power and sufferance **that ye** shine:
I live in light and all your **light is mine.**
Be dark! said God. Night was. **Each glowing**
   sphere
Dulled. Night seemed every thing and everywhere,
Save that in utter space a feeble flare
Told that the pits of hell were sunken there.
Shuddered in fear the universe the while,
Till God again embraced it with a smile.
And all things made were **glad.** Come **now and**
   hear,
Ye worlds! said God, the truth **I** thus make clear:
My words are mercy, wherefore should ye fear?
And straight, obedient to his sacred will,
One great concentrate globe they crowd to fill;
Systems and suns pour forth their glowing **urns;**
Full in the face of God the glory **burns.**
Hearken, thou host! thy trembling hope **to raise,**
I to all Being thus make plain my ways;—
God, the Creator, bade creation rise,
And **matter** came in void like clouds in skies;
Lifeless and cold it spread throughout all space,
And darkness dwelt and frowned upon its face:
Chaos I bade depart this work of mine,
And straight **the** mighty elements disjoin.
Then light I lit; then order I ordained,
And put the dance of atoms to an end.
Matter I brake, and scattered into globes,
And clad ye each in green and growing robes:
Your sizes, places, forms, I fixed with laws,
And wrought the link between effect and **cause.**

Then formed I lives for each, which might inherit
Will, reason, form, and power — **not** deathless **spirit.**
Then I made spirits, things of heavenly worth,
Deathless, Divine.   Round these, from every earth,
I gathered forms and features fit for love,
Trust, pleasure, power, and all I could approve.
To every spirit I disclosed my name,
My love, my might, and whence all Being came:
To deathless souls I righteously decreed
Accountability for thought, word, deed.
Then every orb complete, along the sky,
In glory, beauty, order, harmony,
I launched.   Souls, worlds **did** every thing **possess**
Which could a mortal and immortal bless.
To all the hope of happier state was given —
For all I keep one common boundless Heaven.
Ye all have freedom, and ye all do sin,
For ye are creatures : but ye all may win
Life everlasting — everlasting joy,
If ye do but the love of sin destroy :
This only **is** offence ; for sin ye must
Not by my will ; but weakness dwells with dust,
Unless **ye** have sinned ye cannot enter Heaven.
How shall a sinless creature be forgiven ?
And by forgiveness only can ye claim
Hope in my mercy, trust upon my name.
I knew that ye would **all to** sin be **given ;**
But I, even God, have **paid** your price to **Heaven :**
And if ye will not journey on that way —
The truth — the life — what do **ye** merit ? say !
Death is the **gate** of life, and sin, of bliss :
Mark the dread truth ! but mourn your deeds
        amiss.
Cast off your guilt ! abandon folly's path !
Turn to **the** Lord your God ere hell His wrath !
Turn from your madness, wicked ones, and live !
Take, take the bliss which God alone can give.
God, **the** Creator, me all beings **own** —
God, the Redeemer, **I** will still be known —

God, too, the Judge — the each — the three — the
        one.
Again the Everlasting cried — Repent !
To bless or curse I am Omnipotent.
And what art thou, created Being ?   Round
That world of worlds His arm the Almighty wound ;
The bright immensity He raised, and pressed,
All trembling, like a babe, unto His breast.
There, in the Father's bosom rose again,
Of filial love, the universal strain ;
Strong and exultant — blissful, pure, sublime,
It rolled, and thrilled, and swelled in notes unknown
        to time.
Think ye that I, who thus do ye maintain ;
Thus always cherish ye, or all were vain —
Ye all would drop into your native void,
If by my hand ye were not held and buoyed :
Think ye that I cannot uphold in Heaven,
In righteous state, the souls I have forgiven ?
Is this a weightier task ? with God, 't is one
To guide a sunbeam or create a sun —
To rule ten thousand thousand worlds or none.
Go, worlds ! said God, but learn, ere ye depart,
My favored temple is an humble heart ;
Therein to dwell I leave my loftiest skies —
There shall my holy of all holies rise !
He spake ; and swiftly, reverent to His will,
Sprang each bright orb on high its sphere to fill.
Glory to God ! they chanted as they soared —
Father Almighty ! be Thou all-adored.
Thou art the glory — we, Thine universe,
Serve but abroad Thy lustre to disperse.
Unsearchable, and yet to all made known !
The world at once Thy kingdom and Thy throne —
Pity us, God ! nor chase us quite away
Before Thy wrath, as night before the day.
In Thee, our God, we live ; from Thee we
        came —
The feeble sparks of Thine eternal flame.

Thy breath from nothing filled us all at first,
And could again **as** soon the bubble burst.
In Thee, like motes in the sunbeam, **we move ;**
Glow in Thy light, and gladden in Thy love.
And midst this praise, **earth was** the only **one**
Sullen remained **in** that grand **union**
Of joy and harmony.   Word spake she **none.**
  CLARA.   **Earth** only had been chidden.
  FESTUS.					Not **alone.**
High **o'er all** height, **God gat** upon His throne.
Downwards He bent ; **and, as** a grain of sand,
He lifted up our globe.   **Then** from His hand,
As 't were in pity, bowled **the ingrate sphere,**
Which rushed like **ruin** down **its dark career.**
And high the air's **blue** billows **rolled and swelled**
On many an island world mine **eye beheld.**
  CLARA.   And where **and what is he,** this mighty
      friend,
Who to thee, human, **thus his** might doth lend ?
Who bore thee **harmless, as** thou **sayst,** through
      space,
And brought thee **front before thy Maker's face ?**
  FESTUS.   I know **not where he is.   It is but at**
      times
That he is with me ; but he aye sublimes
His visits thus, by lending me his **might**
O'er things more bright than day, **more deep than**
      night.
And he obeys **me — whether good or ill**
His **or my** object, he obeys me still.
  CLARA.   O Festus ! I **conjure** thee **to beware**
Lest thus the Evil **one thy soul** ensnare.
  FESTUS.   What ! **may not a** free spirit **have pre-**
      ferred
A mortal to his heart — as thou thy **bird**
Lovest, because it singeth of the sky,
Although it is as far below thy soul
As I 'neath an archangel's majesty ?
God will protect the atom as the **whole.**

Clara. Him, then, I pray: the spirit full must
  share
The truths it feels with God Himself in prayer.
So guide us, God! in all our works and ways,
That heart may feel, hand act, mouth show Thy
  praise;
That when they meet, who love, and when they
  part,
Each may be high in hope, and pure in heart:
That they who have seen, and they who have but
  heard
Of Thy great deeds, may both obey Thy word!
  Festus. Unto the wise belongs the sphere of
  light,
And to the spirit world-compelling might.
Yon sun, now setting in the golden main,
Shall count me his ere next he rise again.
Would that the earth had nothing fair to lure,
Nor being more to answer or endure!
But I foresee, fore-suffer. Bound to earth,
Wrecked in the deeps of Heaven, in Death's ex-
  piring birth!

Scene — *The Sun.*

  Festus. Soul of the world, divine Necessity,
Servant of God, and master of all things!
Here, in the Heaven of light's eternal noon,
First see I all things clear: from end to end
The divine cycle of the soul of man;
How spirit, soul, mind, life, flesh, feeling, mix,
And how, withal they each reciprocate,
As ocean, earth, air, fire, and wind; how flow
The streams of feeling, and the cataracts
Of passion; mine and mountain, this of pride,
And that of covetousness. Man I know;
The human universe, and the divine
And central fate; know all must be fulfilled

Of nature that there is ; of sin and strife,
Peace, righteousness, **change,** self-delusion, **self-**
Destruction, ere **the earth can take new** life,
Or man become **the minister of God.**
The world and man are just **reciprocal,**
Yet contrary. Spirit invadeth **sense**
And carries captive Nature. Be this true,
All good is Heaven, and all ill is Hell.
All things are means for greater good. **Thou, Sun,**
Art just a giant slave, a god in bonds.
The summit-flower of all created life
Is its unition with **Divinity,**
In essence, yet **existence separate.**
High o'er my **own existence, here then I**
Look down upon the **nature and** the earth,
Yet mine, whose separate **and** combined ends
Have still to be evolved. How wide men miss,
While in the lower world of soul and sense,
In aiming even at life-ruling Truth —
Formless as air, simple and one as Death.
If Heaven and all its stars depend on earth,
Then may eternity on time ; — not else.
But since now earth is as a crumb of Heaven,
And **time** an atom of eternity,
Neither depends upon the other, **both**
One essence being emanant **from God,**
Whose flowings forth **are aye and infinite,**
And radiant as the **rivers of the skies.**
One only truth **hath consequence, God's truth**
Inspirited in **man.** Mere **human truth**
Or falsehood **matters not.** The **world may act,**
Believe, or bless, or curse, as best it lists.
Yet men expend life, solemnizing points
Uncertain as the site of Paradise
And area **of Hades.** Not the less,
There is no disappointment we endure
One half so great as that we are to ourselves.
We make our hearts the centres of all hopes,
All powers, all rewards, remembering not

That centres are imaginary points.
Imaginary circles only too
Are perfect ; therefore, draw life as we may,
Round as a world, or as an atom round,
And pure as virgin visionary's dream,
Or perfect faith's regenerative wave —
It fails to match the true invisible
Whereof we labor.   It is come to this.
One state of life with me hath passed away.
Aught henceforth that may matter be of doubt
To me is matter of indifference.   I
Love only that is certain.   Me no more
The spirits of the bright invisible
Shall throng round as the winds some mountain-
       top ;
Nor watery lightfulness of ghostly eyes,
Belonging heavenly forms informed with light,
Impose their spell of record under pain.
The inspiration quits me — it is gone —
Like a retreating army from the land
Which it hath wasted — the long gleaming mass,
Snakelike, at last hath wound itself away,
And left me weak and wretched.   None again
Of all the starry tribes of shining mien —
Swifter than undulations of the light,
A million in a moment, multiform
As atomies of air, shall visit me ;
Their word of leave is taken back — henceforth,
Restricted to perfection, earth they quit.
True, albeit, I loved them more than life ;
I felt myself made sacred by their touch :—
But they are gone, and there is nought on earth
Left acceptable.   Fiery shadows, hence !
I have outbraved ye once.   It matters not.
I have left all for one ; Truth's countless rays
For Truth itself ; the mean for the supreme,
The dubitable for the throned power.
Yet thus I cannot rest.   The mightiest sphere

Is not for man.   The elements of mind
And matter are proportioned in all **worlds;**
The father they and mother of all things.
And earth hath **favor over crowds** of stars.
I must reseek earth.   **Still what** boots it now,
To plunge in pleasure **or to** passion bow,
The very lion-honey of the heart
Which dwelleth in corruption ?   **Yet, perchance,**
'T were wisdom to extract it while **we may.**
The oak, as lily, feels the lightest breeze.
The ineradicable seed is sown
Of love in life, and tide-like **'t will have way**
O'er the impalaced prisoner **of the breast.**
The thirst for power and knowledge **still exist,**
And meet with **dizzy mixture in** the **brain.**
If suffering could expiate **offence,**
They who have most **enjoyed have most atoned,**
It may be, humanly; — **but it cannot.**
Earth-like, the heart **must undergo all change**
Ere the superior life **be formed therein,**
The chastity **of heart** which loves but **God.**
Life's sensuous warmth, the spirit's holy **chill,**
Time's week-day work, have yet **to be gone**
          through.
The hortus siccus of **a Paradise**
Is all **earth now can boast.   To God belongs**
The autumn **of all nature.   But, alas !**
Not yet can **we o'ercome our nature here,**   .
Would **we.   If therefore passion strike the heart,**
Let it have length **of line and** plenteous **play.**
The safety of superior principles
Lies in exhaustion of the lower ones,
However vast **or violent.**   Men and angels
Obey the order **of existence.**   Fate !
Who seeks **thee everywhere,** will find **thee there.**

SCENE — *A Drawing Room.*

FESTUS *and* ELISSA.

FESTUS.   Who says he loves and is not wretched,
        lies ;
Or that love is madness came mad from his mother.
'T is the most reasonable thing in nature.
What can we do but love ? It is our cup.
Love is the cross and passion of the heart,
Its end — its errand.   In the name of God,
What made us love, Elissa ?
        ELISSA.   I know not.
I am not happy.   I have 'wept all day.
    FESTUS.   'T was thine own fault.   What wouldst
        thou have of me ?
I tell thee we must — no, I cannot tell thee.
Nor can I bear those tears.   Thou know'st I love
        thee,
Worship thee ; oh ! it's a world more than worship,
The cold obedience which we give to God.
Elissa ! turn to me !
        ELISSA.   I cannot.   Go ! —
    FESTUS.   Thou hadst no need, no business to
        have loved me.
One loved thee well.
        ELISSA.   I could not help his loving
Me, nor my loving thee.   It was our fate.
    FESTUS.   Then Fate hath fee'd the passion for
        our death,
And we are sold.
        ELISSA.   Well !   Let us die together.
Together we will quit our bodies here.
    FESTUS.   Together will we go to God and judg-
        ment.
    ELISSA.   Festus ! I will, I can love none but
        thee.
    FESTUS.   Thou must not

ELISSA.   But I must.   I cannot **help it.**
Look at me — heart and arms, I am thine own.
Thou knowest I am and have been.   Wilt not love
          me ?
Festus ! **mine own and** only ! wilt thou not ?
Have **I** done nothing, suffered and abandoned
Nothing for thee ?   Oh !   I was happy once ;
Ere I knew thee.   Why wast thou kind **to me ?**
Cruelly kind — or this had never been.   .
But now thou **mayst** be cruel **if** thou wilt.
Hate **me !** still **I** am thine : disown **me, thine !**
Desert me ! **no —** thou canst **not.**   **I am thine ;**
I am ! look at me, Festus ! **look at me !**
I am half blind with **weeping ; and** mine eyes
Have not a tear left **in them.**   **But I** know
How it will end.   **Thou wilt leave** me **as I am —**
Loveless and lonely.
          FESTUS.   Nay, not so ; my love
Shall aye be with thee, and my soul with both.
But we must part !   Think that I come again.
     ELISSA.   Not be again with thee ! nor thou with
          me !
It is **too** much.   **Let** me go mad, or die.
     FESTUS.   Live, mine Elissa ! and thou shalt live
          with me,
And I will love thee ever **as I now love.**
Wilt thou ?
     ELISSA.   Oh ! make me happy ! **say I may**
Believe thee.
     FESTUS.   **May ?**   **Thou** must.
     ELISSA.   **Say it** again !
I cannot know too often of my bliss.
But dost thou love me ? tell me — wilt thou love
          me ?
     FESTUS.   Since I have known thee I have done
          nought else.
All hours not spent with thee are blanks between
          stars.
I love thee ! love thee ! **love** thee ! madly love thee

Oh ! thou hast drank my heart dry of all love !
It will be empty to aught after thee.
Come, dry thine eyes. Blessings on those sweet
    eyes !
By Heaven ! they might a moment win the glance
Of any seraph gazing not on God.
    ELISSA. No wonder they drew thine. There
        is a tear !
    FESTUS. Ay ; strange and startling is the first
        hot tear
That we have shed for years ; and which hath lain
Like to a water-fairy in the eye's
Blue depths — spell-bound in the socket of the soul.
Death brought it not — pain brought it not — nor
    shame ;
Nor penitence — nor pity — nor despair :
Nothing but love could. For a fearful time
We can keep down the floodgates of the heart,
But we must draw them sometime ; or it will burst
Like sand this brave embankment of the breast,
And drain itself to dry death. When pride thaws —
Look for floods !
    ELISSA.   Now, thou wilt be very kind
When next we meet ? Our time will soon be
    gone.
    FESTUS. I cannot think of time : — there is no
        time !
Time ! time ! I hate thee — with the hate of Hell
For aught that's good — but thou art infamous.
I will give thee half my immortality
To keep back for one hour. Leave me, to-night ;
And wither me, to-morrow, like a weed !
    ELISSA. Where is he now ?
    FESTUS.   In Hell, — I hope.
    ELISSA.   What mean'st thou ?
He wronged thee never. Say, when cometh he ?
    FESTUS. To-night.
    ELISSA.   He comes to sever us, like fate.
But shall he part us ?

FESTUS.   Never !   Let him part
The sun in two first.
    ELISSA.   It was ever thus :
I am made to make unhappy all around me.
    FESTUS.   I will not hear of thy being wrong, —
        it is I.
I am the false usurper.   And since one
Out of the three must be a sacrifice,
Let it be me.   It shall be.
    ELISSA.   Thou didst swear,
Even now, to love me ever.
    FESTUS.   Be it so.
I have sworn — and now and then I keep my oath —
I will not give thee up, so save me, God !
    ELISSA.   Oh ! we have been too happy, have
        we not ?
But, now I think of it, we might have known
It could not last.   Woe follows bliss as close
As death does life — as naturally, may be.
We might have thought —
    FESTUS.   I never thought about it.
My love — Elissa ! ah, how cold thy hand is !
Here — warm it on my heart.   Nay, let it be.
The hand that is on the heart is on the soul.
And it is thus some moments take the wheel,
And steer us through eternity.   Believe me,
Could I but crowd life, love too, in one throb,
I would beat it out, this moment, in thy hand,
And would die blessing.
    ELISSA.   Give me my hand back !
    FESTUS.   My sweet one ! if this heart hath
        warmed thy hand,
It hath not beaten in vain — it but returns
A pleasure, and a passion, and a power :
For oft at touch of thine this bosom burns.
    ELISSA.   Love hath no end except itself.   We
        only
Felt we loved and were happy.
    FESTUS.   Ah '   It was so.

ELISSA.   Our sole misfortune is, we have been
          happy:
We never shall be happy here again.
   FESTUS.   Nay, say not so. Let us be happy now
Happy?   To fling aside thy wavy locks,
And feed mine eyes on thy white brow — to look
Deep in thine eyes till I feel mine have drank
Full of that soft, wet fire which floats in thine —
Eyes which I ne'er would leave — yet when most
          near,
Then most astray I — oh! to lay my cheek
Upon thy sweet and swelling bosom thus;
Where midst upon the beauty of thy breast
Sits love like God between the cherubim —
To crop the red budding kisses from thy lips —
To name thee, make thee, but one moment, mine —
Delights me more than all that earth can lend
The good or bad — or Heaven can give the saved.
One long, wild kiss of sunny sweets, till each
Lack breath, the lips half bleed, and, come — thou
          knowest!
I ask but one such — let it last for ever!
   ELISSA.   Now, Festus! this is wrong.
   FESTUS.   What? — what is wrong?
Shall my blood never bound beneath beauty's touch,
Heart throb, nor eye thaw with hers — when her
          tears
Drop, quick and bright, upon the glowing brow
Plunged in her bosom — because, forsooth, it is
          wrong?
Let it be wrong! it is wrong, it is wretchedness
That I would lose both sense and soul to suffer.
   ELISSA.   How dare we love each other as we do?
   FESTUS.   Give me some wine! more — more,
          love!
   ELISSA.   Drink and drain
The bowl! the vintage of a hundred years
Would never slake the memory of shame;
Nor quench the thirst of folly.

FESTUS.   Fill again!
My beauty! sing to me, and make me glad.
Thy sweet words drop upon the ear as soft
As rose leaves on a well: and I could listen,
As though the immortal melody of Heaven
Were wrought into one word—that word a whisper
That whisper all I want from all I love.
    ELISSA.   I am not happy, and I **cannot sing.**
Thou lookest happy.   I wish I were so.
    FESTUS.   They tell us that the body **of the sun**
Is dark, and hard, and **hollow;** and that light
Is but a floating fluid veiling him.
Ah! how oft, and how much, **the** heart is like him!
Despite the electric **light it** lives **and** hides in.
    SERVANT *entering*.   **A singer who was** told to
        come is here.
    FESTUS.   Wilt hear him?
    ELISSA.   Yes, love — gladly.
    FESTUS.   Show him in.
What have **you** there?
    SINGER.   Oh! I think, every thing.
    FESTUS.   Well, any thing will be enough this
        once.
The last new song?
    SINGER.   Certainly; here **it is.**   [*Sings.*

    Oh! let not a lovely form
        With feeling fill thine eye;
    Oh! let not the bosom warm
        At love-lorn lady's sigh —
    For how false is the fairest **breast;**
        How little worth, if true:
    And who would wish possessed,
        What all must scorn or rue?
    Then pass by beauty with looks above;
    Oh! seek never — share never — woman's love

    Oh! let not a planet-like eye
        Inbeam its tale on thine;

In truth 't is a lie — though a lie
  Scarce less than truth divine.
And the light of its look on the young
  Is wildfire with the soul ;
Ye follow and follow it long,
  But find nor good nor goal.
Then pass by beauty with looks above ;
Oh ! seek never — share never — woman's love

ELISSA.   Methinks I must have heard that voice
    before,
FESTUS.   And I.
ELISSA.   Where ?
FESTUS.   I forget.
ELISSA.   And so do I.

SINGER.   Oh ! let not a wildering tongue
  Weave bright webs o'er thine ear ;
Nor thy spirit be said nor sung
  To the air of smile or tear.
And say it hath melody far
  More than the spheres of Heaven,
Though to man and the Morning star
  They sang, Ye be forgiven !
Yet pass by beauty with looks above ;
Oh ! seek never — share never — woman's love !

Oh ! let not a soft bosom pour
  Itself in thine ! It is vain.
Love cheateth the heart, oh ! be sure,
  Worse even than wine the brain.
Then snatch up thy lip from the brim,
  Nor drain its dreamlike death ;
For Love loves to lie down and dim
  The bright soul with his breath.
Then pass by beauty with looks above ;
Oh ! seek never — share never — woman's love !

FESTUS.   Come hither, man ! I wish to look at
    thee

A moment.   No ! it **can't be.   Yet I have seen**
Some one much like thee.
    ELISSA.   It was a brother, may be
    SINGER.   I have none, lady.   Have ye done with
        me ?
  FESTUS.   **Yes — go ! and we** will take your song
    of you.
    SERVANT.   Here, follow me !   [*They go.*
    FESTUS.   Weeping again, my love ?
Thou art, by turns, the proudest and the humblest
Creature I **ever** met with.   The least thing
Dints thy soft **heart.**   Come, **cheer** thee, sweet **one —**
    do !
Oh ! if to say, I love, laid **all the sins**
Of all the worlds upon **me, I would say it**
Till I was **out of** breath : **and will till I die.**
    ELISSA.   **If Love be blind, it must be by his**
        tears ;
For love and sorrow alway come together —
Love with his sister, **sorrow,** by the hand.
    FESTUS.   **Nay,** I will conquer thee again to smile,
Or lose my right to love thee.   Let me kneel !
Come ! I will have no other gods but thee ;
To none but thee will I bow down and **worship ;**
Thy bosom is mine altar — **and** thine **eyes**
Are the divinity that preys upon **me.**
Oh ! cruel as the week-day gods of **old,**
Thou wilt have **human victims ; not content**
With tears and **kisses — fire and** water — **thou**
Wilt have the **subtler** element of life ;
Thou needs must live on immortality !
Here — take me then ! I offer up **myself**
A sacrifice to thee.
    ELISSA.   Thou foolish **boy .**
Where will thy passionate folly end ?   **I love thee.**
    FESTUS.   Well, then, let me conjure **thee ! let me**
    swear
By some sweet **oath** that shall **to** both be holy, —
By arms which hold, by knees which worship thee .

By that dark eye, the dark divine of beauty,
Yet trembling o'er its lid all tears and light —
Glory and eye of eyes which yet have shone!
By this lone heart, which longeth for a mate!
By love's sweet will, and sweeter way! by all
I love — by thyself, myself! let me, let me,
Let me — but draw the lightning from thine eye : —
Kisses are my conductors : do not frown ;
Nor look so temptingly angry.   I was but trifling.
The cold calm kiss which cometh as a gift,
Not a necessity, is not for me,
Whose bliss, whose woe, whose life, whose all is love.

   ELISSA.   We both wrong whom we love, love
       whom we wrong.

   FESTUS.   But I am as a dog that fondles o'er
And licks the wound he dies of.   Would I could
Suffer or feel enough of love to kill !

   ELISSA.   Thou lovest one whom thou oughtst not
       to love.

   FESTUS.   And what of that ?   Love hath its own
       belief —
Own worship — own morality — own laws :
And it were better that all love were sin
Than that love were not.   It must have by-laws —
Exceptions to the rules of earth and Heaven —
For it means not the good it doth nor ill.

   ELISSA.   It is wrong — it is unjust — unkind.
   FESTUS.   It is.
But I am half mad and half dead with it.
I have loved thee till I can love nought beside.
My heart is drenched with love as with a cloud.
I have too much of life, that I scarce can live.
I hate all things but thee — shun men, like snakes —
Women, like pits.   To me thou art all woman —
All life — all love, and more than all my kind.
I love thee more than I shall love and look for
Death, if he takes thee from me.   But who dreams
Of death and thee together !

   ELISSA.   I do oft :

And as oft wish dreams would, for once, come true.
The best of all things are dreams realized.
    FESTUS. Dreams such as gods may dream thy
        soul possess
For ever in the Hadeän Eden — Death:
But bless thy lover with reality!
Then, thou shalt live for ever, and with me.
I have gone round the compass of all life,
And can find nought worthy **of** thee.   I but **feel,**
That were I — as I ought to be — a god,
I would just sacrifice the sun to thee,
In bright and burning honor of thy love.
Miracles are not miracles with gods.
    ELISSA.   Dearer thou canst not be to me, unless
I die in telling how dear.
    FESTUS.   My Elissa!
I — I am bewildered: open but thine arms!
And make me happy and all **wise of thee.**
My soul is stung with thy beauty to the quick.
Oh! but thou art too good, or else too bad:
Be colder or be warmer!
    ELISSA.   Leave me!
    FESTUS.   **Well:**
It is most cruel — first, to light the heart
With love completely — boundlessly; and then
Moonlike, slowly to edge aside, and leave
One only little line of all so bright,
Once — teach and unteach — nay, to **use more arts**
Than would outdo the devil of his throne,
To make us ignorant of all we know: —
To take the heart to pieces carefully —
For it is love alone can build the heart —
To root the tree up 'neath whose shade we have lived,
And give us back a sliver.   Let it die!
    ELISSA.   Hark! he is coming.
    FESTUS.   No! **He** cannot come;
For I have driven an oath into his heart,
And I have hung a curse about his neck
Might sink the prince of air into the centre.

ELISSA.   All I have done, I have done to save
       ourselves.
FESTUS.   Then let us perish! But unless we sin
We cannot perish.   Have! Have! cries a voice,
As of a crowd, within me.   I would do aught
To throw this dark desire which wrestles with me.
It answers not to hold it at arms' length:
It must be hurled, dashed, trampled down. — I
       can't.
Lady! how long am I to love thee thus?
Never did angel love its Heaven — nor God
Man, as I thee.
       ELISSA.   I feared how it would end.
Can nothing less than sinning sate the soul?
Can nothing but perdition serve to nest
Our hearts, after so sweet a flight of love?
       FESTUS.   The might and truth of hearts is never
          shown
But in loving those whom we ought not to love —
Or cannot have.   The wrong, the suffering is
Its own reward.
       ELISSA.   Let me not wrong thee, Festus.
Let me not think I have thought too well of thee.
Be as thou wast.   What will become of us?
       FESTUS.   Be mine! be me! be aught but so far
          from me!
Give me thyself!   It is not enough for me,
That I have gazed and doted on thee till
·Mine eye is dazzled and my brain is dizzied:
Thou must exhaust all senses; not enough
That in long dreams my soul hath spread itself
Like water over every living line
Of this sweet make, dreaming thou wast all lips;
Nor that it now sinks in the face of thee,
Like a sea-sunset, hot and tired with the long,
Long day of love; — it is not enough.   I must
Have more — have all!   For I have sworn to fill
Mine arms with bliss — thus — thus — thus!
       ELISSA.   Festus!

LUCIFER, *entering.*   Friend!
Did ye not know me?   **It** was I who sang.
    ELISSA.   It was he!
    FESTUS.   Thou —
    LUCIFER.   **Hush! thou art not to utter what
I am.**   Bethink **thee; it was our covenant.**
I said that I would see thee once again.
    ELISSA.   Thou didst; and I must thank thee.
    LUCIFER.   Hear me now!
Thou knowest **well** what once **I** was to thee:
One who for love of one I loved — for thee —
Would have done or borne the sins of all the **world;**
Who did thy bidding at thy lightest look;
And had it been to have snatched **an** angel's
        crown
Off her bright brow as she sat singing, throned,
I would have cut these heartstrings that tie down,
And let my soul have sailed **to** Heaven, and done
        it —
Spite of the thunder and the sacrilege,
And laid **it at** thy feet.   I loved thee, lady!
I am one whose love was greater than the world's,
And might have vied with God's; a boundless ring,
All pressing on one point — that point thy heart.
And now — but shall I call on my revenge? —
It is at hand in armies.   Thou art a woman;
And that is saying **the** best and worst **of thee.**
I know that vengeance is the part of **God:**
And can make myself **almighty for** the moment.
For what? for nothing.   **Thou** art utter nothing.
Thus it was always with me when with thee;
And I forgot my purpose and my wrongs,
In looking and in loving.   But I hate thee.
To say thou didst love me!   Curse the air
That bore the sound to me!   Forgive me, God!
If **I** blaspheme, it is not at Thee, but her.
I'd not believe her were she saved in Heaven!
There is no blasphemy in love but doubt;
No sin, but to deceive.

FESTUS.   Then is she sinless.
She loved thee first—then me. What wouldst thou
        more ?
Thy heart's embrace, **though** close, was snake-like
        cold ;
And mine was warm, and what is more, was wel-
        come.
    LUCIFER.   Patience ! I spake not, cared not,
        thought **not, of** thee. —
Now I forgive thy having loved **another** ;
And I forgive — but never mind it now ; •
I have forgiven so much, there is nothing left
To make more words about ; but, for the future,
I will as soon attempt to entice a star
To perch **upon my** finger ; or the wind
To follow me like a dog, as think to keep
A woman's heart again.   Answer me not !
Let me say what I have to say and go.
Thou art all **will and** passion ; **that** is **thine**
Excuse and condemnation.
    ELISSA.   /   While that will
Was love to thee, I saw no harm, nor thou.
And if my heart hath gained, it was not I
Who put it on — nor could help it going wrong.
    LUCIFER.   Oh ! I have heard, what rather than
        have heard,   •
I would have stopped **mine ears with thunder :**
        words,
That have gone singing through my soul, like arrows
Through the air.
    ELISSA.   I never will defend myself.
For I despise defence like accusation —
And now look down on them and thee together.
    LUCIFER. **Now let us part,** or I shall die of
        wrath.
Be my estrangement perfect as my love !
    ELISSA.   Part then !
    LUCIFER.   Thank God it is for eternity !
    ELISSA. I do. Away.

LUCIFER.   Festus! I wait for thee.
  FESTUS.   Come, thou art not the first deceived
        in love ;
Yet love is not so much love as a dream,
Which hath, it seems, like guerdon with the thing—
The staring madness when we wake and find
That **what** we have loved, must love, is not **that**
We meant to **love.**   Perhaps I profited
Too much by **thy** good lessons.   **Go! I** follow.
  LUCIFER, *going.*   Now therefore would I **wager,**
        and I might
The great archangel's trump **to a dog-whistle,**
That whatsoever happens, **worse ensues.**
  FESTUS.   Forgive **me, love, for having brought**
        this on thee.
  ELISSA.   **The** love which giveth **all, forgiveth**
        aught.
And thou **art more** to me than earth or Heaven.
They have but given life : thou gavest **me** love,
The lord **of** life — thou, my life ! love, and lord !
Take me again ! my kindest — dearest — best !
Him who hath gone I never loved like thee.
There was a desolation in his eye
I could not brook to look **on ;** for it **seemed**
As though it ate the light out of mine own.
I think that thou dost love **me.**
  FESTUS.   And I think,
For perfect love there should be but one god —
One worshipper.
  ELISSA.   We know the gods of **old**
Worshipped each other — equal deities.
For the sweet poets surely spake the truth
About the gods ; they dare not speak **but** truth.
  FESTUS.   Who but thyself would speak of
        poetry,
While thou art by ? who art the very breathing
Beauty which bards may seek ideally.
And dost thou, then, believe the gods of old —
Those toys and playthings of **an** infant world ?
22

Elissa. If I do not believe, I do not scorn
      them.
Nay, I could mourn for them and pray for them.
I can scorn nothing which a nation's heart
Hath held, for ages, holy: for the heart
Is alike holy in its strength and weakness:
It ought not to be jested with, nor scorned.
All things, to me, are sacred that have been.
And, though earth, like a river, streaked with blood,
Which tells a long and silent tale of death,
May blush her history and hide her eyes,
The past is sacred — it is God's, not ours.
Let her and us do better if we can.
    Festus. There are whole veins of diamonds in
      thine eyes,
Might furnish crowns for all the Queens of earth.
Oh! I could sooner set a price on the sun,
My love, than on thy lightest look. Look on me!
Speak! if it only be to say thou wilt not.
Look! I would rather look on thee one minute,
Than paradise for a whole day — such days
As are in Heaven. I love thee more and more.
    Elissa. To love, and say we love — to suck
      the sting
Out of the heart, and put its poison on
The tongue.
    Festus. Yet it is luxury to feel
Inflamed — to glow within ourselves, like fire-opals.
Now, stay thy pretty little tuneful tongue,
Nor silver o'er thy syllables! They will not
Pass. No, not one more word! I must away;
I have staid too long, already, for my word.
    Elissa. I cannot part with thee: nay, sit again!
Parted from thee I feel like one half riven,
And my soul acheth to spring to — as thus!
    Festus. There! let me leave love! let me
      loose these arms.
Another time and, ah! well — never mind!
We shall be happier — I know we shall.

Thou hast been mine — thou art mine — and thou
    shalt be!
  ELISSA. My life is one long loving thought of
    thee.
If any ask me what I do, I could say
I love, and that is all.
  FESTUS.   It is enough.
One kiss! another! one more — there! farewell!
                     [Goes.

  ELISSA. And he is gone! and the world seems
    gone with him.
Shine on, ye Heavens! why can ye not impart
Light to my heart? Have ye no feeling in ye?
Why are ye bright when I am so unhappy?
But oh! I would not change my woes for thrice
The bliss of others, since they are for thee, love.
Our very wretchedness grows dear to us
When suffering for one we love. Sweet stars!
I cannot look upon your loveliness
Without sadness, for ye are too beautiful;
And beauty makes unhappy: so men say.
Ye stars! it is true — we read our fate in ye.
Bright through all ages, are ye not happy there?
With years, many as your light-rays, are ye not
Immortal? Space-pervading, oh! ye must be,
Spirit-like, infinite. All-being God!
Who art in all things, and in whom all are! —
And it is thus we worship Thee the most;
When heart to heart with one we love we are
    gods; —
Let us believe that if Thou gavest earth
For our bodies, then the stars were for our souls;
For perfect beauty and unbounded love!
Let us believe they look upon us here
As their inheritors, and save themselves
For us, as we for Thee, and Thou for all!

SCENE —*Garden and Bower* **by the Sea.**

ELISSA, *alone.*   Come, Festus, let me think on
    thee, my love!
And fold the thought of thee unto my soul,
Until it fills it, and is one with it.
Ah! these poor arms are far from where they
    should be;
And this heart further still. Mine only love!
Why art thou thus so long away from me?
I have whispered it unto the southern wind
And charged it with my love: why should it not
Carry that love to thee as air bears light?
And thou hast said I was all light to thee.
The stars grow bright together, and for aye,
Lover-like, watch each other; and though apart,
Like us, they fill each other's eyes with love
And beauty: and mine only fill with tears.
Oh! life is less than nothing without love!
And what is love without the embrace of love?
I would give worlds for one more ere I die.
Festus! come to me. I do think I am dying.
Let me bequeathe my life to thee, that so,
In doubling thine, I may live alway with thee.
I know that I am dying. It is my heart
Which makes me live that kills me. But I want
To see him ere I do die. Oh! he will come!
He must know how I love him. It is long —
Long since I saw him: I am ill with waiting.
And I will fancy him coming to me now —
Now he is thinking of me, loving me —
He sees me — flies to me, half out of breath —
His hand is on my arm — he looks on me —
And puts my long locks backwards — God! Thy
    ban
Lies upon waking dreams. To weep and sleep —
Dream — wake, and find one's only one hope
    false, —

Is what we can bear, for we do endure it,
And bear with Heaven still.   Just one year ago,
I watched that large bright star where it is now : —
Time hath not touched its everlasting lightning,
Nor dimmed the glorious glances of its eye —
Nor passion clouded it — nor any star
Eclipsed — it is the leader still of Heaven.
And I who loved it then can love it now ;
But am not **what** I was, in one degree.
Calm star! who was it named thee Lucifer,
From him who drew the third of Heaven down **with**
     him ?
Oh! it was but the tradition of thy beauty !
For if the sun hath one part, and the moon one,
Thou hast the third part of the host of Heaven —
Which is its power — which power is its beauty !
    LUCIFER.   It was no tradition, lady, but of truth !
    ELISSA.   I thought we parted last to meet no
      more.
    LUCIFER.   It was so lady ; but it is not so.
    ELISSA.   Am I to leave, or thou, then ?
    LUCIFER.   Neither, yet.
I mean that thou shouldst fear me and obey.
    ELISSA.   And who art thou that I should fear
      and serve ?
    LUCIFER.   I am the morning and the evening
      star,
The star thou lovest and thy lover too ;
I am that star! **as** once before I told thee,
Though thou wouldst not believe me, but I **am**
A spirit, and a star — a power — an ill
Which doth outbalance being.   Look at me !
Am I not more than mortal in my form ?
Millions of years have circled round my brow
Like worlds upon their centres ; — still I live ;
And age but presses with a halo's weight.
This single arm hath dashed the light of Heaven ;
This one hand dragged the angels from their
      thrones : —

Am I not worthy to have loved thee, lady?
Thou mortal model of all Heavenliness!
And yet I have abandoned all these spoils,
Cowered my powers, and becalmed my course,
And stooped from the high destruction of the skies
For thee, and for the youth who loveth thee —
And is lost with ye: ye are both, both — lost!
Thou hast but served the purpose of the Fiend.
And thou art but the vessel of the sin
Whose poison hath made drunk a soul to death;
And he hath drunk; and thou art useless now.
And it is for this I come; to bid thee die!
    ELISSA.   I said that I was dying.   God is good.
The Heavens grow darker as they grow the purer
And both, as we do near them; so, near death,
The soul grows darker and diviner, hourly.
Could I love less I should be happier!
But it is always to that mad extreme,
That death alone appears the fitting finish
To bliss like that my spirit presses for.
    LUCIFER.   Thy death shall be as gentle as thy
        life.
I will not hurt thee, for I loved thee once.
And thy sweet love, upon my burning breast,
Fell like a snowflake on a fevered lip.
Thy soul shall pass out of thee like a dream.
One moment more, and thou shalt wake in Heaven!
    ELISSA.   I ever thought thee to be more than
        mortal.
And if thou art thus mighty, grant me this! —
Since now we love no more — as friend to friend —
Bring him I love, one moment, ere I die.
    LUCIFER.   Thou judgest well; I am all but al-
        mighty.
And I have stretched my strength unto its limits
To satisfy the heart of him who loves thee:
In proof whereof, did I not give up thee,
Because he loved thee? I have given him all
        things

Body or spirit could desire or have.
And even, at this moment, now he reigns
King of the sun, and monarch of the seven
Orbs that surround him — leaving earth alone —
The earth is in good keeping as it is.
I know that he is hasting hither now;
But may not see thee living.
   ELISSA.   **It is not thou**
Who takest life : it **is God, whose I shall be!** —
And his, with God, whom **here my heart deifies.**
I glory in his power **as in** his love.
But I will, will see him while **I am alive.**
I hear **him** — he is **come** — it is he ! it is he !
  LUCIFER.   Die ! **thou shalt never look on him**
     again.
  ELISSA.   **My love ! haste, Festus !** I am dying —
  LUCIFER.   **Dead !**
A word could kill her.   **She** hath gone to Heaven.
  FESTUS.   Fiend ! **what is** this ?   Elissa — she is
     not dead.
  LUCIFER.   She **is.**   I bade her die, **as I had**
     reason.
  FESTUS.   Now do I hate thee and renounce **for**
     ever ! —
Abhor thee — go !
  LUCIFER.   **Who seeks** the other **first ?**
I am gone.
  FESTUS.   **Away,** Fiend ! **Leave me !   My Elissa !**

SCENE — *A Library* **and** *Balcony — A Summer
Night.*

  FESTUS *alone.*   The last high upward slant of
     sun on the trees,
Like a dead soldier's sword upon his pall,
Seems to console earth for the glory gone.
Oh ! I could weep to see the day die thus ;
The death-bed of a day, how beautiful !

Linger, ye clouds, one moment longer there;
Fan it to slumber with your golden wings!
Like pious prayers ye seem to soothe its end.
It will wake no more till the all-revealing day;
When, like a drop of water, greatened bright
Into a shadow, it shall show itself
With all its little tyrannous things and deeds,
Unhomed and clear.   The day hath gone to
          God, —
Straight, like an infant's spirit, or a mocked
And mourning messenger of grace to man.
Would it had taken me too on its wing!
My end is nigh.   Would I might die outright!
And slip the coil without waiting its unwind.
Who that hath lain lonely on a high hill,
In the imperious silence of full noon,
With nothing but the clear dark sky about him,
Like God's hand laid upon the head of earth —
But hath expected that some natural spirit
Should start out of the universal air —
And gathering his cloudy robe around him,
As one in act to teach mysterious things,
Explain that he must die? — that having got
As high as earth can lift him up — as far
Above that thing, the world, as flesh can mount —
Over the tyrant wind, and the clouded lightning,
And the round rainbow — and that having gained
A loftier and a more mysterious beauty
Of feeling — something like a starry darkness
Seizing the soul — say he must die — and vanish?
Who hath not, at such moments, felt as now
I feel, that to be happy we must die?
And here I rest — above the world and its ways;
The wind, opinion — and the rainbow, beauty —
And the thunder, superstition — I am free
Of all : — save death, what want I to be happy?
And shall I leave no trace, then, of my life?
The soul begetteth shadows of itself
Which do outlive their author : and are more

Substantial than all nature, and the red
Realities of flesh and blood, as echo
Is longer, louder, further than the voice
Of man can thunder, or his ear report.
And oft the world hath Deified its echoes.
A year! — and who shall find them ?   Can it be
The mind's works have been deathless — **not the**
    mind ?
Or will the world's **immortals die with me ?** —
The sages, and the heroes, and the **bards,** —
Whose verse set to the thunder **of the seas,**
Seems as immortal as their **ceaseless** music !
O God! I fain would **deem** Thou livest not :
And that this world **hath** sprung up from **chance**
    seed,
Unknown to thee ; and is not reckoned on.
Hell solves all doubts. — **Come to** me, Lucifer !
   Lucifer.   Lo! I am here : and ever prompt
    When called for.
How speed thy **general pleasures ?**
   Festus.   Bravely ! **joys**
Are bubble-like — what makes them, bursts **them,**
    too.
And, like the milky way, there ! dim with **stars,**
The soul that numbers most will shine **the less.**
   Lucifer.   No matter — mind it not !
   Festus.   Yet, joys of **earth !**
That ye should ruin spirits is **too** hard.
Who can avoid ye ? who can say ye nay ?
Or take his eyes from off ye ? who so chaste ?
   Lucifer.   **They** have well-nigh unimmortalized
    myself.
   Festus.   Yet have **they nought to** sate **the**
    pining spirit
Which doth enamor immortality.
No! they are all base, impure, **ruinous** —
The harlots of the **heart.**   Forgive me, God :
I am getting too forlorn to live — too waste.
Aught that I can or do love, shoots by me,

Like a train upon an iron road.   And yet
I need not now reproach mine arm or aim;
For I have winged each pleasure as it flew,
How swift or high soever in its flight.
We cannot live alone.   The heart must have
A prop without, or it will fall and break.
But nature's common joys are common cheats.
As he who sails southwards, beholds, each night,
New constellations rise, all clear, and fair;
So, o'er the waters of the world, as we
Reach the mid zone of life, or go beyond,
Beauty and bounty still beset our course;
New beauties wait upon us everywhere;
New lights enlighten and new worlds attract.
But I have seen and I have done with all.
Friendship hath passed me like a ship at sea;
And I have seen no more of it.   I had
A friend with whom, in boyhood, I was wont
To learn, think, laugh, weep, strive, and love,
        together;
For we were alway rivals in all things —
Together up high springy hills, to trace
A runnel to its birthplace — to pursue
A river — to search, haunt old ruined towers,
And muse in them — to scale the cloud-clad hills
While thunders murmured in our very ear;
To leap the lair of the live cataract,
And pray its foaming pardon for the insult;
To dare the broken tree-bridge across the stream;
To crouch behind the broad white waterfall,
Tongue of the glen, like to a hidden thought —
Dazzled, and deafened, yet the more delighted;
To reach the rock which makes the fall and pool
There to feel safe, or not to care if not;
To fling the free foot over my native hills,
Which seemed to breathe the bracing breeze we
        loved
The more it lifted up our loosened locks,
That nought might be between us and the skies;

Or, hand in hand, leap, laughing, with closed
    eyes,
In Trent's death-loving deeps ; yet was she kind
Ever to us ; and bare us buoyant up,
And followed our young strokes, and cheered
    us on —
Even as an elder sister bending above
A child, to teach it how to order its feet —
As quick we dashed, in reckless rivalry,
To reach, perchance, some long, green floating
    flag —
Just when the sun's hot lip first touched the stream,
Reddening to be so kissed ; and we rejoiced,
As breasting it on we went over depth and death,
Strong in the naked strife of elements,
Toying with danger in as little fear
As with a maiden's ringlets.   And oft, at night,
Bewildered and bewitched by favorite stars,
We would breathe ourselves amid unfooted snows,
For there is poetry where aught is pure ;
Or over the still dark heath, leap along, like
    harts,
Through the broad moonlight ; for we felt where-
    e'er
We leapt the golden gorse, or lowly ling,
We could not be from home. — That friend is
    gone.
There's the whole universe before our souls.
Where shall we meet next? Shall we meet again ?
Oh ! might it be in some far happy world,
That I might light upon his lonely soul,
Hard by some broad blue stream, where high the
    hills,
Wood-bearded, sweep to its brink — musing, as
    wont,
With love-like sadness, upon sacred things ;
For much in youth we loved and mused on them.
To say what ought to be to human wills,
And measure mortals sternly ; to explore

The bearings of men's duties and desires;
To note the nature and the laws of mind;
To balance good with evil; and compare
The nature and necessity of each;
To long to see the ends and end of things;
Or, if no end there be, the endless, then,
As suns look into space; these were our joys —
Our hopes — our meditations — our attempts.
And, if I have enjoyed more love than others,
It is but superior suffering, and is more
Than balanced by the loss of one we love.
And love, itself, hath passed.   One fond, fair girl
Remains; one only, and she loves me still.
But it is not love I feel: it is pure kindness.
How shall I find another like my last?
The golden and the gorgeous loveliness —
A sunset beauty!   Ah! I saw it set.
My heart, alas! set with it.   I have drained
Life of all love, as doth an iron rod
The Heaven's of lightning; I have done with it,
And all its waking woes, and dreamed-of joys.
No more shall beauty star the air I live in;
And no more will I wake at dead of night,
And hearken to the roaring of the wind,
As though it came to carry one away —
Claiming for sin.   Ah! I am lost forever.
To earn the world's delights by equal sins
Seems the great aim of life — the aim succeeds.
Here it is madness, and perdition there.
And, but for thee, I had renounced these joys —
These cursed joys my soul now writhes among,
Like to a half-crushed reptile on a rose: —
Ay, but for thee, I might have now been happy!
    LUCIFER.   Why charge, why wrong me thus?
        When first I knew thee,
I deemed it thine ambition to be damned.
Thine every thought, almost, had gone from good,
As far as finite is from infinite;
And then thou wast as near to me as now.

Thou hadst declined in worship, and in wish
To please thy God ; nor wouldst thou e'er repent.
What more need I to justify attempt ?
Have I shrunk back from **granting aught I** prom-
    ised ?
Thy love of knowledge — is that satisfied ?
   FESTUS. It is. Yet knowledge is **a** doubtful
    boon —
Root of all good **and** fruit of all that's **bad.**
I have caused face to face with elements,
Yea, learned the luminous language of **the skies,**
And the angelic kindred **of** high Heaven ;
The bright articulations **of all** spheres, —
Impetuous hearted **orbs,** and mountain-maned,
Aye circling onwards breathless through the air —
And wisest stars which speak themselves **in** signs
Too sacred to be explicable **here ;**
And now what better am I ? — nearer God ?
When the void finds a voice mine answer know.
   LUCIFER. What better or what **worse** thou
    canst not tell.
For, good and **evil !** **Wherein** differ they ?
Do they not both accrue from the same cause, —
As ripeness and decay ? Light, light **alone**
Of hues, **how** contrary soever, **is**
The common cause.
   FESTUS. Distractor **of** God's **truth !**
Shall not His word suffice the living world ?
   LUCIFER. Thou canst **not** have lacked **joys ?**
   FESTUS. We **seek them oft**
Among our **own delusions,** pains, and follies.
   LUCIFER. Hath **not care** perished from **thy**
    heart, as did
The viper' flung from the apostle's hand ?
   FESTUS. Ay ; and, like that, **all** care will **cease**
    in fire.
Dark wretched thoughts, like ice-isles in a stream,
Choke up my mind, and clash ; — and to no end.
In spite of all we suffer and **enjoy,**

There comes this question, over and over again,
Driven into the brain as a pile is driven,—
What shall become of us hereafter ? what
Is it we shall do ? how feel, how be ?
And there are times when burning memory flows
In on the mind, that saving it would slay,
As did the lava-floods which choked of yore
The Cyclopean cities — brimming up
Brasslike their mighty moulds.   And shall the past
Thus ruinously perfect aye remain ;
Or present, past, and coming, all be one,
In natural mystery ?   Like snow, which lies
Down-wreathed round the lips of some black pit,
Thoughts which obscure the truth accumulate,
And those which solve it in it lose themselves ;
And there is no true knowledge till descent,
Nor then till after.   What shall make the truth
Visible ?   Through the smoky glass of sense
The blessed sun would never know himself.
All truth is one.   All error is alike.
The shadow of a mountain hath no more
Substance than hath a dead and moss-mailed
        pine's ;
But only more gigantic impotence.
    LUCIFER.   Hast thou not had thine every
        quest ?
    FESTUS.   Save one.
    LUCIFER.   I proffer now the power which thou
        dost long for.
Say but the word, and thou shalt press a throne
But less than mine — the scarcely less than
        God's ; —
A throne, at which earth's puny potentates
May sue for slavedoms — and be satisfied.
    FESTUS.   I have had enough of the infinities:
I am moderate now.   I will have the throne of
        earth.
    LUCIFER.   Thou shalt.   Yet, mind !—with that,
        the world must end.

FESTUS. I can survive.

LUCIFER. Nay, die **with** it must thou.

FESTUS. Why should I die? I am egg-full of
life:
And life's as serious a thing as death.
The world is in its first young quarter yet;
I dare not, cannot credit it shall die.
I will not have it, then.

LUCIFER. **It matters not;**
I know thou **wilt never have ease at heart**
Until thou hast thy soul's whole, **full desire;**
Whenever that **may** happen, all **is done.**

FESTUS. **Well,** then — be it now! **I live but**
for myself —
The whole world **but for me. Friends, loves, and
all**
I sought, abandon me. It is time **to die.**
I am yet young; yet have I **been deserted,**
And wronged, by those **whom** most **I have loved**
and served.
Sun, moon, and stars! may they all fall on me,
When next I trust another — man or woman.
Earth rivals Hell too often, **at** the best.
All hearts are stronger for the being hollow.
And that was why mine was no match for theirs.
The pith is **out of it now. — Lord** of the world!
It will not **directly perish?**

LUCIFER. **Not,** perhaps. —
Thou wilt have all fame, while thou livest, now.

FESTUS. **I care not:** fame **is folly:** for, it is, sure,
Far more **to be** well known **of God** than **man.**
With all my **sins** I feel that I am God's.

LUCIFER. Farewell, then, for **a time!**

FESTUS. **I am alone. —**
Alone? He clings around me like the clouds
Upon a hill. When will the clouds roll off?
When **will** sun visit me? Oh! Thou great **God!**
In whose right hand the elements are atoms —
In whose eye, light and darkness but a wink —

Who, in Thine anger, like a blast of cold,
Dost make the mountains **shake** like chattering
        teeth —
Have mercy!   Pity **me**!   For it is Thou
Who hast fixed me to this test. Wilt Thou not save ?
Forgive me, Father! but I long to die : —
I long to live **to Thee, a pure,** free mind.
Take again, God! **and thou, fair** Earth, the form
And spirit which, at first, **ye lent me.**
Such as they were, I have **used them.   Let them**
        part.
I weary of this world ; and, like the dove,
Urged o'er life's barren flood, sweep, tired, back
To thee who sent'st me forth.   Bear with me, God !
I am not worthy of thy wrath, nor love ! —
Oh! that the things which **have** been were not now
In memory's resurrection !   But the past
Bears in her arms the present and the future ;
And what can perish while perdition is ?
From the hot, angry, crowding courts **of** doubt
Within the breast, it is sweet to escape, and soothe
The soul in looking upon **natural** beauty.
Oh! earth, like man her son, is half divine.
There is not a leaf within this **quiet spot,**
But which I seem to know ; **should miss, if gone.**
I could run over its features, hour by hour.
The quaintly figured beds — the various flowers —
The mazy paths all cunningly converged —
The black yew hedge, like a beleaguering host,
Round some fair garden province — here and there,
The cloud-like laurel clumps sleep, **soft** and fast,
Pillowed by their own shadows — and beyond,
The ripe and ruddy fruitage — the sharp firs'
Fringe, like an eyelash, **on** the faint-blue west —
The white owl, wheeling **from** the gray old church, —
Its age-peeled pinnacles, **and** tufted top —
The oaks, which spread their broad arms in the blast,
And bid storms come, and welcome ; there they stand,
To whom a summer passes like a smile : —

And the proud peacock towers himself there, and
        screams,
Ruffling **the** imperial purples of **his** neck.
O'er all, **the** giant poplars, which maintain
Equality with clouds half way up Heaven;
Which whisper with the winds none else **can** see,
And bow to angels as they wing by them;—
The lonely, bowery, woodland view before—
And, making all more beautiful, **thou, sweet moon,**
Leading slow pomp, as triumphing **o'er Heaven!**
High riding in thy loveless, deathless brightness,
And in thy cold, unconquerable beauty,
As though there were nothing **worthy in the** world
Even to lie below thee, **face** to **God.**
And Night, in her own name, **and God's** again,
Hath dipped the earth in dew;— **and there** she lies,
Even like **a heart** all trembling **with delight,**
Till passion murder power to **speak — so mute.**
Young maiden moon! just looming into light—
I would that aspect never might be changed;
Nor that fine form, so spirit-like, be spoiled
With fuller light.   Oh! keep that brilliant shape;
Keep the delicious honor of thy youth,   ·
Sweet sister of the sun, more beauteous thou
Than he sublime.   Shine **on,** nor dread **decay.**
It may take meaner things; **but thy bright look,**
Smiling away an immortality,
Assures it **us — nay,** it seems, **half, to** give.
Earth may **decease.**   God will not part with thee,
Fair ark of light, and every blessedness!
Yes, earth, this earth, may foul the face **of life,**
Like some swart mole on beauty's breast — **or dead,**
Stiff, mangled reptile, some clear well — **while thou**
Shalt shine, aye brilliant, on creation's corse,
Like **to a** diamond on a dead man's hand;
Whence God shall pluck thee to his breast, or bid
Beam 'mid His lightning locks.   What are earth's
        joys
To watching thee, tending thy bright flock over
23

The fields of Heaven?   Thy light misleadeth not,
Though eyes which image Heaven oft lure to
      Hell;—
Thy smile betrayeth not—though sweet as that
Which wins and damns. Mother, and maid of light!
That, like a God, redeems the world to Heaven—
Making us one with thee, and with the sun,
And with the stars in glory—lovely moon!
I am immortal as thyself; and we
Shall look upon each other yet, in Heaven,
Often—but never, never more on earth.
Am I to die so soon?   This death—the thought
Comes on my heart as through a burning glass.
I cannot bend mine eyes to earth, but thence
It riseth, spectre-like, to mock—nor towards
The west, where sunset is, whose long bright pomp
Makes men in love with change—but there it
      lowers
Eve's last, still lingering, darkening, cloud; and on
The escutcheon of the morn, it is there—it is there!
But fears will come upon the bravest mind,
Like the white moon upon the crimson west.
I have attractions for all miseries:
And every course of thought, within my heart,
Leaves a new layer of woe.   But it must end.
It will all be one, hereafter.   Let it be!
My bosom, like the grave, holds all quenched pas-
      sions.
It is not that I have not found what I sought—
But, that the world—tush! I shall see it die.
I hate, and shall outlive the hypocrite.
Stealthily, slowly, like the polar sun,
Who peeps by fits above the air-walled world—
The heavenly fief, he knows and feels his own,
My heart o'erlooks the Paradise of life
Which it hath lost, in cold, reluctant joy.
I live and see all beauteous things about me,
But feel no nature prompting from within
To meet and profit by them.   I am like

That fabled forest of the Apenn.ne,
Which leafless lives ; whereto the spring's bright
        showers,
Summer's heat breathless, autumn's **fruitful** juice,
Nothing avail ; — nor winter's killing cold.
Yet have I done, said, thought, in time **now past,**
What, rather than remember, I would **die,**
Or do again.   It is the thinking on 't,
And the repentance, maddens.   I have thought
Upon such things **so** long and grievously,
My lips have grown like to **a** cliff-chafed **sea,**
Pale with a tidal passion ; and **my** soul,
Once high and bright and self-sustained as **Heaven,**
Unsettled now for life or death, **feels** like
The **gray gull** balanced **on her** bowlike **wings,**
Between two black waves seeking **where to dive.**
Long we live, thinking nothing of **our fate,**
For in **the morn** of life **we** mark **it not** —
It falls behind ; but as our day goes down
We catch it lengthening with a giant's stride,
And ushering us unto the feet of night.
Dark thoughts, like spots upon the sun, revolve
In troops for days together round my soul,
Disfiguring and dimming.   Death ! oh death !
The past, the present, and **the future,** like
The dog three-headed, by the **gates of woe**
Sitting, seem ready to devour **me each.**
I dare not look **on them.**   I dare **not think.**
The very best **deeds I have ever done**
Seem worthy **reprobation, have** to **be**
Repented of.   **But have I done** aught good ?
Oh that my soul were calmer !   Grant me, God !
Thy peace ; **that** added, **I can smile** and die.
Thy Spirit only is reality :
All things beside are folly, falsehood, **shame.**

SCENE — *Elsewhere.*

FESTUS, *a one.* I feel as if I could devour the
    days
Till the time came when I shall gain mine end ;
God shall have made me ruler, and all worlds
Signed the sublime recognizance. Till then, —
Even as a boat lies rocking on the beach,
Waiting the one white wave to float it free,
Wait I the great event ; — too great it seems.
Yet, Lord, thou knowest that the power I seek
Is but for others' good and Thine own glory,
And the desire for it inspired by Thee.
So use me as I use it. Thou hast passed
Thy word that such I shall enjoy, and then
My mission is accomplished in this world.
I go unto another, where all souls
Begin again, or take up life from where
Death broke it at. I cannot think there will be
Like disproportion there between our powers
And will, as here ; if not, I shall be happy.
I feel no bounds. I cannot think, but thought
On thought springs up, illimitably, round,
As a great forest sows itself ; but here
There is nor ground nor light enough to live.
Could I, I would be everywhere at once,
Like the sea, for I feel as if I could
Spread out my spirit o'er the endless world,
And act at all points ; — I am bound to one.
I must be here, and there, and everywhere,
Or I am nowhere. Sense, flesh, feeling, fail
Before the feet of the imperious mind,
To which they are but as the dust she treads, —
Windlike treads o'er, uplifts and leaves behind.
How mind will act with body glorified
And spiritualized, and senses fined,
And pointed brilliantwise, we know not. Here,
Even, it may be wrong in us to deem

The senses degradations, otherwise
Than **as fine** steps, whereby **the** queenly soul
Comes down from her bright throne to view **the**
      mass
She hath dominion over, and the things
Of her inheritance ; and reascends,
With an indignant fiery purity,
Not to be touched, her seat.   The **visible world,**
Whereby God maketh Nature known **to us,**
Is not derogatory to Himself
As the pure Spirit Infinite.   **A** world
Is but, perhaps, **a** sense of **God's,** by **which**
He may explain **His nature, and receive**
Fit pleasure.   But **the hour is hard at hand,**
When Time's gray **wing shall winnow all away,**
The atoms of the earth, the stars **of Heaven ;**
When the created and Creator mind
Shall know each other, worlds and bodies both
Put off **for** aye ; man and his Maker meet
Where all, who through the universe do well,
Embrace their heart's desire ; what things **they**
      will,
And whom remember ; live, too, where they list ;
And with the beings they love best, and God,
Inherit and inhabit boundless bliss.
Hear me, all-favoring God ! my latest prayer ;
Thou unto whom all nations of the world
Lift up their hearts, like grass-blades to the sun ;
Thou who hast all things and hast need of nought ;
Thou who hast given **me** Earth and all it holds,
Give me, from out Thy garner stored with good,
Some sign, **Lord** ! while I live, in proof to earth
My prayers are with Thee ; that they rend the
      clouds,
And, rising through **the** sightless dark of space,
Reach to Thy central throne.   Oh ! let me feel,
What **was my** constant dream in my young years,
And is in **all** my better moments now, —
My hope, my faith, **my** nature's sum and end,

Oneness with Thee and Heaven. Lord! make me
    sure
My soul already is in unison
With the triumphant. Ah! I surely hear
The voices of the spirits of the saints,
And witnesses to the Redeeming Truth;
Not, as of old, in scanty scattered strains,
Breathed from the caves of earth and cells of
    cities,—
Nor as the voice of martyr choked with fire —
But in one solemn Heaven-pervading hymn
Of happiness impregnable, as when
From the bright walls of the Son's city they
Looked on the war of Hell, host upon host,
Foiled by God's single sword before their gates,
Of perfect pearl; — nearer and nearer now!
This is the sign, O God! which Thou hast
    given,
And I will praise Thee through Eternity.

THE SAINTS *from Heaven.*
  Call all who love Thee, Lord, to Thee!
    Thou knowest how they long
  To leave these broken lays, and aid
    In Heaven's unceasing song;
  How they long, Lord, to go to Thee,
    And hail Thee with their eyes, —
  Thee in Thy blessedness, and all
    The nations of the skies;

  All who have loved Thee and done well,
    Of every age, creed, clime,
  The host of saved ones from the ends
    And all the worlds of time:
  The wise in matter and in mind,
    The soldier, sage, and priest,
  King, prophet, hero, saint, and bard,
    The greatest soul and least;

The old and young and very babe,
  The maiden and the youth,
All **re-born** angels **of** one age —
  The age of Heaven and truth;
The rich, the poor, the good, the bad,
  Redeemed, alike, from sin;
Lord! close the book of time, and let
  Eternity begin.

FESTUS.   **Will ye away, ye blessed ones?   To**
      God
I then commend ye, and my soul with **yours.**
And midst the light in which ye live, **oh! mind**
Of all the sunless **days** and starless **nights**
Which myriads pass on earth, **and** pray for them!
Oh! pray for those who in the world's dark womb
Are bound, who know not yet their Father, God!—
Lord of all earth, **all** worlds, **all** Heaven! lift **up**
My **spirit to** Thy glory!   Let me share
The **comfort** of Thy love, and while ordained
To **the** great task I have to go through, let
No more misgivings, fears, nor mortal doubts,
With the cold dew of darkness chill the soul
Which thou hast hallowed with Thy love, **and**
      which,
Like molten gold within **its mould, hath made**
The thing **that** holds it **precious; — or** if, Lord!
For Thine **own** purpose, **Thou wilt** suffer such,
May they pass quick and perish tracelessly;
So, too, all thoughts of earth and pangs of death
May I o'ercome at last, and with Thy chosen,
Seraphs and saints, and all-possessing souls,
Which minister unto the universe,
Enthroned in spirit and intensest bliss,
Succeed **to** Heaven for ever.
  GUARDIAN ANGEL.   Mortal, hear!
The soul once saved shall never cease from bliss,
Nor God lose that He buyeth with his blood.
She doth not sin   The deeds which look like sin,

The flesh and the false world, are all to her
Hallowed and glorified.   The world is changed.
She hath a resurrection unto God
While in the flesh, before the final one,
And is with God.   Her state shall never fail.
Even the molten granite which hath split
Mountains, and lieth now like curdled blood
In marble veins, shall flow again when comes
The heat which is to end all ; when the air
Is as a ravening fire, and what at first
Produced, at last consumeth ; but the soul
Redeemed is dear to God as His own throne,
And shall no sooner perish.   Hearken man !
Wilt thou distrust God ?   Doubt on doubt no
          more.
Prepare thee for the power and lot sublime
Whereto the Lord hath called thee.   He hath
          heard
The prayers with which thou hast entreated Him,
And bids me tell thee, shrink not, doubt not.   He
Will comfort and uphold thee at the end ;
For after God the Chooser, God the Slain,
Cometh the God of Comfort to the heart,
Whose action and effect is ministrant
For ever after — consummating all.
     FESTUS.   I fear, I fear this miracle of Death
Is something terrible.   But go to God,
Thou angel, and declare that I repent
Of all misdeeds ; that but for His own grace
I should repent of my whole life ; that on
That grace, which now hath sanctified the whole,
I trust for all the rest of it, and then
For ever ; that I am prepared to act
And suffer as He bids, and in all things
To do His will rejoicing.
     ANGEL.   It is done.
     FESTUS.   Oh !   I repent me of a thousand sins,
In number as the breaths which I have breathed.
Am I forgiven ?

ANGEL.   Child of God, thou art.
It is God prompts, inspires, and answers prayer:
Not sin, nor yet repentance, which avails:
And none can truly worship but who have
The earnest of their glory from on high —
God's nature in them.   The world cannot **worship.**
And whether the lip speak, **or** in inspired
Silence we clasp our hearts as a shut book
Of song unsung, the silence and the speech
Is each His; and as coming from and going
To Him, is worthy of Him and His Love.
Prayer is the spirit speaking truth to Truth;
The expiration **of** the thing inspired.
I go.   Thy God **is** with thee.   We shall meet
Again in Heaven, no **more to part.**
    FESTUS.   **Thou** art gone!
'T is sweet **to feel we** are encircled here
By breath of angels **as** the stars by Heaven;
And the soul's own relations, all divine,
As kind as even those of blood; — and thus
While friends and kin, like Saturn's double rings,
Cheer us along our orbit, we may feel
We are not lone in life, but that earth 's part
Of Heaven and all things.   Praise we, therefore,
        God!
O all ye angels, **pray and praise with us!** —

SCENE — *A Gathering* **of Kings and** *Peoples.*

FESTUS, *throned.*   Princes and Peoples!   **Pow-**
        ers once, of earth!
It suits not that I point to ye the path
By which **I** reached this sole supreme domain —
This mountain of all mortal might.   Enough,
That I am monarch of the world — the world.
Let all acknowledge loyally my laws,
And love me as I them love!   It will be best.
No rise against me can stand.   I rule of God;

And am God's sceptre here.   Think not the world
Is greater than my might — less than my love —
Or that it stretcheth further than mine arm!
Kings! ye are Kings no longer.   Cast your crowns
Here — for my footstool.   Every power is mine.
Nobles! be first in honor.   Ye, too, lose
Your place, in place: retrieve yourselves in good.
Peoples! be mighty in obedience.
Let each one labor for the common weal.
Be every man a people in his mind.
Kings — nobles — nations! love me and obey.
I need no aid — no arms.   Burn books — break
      swords!
The world shall rest, and moss itself with peace.
Stand forth, and speak, sole servant of my throne!
If aught thou hast to settle and explain —
Or send away these nations to their homes.
    LUCIFER.   Ye mighty once — ye many weak
      give ear!
I and my god — for god he sure must be,   .
In human form, who sitteth there enthroned —
For readier rule, and for the good of all,
Have cast again the dynasties of earth
According to the courses of the air : —
Therefore, from east, and west, and north, and
      south,
Four element-like ministers shall bend
Before his feet.   Hearken, thou unkinged crowd!
Ye have not sought the good of those ye governed.
The people only for the people care.
Ye seem to have thought earth but a ball for kings
To play with : rolling the royal bauble, empire,
Now east — now west.   Your hour and power is
      past.
Ye are the very vainest of mankind,
As loftiest things weigh lightest.   Ye are gone!
Nations, away with them!   Nor do ye boast!
Ye find that power means not good, not bliss.
But ye would wed delusion : — now, ye know her.

And she is yours for life — and death — **and judg-**
  ment.
There is no power, nor majesty, **save his :**
His is the kingdom of **the** world and glory.
His throne is founded centre-deep by Heaven :
And the whole earth doth bless him.   Unto **all**
He hath laid out one perfect level law —
His will.   For as the people cannot **rule**
Themselves, so neither may a crowd **of kings :**
And hence hath been the evil of the earth —
Now ceased for ever.   War will be no more.
His is the sway of social sovereign peace :
His tyranny **is love** and **good to** all : —
His is the vice-royed, vouched-safe sway of God : —
And he **will** turn **the** world, at **will ; as** light
Turneth the world round.   **Greet your** Lord, and
  go !
Depart, ye nations !
    Festus.   Hark ! **thou fiend !** dost hear ?
    Lucifer.   **Ay !** it is the death groan of the sons
  of men —
Thy subjects — King !
    Festus.   Why hadst thou this so **soon ?**
    Lucifer.   It is **God** who brings it all **about** —
  not I.
    Festus. **I am not ready — and — it shall not**
  be !
    Lucifer.   **I cannot** help **it,** monarch ! **and —**
  it is I
Hast not **had time for** good !
    Festus.   One day — perchance.
    Lucifer.   Then hold that day as an eternity.
    Festus.   All around me die.   The earth is one
  great death-bed.
    Clara.   **Oh !** save me, Festus ! **I** have fled to
  thee,
Through all the countless nations of yon dead —
For well I knew it was thou who sattest there,
To die with thee, if that thou art not Death :

And, if thou wert, I would not shrink from thee.
I am thine **own, own** Clara !

    FESTUS.   Thou art safe !
Here in the holy chancel of my heart —
The heavenly end of this our fleshly fane,
I hold thee to communion.   Rest thee safe !

    CLARA.   Men thought I **was** an angel, **as I**
        passed ;
And caught **up** at my feet — but I 'scaped all.
I knew — I was sure, that I should die by thee.
The heart is a true oracle — I **knew it** !

    FESTUS.   Then there is faith among these **mor-**
        tals yet.
Thy beauty cometh first, and goeth last —
Willow-like.   Welcome !

    CLARA.   Oh ! I am so happy !

    FESTUS.   **I speak of thee as** of the dead ; the
        dead
Are alway faithful.

    CLARA.   I will stay with thee —
Though angels beckon — may I ?   Let me, love !
I dare not — cannot, take mine eyes from thee,
For fear of looking on the dead.   Dear Festus !

    FESTUS.   Thou art the only **one hast** answered
        me,
Love to love — life to life.

    CLARA.   Oh ! I am dying !
Give me one kiss — the kiss of life and death —
The only taste of earth I will take to Heaven.
Here ! let me die, die in it.   [*Dies.*

    FESTUS.   Last and best !
Now am I one, again.   **Oh ! memory** runs
To **madness,** like a river to the sea.
Happy **as Heaven** have I been with thee, love !
Thine innocent heart hath passed through a pure
        life,
Like a white **dove,** wing-sunned through the blue
        sky.
A better heart God never saved in Heaven.

She died as all the good die — blessing — hoping.
There are some hearts, aloe-like, flower once, and
        die :
And hers was of them. Ah ! all life hath ceased.
And silence reads the dead world's burial tale.
And Death sits quivering there, and watering,
His great, gaunt jaw at me. When must I die ?
    LUCIFER. Say ! dost thou feel **to** be mortal, or
      immortal ?
    FESTUS. Away ! — and let me die alone.
    LUCIFER.   **I go :**
And I will come again : **but spare thee, now,**
One hour to think —   [*Goes.*
    FESTUS.   On all things. **God,** my God !
One hour to sum a life's iniquities !
One hour to fit me for eternity —
To make me up for judgment and for God !
Only **one** hour to curse thee ! Nay, for that,
There may be endless hours. God ! I despair, —
'And I am dying. Let me hold my breath !
I know not if I ever may draw another.
I feel Death blowing hard at the lamp of life.
My heart feels filling like a sinking boat ;
It will soon be down — down. What will come **of**
    me ?
It is as I always wished it ; — I shall die
In darkness, and in silence, and **alone.**
Even my last wish is petted. God ! I thank **Thee.**
It is the earnest of Thy coming — what ?
Forgiveness ? Let it be so : for **I** know not
What I have done to merit endless pain.
Is pleasure crime ? Forbid it, God of bliss !
Who spurn at this world's pleasures, lie to God ;
And show they are not worthy of the next.
What are Thy joys we know not — nor can we
Come near Thee, in Thy power, nor truth, **nor**
    justice ;
The nearest point wherein we come towards Thee,
Is loving — making love — and being happy.

Thou wilt not chronicle our sand-like sins;
For sin is small, and mean, and barren.   Good,
Only, is great, generous, and fruitful.
Number the mountains, not the sands, O God!
God will not look as we do on our deeds;
Nor yet as others.   If He more condemn,
Shall He not more approve?   A few fair deeds
Bedeck my life, like gilded cherubs on
A tomb, beneath which lie dust, decay, and dark-
        ness.
But each is better than the other thinks.
Thank God! man is not to be judged by man: —
Or, man by man, the world would damn itself.
What do I see?   It is the dead.   They rise
In clouds! and clouds come sweeping from all sides.
Upwards to God: and now they are all gone —
Gone, in a moment, to eternity.
But there is something near me.
    SPIRIT.   It is I.
    FESTUS.   Go on! I follow, when it is my time:
There is no shadow on the face of life:
It is the noon of fate.   Why may not I die?
Methinks I shall have yet to slay myself.
I am calm now.   Can this be the same heart
Which, when it did sleep, slept from dizziness,
And pure rapidity of passion, like
The centre circlet of the whirlpool's wheel?
The earth is breaking up; all things are thawing
River and mountain melt into their atoms;
A little time, and atoms will be all.
The sea boils; and the mountains rise and sink
Like marble bubbles, bursting into death.
O thou hereafter! on whose shore I stand —
Waiting each toppling moment to engulf me —
What am I?   Say, thou Present! — say, thou Past!
Ye three wise children of Eternity!
A life? — a death? — and an immortal? — all?
Is this the threefold mystery of man?
The lower, darker Trinity of earth?

It is vain to ask.   Nought answers me — not God.
The air grows thick **and** dark.   The sky comes
      down.
The sun draws round him streaky clouds, like God
Gleaning up wrath.   Hope hath leapt off my heart,
And overturned it.   I am bound to die.
God, why wilt Thou not save ?   The **great round**
      world
Hath wasted to a column beneath my **feet.**
I will hurl me off it, then ; and search **the depth**
Of space, in this one infinite plunge ! — **Farewell,**
To earth, and **Heaven, and** God !   **Doom !** spread
      thy lap !
I come — I come !

God.

Forbear !

Festus.   I am God's !

God.

Man, die !

SCENE — The Skies.

God, Angels, Angel **of Earth, Lucifer.**

God.

The age **of matter consummates itself.**
All things that are **shall end, save that is mine.**
As with one world, **so shall it be with all ;**
For all are human, fallible, **and false,** —
As creature towards Creator **must be** aye.
But for the whole prepare ye, **not** the less
Grade upon grade of glory, **sons** of God !
And Earth shall live again, and **like her** sons
Have resurrection **to a** brighter **being :**
And waken like a **bride, or** like a morning,
With a long blush **of love to a** new life.
Another race of **souls shall rule in her,**

Creatures all loving, beautiful, and holy.
Go, angel! guide her as before through Heaven.

ANGEL OF EARTH.   **On**! on! my world **again**!
    Away we fly
    - Through Heaven's blue plain,
    Like thought through the eye.
   Ye angels, **keep your** Heaven!
    I, Earth!
  For that with God **I have striven,**
    And have prevailed.
    I come once more,
    I come to thee, Earth!
    Like a ship to shore.

LUCIFER.   **Have not I** triumphed o'er the earth
   that was ?

            GOD.
Prince of the powers of air! thy doom **is nigh.**
The prison place of spirits is for **thee** —
As for **all** others thou **hast** wronged, for a time —
But those **who** by my favor die not.   Him
Conduct, ye angels, into Hades; **there**
To wait my will while the **world's** sabbath lasts.

SCENE — *The Millennial Earth.*

SAINTS *and* ANGELS *conversing;* FESTUS.

ANGEL.   The Earth is **all one** Eden.   Pity, sure,
That it should ever end.
  SAINT.   I say not so ;
Although I have a thousand plans in hand,
Some interwoven with the farthest stars —
Each **one of** which might **ask a year** of years
To perfect.
  ANGEL.   **True ;** our Maker knoweth best

What thought or deed may best belong to **time**
Or to eternity.
   Saint.   All prophecy
Hath said the **earth** shall cease, and that **right**
      soon.
   Festus. 'Tis like enough. Beauty's akin **to**
      Death.
   Angel. Behold, our sister Graces **of the skies,**
Faith, Hope, and Love, descend! **Methinks of**
      late
Ye chiefly dwell on earth.
   Love.   **Where lives and reigns**
The Son of God, there are we ever seen,
Successive, as **the seasons to the** sun.
   Saints. Well are ye known and welcome in all
      worlds.
Wherever lofty thought or godly deed
Is lodged or compassed, there your blessings rest.
   Hope. How sweet, how sacred now, this earth
      of **man's!**
The prelude of a yet sublimer bliss!—
I marked it from the first, while yet it lay
Lightless and stirless; ere the forming fire
Was kindled in its bosom, or the land
Lift its volcanic breastwork up from sea.
The deluge and idolatries of men
I viewed, though shuddering, **and with** faltering
      eye,
E'en to the incarnation of Heaven's Lord,
And dawning of His faith; that faith which **was**
An infant and anon a giant; was
A star, and grew **a** Heaven-fulfilling sun;
Which was an outcast, and become, ere long,
A dweller in all palaces; which hid
Its head in dens of deserts, and sat throned,
After, in richest temples high as hills;
Which was poured out in mortal blood, and rose
In an immortal spirit; as **a** slave
Was sold for gold and prostrated to power;—

And now that lowly bondmaid is a Queen;
And lo! she is beloved in earth and Heaven;
And lieth in the bosom of her Lord,
The Bride of the all-worshipped, one with God.
    LOVE.   We even of divinest origin
In infinite progression view all worlds;
And we are happy.
    FAITH.   The dead sleep as yet;
But their time cometh, and the bonds of death
Already slacken round the living soul;
The mortal sleep of ages, which began
When Time sank down into his slumberous west,
Thins even now o'er the reviving eyes
Gathering their Heaven-lent light, no more to
            wane
In woe or age; never be quenched in tears
Like a star in the sea.   'T is as I ever knew;
My life is to receive and to believe
The Word and words of God.
    LOVE.   I, who am Love
And Grace and Charity, rejoice with you;
Whither ye wend I with ye; whether here,
Or on the utmost rim of Light's broad reign —
The least and last of stars which even seems
To tremble at its insignificance
In presence of Infinity; where yet
No angel's wing hath waved, nor foot of fiend
Left its hot imprint; — still, in all do we
Find fit delight and honor, as now here.
Now earth and Heaven hold commune, day and
            night;
There's not a wind but bears upon its wing
The messages of God; and not a star
But knows the bliss of earth.
    FESTUS.   The earth hath God
Remade, and all its elements refined,
Fit for sublimer Being. Flesh hath passed
Its fiery baptism, and come forth clear
As crystal gold: all that of vile or mean

Pertained to it hath perished **atomless.**
Earth, like a diamond, basks **in her own free light;**
Unfed, unaided, unrequiring aught.
All now is purity **and** power and **peace.**
The first-born of creation, they **who** hail
Archangels as their brethren, mountainlike
Reign o'er the plains of men, converting all;
Reaping the fields of immortality,
Each one his sheaf, for Him the Harvest-Lord,
To whom belongs earth's whole estate and life
And every world's.

    Angel.   **And He** shall garner **all.**
The awful tribes **which have** in Hades **dwelt,**
Past count of time, await their rising. **God's**
Great day, the sabbath **of the** world's long week,
Is **at** high noon; and **Christ hath** yet to come
To judge and **save** the living **and** the dead.

    Saint. The shadows **of** Eternity o'ercast
Already Time's bright **towers.** The Heavens shall
       come
Down like **a** cloud upon **a** hill, and sweep
Their spirit over earth, and the whole face
And form of things shall be dissolved and **change.**
Nothing shall be but essence, perfect, pure,
And void of every attribute but God's.
This even **is too gross** for **that which is**
To come. **The holy have both earth and Heaven.**

    Festus. **Nor pain, nor toil of mind or frame,**
     nor doubt,
Nor discontent, nor enmity **to God,**
Disturb the steady joy the **spirit feels;**
Nor element **can** torture, nor **time** tire;
Nor sea nor mountain make **or bar** or fear;
Sickness and woe and death are things gone **by;**
Destroyed with **the** destruction **of** the world: —
Shadows of things which have **been,** never more
To waste the world's bright **hours,** nor grate the
     heart
Of mighty man; **now** fit for thrones and wings;

Ruler of worlds, main minister of Heaven,
Inheritor of all the prophecies
Of God fore-uttered through the tongues of Time,
Ages of ages.   Evil is no more.
      ARCHANGEL.   **And** does earth satisfy thee now ?
      FESTUS.   As earth.
There is a brighter, loftier life for man
Even yet, **the very** union **with** God.
      ARCHANGEL. **God works by means.**   Between
            the two **extremes**
Of Earth and Heaven there lies **a** mediate **stat** —
A pause between the lightning lapse of life
And following thunders of eternity ; —
Between eternity and time a lapse,
To **soul** unconscious, though age-lasting, where
Spirit is tempered to **its** final fate ;
When every interfulgent conscious state
Within or between worlds, repose or bliss,
Divested, man shall mix **with** Deity,
And the Eternal and Immortal make
One Being.   As in earth's first paradise
God's Spirit walked with man, and **commune**
            made
With him, so in **the second, after death,**
Man's spirit walks **with God in an elect**
Existence, and a vigil of the great,
The holy day which is to break in Heaven.
Thither the Lord of Life went, in the hour
That Hell by earth revenged itself on Heaven,
With one soul penitent accompanied ; —
Nor long remained He there, yet long enough
To cheer earth's faithful, who received Him then
In silent, unknown blessedness of soul,
With time-outwearing hope that yet in Him
They should partake the Godhood of His love.
And with Him rose then, in prophetic proof
Of His Divinity, many a deathless ghost,
Triumphant o'er that blind revenge which wrought,
Hell ! thy destruction — thy salvation, Earth !

FESTUS.   That such will be, the just well know,
        and all
Earth's great events and changes tend thereto;
Its fiery dissolution in **the** past,
And supernatural recommencement now
Under the universal creed of Christ.
The chosen and the world-redeemed partake
His personal and spiritual reign.
    ARCHANGEL.   And **this** shall **last, till, like the**
        setting sun
Deserting earth, He shall **retire** to Heaven,
With all His captive **victors in** His train,
Triumphant, and **translated evermore**
Into the **hierarchal** skies.   **Wilt see,**
While yet time is, earth's shadowy **world** within —
The inward living death she bears about
Her heart, hath **ever** borne — and, augur-like,
Explore the ominous bowels of the earth?
To me are given the secrets of the centre,
The keys of earth, to lock and to unlock,
Coffer-like.   I, it was who seized and bound,
At His behest who wills and it is done, —
Even on their thrones, the mighty thou wilt see.
    FESTUS.   Angel of Heaven!   I would view these
        things.
    ARCHANGEL.   **Nor these alone, but other won-**
        ders yet.
The valley where Death's **dark** wings brooded o'er,
A God-offending night, unvisited
By sun or star, where but the fatuous fire
Of man's weak judgment wandered, till God's Son
Laid o'er the black abyss a bridge of light,
And married earth to the mainland of Heaven —
This shalt thou see, Death's grave; and over him,
And over it, that monument of light.
Enlightening earth.   The gods and fiends of old,
And all the fictions of the heart of man,
Imagined of the future past for aye,
Thou shalt inspect.   Behold this mountain!   **We**

Must pass through it; for under lie the **gates**
Of the invisible regions whereunto
We tend, for a brief season.
   FESTUS.   **On,** then!
   ARCHANGEL.   Bare
Thy marble breast, O mountain, to its depths!
An angel and a man divine demand
A way through these foundations.
   FESTUS.   And the rocks
Open like mists before thee.
   ARCHANGEL.   Follow me!

SCENE — *Hades.*

ARCHANGEL, FESTUS, DEATH, LUCIFER.

FESTUS.   Almighty God! sustain me.   This is
       Death; —
And this — I knew not, angel! he was here —
Is Lucifer — the fallen, like a bolt
Of thunder forged in intramundane air,
Self-buried in the centre. Lucifer!
Wake from thy sea-like sleep; in peace or wrath,
Rouse from thine age-long trance; arise and
       see;
The representatives of earth and Heaven
Stand by thee. As for me, I blame no more
The part thou tookest in my mortal life;
'T is gone, — nor spurn thee for delusions dead.
The blood that hath been spilled is sunk in earth,
And run into the rivers, and dried up
Into the air; — and there's an end of it.
What good hath come of it alone I bear
At heart. And we have both offended God.
Let me, though not in nature to forget,
Forgive, what every one hath sometime felt —
The Devil's burning gripe upon his heart.
I see thee with compassion, half with hope.

LUCIFER.   Mortal! I bow to thee, and **would do to**
The least and lowest spirit God hath made :
But still the curse that I am cursed with
Outlasts the elements — outlives all time.
    FESTUS.   **All** curses cease with time ; all ill, all **woe.**
Blessings star forth forever ; but **a curse**
Is like a cloud — **it** passes.
    LUCIFER.   'T was by him —
Yon angel, only not **almighty, there** !
As with **a** chain of **mountains I was bound**
And hurled **into this** unformed nebulous **life** ;
Stripped **of all** might when mightiest, **struck down**
While triumphing the loftiest, — enslaved
When most a monarch o'er both earth and hell,
And made a shadow among shadows here.
It recks not.   Let the impenetrable soul
Be ground as through a mill, I only know
In action or inaction equal woe —
Suffering, doing, being, **one** extreme.
Pass on ! we meet again !
    FESTUS.   And when we do,
May God forgive, as **I** ! —
    ARCHANGEL.   **Behold there, Death !**
Throned **on his tomb** — entombed in **his throne** ;
Just as he **ceased he rests for aye** — his scythe,
Still **wet out** of its **bloody swathe, one hand**
Tottering sustains ; the other **strikes the cold**   .
Drops from his bony **brow : his mouldy breath**
Tainteth all **air.**
    FESTUS.   I dread him now no more,
Nor hate.   He is a vanquished enemy.
    ARCHANGEL.   Listen ! he speaks.
    DEATH.   To you, **ye** sons of God,
My latest words I utter.   Unto him
Who ever lives, and hath for aye destroyed
Me and my reign, give ye this crown usurped,
And lay it at His feet ; and this dulled dart

Which was my sceptre.   **To** the conqueror
Belong these trophies.   All the progeny
Of time will soon cease.   Lo! the end's at hand.
   Archangel.   **Thus** shall it be, O Death! and
     thus **it** is.
   Festus.   And who are these gigantic awful
     shades
Which fill the midst — the present **of the place?**
   Archangel.   **These** are the **mighty nothings**
     man
Made; the dread unrealities by whom
He swore, to whom he prayed, and **at whose**
     shrines of old
He sacrificed a thousand times a day:—
His brother falsehoods these, men like himself,
Which mere imagination changed to gods,
Some for their good deeds, others for their bad:
Bel, Odin, Bramh, and Zeus, the Lords of death,
And fire, and judgment, waiting here their death
And fiery judgment — Time and Titan — war —
Beauty, and strength, **and** light, and the long
     roll
Of creatural powers and **passions** Deified; —
Who gave their **names to stars** which **still roam**
     round
The skies, all worshipless, even from climes
Where their **own** altars once topped every hill.
   Jove.   Before the Christian cross and Moslem
    ·   mosque
My marble fanes have fallen, and my shrines
Shrunk like a withered hand ages ago.
But now all signs and sacred domes for **gods**
To **dwell** in are extinct.   **The world** is **all**
One Temple of the Truth.
   Bramh.   **The ages** feigned
That made Time groan to think **how old** he was,
And Deities in millions are no more.
Ageless eternity and God the sole,
The royalty of Heaven, is at hand.

Boodh.   All things that are shall nothing be at
		last,
Save what's resolvable in Deity.
	Festus. And all these lesser shades, which
		move like moons,
Half-darkened by the greater — half-illumined —
Are priests and prophets of the mightier ones?
	Archangel. They are; — and further round
		thine eye can mark,
The myriads of adorers of each god,
Confused and prostrate, as their souls awake
To the demoniac madness of their creeds.
Behold! they kneel **to** those they hailed **on earth**
As makers — as omnipotent — eterne —
And cry for help, for comfort; none have they
To give **to** others or themselves.   The false,
The base, the brutish Deities give way,
And all their sacred follies **in** their train,
Before the earthquake truth, engulfing all.
Woe to the false gods, woe! to prophet, priest,
And worshipper, all woe!
	Festus.					**Hark**! round the earth
Each soul hath found **a** tongue and uttereth woe.
Lo! from their thrones the man-made gods descend,
And rend their robes and trample on their crowns,
And hurl away their sceptres.   Woe to all
The gods and idols **of** the heart **of** man!
Their sun is set forever in **the** night
Which was ere Light was.   Surely **it is** more
To be true man or woman than false god
And falser prophet.   God alone the true,
The God of Heaven, shall be witnessed to
And worshipped.
	Archangel. Witnessed, worshipped, too,
By all: the faithful and the faithless — saint
And sinner.
	Festus. Lo! the nations of the dead,
Which **do** outnumber all earth's races, rise,
And **high in** sumless myriads over head

Sweep past us in a cloud, as 't were the skirts
Of the Eternal passing.
    A VOICE.   Souls, arise
To deathless life !
    ARCHANGEL.   'Tis God speaks. Let us hence.
The general judgment is in hand, — God's hand.
The souls of those whom God loves circle us.
For thee, thy lot thou knowest. As a seed
Buried in earth doth multiply itself
Full fifty fold, so will thy nature when
Changed, it lifts head in the air divine of Heaven.
    FESTUS. Out of the depths of earth and the
        world's womb
Thine unborn angels seek thee, God, all Love !
Now is Thine hour for which all hours were made,
All life created, all things else ordained ;
Be it the hour of mercy, Lord ! to all,
For Thy Son's sake, who, for the sake of man,
Came down from Heaven into the pit of earth,
And lived as one of us and died ; — He died
The death of all at once of every age ;
The world's accumulated weight of woe,
From its first life unto its last, which none
But the Omnipotent could bear — He bore ;
And all for us. God became man that man
Might become God. Oh, favor infinite !
Now reap the righteous, righteous but in Him
Any, their guerdon. Evil to repay   [Heaven
With good was Christ's command, and earth with
Is thus the great example of His word.
Enough for sinners this, for all which live.
Do Thou, Lord ! be with us. In Thee we live ;
Our treasure, trust, and triumph is in Thee.
Behold the day of our salvation come
Unto the countless all Thou hast redeemed !
The ages sweep around me with their wings
Like angered eagles cheated of their prey,
The ages of all time : the glowing Heavens
Are rushing to receive us. Oh, rejoice

All ye that are immortal — and whate'er
Hath been predestined to eternal end,
The day determined **ere all** time was dawns!

SCENE — *Earth.*

ANGELS *and* SAINTS — AN ANGEL *descending;*
FESTUS.

SAINT.   Whence art **thou ?**
ANGEL.   I ? **from** Heaven, **and thither tend ; —**
One moment **here to** bid **ye** to prepare.
Our Lord the Eternal Son comes hither, girt
With His victorious hosts, to judge the world.
SAINT.   What victory hath our Almighty gained ?
ANGEL.   One final, over Death and Hell. Shout,
      earth!
Thy freedom is accomplished, and thy foes
Brought down to endless ruin.
SAINT.   Angel, speak !
We burn to learn the tidings of this war,
Whereof thou tell'st, and doubtless wast a part.
ANGEL.   Hot from the fight I **come.** This light-
      ning blade
Hath holpen well to **thin the infernal rout,**
Which back hath fled **to hell, howling like winds.**
But let me, **at your will, ye peaceful saints,**
Relate what happened to **us from first to last.**
The time was come in Heaven when **God** the Son,
Bowing his head before the Omnipotent,
Who doubled every blessing infinite
Wherewith he had enriched His Only One
From first, **rose** from his glorious throne, and stepped
Into His sun-bright car, calling aloud
His angels to attend Him while He went
To judge the earth, as fore-ordained of old :
That Heaven and earth might view the majesty
And mercy of the God of all. We came,

Selectest spirits, countless — crowded bright
As the great stream of stars which flows through
          Heaven
Fast by the foot of God, each wave a world —
Eager to the eye this act of glory long   ·
Talked of in Heaven, and now to be achieved.
Forth from the starry towers, and world-wide walls,
Of Heaven, we sat in high and silent joy,
And journeyed half our way through Heaven, when
          lo !
A sight which checked the foremost flaming ranks,
That halted frontwise, working doubt at first,
But triumph after.   Shielded and drawn up close,
Behind a broken and decaying world,
From which the light had vanished like the light
Out of a death-shrunk eye, sat Lucifer —
Midst in the powers of darkness, and the hosts
Of hell, enthroned sublime ; and all were still
As ambushed silence round the Foe of God.
But oh ! how changed from him we knew in Heaven,
Whose brightness nothing made might match nor
          mar ;
Who rose, and it was morn ; — who stretched his
          wing,
And stepped from star to star ; — so changed he
          showed
Most like a shadowy meteor, through which
The stars dim glint — woe-wasted, pined with pain.
And by his side there sat or shrank a shape   ·
We angels knew not, but the Son of God
Knew him, and called him Death ; whom, when he
          saw,
Arousing, after, out of sleep intense,
That unrealmed tyrant drew his mortal dart,
And drave it through himself, — a shade, shade·
          quelled.
Then to that chief of mischief and his fiends,
Who, thick as burning stones that from the throat
Of some volcano foul the benighted sky,

Shot up triumphant into air as they
Beheld our ranks move on, thus spake our Lord,—
Not wrathfully, but sternly pitying:
Hell's wretched remnant! **wherefore crouch ye**
     here ?
Is it to sue destruction, or to bar
My passage ? If it **be, in** both **ye err.**
And will ye trust yourselves again to war
With me, Almighty ? Have I not overcome
Ye separately, both ? Speak, brutal **Death !**
Fit follower and fellow to **all woes,** —
Wherefore **this** instantaneous **haste from hell,**
And both **from** Hadeän **bondage, thus again**
So soon to compass **mightiest wickedness,**
And tempt the extremest wrath ? Speak, head of
     hell !
To Him thus Lucifer : Almighty Son !
Thy power I defy not ; but in peace
I war with fate. My life is to destroy.
Evil hath more activity, if good
More strength : and one must wear the other out.
The more august the sin, so much the more
Is my necessity. Yon earth hath been
The battle-plain of Heaven and hell. From **Thee,**
Who knowest all things, it were vain to hide
My purpose, which for a **thousand** years, the years
Of bondage, hath grown **in** me and lived **on,**
Toad-like within a rock — vital where all
Beside was death — to seize the nascent souls
Of men as they rerose from death to life,
And sweep them off in midst of all these hosts,
Assembled for that cause here as Thou seest,
To hell ; — **the** universal race **of** man.
But if ordained that not on them, but Thee
And Thine, old hate shall satisfy itself,
Approach no nearer ; for we live by death ; —
Or turn the tide of fate, Thou sole who canst !
Ceasing thereat, **his host** upraised a shout
Which shook the stars, and made them ring again.

Our Lord to him then spake thus, mild as Spring,
Addressing earth when smiling she lets fall
All flowerets from her lips—'Tis well there is a
       God!
Lo! to what base extremes infernal pride
Can push a princely spirit once in Heaven.
Thee we will not destroy now, for thine hour
Hath yet to come—when least thou thinkest it.
God's wrath thou hast endured in punishment.
Not yet His power. Away! I warn ye hence
Ere wrath ride forth again. To Him the Fiend
Answered: God rules not us, the unordered
       damned,
Nor recks of hell. For ages past belief,
Unless by those who like ourselves denied
Thine own eternity — by creature mind,
However lofty, hardly compassed — we
Have borne our pain without remorse, or sign
Of pity from our Maker. Shall we now
Believe, while thus confronting Him again,
He means us better? Never worse than now.
Therefore I say to ye, on! mightiest fiends,
On! Let us reap companions for our woes,
Or earn annihilation ! At the word,
His fiery phalanx rushed to bar the way
Of Him whose ways are over all his works.
A million spears blazed forth their answer bright,
As of as many tongues. Serene our ranks
Stood as the stars o'er thunder. God the Son
Sate in His orbèd car, and breathed on them;
And they were rolled up like the desert sands
Before the burning wind, — throne wrecked on
       throne,
All ruined and fordone. Pursue ! He cried,
Nor let them near the earth I go to judge.
And we pursued, as many as He chose,
And chased from sphere to sphere that wretched
       wreck
Of falsest fiends : — and I, it seems, am first

Of all my victor brethren to declare
The triumph past and coming, and to cheer
Your hearts with tidings of our Lord, to whom
Be glory for His universal deeds,
And to him, only God!
　　SAINT.　　　　　　Behold where comes
Another warrior-angel from on high ;
Like angels, always singly or in hosts.
　　ANGEL.　It is the most dread Azrael, unto whom
The sword of Death is given as a boon.
　　SAINT.　What sayst thou, heavenly one ?
　　AZRAEL.　　　　　　To the extreme bound
Of Light's domain we chased the flying foe,
Who on the confines of the lower air
Once rallied at their leader's stern command,
Whom more they fear, or seem to fear, than God.
They halted, formed, and faced us.　I and mine,
As on we came in order, full career,
Exalted by success, hoped ardently
One more convincing contest ; but in spite
Of future woe or the tempestuous threats
Of the great Fiend who marshalled them, each
　　　eyed
His neighbor pale ; their trembling shook all air ;
And each one lift his arm, but no one struck.
Awhile in dead throe-like suspense they stood,
Or like the irresolution of the sea
At turn of tide — then wheeled and fled amain,
And in one mass immense broke down from Heaven,
Cliff-like ; — there let them lie ! such fate have
　　　fiends.
And we returned, hoping to meet, as charge
To all was given, the Lord our glory here.
　　ARCHANGEL.　Let all the dead rejoice ! their
　　　Saviour comes.

SCENE — *The Judgment of Earth.*

THE SON OF GOD, THE ARCHANGEL, SAINTS,
and ANGELS.

ARCHANGEL. Let all the dead rejoice! their
    Saviour comes;
With clouds of angels circled like a sun,
Belted with light, and brighter than all light,
Lo! He descends and seats Him on His throne,
Alighting like a new made sun in Heaven.
The world awaits Thee, Lord! Rise, souls of men,
Buried beneath all ages from the first;
Ye numbered and unnumbered, loathed and loved,
Awake to judgment! Rise! the grave no more
Hath power upon ye than the ravening sea
Upon the stars of Heaven. Ye elements!
Give back your stolen dead. He claimeth them
Whose they both were and are, and aye shall be.
             SON OF GOD.
I come to repay sin with holiness,
And death with immortality; man's soul
With God's Spirit; all evil with all good.
All men have sinned; and as for all I died,
All men are saved. Oh! not a single soul
Less than the countless all can satisfy
The infinite triumph which to me belongs,
Who infinitely suffered. Ye elect!
And all ye angels, with God's love informed,
Who reign with me o'er earth and Heaven, assume
Your seats of judgment. Judge ye all in love,
The love which God the Father hath to you —
For His Son's sake, and all shall be forgiven.
  SAINTS. Lord! let us render back to Thee the
    love
Which is Thine own : none else is worthy Thee.

Son of God.

Behold this day I dwell with thee on earth,
E'en to the last; the next shall be in Heaven,
Where ye shall meet the Father, and remain
In the Eternal presence, He through me
Blessing all spirits overflowingly.
  Saints. Dear Lord, our God **and** Saviour! **for**
    Thy gifts
The world were poor in thanks, though every **soul**
Were to do nought but breathe them, every blade
Of grass and every atomy of earth
To utter it like dew. Thy ways are **plain**
Only in Thine own light. And this great **day**
Unveils all nature's laws and miracles—
All to Thee all as one. Thy death was life;
Thy judgment is all mercy, Lord of Love!
The world's incomprehensible no more
To man, but all is bright as new-born star.

Son of God.

The Book of Life is opened. Heaven begins.

Scene — The Heaven of Heavens.

The Recording Angel, Lucifer, Festus,
Angels.

  The Recording Angel. **All men are judged**
    save one.

Son of God.

        He too **is saved.**
Immortal! **I have** saved thy **soul to** Heaven.
Come hither. All hearts bare themselves to me,
As clouds unbind their bosoms to the sun,
And thine was wealthy in the gifts of good.
And, if its guilt and glory lay in love,
Let light outweigh the darkness! Thou art saved.
  Saints. Rejoice! Rejoice!
  Festus.   Could **I,** Lord! pour my soul out,

25

In thanks, even as a river rolling ever,
'T would be too scant for what I owe to Thee.

SON OF GOD.

Nay; immortality is long enough,
As life, or as a moment is, to show
Thy love of good, thy thanks to me and God.
One heart-throb sometimes earneth Heaven — one
　　　tear.

FESTUS. My **Maker! let me thank Thee, I
　　　have** lived,
And live a deathless witness of Thy grace.
And Thee, the Holy One, who hast chosen **me,**
From old eternity, while yet I lay
Hid, like a thought in God, unuttered — Thou,
Who makest finite full with the Infinite,
As is a womb with an immortal spirit,
Oh! let me thank Thee that I witness to Thee.
And Thou, mid-God! my Saviour, and my Judge!
Sun of the soul, whose day is now all noon —
Who makest of the universe one Heaven —
I praise Thee. **Heaven doth** praise Thee. God
　　　doth praise **Thee.**
The Holy Ghost doth praise **Thee. Praise Thy-
　　　self**!

LUCIFER. Is he not mine?

GOD.

　　　　　　　　Evil! away for aye!
In the beginning, **ere** I bade things be —
Or **ever** I begat the worlds on space,
I knew of him, and saved him in my Son,
Who now hath judged; for, fraught with God-hood,
　　　He
Yet feels the frailties of the things He has made;
And therefore can, like-feelingly, judge them.
For I abide not sin; and in my Son
There is no sin — not that He takes away.
It is destroyed forever and made nothing.

SON OF GOD.

Spirit, depart! this mortal loved me.

With all his doubts, he never doubted God:
But from doubt gathered truth, like snow from
        clouds,
The most, and whitest, from the darkest.   Go!
    LUCIFER.   I leave thee, Festus.   Here thou
        wilt be happy.
To be in Heaven is to **love** forever
God — and **thou must** love here.   **Here** thou wilt
        find
All that thou canst and oughtst to love: **for souls,**
Re-made of God, and moulded over **again**
Into his sun-like emblems, multiply
His might and **love: the** saved are suns, not
        earths;
And with original glory shine of God.
While **I** shall keep on deepening in my darkness,
With not one gleam across the gloom of being.
    FESTUS.   Let us part, spirit! it may be, in the
        coming,
That as we sometime were all worth God's making,
We may **be** worth forgiving; taking back
Into His bosom, pure again — and then,
All shall be one with Him, who is one in all.
    LUCIFER.   It **may** be, **then, that** I shall **die.**
        Farewell.
Forgive me that **I tempted thee!**
    FESTUS.   **I am glad.**
                GOD.
Stay, spirit! all created things unmade
It suits not the eternal laws of good
That Evil be immortal.   In all space
Is joy and glory, and the gladdened stars,
Exultant in the sacrifice of sin,
And of all human matter in themselves,
Leap forth as though to welcome earth to Heaven —
Leap forth and die.   All nature disappears.
Shadows are passed away.   Through all is light.
Man is as high above temptation now, —

And where by **Grace** he alway shall remain
As ever sun o'er sea; and sin is burned
In hell-to ashes with **the dust** of death.
The worlds themselves are **but as dreams** within
Their souls who lived in them, and thou art null,
And thy vocation useless, gone with them.
Therefore shall Heaven rejoice **in thee again,**
And the lost tribes of angels, who **with thee**
Wedded themselves **to woe, and** all **who dwell**
Around the dizzy centres **of all** worlds,
Again be blessed with the blessedest.
Lo! ye are all restored, rebought, rebrought
To Heaven by Him who cast ye forth, your God.
Receive ye tenfold of all gifts and powers.
And thou who cam'st to Heaven **to** claim **one**
    soul,
Remain possessed by **all.** The sons of bliss
Shall welcome thee again, and **all** thy hosts,
Whereof thou first **in** glory as in woe —
In brightness as in darkness **erst — shall shine.**
Take, Lucifer, thy place. **This day art thou**
Redeemed to archangelic state. **Bright child**
Of morning, **once** again thou **shinest fair**
O'er all the **starry ornaments of light.**
    Lucifer. **The highest and the humblest I of**
      all
The beings Thou hast made, Eternal **Lord!**
    Angel. Behold they come, the **Legions of the**
      lost,
Transformed already by the bare behest
Of God **our** Maker to the purest form
Of seraph **brightness.**
    The restored Angels. His be all the
      praise!
And ours submissive thanks. When evil had done
Its worst, then God most blessed us and forgave.
Oh, He hath triumphed over all the world,
In mercy, over death, and earth, and hell!

SON OF GOD.
All God hath made are saved.   Heaven **is** complete.
GUARDIAN ANGEL.   Hither with me !
FESTUS.   But where are **those I** love ?
ANGEL.   **Yon** happy troop !
FESTUS.   Ah ! blest ones, come to me !
Loves of my heart, on earth; and soul in Heaven !
Are ye all here, too, **with me ?**
ALL.   **All.**
FESTUS.   **It is** Heaven.
ANGEL.   Come, **let us** join our **souls** into the
    song
Of glory, which the Saved all sing, to God.

THE SAVED.   **Father of goodness,**
        Son of love,
        Spirit of **comfort,**
        Be with **us !**
        God who hast made us,
        God who hast saved,
        God who hast judged us,
        Thee we praise.
        Heaven our spirits,
        Hallow our hearts;
        Let us have God-light
        Endlessly.
        Ours is the wide world,
        Heaven on Heaven ;
        What have we done, Lord,
        Worthy this ?
        Oh ! we have loved Thee ;
        That alone
        Maketh our glory,
        Duty, meed.
        Oh ! **we** have loved Thee !
        Love we will,
        Ever, and every
        Soul of us.

> God of the saved,
> God of the tried,
> God of the lost ones,
> Be with all!
> Let us be near Thee
> Ever and aye;
> Oh! let us love Thee
> Infinite!

FESTUS.   So, soul and song, begin and end in
        Heaven,
Your birth-place and your everlasting home.
                THE HOLY GHOST.
Time there hath been when only God was all;
And it shall be again.   The hour is named,
When seraph, cherub, angel, saint, man, fiend,
Made pure, and unbelievably uplift
Above their present state — drawn up to God,
Like dew into the air — shall be all Heaven;
And all souls shall be in God, and shall be God,
And nothing but God, be.
                SON OF GOD.
                        Let all be God's.
                GOD.
World without end, and I am God alone;
The Aye, the Infinite, the Whole, the One.
I only was — nor matter else, nor mind,
The self-contained Perfection unconfined.
I only am — in might and mercy one;
I live in all things and am closed in none.
I only shall be — when the worlds have done,
My boundless Being will be but begun.

L'ENVOI

READ this, **world!** **He who writes is** dead to **thee,**
  But still lives **in these leaves.** He spake **inspired:**
  Night and day, thought came **unhelped, undesired,**
Like blood to his heart. The course of study he
Went through was of **the soul-rack.** The degree
  He took was high : it was wise wretchedness.
  He suffered perfectly, and gained no less
A prize than, in his own torn **heart,** to see
    A few bright **seeds: he sowed** them — hoped
      them truth.
The autumn of that seed is in these pages.
God was with him, and bade old Time, to **the youth,**
Unclench his heart, and teach the book of ages.
    Peace to **thee, world!** — farewell!. May God the
      Power,
And God the **Love!** — and God the Grace, **be ours**

www.ingramcontent.com/pod-product-compliance
Lightning Source LLC
Chambersburg PA
CBHW032147110726
47902CB00003B/726